THE AWAKENING

THE AWAKENING

Age Of Faith: Book Seven

TAMARA LEIGH

Cover Design: Ravven

ISBN-10: 1942326300
ISBN-13: 9781942326304

TAMARA LEIGH NOVELS

CLEAN READ HISTORICAL ROMANCE
The Feud: A Medieval Romance Series
Baron Of Godsmere: Book One
Baron Of Emberly: Book Two
Baron Of Blackwood: Book Three

Lady: A Medieval Romance Series
Lady At Arms: Book One
Lady Of Eve: Book Two

Beyond Time: A Medieval Time Travel Romance Series
Dreamspell: Book One
Lady Ever After: Book Two

Stand-Alone Medieval Romance Novels
Lady Of Fire
Lady Of Conquest
Lady Undaunted
Lady Betrayed

INSPIRATIONAL HISTORICAL ROMANCE
Age of Faith: A Medieval Romance Series
The Unveiling: Book One
The Yielding: Book Two
The Redeeming: Book Three
The Kindling: Book Four
The Longing: Book Five
The Vexing: Book Six
The Awakening: Book Seven
The Raveling: Book Eight

Prologue

Barony of Owen, England
Spring, 1152

BEWARE THE DELILAH, my son. Beware the Jezebel.

That warning again, ever near though it did not belong in the space between this young woman and him. She was no Delilah. No Jezebel. Were she, his mother would not have chosen her to wed the heir of Lexeter.

She was pure, younger than he, and only pretty enough to please so he did not stray from vows exchanged a year hence when she attained her fifteenth year and he his nineteenth. Only pretty enough to ensure those who sought to make a cuckold of him were not overly tempted to make a harlot of her.

He nodded.

She laughed. "If you are done conversing with yourself, Lord Soames..." She leapt in front of him and danced backward to accommodate his stride. "...mayhap you would like to converse with me."

Lothaire scowled amid embarrassment warming his face. "You are too expressive, Lady Laura."

She arched eyebrows above eyes so dark they might haunt did they not sparkle like stars on a moonless night. "You make that sound a bad thing. Fie on you! I shall not be ashamed I am pleased to see you again."

She bobbed her head forward. "And more so in the absence of your mother."

He halted. "What is wrong with my mother? You do not like her?"

She stilled her own feet, clapped a hand over her mouth, and smiled on either side of it.

The sight of her—so lovely and happy—made his heart convulse. And stirred his body as it should not. "Lady Laura!"

She dropped her hand but not her smile. "Do not take offense, Lord Soames. I did not say I do not like her, severe though she is. I am simply pleased to be alone with you."

Only possible because the Lady of Lexeter had taken ill. Despite his mother's attempt to sit the saddle, they had barely gained the drawbridge before she became so light of head she had to accept he alone would journey to visit his betrothed. Lothaire had been secretly heartened, her constant attendance making him feel like a boy—and appear one.

"As we are to wed," Lady Laura continued, "we ought to know each other better, and now we can." She threw her arms wide, dropped her head back, and whirled. "'Tis a beautiful day to fall in love!"

Appalled yet entranced, he stared. Such frivolity had not been apparent six months past when his mother accompanied him to the barony of Owen to determine if the girl fostered by Lady Maude D'Arci would make a suitable wife.

For hours, the young lady who was to bring a generous dowry to the marriage had sat quietly with hands folded and slippered feet tight against each other, speaking only when spoken to. She had seemed shy, and only twice had he caught her looking at him. What had happened these past months to make her think it appropriate to behave in this manner? And to speak of love!

She ceased whirling, gave a great sigh. "I will make you talk to me, Lord Soames. I vow I shall! And you will laugh, as I know you wish to do."

"My lady!"

She held up a hand. "If we are to wed, you must accept that though I shall be the proper and gracious noblewoman in the company of others, when 'tis but you and me, I shall be…Well, I shall be me, as I would have you be you. Now the question is"—she stepped nearer, tilted her head—"who are you?"

He could hardly breathe for how close she stood. More, for how much he wanted to wrap his arms around her and match his mouth to hers.

She raised an eyebrow. "I wait."

He swallowed loudly, said tightly, "I am your betrothed, the man for whom you will bear children and keep a good household."

She groaned. "That is not who you are. Lady Maude assured me 'tis not."

"Lady Maude?"

"She said once you are away from your mother, you will not be dull as I fear—"

"I am not dull!"

She wrinkled her nose. "I believe what I see and feel, not merely what is told me. So show me, Lord Soames, the life we share will be blessed with far more laughter than tears."

Again, he stared. Again, his body stirred.

She swung away. "Chase me!"

"What?"

"I wish to be chased," she called over her shoulder. "And caught." Hitching up her skirts, she ran, unbound hair flying out behind her, sunlight gliding over strands of red amid brown.

"This is unseemly, Lady Laura!"

More laughter, but not mocking. It called to the boy in him he had thought shut away. Still, he held his feet to the beaten path that led to the pond she told lay just beyond the castle walls.

That had been his first mistake, allowing her to persuade him to leave the garden. And his second mistake would be to give chase. But she grew so distant she would soon go from sight.

A lady alone in the wood. *His* lady.

He gripped his sword hilt and ran on long muscled legs. And she made it even easier for him to overtake her by staying just enough ahead to reach the bank of the promised pond.

She spun, propped her hands on her hips, and with an open-mouthed smile, said, "Methinks Lady Maude is right. You are not dull."

He should have drawn up far short of her, but his feet carried him to within arm's reach. "Lady, we must return to the castle."

"Aye, but first…" She stepped near and laced slender fingers with his that had never seemed so large and clumsy. Before he could correct her brazen familiarity, she turned and settled her shoulder against his. "Look, Lothaire. Is it not lovely?"

She was lovely. Not simply pretty as was required.

"I am fond of this place," she said as he followed her gaze around the pond. "When I was little, Lady Maude brought her son and me here on the hottest days and we played and swam."

"You speak of Simon?" he said to distract himself from the soft hand he should not be holding. He knew it was Lady Maude and her departed husband's only child she spoke of. Though he liked the lady's stepson who was now Baron of Owen, there was something amiss about Joseph D'Arci's half-brother—something beyond the feeling Simon disliked Lady Laura's betrothed. Their one encounter this day was brief as the young man prepared to return to the lord from whom he received knighthood training, but it had disturbed. And Lothaire was strangely relieved when Simon departed two hours past.

He frowned. "Surely you do not still swim here with Lady Maude's son?"

Lady Laura looked up. "I do not. 'Twould be improper now we are no longer children."

His mother would not like that Simon and she had frolicked here, and neither did he, but though that might cause Raisa Soames to reject this young woman, Lothaire was now a man. *He* would determine what was acceptable.

"But once you and I are wed"—she made a song of her words and angled her head toward the pond—"methinks it permissible for husband and wife to swim together."

The thought of going into the water with her once more making him much too aware of their bodies, he told himself to release her hand and put distance between them.

Told himself.

Her sparkling eyes returned to his. "Perhaps even bathe together, hmm?"

He caught his breath, heard his mother's words again—*Beware the Delilah, my son. Beware the Jezebel.*

He cast off her hand. "You should not speak thus, Lady. 'Tis sinful!"

She blinked as if slapped, and as the light in her eyes fell to earth alongside her smile, whispered, "Forgive me. Oh, Lady Maude shall be disappointed. I am a lady. Truly, I am. I just…" She peeked at him from beneath her lashes. "I am pleased you wish to take me to wife, Lord Soames. You are young and handsome, and I am certain you are kind. I but wish you to be as happy with me as I am with you."

Though his mother would not overlook her behavior, the man before her decided she could be forgiven. She was young and would mature ere they wed, and once Lady Maude was made aware of her ward's deficiencies, she would correct them.

His betrothed lifted her chin, and he saw her eyes sparkled again, but not with joy or mischief. "You are not pleased with me, are you?"

Struggling against the impulse to pull her close and wipe away her tears, he clenched his hands at his sides. "I make allowances for your age and am confident a year hence you will be nearer a woman than a girl."

His words offended, as evidenced by a different sort of light in those eyes, but it scattered and she said, "Much can happen in a year. Be patient, and I shall not disappoint you or Lady Maude who has been so good to me."

The lady *had* been generous, fostering Laura Middleton since the age of five when her mother's passing left the girl's father with one female child to raise amidst six males.

"You…" She moistened her lips, and he saw they trembled. "…will not be too harsh in telling Lady Maude of my failings, will you? She will count herself responsible, and she is not. Ever I have been excitable." A tear spilled, and she clapped a hand to her cheek as if to hide it. Another fell. "Oh, how the fluff upon the air irritates my eyes!"

Dear Lord, Lothaire silently appealed, *she should not captivate so.*

But she did, and he had only himself to blame when he breached the space between them and set his mouth on hers. He had kissed a few chambermaids—the extent of his carnal sin—but he was familiar enough with the intimacy to know this was different. The taste of Laura was more than pleasant. It was sweet, like the honey milk of his childhood.

It was she who ended the kiss. Dropping from her toes he had not realized he had dragged her onto, she said, "I like that, Lord Soames, but now I must prove Lady Maude has made a lady of me."

"This is good," he said as if he but tested her—and wished he did. How many hours must he now spend praying for forgiveness?

"My lord?"

"My lady?"

She was smiling again, though more demurely, cheeks prettily flushed. "Methinks you ought to release me."

He lurched back. And had only a moment to miss the press of her body before what sounded like a large insect passed between their faces and skittered across the pond.

He snapped his head around, considered the rippled surface. "What was that?"

"Simon?" she called with what seemed rebuke.

Lothaire followed her gaze to the trees between pond and castle. "You think 'twas him?"

"I…" She looked sidelong at Lothaire, pressed pretty white teeth into her lower lip.

"He is gone from Owen," he reminded her, then wondered if he erred when he recalled the slingshot looped over the young man's belt—of note since Lothaire was fond of that childhood weapon. Though these past years of training were mostly spent mastering the sword, he was certain he could still make his mark.

"You are right, it cannot have been him," she said. "Do you think 'twas a dragonfly?"

He studied the trees again. No movement. No sound that did not belong.

Might it have been a large insect? Possible. Regardless, it would have struck him in the temple had he not released her. "We ought to return, Lady Laura." He stepped past her. And halted.

We are going to wed, he assured himself. *She will be my wife. We will swim in the lake near Thistle Cross. Mayhap bathe together.*

He peered over his shoulder and met her wary gaze. Longing to see the sparkle return to it, he reached to her.

There. So much light shone from her he felt its rays enter him. And as she slid her palm over his and worked her fingers through his, he was so warmed he discovered within him places he had not known were cold.

It *was* a beautiful day to fall in love. Perhaps he would.

As they walked side by side, skirts brushing chausses, brown hair caressing muscled forearm, neither saw the one who pressed his back to the bark of an ancient oak. Neither saw calloused fingers gripping straps of leather whose missile should have turned Lord Soames's dark blond hair red…knocked him to his knees…made him cry like a boy…

Neither heard him rasp, "She is mine. Shall ever be mine. She promised!"

1

Barony of Owen, England
April, 1163

AWAKEN, LAURA. IT is time.

She shook her head, felt the lingering caress of hair across cheeks, nose, and throat.

Open your eyes, the voice persisted.

She squeezed her lids tighter, ignored the ache of lungs that had expelled their last breath.

Do not do it for you. Do it for Clarice.

She sprang open her lids, peered at the clouded, candle-lit ceiling. It *was* time. Past time. But she was not yet clean.

That made her laugh, causing a bubble to burst from her lips and further distort the ceiling.

Her lungs lied. In the deepest of her, she yet had breath. And *she* lied. Never would she be truly clean, no matter how hard she scraped her scalp or urged her maid to scrub her flesh until so abraded pricks of blood surfaced.

A moment later, that woman appeared above—wide-eyed and disapproving.

Pushing her feet against the tub's bottom, Laura slid up the side with a great slop of water.

Tina jumped back. "Oh milady! Ye got me skirts. Again!"

Water streaming Laura's face and shoulders and over breasts she knew more by weight than sight, she managed one of the few smiles of which she was capable—that of apology. "I was in need of air."

"Then ye shoulda come up sooner." Tina snorted. "Sometimes ye worry me no end."

Laura flicked water from her fingers, dragged a hand across her eyes. "I come up when I must."

"As Lady Maude said, ye be a creature of the water."

Maude. Gone six months now. Thus, Laura must awaken. For Clarice, who needed her mother now the woman she had not known was her grandmother had died. But there was something Clarice needed more—a father. Rather, a provider.

And so I shall sell this used body to the highest bidder, Laura silently vowed. It mattered not were he young or old, only that he had sufficient income to support a wife and child and could be trusted to treat Clarice well and protect her.

It seemed easily attainable, as if Laura would have many to choose from, but she would be fortunate to find one, and only then were she given aid. Would Queen Eleanor help her distant cousin who had borne a child out of wedlock, so shaming her family she was disavowed? No chance if the truth of Clarice remained a secret, but now Maude was gone…

"Come, milady, give me yer back."

Laura scooted forward and lowered her chin in preparation for the stiffly bristled brush.

As Tina piled her lady's wet tresses atop her head and began working the brush over a shoulder blade, that voice persisted in reminding Laura it was time. Drawing a deep breath, she peered over her shoulder. "Not the brush, Tina. A washcloth."

The maid's eyes grew so round, Laura knew in her first life—before Clarice—she would have laughed. "I do not know I heard right, milady. Did ye say washcloth?"

"I did."

"Huh!" She dropped the brush to the floor and snatched up the cloth she had earlier worked over face and hands.

It was so lightly felt that twice Laura looked around lest she imagined the soft fibers.

"Are ye comin' into sickness, milady?"

Laura lowered her chin again, caught her reflection in water so clouded with soap she could see no more than the outline of her torso and limbs—as preferred.

"I am not." She stared into eyes one would never know had once shone with happiness. "'Tis just..." She nearly said it was time, but that would make as little sense to Tina as using the washcloth. "I am clean enough."

Rather, she could get no cleaner. She was sullied and would ever be. More, were she to capture a husband, he would expect soft unmarred skin, and for the sake of Clarice, she would have to keep him content. Especially in bed.

Bile shooting into her mouth, she convulsed.

"Ye *are* ill, milady!"

Laura grimaced as the acid burned its way back down. "'Tis but something I ate."

After a long moment, Tina said, "Or something ye did not eat. I saw ye nibble all 'round yer bread, and did ye even taste the soup? Methinks not."

Though Laura's appetite was often lacking, it had been absent this eve after the incident with Clarice and the lady of the castle's son, which had propelled her in a direction she had not yet fully accepted she must travel.

Laura sat back. "I am done with my bath. Pray, bring a towel near."

Tina shook out the large cloth and stretched it between her hands.

Gripping the tub's rim, Laura set her chin high and stood. Yet another thing she must overcome—distaste for an unclothed body. As difficult as it was to look at her own, how was she to look upon a husband's?

More bile, but she was prepared, and Tina did not notice her lady's discomfort as she enfolded her in the towel.

"I shall get ye into yer chemise and braid yer hair, then to bed."

"Clarice—"

"*Tsk,* milady. Worry not, I shall go for her and see her upon her pallet."

The one alongside Laura's bed, which her daughter had rarely used before Maude's passing. Most nights the girl had slept in her grandmother's chamber. Though Laura told herself it was because of her own restless sleep, it was a lie. Clarice had loved her grandmother more. She still did, and with good cause.

But I am awake now, she assured herself.

Another lie, though she *was* awakening, and would do right by her daughter as had not seemed necessary until now. Maude had made it too easy for Laura to live inside herself—to be more a creature of the water than the air.

Guilt had done that to the older lady. And love of Clarice.

I am sorry, Laura sent her thoughts in search of the dead. *I did not say it often enough, but you were too good to me. I should have been stronger for Clarice. Should have been a mother not a...*

What was I? What am I? Not even a sister.

Tina pressed her onto the stool before her dressing table and, in a moment of unguardedness, Laura caught her reflection in the mirror.

Forcing her awakening self to confront the stranger there, she wondered how she was to secure a husband. Though with Maude's guidance and encouragement she had maintained the facade and carriage of a fine lady, these past months had been less kind to her appearance than all the years before. She was thin and pale, eyes shadowed, lips low, shoulders bent.

Awaken, Laura. That voice again. *For Clarice.*

She opened her eyes wider, raised her shoulders, and watched as Lady Laura's hair was gently combed and worked into braids.

A quarter hour later, Tina swept the covers atop her, fussed over the placement of the braids on the pillow to ensure the crimps lay right when she uncrossed them in the morn, then snuffed all but one candle.

"Sleep in God's arms, milady," she said and closed the door.

Laura stared at the ceiling and thought how much more she liked it seen through water. "God's arms," she whispered. "Ever too full to hold me. Lest I drop Clarice, I shall have to hold myself."

2

Barony of Lexeter, England
Mid-May, 1163

KING HENRY WAS returned, and with him his queen. For four years he had occupied his French lands, not once setting foot in his island kingdom. But now he was everywhere, traveling across England at a furious pace, setting aright wrongs, and—it was said—increasingly disillusioned with his old friend, Thomas Becket.

The archbishop, a favorite to whom the king had entrusted the education of his heir, was not behaving. At least, not how Henry wished Thomas to behave.

As for Queen Eleanor, she was also making her presence felt. In this moment. Inside these walls.

"What does that harlot want?"

Lothaire stiffened. He had heard footsteps, but since they did not scrape or land heavily, he thought they belonged to a servant come to prepare the hall for the nooning meal. When his mother wished to be stealthy, she made the effort to lift and softly place her feet.

Setting his teeth, he turned.

She stood before the dais upon which the lord's table was raised. Wisps of silver hair visible beneath her veil, face loose and heavily lined, she arched eyebrows above eyes so lightly lidded they seemed unusually large.

Having wed a man six years younger than she and birthed Lothaire just past the age of thirty, Raisa Soames could more easily be his grandmother. Though fifty and nine, she looked older. But then, she had always appeared aged beyond her years. For that and her temperament, it was told her now departed husband had often strayed from the marriage bed.

"My son," she said with an imperious lift of her chin, "I asked a question."

And he would answer when he answered. They were years beyond her ability to dominate him, but ever she tried to take back ground lost a decade past after his betrothal to Lady Laura Middleton was broken.

Resenting that even a glancing thought for that young lady yet felt like a blade between the ribs, he rolled the missive and slid it beneath his belt.

His mother stared at what he refused her greedy eyes, the color blooming in her cheeks proving blood yet coursed beneath her skin.

"I am summoned to court, Mother."

She drew a sharp breath. "For?"

"What we knew would call me to Eleanor's side if I failed to find a bride with a sizable enough dowry to make Lexeter whole."

She hastened onto the dais and would have dropped to her knees had he not caught her arm. As he pulled her up beside him, she gripped his tunic so fiercely her nails scraped his chest through the material. "You have not searched far enough!" Saliva sprayed his face. "Now see, our future is in the hands of that French harlot."

She was not entirely wrong. Since the annulment of his unfortunate marriage to Lady Beata Fauvel a year past, he could have searched harder, but the thought of awakening beside another woman he wanted only for her wealth had put him off the hunt. Too, when he was not working the land to turn it profitable, he pursued his only other passion—becoming worthy to don a Wulfrith dagger.

Of that his mother remained unaware, though not for lack of trying to discover where twice now he had gone for three and four weeks—Wulfen Castle where he suffered humiliation after humiliation, ofttimes at the hands of mere squires. And where he was to have traveled a sennight hence.

Much to Abel Wulfrith's displeasure, Lothaire had slammed his pride to the ground and accepted the man's offer to train him into one of England's most formidable warriors. Lothaire had known it was but a taunt, but he had dared. And Sir Abel's brother, Everard, had said if the offer was made it must be fulfilled.

Despite the pain and shame endured, Lothaire had discovered a liking for the two brothers, and even the eldest, Baron Wulfrith. More surprising, Sir Abel had become easier in his pupil's company during the second training. They could never be friends, Lothaire having no use for such, but there was something appealing about spending time with men his own age who shared similar interests.

Now he must send word he would not avail himself of next month's training. More unfortunate, even if he returned from court with a wife, it would be months before he could journey to Wulfen Castle since he must wait until next Sir Abel relieved one of his brothers of the task of training up England's worthiest knights.

"I shall accompany you," his mother broke into his thoughts. "King Henry's harlot will know exactly what you require in a wife—virtuous, wealthy, pretty, but not too pretty."

"I go alone." Lothaire unhooked his mother's hands from his tunic.

"But my son—!"

"You shall remain here." Ensuring she had her balance, he stepped back. "If the queen provides a wife, you will relinquish the title of Lady of Lexeter without protest, else I will see you removed to your dower property." Which he should have done years ago.

Light leapt in her eyes, but naught resembling the sparkle of stars on a moonless night. This was fire. And here came the threat that was the greatest control she had over him.

"Sebille will go with me. You know she will."

His older sister whom their parents had once called their *miracle* for the Lord's healing of an affliction in her infancy. Though Lothaire could have secured a marriage for Sebille, Raisa Soames had deemed a landless knight unworthy of her daughter and persuaded the young woman that her place was at her mother's side.

"For years, Sebille's devotion to you and your poor health has stayed my hand," he said, "most notably when I did not send you away after you risked all of Lexeter by hiring men to murder Lady Beata and Baron Marshal."

Her eyes burned brighter. Would she now deny the wrongdoing as she had not a year past after he and his men intercepted the assassins shortly before Lady Beata's husband challenged those who trespassed on his lands? Lothaire had sensed she wanted to deny it, but she had gone silent, and he had been glad lest she demand proof it was of her doing. That he could not have provided, not only because it was his sister who secretly alerted him to their mother's plans but because the assassins had escaped High Castle's prison before they could be made to talk.

Lothaire narrowed his eyes. "It will end differently if you threaten *my* wife, Mother."

"Foolish boy! Ever you do not see the Delilah who would make of you a Samson, who would steal your strength and leave you weak as a woman."

Many times he had heard this. Indeed, one of his first acts of rebellion against her tyranny had been to grow his hair. She had hated it, though it had been only long enough to catch back at the nape when he was first betrothed. After Lady Laura's betrayal, he had meant to cut it so he might more easily forget their hands in each other's hair, but that would have pleased his mother. Upon learning the cause for the broken betrothal and seeing her son's misery, over and again she had cursed Lady Laura for *cutting* her Samson's hair.

"Nor do you see the Jezebel!" She jabbed a finger at him. "She who would make an Ahab of you, provoking the Lord and bringing ill upon your house. But I see her. And would not have you suffer again as that wicked—"

"Enough!" Lothaire stepped from the dais and tossed over his shoulder, "You may wish me still a boy, but I have not been since—"

"Since that harlot made a cuckold of you, just as over and again your father made a mockery of our wedding vows."

He did not break stride.

"You still think on her. I know you do."

He halted. Though she spoke of Laura, neither had his first wife, Lady Edeva, been pure.

Do I hate my mother? he wondered. He did not, but she gave him little cause to love her.

He turned. "That would please you, aye? For me to more greatly regret not heeding your advice than that she lay with another."

"You should have listened to me! How many times did I warn—?"

"I did listen. You said she would make a fitting wife."

"Until time and again she called you back to her, like a siren seeking to drag you down into the dark. Into sin!"

It was as Raisa Soames wished to believe, though he knew her objections thereafter were rooted in jealousy. She had never fully recovered from the wasting sickness that prevented her from accompanying him to Owen for his second visit with his betrothed. Hence, four more times he had visited Laura unchaperoned, and each time was sweeter than the last.

But not the very last when he learned the truth of her—she who had assured him she would mature…would not disappoint…that much could happen in a year. Much had happened, though not as expected. Even now, ten years gone, he could see her standing before the pond. Alone, but not entirely alone.

Of the ride home to Lexeter, he recalled little. Nearly all was a blur, though less so his stop at the village of Thistle Cross to seek solace at the church whose priest had once ministered inside the castle walls.

A year after his lord's disappearance, Father Atticus had displeased Lady Raisa. Like others in his lord's service, he had been cast out. But rather than leave Lexeter, he had withdrawn to the nearest village and ministered alongside its aging priest. When the latter passed, Atticus had assumed the other man's duties, returning to the castle only when called upon on the rare occasion Lady Raisa hosted other nobles and the presence of a man of God was required.

On that day of Laura's betrayal, Lothaire had hated himself for the tears shed over the faithless woman, and Atticus had consoled him by listening and praying with him—as had become habit over the years since.

"Ah, but ever I am to blame," Lady Raisa returned her son to her presence.

"Leave it be, Mother," he said and strode to the stairs off which stepped Martin, his mother's physician of too many years to number. A coincidence? Possible. Had he been listening in on the exchange between mother and son? More possible. If not that Lady Raisa was so dependent on the man, he would have been replaced years ago.

"My lord," the physician acknowledged him.

Lothaire inclined his head and continued past. As he ascended the stairs, he glanced over his shoulder. Martin had hold of his mother's arm and guided her toward the kitchen.

Moments later, Lothaire closed himself in the solar. When his breathing calmed, he read the queen's missive again. He did not like the wording. It begged a question. Did she or did she not have a wife for him? She said she did, and yet in closing she wavered.

We shall expect you within a fortnight, Lord Soames. Do you present well, we believe you will gain the hand of the lady who shall bring to her marriage the relief many a lord seeks to save his lands. Do not disappoint us.

3

Windsor Castle, England
Late May, 1163

SHE KNEW SHE was awake, but it seemed a dream she inhabited as she stared at the lady before her.

It was the finest mirror, with so little distortion she wondered if she had truly seen herself before. The pond she had not visited since before Clarice's birth had offered the truest reflection, but she had never presented as clearly as this.

She did not think herself beautiful, but she was quite fair, especially after a month beneath the queen's eye and that woman's sighing over all that must be done to transform her cousin from disagreeably delicate to agreeably desirable.

Desirable. Laura detested the word. It told of things that happened in the dark whether a woman wished it or not.

"Milady?"

She blinked, looked to the maid beside her. "Am I ready, Tina?"

"Oh, lass." She patted her lady's cheek. "More ready than ever I have seen ye. And it has been six years since Lady Maude gave ye into me care, eh?"

Six years—following the visit to Simon's half-brother whose wife had nearly suffered the same as Laura.

How she adored Michael and Lady Beatrix. How she wished she could accept their offer for Clarice and her to live at Castle Soaring. The temptation was great, but were she to agree, she would not fully awaken. And she was determined not to be a burden to anyone again— excepting whomever she wed, but he would have payment enough in the bedroom.

She almost smiled at the realization her throat did not burn with bile. She was growing accustomed to the idea of violation. That was good, for a poor marriage it would be—and of detriment to Clarice—if the man whose ring Laura wore discovered how she felt about what he did to her.

Still no bile.

"Six years, Tina. I pray we have many more."

Blessedly they would, Maude's stepson having agreed the maid could leave Owen, and Queen Eleanor concurring that Laura's husband would accept Tina's services.

"'Tis time," the maid said.

Laura slid her palms down the skirt of one of a dozen gowns gifted her by Maude over the years.

The queen had been pleased with the quality and colors of Laura's wardrobe, surely having expected the royal coffers to bear the cost of clothing her cousin in finery needed to capture a husband. Though a few gowns were no longer fashionable, a seamstress had been engaged to alter their fit and design.

Were I happy, Laura thought, *I would feel like a princess.*

"I am ready," she said and followed Tina to the door of the luxurious apartment that had been hers these past weeks. Soon she would leave here, collect her daughter from Michael D'Arci and Lady Beatrix, and journey to wherever she would spend the remainder of her life with the man to whom she must give herself to provide her daughter a good future.

Now to see which lord so badly needed funds he would pay the price of a used lady newly awakened.

Which one was she?

The tall lady whose eyes rushed about the hall as if in search of someone? The freckled lady twisting a tress of glorious red hair? The elegant blond lady of an age several years beyond his own? What of the lady with hair the color of burnished bronze?

Lothaire looked nearer upon the latter. She stood in profile, but there was no denying she was lovely, albeit thinner than he liked.

He grunted. Though given a choice, he would pick a wife pure of body and passing pretty, he grudgingly accepted that what mattered was she possess dowry enough to return Lexeter to the prosperity it had enjoyed before his father's murder over twenty years past.

He pushed that remembrance aside. Though determined to learn where Ricard Soames was buried so the old baron could be moved to consecrated ground, Lothaire was here to secure a wife.

He looked to the queen who had yet to grant him an audience though he had arrived at Windsor last eve. Likely, she remained displeased with him for wedding Lady Beata Fauvel without her permission, forcing her to arrange an annulment of the unconsummated marriage before she could see her favorite—Sir Durand Marshal—wed to the lady.

As Lothaire started to move his gaze from Eleanor, she settled hers on him. And smiled.

That he did not expect. Though he did not like her, he returned the smile.

She inclined her head and pointedly looked toward a gathering to her left.

Then it was to be the lady with the burnished bronze hair, she who had added another nobleman to her audience.

Lothaire was not averse to the queen's offering. Of all those whose unveiled hair proclaimed them unwed, she was among the few with whom he would have sought an acquaintance. Young enough to bear children, but not so young he would suffer the foolishness of a girl who believed her maturing body made her a woman. Though more pleasing to the eye than he liked, he would simply have to be vigilant. As for her weight, once she knew he did not find half-starved women desirable, she would eat more.

He looked back at Eleanor who gestured for him to approach the lady.

Wishing he had a name by which to call his future wife, he strode forward. As he neared, he studied her face in profile and revised his opinion. Given a choice, he would not make this lady's acquaintance. Too much she resembled the first woman to whom he had been betrothed, albeit more mature. But he dare not further displease the queen, and he must wed a lady who brought a good dowry to the marriage.

He was several strides distant when she tapped the air between her and a nobleman of middling years and said, "Fie on you, Lord Benton."

Now he had a name, one that stopped him and blew warm breath into his cold places. But it could not be her. She had no dowry, her father having disavowed her.

At what did the queen play? Eleanor had to know that once he had been betrothed to this lady. Might this be punishment for his defiance?

Feeling his chest and shoulders rise and fall, hearing blood thrum through his veins, he looked to the queen.

She raised her eyebrows, motioned for him to resume his approach.

Dear Lord, make me stone, he silently beseeched. *Open wide a path to sooner see me away from here.*

Continuing forward, he altered his course and inserted himself between Lord Benton and another nobleman. He had only a moment to take in the lady's lovely face before shuttering his own against her gaze.

Lids fluttering, breath catching, she stumbled back and dropped her chin.

"Lady Laura?" Lord Benton gripped her arm.

"Forgive me! The heel of my slipper has failed." She put its toe forward, providing no evidence of what remained hidden beneath the elaborately embroidered skirt of a gown that bore little resemblance to the simple gowns she had worn ten years past.

She sighed, looked up. As if Lothaire were not a flicker of the eyes away, she smiled at Lord Benton. "Pray, excuse me. I shall remedy the situation as soon as possible."

"Do not forget your promise to sit with me at meal," said a short, attractive man to Lothaire's right.

"I shall not, Lord Gadot." She swung away and, absent a hitch in her step, moved toward the stairs.

Lord Benton looked to Lothaire. "You are?"

"Baron Soames."

The man's brow lowered. "Another rival? Or just passing through?"

"Rival?"

"For the lady's hand," Lord Gadot said and winked. "Quite the surprise she is so lovely, hmm? I was certain she must be the freckled one, else the lady nearing the end of her child-bearing years, but the Lord is kind. I would very much like Lady Laura in my bed."

For a moment, Lothaire did not know himself. But a reminder of who the lady was—a Jezebel from the top to the bottom of her—kept his hand from his dagger.

"Ah, but whoever wins her must needs watch her closely," said the third nobleman who, were he capable of wielding a sword, would find his swing hindered by excessive weight. "I have no wish to be made a cuckold."

As the others murmured agreement over the comment surely meant to discourage the other suitors, Lothaire ached that Laura's sin should be so well known. And resented her for it. Blessedly, none looked upon him in any way to indicate they knew he was a victim of her cuckolding.

"Are you a rival, Baron Soames?" Lord Benton asked again.

"Just passing through." Lothaire pivoted away from the three who sought to wed the woman he had once wanted. But no more. Not ever again. As soon as he gained an audience with the queen, he would make it known Laura Middleton was unacceptable. If Eleanor insisted on finding him a wife, it would have to be another.

Upon reaching a sideboard, he accepted a goblet of wine from a servant. Once his face was composed as much as possible, he turned.

Though the queen remained seated and conversed with one of her ladies, her eyes were on him.

She liked this game—wanted to watch the players dance on their twisted and knotted strings. But he would not, and eventually she would weary of her sport and summon him.

Unless she had another lady able to raise Lexeter out of its financial difficulties, he would depart on the morrow, ride for Wulfen, and make good out of bad by sharpening his sword skill with the anger coursing his veins.

Abel Wulfrith's opponent would prove worthier yet. Mayhap near deadly.

4

Blinded by tears, she knew not how she made it to her chamber. But it was the one given her, as evidenced by Tina who leapt to her feet in response to the door's slam.

"What has happened?" the maid exclaimed as she hastened to where her lady pressed herself back against the door. "Ye have displeased the queen?"

Though Laura knew Eleanor would be unhappy with her departure, she shook her head. Panting so deeply her laces strained, she choked, "He is here," and the face of the man who had once called her *Laura love* rose before her—more weathered than she would have expected, and more fit with condemnation than the last time she had looked upon it. Though a goodly distance had separated them ten years past, his judgment then had been tempered by hurt.

"Who is here, milady?"

"Lo—" She whimpered. She had thought his name a thousand times, but it had not passed her lips for longer than she could recall.

Tina gasped. "Tell me ye do not mean Lothaire Soames."

The maid did not know the exact circumstances that led to the dissolution of Laura's betrothal, but all of Owen and many beyond knew that once the two were to have wed. And Clarice was the reason they had not.

"Aye, Tina." She saw him again, from wheat-colored hair springing back from his brow to tall leather boots encasing muscled calves and large feet. "Him."

"Mercy, such ill timing! Or do ye think…? Nay, he cannot be amongst those seeking yer hand."

Laura startled so hard her head knocked against the door. *That* had not occurred. Though Eleanor said she had four noblemen prepared to vie for her, what had not needed to be told was they were in such desperate need of funds they would accept as wife and mother of their children one whose taint was all the more visible in the misbegotten daughter who would also share hearth and home.

But Lothaire could not be that desperate. At worst, he had been summoned to allow the queen to test Laura's claim she was lady enough not to succumb to the carnal outside of marriage and that her love for Lothaire had been too complete to make a cuckold of him.

"Milady, ye are twisting yer skirt into a mess, makin' wrinkles I shall have to smooth again." Tina closed her hands over Laura's and gently pried them open. "And yer face!"

A sharp knock sounded, and Laura lurched away from the door. If not for Tina's sturdy build, the two might have tumbled to the floor.

"Lady Laura, the queen approaches," a voice called and knocked again.

Having steadied her lady, Tina whipped up her own skirt and wiped at Laura's face. She dropped back, winced. "Well 'tis not as if Her Majesty is not expecting this, eh?" She squared her shoulders and opened the door—with no time to spare.

"Lady Laura!" Eleanor's voice was like a whip against its recipient's back. "Do we waste our time finding you a husband and your daughter a protector?"

Laura splayed her hands amid her skirts, turned.

The queen's frown deepening, she made a sound of disgust and peered over her shoulder at Tina. "You. Close the door."

"I should remain, Yer Majesty?"

"You should."

As Tina swung the door in the faces of the queen's ladies who stood in the corridor, Eleanor motioned Laura forward.

"Forgive me, Your Majesty." Laura halted before her sovereign. "I know I should not have left the hall, but would that you had told me Baron Soames was in attendance. As you must know, it was a shock to see him again. 'Tis difficult enough accepting I am to wed a man I do not want without so painful a reminder of the man I..."

"Loved," the queen said. "Perhaps still love, hmm?"

"I do not. Can not. It has been ten years, and I would be a fool to love one who feels only loathing and revulsion for me." A tear fell. "Pray, send him away so I may do what I came for."

The queen studied her so long a half dozen more tears fell ere she spoke again. "What you told us is true, Lady Laura?"

That which had remained a secret to nearly all while Lady Maude lived. "It is, Your Majesty." She felt the presence of Tina who may have guessed but did not know with certainty the circumstances of Clarice's conception. "'Twas not I who made a cuckold of Lord Soames."

Eleanor's smile was slight. "Then you have four prospects. By week's end, you shall be betrothed."

"Four! Surely you do not mean Baron Soames—"

"We do, and him most of all."

Not ill timing. The *queen's* timing. Laura's knees softened, but she snapped them back lest she drop at her sovereign's feet and make Eleanor further regret the aid given her cousin. "Pray, reconsider, Your Majesty. I do not know I can do this with him present. 'Twill be torture."

The queen put her head to the side. "Have we not given counsel every day since your arrival? Have we not been heartened to see your body and resolve strengthen? Have we not summoned these men to court given your assurance you are ready to be a wife to the one we deem best for your daughter and you?"

Laura was ashamed by the spill of more tears. "Aye, Your Majesty, but—"

"Then enough! You will not disappoint us." Eleanor raised her hands and stepped forward so suddenly Laura startled. But the queen did not slap at her. She took the younger woman's face between her soft, fragrant palms. "Listen to me," she eschewed the royal *us,* her reference to her singular self nearly setting Laura to sobbing. "If Baron Soames loved you as you say you loved him, he is the one. And when he learns the truth of your daughter, a good marriage you can make."

Dear Lord, Laura silently bemoaned, *she as good as tells she will choose him!*

The queen lowered her hands and stepped back. "And he shall right another of his wrongs."

Another? Laura wondered.

"Providing," Eleanor added, "he is the man *we* believe him to be and is willing to take our advice on removing his mother from his home." She shook her head. "That woman will be the ruin of him does he not sever her influence—as she would be the ruin of you and your daughter. Such bitterness over her husband's faithlessness, his disappearance, and now…" She waved away whatever else she meant to say.

However, what she had revealed was intriguing enough to distract Laura. She knew Lothaire's father had gone missing when his son was six years old and that he was never found, but Lothaire had not revealed his father was unfaithful. It accounted for his mother's severity and portended how deeply Lothaire and Lady Raisa must have felt what they perceived as Laura's faithlessness.

"You will return to the hall, Lady Laura." It was not a question. "And you will spend time with your suitors in our sight so we may observe."

Laura longed to fall on the bed and only be bodily moved from it, but she would appear ungrateful for all Eleanor had done. More, though at times the queen was nearly as severe as Lothaire's mother, Laura sensed she genuinely cared for her scandalous relation.

"If you will allow me some minutes to put myself in order, Your Majesty, I shall rejoin you belowstairs."

"And charm your suitors?"

She inclined her head.

"Even Lord Soames?"

She hesitated, asked, "Ere he appeared before me, did he know my purpose—that I am the one he must take to wife to ease his financial difficulties?"

"He did not, but whatever the others said of you following your departure, he did not like. And we venture it nearly moved him to a display of jealousy."

That Laura did not believe. He was angered, but only by her presence and the waste of his time. Thus, he would surely be gone by the morrow, leaving her with three suitors.

And were he desperate enough to stay? Then within days he would depart. Painful though it would be, Laura would charm him as much as the others—nay, more. If purity and modesty were as important to him as once they had been, he would find her seriously lacking.

"Lady Laura?" Irritation edged the queen's voice.

Laura forced a smile. "I shall charm all my suitors, Your Majesty."

Eleanor's lids narrowed, and though Laura expected her to warn her cousin about the lengths to which she could go to charm, she said, "A quarter hour. No more." She turned, and Tina opened and closed the door behind her.

"I know what ye are thinking lass." She drew her lady to the dressing table. "I saw the steel straightening yer back—and I am glad of it—but proceed carefully. Ye do not want to fall out of favor with a woman such as that."

Laura lowered to the plump stool before the mirror, looked near upon her reddened eyes and cheeks. "Worry not, Tina. Cruelty by cruelty I am finding my way through the world."

And shall leave a well-marked path for Clarice to follow, if necessary, she did not say. Then she silently prayed, *Lord, let it not be necessary. Let me do for her what I should have done long ago. Do not let her life mirror mine.*

When he was not discreetly tracking the woman who had betrayed him, ensuring their paths did not cross, he watched the queen. But though he did so with the hope of receiving permission to approach, whenever she bestowed her gaze, it was dismissive.

But he would not play her game. And that she would have to accept.

Moments later, Lothaire heard *her* voice and looked around to discover the distance between Laura and himself had narrowed considerably.

She was in the company of Lord Benton, having shed Lord Gadot with whom she had sat at meal, and the two strolled the path upon which Lothaire stood.

He nearly turned opposite, but when she looked up, pride demanded he not scurry away.

Something flashed in her dark eyes—nearer a fire than a sparkle—then she returned her attention to her companion and said, "She is nine years aged."

Lothaire ground his teeth. He did not wish to hear of the child she had made with another. Hoping Lord Benton and she would alter their course, he remained unmoving.

"As lovely as her mother?" The nobleman asked.

Lothaire would not know her smile was forced were he not acquainted with the true turn of her lips.

"Clarice is still very much a girl, my lord, but I believe she will be far lovelier than I. She has the most beautiful sable hair."

Likely given by her father, Lothaire succumbed to bitterness. But that emotion was short-lived, for the two were nearer yet, and he would not have her know how much she disturbed him.

"I look forward to meeting her, my lady."

She inclined her head, moved her gaze to Lothaire. As if surprised, she gasped, "Baron Soames, I meant to seek you out." She and Lord Benton halted. "I apologize for not acknowledging you earlier. I did not intend to be rude, but I had to change slippers."

Though Lothaire had no desire to converse with her—and would not outside Lord Benton's company—it was she who provided him with satisfying small talk. He looked down her skirt, eyed the fine shoe visible beneath the hem. "Do you not wear the same slippers, my lady?"

She gave a little laugh. "'Tis a style and color I quite like."

How easily she lied between her words. "Indeed."

"Oh!" She angled toward the man at her side, touched his arm. "In my absence, did you have the chance to introduce yourself to Lord Benton?"

"Well enough," Lothaire said sharply. And berated himself for not controlling his tongue. And he paid for it when she clapped a hand to her mouth and smiled on either side of it. That expression making him ache, he steeled himself for what was to come.

"Is this jealousy, Baron Soames?"

"Jealousy?" Lord Benton jerked as if his chin were clipped. While behind Lothaire's face, distaste and anger jerked through him.

"Ah, we must remedy this," the lady said. "'Tis only fair all my suitors know who they must better to win my hand."

Almighty! Lothaire sent heavenward. *She does not even try to disguise the Daughter of Eve who bore a child out of wedlock.*

And there was more. She stepped forward and placed on Lothaire's arm the slender fingers recently familiar with the other man. "Your rival, Lord Benton, the handsome Baron Soames of Lexeter. The fourth of four—well, I believe 'tis only four—suitors." She made a face that once more sent Lothaire into the past. "We shall see, hmm?"

She released him, and he breathed again. But only for a moment. As she turned away, the ends of her unbound hair swept his wrist and the back of his hand, and he remembered the feel of strands he should never have drawn his fingers through.

Not for the first time, though it was long since he had pondered it, he questioned if the kisses and caresses shared prior to the wedding that had not taken place were responsible—at least in part—for making a Jezebel of her. He had liked the intimacies. Had she felt as much as he, perhaps she had gone in search of one willing to show her what came next.

"Now I must find Lord Thierry," she returned him to the present he longed to leave behind. "I promised I would sit with him whilst the troubadours encourage us to fall in love. Lord Soames," she said, then touched the other man's arm again. "Lord Benton. Good eve."

Head high, she left what she wrongly believed to be two rivals.

"Just passing through, hmm?" Benton grumbled.

"The lady has a high opinion of herself and her charms," Lothaire said. "Aye, just passing through." He turned, gained the queen's gaze, and lost it. Not as dismissive as before. There had been interest in the arch of an eyebrow, but not enough to grant him an audience.

"Curse you, Eleanor," he muttered and strode toward the stairs that would deliver him from the presence of the woman who would make one of her suitors wish he had found another way to return prosperity to his lands. Just as Lothaire had long sought to do. And would continue to do.

Even if every day the rest of my life I must work the land myself, he vowed.

"Lothaire."

There. She had spoken his name. It swept her back to when she had called it over her shoulder as he chased her across soft spring grass, dry summer grass, leaf-covered autumn grass, frost-bitten winter grass. But most painful were memories of when she had whispered his name against his lips and he had groaned over hers.

Laura love, he had called her.

Though they had both wanted more than kisses and caresses, neither had tempted the other too far past want. And there had been no need, certain as they were of a nuptial night and every night thereafter.

Laura drew a shuddering breath. Assured Tina slept on her pallet, snores so soft her lady rarely had difficulty sleeping through them, she said again, "Lothaire." Slowly, so she felt each tap behind her teeth and the warmth of her breath across tongue and palate when she came to the end of his name.

She had been glad she had eaten little at meal, so sickened was she by her behavior which Lothaire would name wanton and her taunting words that confirmed she was not merely thoughtless.

He would be gone on the morrow and, God willing, she would not see him again.

"Please, Lord. Not again. I love him still."

5

"CAN YOU PAY your taxes, Lord Soames?"

Lothaire turned to the queen where she halted just over the threshold of the private apartment to which he had been summoned a half hour past, bowed. "Your Majesty."

She motioned for him to straighten. "Can you, Lord Soames?"

"I can." Though it would strain his coffer's every joint, his purse's every seam.

She looked almost disappointed. "But not easily, hmm?"

Feeling the shame of it, though every year he gained ground lost by his mother ere he had wrested control of Lexeter from her, he said, "Not easily, Your Majesty."

"Then for your family and people it is imperative you prove the best choice of husband for our cousin, Lady Laura."

He opened his mouth to decline, hesitated over her kinship with his former betrothed. He had not known of it, but it explained why the queen took an interest in a woman disowned by her father. Or did it? Lady Laura's scandalous behavior also reflected on the Queen of England.

"Distant cousins," she guessed at what cramped his expression.

"She requested your aid, Your Majesty?"

"She did. Her protector, Lady Maude, passed last year. Hence, Lady Laura and her daughter are in need of a home."

Not his home. It would be barely tolerable seeing her every day, but to also suffer the girl who surely bore some resemblance to the man gifted with Laura's innocence? And even if he could accept both, never would his mother. Lady Raisa would make their lives torture.

A thought struck him. Had he misinterpreted Laura's reaction to his appearance alongside Lord Benton? "Your Majesty, may I ask if Lady Laura requested I be among her suitors?"

"You may. The answer is nay. *We* determined the man she once loved, who is much in need of a wife and funds, to be a good prospect. And this we tell you in confidence—she was distressed to discover you are among our choices."

"One would not know it from her behavior last eve."

"Indeed. She performed better than expected."

"Performed?"

"We insisted she charm all her suitors. And so she did, though we think it likely she intentionally offended you in hopes you would stand before us this day resolved to working yourself to death rather than take her to wife."

Eleanor was not uninformed. Somehow she had learned of the extent to which he went to return Lexeter to prosperity. He nearly looked to hands he had soaked for hours to remove grime from pores and beneath nails. But the long hours and days out of doors laboring alongside commoners was etched in his face. No amount of soaking would wash away those lines. And unlike King Henry, whose face had given its youth to the sun, wind, and rain, Lothaire had no reason to spend so much time in the saddle.

"Have you any other question, Lord Soames?"

"Forgive me, but considering the lady's past, I am surprised you claim kinship. More, that you are willing to gift her a dowry sizable enough to tempt a nobleman to wed her."

"A dowry," Eleanor mused. "We suppose it is that."

Suppose? Lothaire did not have to think long to unriddle her words. The answer was in the question put to him upon her entrance. "Tax relief. That is what you offer the one who takes her to wife."

"We have discussed Lady Laura's situation with our lord husband, and he agrees a reduction in taxes to half for a period of three years is generous compensation."

It *was* generous, but though it would allow him to make great strides in restoring Lexeter, he would make those strides without the lady and her daughter ever a barb beneath his skin.

"Though tempted, Your Majesty, I must decline and request permission to leave court."

She pursed her lips and considered him through narrowed lids. "Reconsider, Lord Soames. And in doing so, know you stand the greatest chance of winning the lady's hand."

He had to ask. "Why me? From what you have told, she does not wish me for a husband."

"She has no say. If she wants a home for her daughter and her, we shall determine whose home that is. As time and again we must make clear to our subjects, we know best what they require."

He wanted to argue, but it would be futile. "Your Majesty, respectfully I decline marriage to Lady Laura and request my leave-taking."

Her nostrils flared, detracting from her carefully constructed elegance, then she sighed. "You may leave Windsor."

He bowed, and she stepped aside to allow him to pass.

"Lord Soames."

One foot over the threshold, he turned. "Your Majesty?"

"You may not believe this, but we like you. Hence, we are compelled to share that to which few are privy. A great honor, we assure you."

He tensed, certain here was how she meant to slip a noose over his head.

"As you know, now the king and queen are returned to England, those things made wrong in our absence are being made right."

He knew it. For this, her husband was absent from Windsor, traveling the length and breadth of England to assess his long-neglected kingdom and make his presence felt.

"Unfortunately, that requires much revenue."

The noose dropped past his ears.

"There will be more taxes, Lord Soames, and we worry you will not be able to pay them."

He would. Somehow. He would not lose his family's lands.

"You are certain you do not wish to reconsider?"

She was conniving. Had he agreed to be a suitor, much of the tax relief gained in wedding Lady Laura would be lost to these new taxes she would not have mentioned. However, if he continued to put in long hours on the land, the tax relief would offset the taxes to come.

Nay, somehow he would save Lexeter without shackling himself to the one who had betrayed him. Somehow.

For all his certainty, the noose that had descended to his shoulders tightened. Imagining the rough knot abrading his throat, he breathed deep against the constriction. Finding too little air to sustain him, let alone Lexeter, he grudgingly accepted the queen had him—that Lady Laura was his *somehow*. But if Eleanor wanted him badly enough for her relation that she made him privy to what would cause great unrest among the landholders, he had *her*.

"As proposed, a three-year reduction in taxes," he said. "And during that time, Lexeter is exempt from all new taxes."

She was slow to respond, but when she did, it was with little censure. "Lord Soames, do you seek to cause a rift between our lord husband and us?"

"I do not. That is but the price of the sacrifice of my happiness."

"Ah, but you are not happy. Thus, if we determine you are, indeed, best for Lady Laura and her daughter, your loss is not as substantial as you would have us believe."

"Call it what you will, Your Majesty, I count it a great price. We are in agreement?"

She inclined her head. "Your task, Lord Soames, is to show us you can be kind to Lady Laura so we are assured she and her daughter are welcome upon Lexeter."

Kind? Lothaire mused. Tolerant would have to suffice. And even that would be difficult.

"Do you win Lady Laura's hand, we think it best you remove your mother to one of your lesser castles. Are we in agreement?"

Raisa Soames would rage, but Lothaire needed none to tell him that, as unpleasant as it would be to live out his days with a Jezebel, far worse it would be with his mother between them. "Agreed, Your Majesty."

She smiled, further proof that, despite advancing age, she remained a beautiful woman. "Now to convince Lady Laura you are the best fit. Not that it is her decision, but we would give her hope for her future and her daughter's. Go to her Lord Soames."

He stiffened. "Now?"

"We told her we would send one of her suitors to her in the garden. That suitor is you."

He who should be spurring away from Windsor. He who might do so at the end of the week in the company of the woman who should have remained cast off.

"I shall seek her there, Your Majesty."

"And you shall be kind, Lord Soames. Most kind."

Lord Benton? Lord Gadot? Or Lord Thierry?

Not that it mattered. Laura wanted none of them. All she required was a home and protection, and she would not feel guilty for it. Certes, none of them truly wanted her, and they would not feel guilty over the funds she brought to the arrangement—nor her body that they could do with as they pleased.

She shuddered. Outside of Clarice, that last was everything. How was she to bear it?

The dark would make it more tolerable, would hide the revulsion of being intimate with one other than—

She shook her head. *He* did not belong near such imaginings. And after what had been done her, even his touch would repulse.

Where was he now? Riding for home, thanking the Lord no man—or woman—could force him to speak vows? Setting his mind to another with whom he would swim and bathe in the lake upon Lexeter as he had promised Laura they would do?

She dropped her head back, sighed over the blue sky, and in the midst of twittering birds, buzzing insects, and murmurings of those strolling the immense garden, closed her eyes.

As I must do should my husband come to me in daylight to lie me down, she counseled. *I shall close them tight and think on good things. My blessed childhood. The love of Lady Maude. The friendship with Si—*

Nay, not that. She would think nowhere near him, not even the good of him. Because of him, she had lost—

She fought off the memory, tried to turn it inside out and gaze instead upon its seams. Though those inward-turned strips of fabric held the memory together, on this side it was possible to look out between the stitches and see only the pond and sky. And if she turned as she had done that day, she could direct her gaze above the man she loved and lose it amid the treetops.

For years, that was as she had done, but this day after the day past...

Lothaire was there, guiding his horse toward her, confusion sprawled across his face. She had longed to call to him...run to him... assure him she had not betrayed his love. But she was ruined, not only by her father's rejection and her loss of dowry, but the secret she had promised to hold close in exchange for a home in which to raise her misbegotten child.

Thus, she had settled her hand on her belly that was familiar with the bulge only from recent awakenings before she snatched her hand away. A deep breath raised her shoulders, then she slowly turned to allow him to see her body in profile.

It had taken some moments for him to understand, then he had jerked the reins, causing his mount to toss its head.

Hurt replaced the confusion on Lothaire's beloved countenance before anger and condemnation transformed it.

How long had he shone them upon her? How long had she with-stood it? All she knew was that when he reined around and set his horse to flight, she had dropped to her knees and wept until Lady Maude's eldest stepson found her on the bank and carried her to the donjon.

She had wept since, but never like that. And never again would she. Such loss she would not know again.

What of Clarice? she reminded herself of her resolve to become the mother she had not been.

"I shall," she whispered. "I will love you more than ever I have loved. And perhaps one day you will grant me a measure of the affection gifted your grandmother."

She breathed deep through her nose, parted her lips, and on the exhale let the scent of grass, flowers, and bread baking in the palace's kitchen slide their taste across her tongue. So intense was it, she smiled.

I am awake, she told herself. *I shall not sleep again.*

She opened her eyes, wondered if the clouds scattered across the sky would join forces to provide a cool drink to the garden's loveliest occupants. By day's end, she thought, and hoped the clouds would not work themselves into a great storm more apt to drown than water all that thirsted.

Now where was one of those who sought to become her lord husband?

She lowered her chin. And there stood the memory that made her question if she were yet inside it.

Nay, this Lothaire's face was not that of a young man, and he was in the garden of Windsor where he ought not be.

She tried to hold onto her smile so he would not know how deeply he affected her, but it quivered so much she lowered it.

"Lord Soames, are you to be my first…" She raised her eyebrows. "What should I name you? Appointment? Ah, that sounds too much like business. Rendezvous? Nay, slightly scandalous. Audience?"

"Appointment," he said, continuing to lean against the tree where he had watched her for how long she could not know.

That realization unsettled her, though she assured herself no matter what had passed over her face, he could not guess what went behind it.

"Then I should invite you to join me on the bench?" She glanced at the place beside her, silently beseeched, *Pray, stay where you are. Better, mount your horse and leave me with three suitors. I do not need a fourth. I do not need you.*

He pushed off the tree and strode forward in tall boots that beautifully fit his muscled calves.

Try though she did to appear relaxed, her back stiffened and hands convulsed amid her skirts when he lowered beside her, leaving barely enough space to allow another to sit between them.

The last time we sat this near, ere long we were nearer yet, her thoughts defied her. *My hands as much in his hair as his were in mine. And his lips smiled upon mine. Has he been as unhappy as I?*

She looked sidelong at him.

His gaze awaited hers, moved down her nose to her mouth, quickly returned to her eyes. "I am to be kind to you." Resentment punctuated his words. "The queen's orders."

That hurt, though it was his due. He had every reason to feel she had betrayed him in the worst way, but having failed on the night past to send him running, she would have to make it very difficult to be kind to her.

"Poor Lothaire." Her heart ached over his name. "As much as you hate me, you must be in dire straits to seek the hand of a whore."

A sharp breath flared his nostrils.

She pushed a sorrowful smile onto her lips. "That is what I am, is it not? And should you be so desperate as to entertain doubt, I have the daughter to prove it."

He did not leave as he ought to, and so she steeled herself for her next words. "Clarice is lovely—has her father's eyes. Of course, if you prevail against my other suitors, you will see for yourself. Every day."

He rose and strode opposite.

Laura kept her chin up and stared after him lest he look back.

He did not.

Better this way, she told herself. *Better for both of us. Better for Clarice.*

Certain he would go directly to the stables and be away from Windsor as soon as his horse could be saddled, Laura sagged, put her face in her hands, and cried. One last time.

Lothaire halted. He was doing exactly what she wanted—fleeing the one who could be Lexeter's only hope, proving she was as much a coward as he. She may have fallen into sin, but the woman who taunted him, seeking to make him forget she was his *somehow*, was not the same he had once called *Laura love*. She whom he had fled was an entirely different creature, just as she wished him to believe.

He turned, with apology sidestepped an elderly couple who strolled the path, and shortly passed beneath the vine-covered arbor.

The sun in Laura's hair revealing there was still red among tresses that had darkened over the years, she sat forward, elbows tight to her sides, face in her hands.

He paused to listen. Though she made no sound, the jerk of her shoulders told she wept, and he was glad. Here was proof some of the young woman he had loved yet breathed. He could not feel for her again, but for Lexeter he would tolerate her. And the daughter who had her father's eyes.

He continued forward. When she did not respond in any way to indicate she was aware of his return, he dropped to his haunches and caught up the hem of a heavily beaded skirt shot through with gold thread—revealing a pretty ankle and shapely calf.

She gasped, lifted her head. As he stared into her moist eyes, he recalled once he had thought them so dark they would haunt did they not sparkle like stars on a moonless night. He had thought right. They haunted. And moved him as he did not wish to be moved.

He thrust the handful of skirt at her. "Dry your tears, Lady, and resolve to turning your efforts to discouraging your other suitors."

Her mouth worked, but no words passed her lips. Then she snatched the material from him and sat back. But rather than wipe at her eyes and cheeks, she swept her skirt down as if modesty were of greater import than erasing evidence of emotions she had not wished him to know she possessed.

He shrugged, straightened, and as her gaze followed him upright, said, "When this farce is done and our queen well-entertained, you shall be going home with me."

She swallowed loudly. "I will not."

"It will not be the life our foolish young selves imagined," he continued, "but it will be of great advantage to my family and people. Even to you, methinks, and your daughter. Many a night I spend away from High Castle, and when I am home, I am oft gone from dawn to eventide. Once you have given me an heir, I will not bother you again."

Sparks flew from eyes he could not help wishing were sparkles, then bitter laughter sprang from her. "So you have become your father."

He frowned, tried to remember what he had revealed of his sire who, at that time, was a dozen years missing from Lexeter. If she referred to Ricard Soames's faithlessness, that he had not revealed, meaning another had.

"How many mistresses?" she confirmed her knowledge of his mother's heartache. "How many more illegitimate children have you than I?"

Realizing it mattered not who had told her—whether it was their all-knowing queen or idle conversation Laura happened upon, he caught up her hand. Before she could snatch it away, he pressed his lips to the backs of her fingers. "I will leave that to you to discover when we wed"—he smiled as she pulled free—"a month hence."

"Go home, Lord Soames," she hissed. "Go home to your mother who will praise the Lord you escaped me again."

More easily he recalled what he had shared about the controlling Raisa Soames who, mostly bedridden throughout their betrothal, had disapproved of how often he visited Laura—heaping guilt on him, bemoaning she should not have accepted such a woman for her son's wife, warning that as entranced as he was, she could prove a Delilah *and* a Jezebel.

That last he had not shared with Laura. Never had he cause to—at least until Lady Maude sent him away, refusing to reveal the reason for his broken betrothal. Minutes later, Laura had turned at the pond's bank, her hand resting on the reason they would never wed.

"Were we not greatly in need of what you bring to the marriage," he said, "my mother would, indeed, praise the Lord you are not to be her daughter-in-law. But she knows what is needed, and you will provide it." He inclined his head. "I shall see you at dinner, my lady."

He stalked away.

A half hour later, in Lothaire's hearing, Lord Gadot was most unfortunate to boast to Lord Thierry of what he would do to Lady Laura on their nuptial night.

6

He was everywhere, would not be discouraged no matter how often she displeased the queen with shows of preference for her other suitors.

Lothaire Soames was *not* the one. Though the effort to prove Eleanor wrong so exhausted that Laura was too worn to complete her prayers before falling asleep each night and every morn had to be pried out of bed by a clucking Tina, she remained determined to wed any but him—especially after their exchange in the garden four days past when he made it clear she would never be more to him than a means of returning prosperity to Lexeter and gaining an heir. Far less it would ache to wed a man she did not love who did not love her than one she loved who would never love her again. And might ever loathe her.

Now once more the two of them sat at meal, a trencher of pheasant stew between them which she was content to allow him to empty. Unlike whilst seated with her other suitors, she was relegated to a lower table. Not as punishment, though she had thought it at first, but to allow the queen to better observe Lothaire and her.

He leaned near, and when she looked sidelong at him, she saw he smiled—doubtless, for Eleanor's benefit. "You do not have to appear to enjoy my company as much as you do the others', but do you not converse with your future husband, our sovereign will be compelled to remind you of proper etiquette. Again."

She turned her face to him, felt the lonely occupant of her chest move toward his fortified one. He knew of her daily summons to the queen's apartments? Of Eleanor's exasperation over Laura's resistance to Lothaire whether at meal, in the garden, or moving about the crowded hall? How? Had the queen told him?

Nay. Laura had noted the interest shown Lothaire by one of Eleanor's ladies, a pretty woman who could not be more than ten and ten and who was often present during Laura's audience with Eleanor. The lady watched Lothaire, at every opportunity given—or made—conversed with him. And he was receptive, especially when Laura came to his notice.

"Lady Elizabeth," she said and returned his false smile. "Have you made her your mistress yet?" As his eyes darkened, she laughed for the queen. "Do not answer that. Truly, I do not care."

He drew nearer, and she felt his warm breath fan her jaw, slip beneath the neck of her gown, brush the tops of her breasts. "No matter how you wish it, no matter how coarse you present, *Lady* Laura, each time you tempt me to abandon my purpose I have but to recall you in the garden—weeping over me."

It had been a blade to the heart to find him returned. Afterward, *she* had been tempted to abandon her purpose and accept Michael and Lady Beatrix's offer to reside at Castle Soaring. But Clarice needed a home of her own and no longer would Laura be a burden to any. As painful as it was to be awake, she would remain in the world her daughter inhabited.

She broadened her smile. "Though you waste your time and mine, Lord Soames, let us please the queen. Converse with me."

Something flickered across his face, and she guessed he had not expected her to bend. But then, she had not the other times he tried to engage her.

"Speak to me of your daughter," he said.

And now something surely flickered across her face. Far more than dismay. Not quite fear. "Already I have told she has her father's eyes, and you must know she is nine years aged. What more need be told? And why?"

He did not try to maintain his smile. "The *why* is obvious. Until I can wed her away, she shall occupy my home. Regardless of whether I am present, she will affect the workings of my household."

"Then no more need be told," Laura said. "Neither my daughter nor I will occupy your home. I *shall* wed another."

"Ever you say, but two days hence, I will take you from here. As for what I would know of...Clarice, her appearance matters not. What matters is her disposition. Is she of a compliant nature and well-behaved, or willful and in need of correction?"

She was glad she had allowed him to draw her into conversation—at least, this one. She would be making more of the truth than it was and not clarifying that much of the difficulty was a result of Maude's passing, but if he could be dissuaded from his pursuit...

For Queen Eleanor and to better gauge his reaction, Laura angled her body toward his. "Compliant? Hmm. Well-behaved?" She shrugged a shoulder. "She can be. Oft is. But her——" She closed her mouth against naming Maude Clarice's grandmother.

"Her?" Lothaire prompted.

She moistened her lips, touched a hand to her chest. "Her mother has been lax and spoiled her. Though she is quite mature for her nine years, sometimes I know not what to do with her, especially when she is in a mood to disrupt the household."

There was promise in the narrowing of Lothaire's lids, but then he laughed. It was at her expense, but she drank it in as the lines of his face eased save those that expressed joy around the eyes and mouth.

Before her was the young man she had taught how to smile often and laugh well. So glad was she to see him that were they alone she might fling her arms around him and weep over their lost years.

When he sobered, his lips remained curved, and she had to avert her gaze lest he think her captivated. It was the queen who came to her regard. Lothaire's laughter having drawn Eleanor's attention, her eyes were all approval, and something told Laura that were she nearer her sovereign, she would glimpse wonder there as well.

No man laughed like Lothaire—providing the laughter was genuine. The sound swelled from depths one would not guess he possessed, so quiet and controlled did he normally present. And so wonderfully forceful was his laughter, Laura was certain it could enter all in its hearing and make even the bitterest soul smile.

"Keep doing that," he said.

She returned his beloved face to focus. "What?"

"Smiling." He glanced toward the high table. "It pleases the queen."

Laura *was* smiling, in the next instant was not.

Lothaire's mouth also eased. "I have not done that in a long time," he said, "but you amuse me."

"How did I accomplish so great a feat?"

"Your belief the prospect of an uncontrollable child will discourage what cannot be discouraged. More, how still you wet your lips and your voice deepens when you seek to convince me of the improbable."

Then he had also been revisiting their past.

"Though of course, whereas now you seek to deceive, *then* you sought to tease."

She momentarily closed her eyes. When she opened them, she beseeched, "If ever you truly felt for me—"

"I did, Laura," he said gruffly. *"Did."*

His familiar use of her name made tears flood her eyes, but she did not look away. "Then do not do this to us, Lothaire. Leave me to another so those memories are not sullied."

His jaw shifted. "They have long been sullied. You fool yourself to think otherwise."

She longed to flee the hall, let the unwounded laugh and judge her as harshly as dared those with sins of their own, but she held against all stuffed inside that wanted out.

A huff of bitter laughter parted her lips, and she thought, *So this is how it feels to be fully awake.*

Lothaire sighed. "I should not have said that, but this cuckold seems determined to cede ground gained with you and the queen. Certes, I must be vigilant in keeping him locked away these next two days."

Laura looked to Eleanor. Where approval had shone was its opposite. And she did not doubt it was directed at her.

Wishing she did not disappoint the one who had answered her appeal for aid, who believed she knew what was best for her relation, Laura determined to present as passably agreeable.

She turned back to Lothaire, but before she could summon idle conversation, he said, "The queen told me of Lady Maude's passing. My condolences. I know how close you were."

Her heart's ache revived, she said, "She is greatly missed."

"A terrible loss, especially for her son."

Now her heart jolted. Her distress must have shone, for he frowned and asked, "How is Simon?"

She could not maintain his gaze. "He is dead."

After a long moment, he said, "I am sorry."

"'Twas a long time ago."

"In battle?"

"It happened whilst in service to his lord." It was true, though there had been no honor in the manner of his death. Hoping to leave Simon D'Arci be, she swept her eyes around the hall and was grateful Lord Gadot handed her a distraction. As with each time she looked upon his handsome face these past days, she winced. Here was something safe over which Lothaire and she could converse.

"Poor Lord Gadot. You noticed his face?" She shook her head. "He says never again will he accept a challenge to mount an untamed horse whilst he has too much drink in him."

Lothaire laughed again, almost as sincerely. "So that is what he told you."

She blinked. "You know different?"

He lowered his goblet and reached a hand to her. "I assure you, my lady, the mounting of a *horse* was not what earned him a beaten face."

She stared at scabbed and abraded knuckles. Did he speak true? The incident had happened the day Lothaire appeared before her in the garden, and she had not noticed the injury to his hand in all the days since. But then, she avoided looking close upon him.

She swept her gaze to his. "Why?" she said, then caught her breath. "As I seek to discourage you, you seek to discourage him—to frighten him away."

She thought he might laugh again, but he smiled. "Were he truly a rival, I might." He raised his goblet.

"Then?" she pressed.

"You would not believe me. So tell, with whom are you to watch the play this eve?"

"Lord Gadot."

"Then you may ask of him the truth about his cuts and bruises and, I believe, a very loose tooth."

Laura made a sound of disgust, reached for her own goblet.

"Food would benefit you more, my lady." Once again, his breath warmed her jaw and wandered downward.

"I eat when I have an appetite, Lord Soames. At the moment, I am without one."

He considered her, then drew back.

It was another hour before she joined Lord Gadot. And time and again, she sought evidence of that loose tooth.

7

THIS IS THE first of all days to come, Laura told herself as she halted before the queen. *Lord, bless it as much as possible. Above all, for Clarice.*

"Rise, Lady Laura."

She straightened, met her sovereign's gaze.

"You are prepared to show gratitude for our time, effort, and wisdom by accepting our decision?"

Deep breath. "I am, Your Majesty."

Eleanor looked past Laura, inclined her head.

Behind, the door opened and closed, then silence as all waited for the lady who had admitted Laura to return with the one chosen by the queen.

They did not wait long.

Laura stopped her breath at the sound of the door opening, suppressed the impulse to peer over her shoulder, hoped it was Lord Benton who drew alongside.

It was Lord Thierry, the last of the three she would have chosen. Not that he was disagreeable—outside of imbibing too often and too much.

But at least he is not Lothaire, she tried to console herself.

More footsteps, and not of the slippered sort. Boots.

She glanced past Lord Thierry, saw Lord Benton halt beside the other man.

Laura looked her question at the queen, but Eleanor's eyes were on whoever next entered.

Then like a horse at auction, Laura Middleton was to stand before its bidders while the winner was named. Worse, one of those bidders was Lothaire, and without looking to her right, she knew from his long-reaching stride he entered last.

She clasped her hands at her waist, prayed to the Lord to calm her racing heart and still her body that one need not look near upon to know it quaked.

"Let us begin," Queen Eleanor said. "The decision is made as to who shall wed Lady Laura, and she has agreed to abide by our determination." She moved her gaze over the five, returned to the man directly to Laura's right. "Lord Thierry, step forward."

He gave a grunt of satisfaction and did as bid.

"We thank you for your time and interest in taking Lady Laura to wife, Lord Thierry. But we find you wanting. Too much you drink. Too much you gamble. And so seriously does your behavior compromise your lands, we do not believe what the lady brings to the marriage will save them. Your leave is granted."

Speaking no word in his defense, he turned and, shame-faced, lumbered opposite.

Eleanor swept a hand toward Laura, and her three remaining suitors closed the gap left by the rejected lord.

Laura glanced at Lord Benton, her first choice of a husband. Was he next to be sent away?

"Lord Gadot, step forward."

No pattern, then.

"We thank you for your time and interest in taking Lady Laura to wife, Lord Gadot. But we find you wanting. Too indiscreet you are in numbering your mistresses."

Laura caught her breath. She had guessed that of Lothaire, not this one.

"Too much you boast of past and future trysts, including those you anticipate having with the lady who might have become your wife."

Laura snapped her chin around, saw color pour into the nobleman's cheeks. Again, not what she would have guessed of him. Though it was obvious he thought well of himself, he had been attentive and spoke no inappropriate word to her.

"Thus," Eleanor continued, "too much you deserve that face. A pity it soon heals."

Laura's knees weakened. Lothaire had not been trying to frighten away a rival. His knuckles had been battered in defense of her.

"Your leave is granted, Lord Gadot."

As he pivoted, a hand gripped Laura's elbow, and Lord Benton said low, "Are you well, my lady?"

She looked up. He was kind, would make a better husband than Lothaire though her heart was pulled past this one. "I am well."

"Lord Benton, I believe Lady Laura can stand on her own."

He released her.

"Lord Soames." Eleanor motioned him to close the space left by Lord Gadot's departure, then looked to Laura. "You are all surprise, Lady Laura. But we know our subjects, and when we must know them better, we spare no effort to discover what they hide—especially that we might protect those too vulnerable and young to protect themselves."

"I understand, Your Majesty."

"Not as much as you shall." Eleanor smiled. "Lord Soames, step forward."

I am glad, Laura told herself. *As shall he be when he rides away. He will make Lexeter prosperous without me.*

"Rather, come stand beside us, Lord Soames."

Laura stared at the queen.

She raised her eyebrows. "As Lord Gadot learned, the Baron of Lexeter is not always in control of his temper."

Laura watched him stiffly cross the apartment and position himself alongside the queen and in front of the knight who stood guard over her.

Did Eleanor fear he would attack Lord Benton when the other man was awarded what Lothaire had boasted would be his?

"Lord Benton, step forward."

Laura felt his eyes upon her. And uncertainty she only now realized had been certainty a moment earlier. Why did the queen make him suffer? It was cruel, and Laura had not thought her bent that way.

"We do not thank you for your time and interest, Lord Benton, for we find you wanting in the extreme."

Of a sudden, Laura was in greater need of a hand to hold her upright. Beyond the implication Lord Benton's character was more warped than the other two, was the shock of who was to be her betrothed. Again.

Stiffening her legs to keep them from folding, she swept her regard to Lothaire. Before he blinked, she glimpsed relief in his eyes—and something akin to happiness. Was it possible? If so, surely for being the victor and making good his promise she would depart Windsor with him.

"Too much appetite you have for very young women, Lord Benton." Eleanor's upper lip curled. "Or should we say girls? We should. Therefore, Lady Laura is too old for you and her daughter too young."

Her meaning slammed through Laura, sent her thoughts spinning back through the encounters with Lord Benton. Often he had asked about Clarice. And unlike Lothaire, he had very much wanted to know of the girl's appearance. Laura had revealed little, but only because she feared he would probe further, trying the doors behind which lay the circumstances of her daughter's conception.

"Your leave is happily granted."

He turned, but rather than shame-faced like Lord Thierry, his countenance was marred by anger. Narrowing his eyes at Laura, he strode past.

Feeling light of head, she lowered her gaze to the rug beneath her feet whose fleur de lis pattern was not as distinct as before.

"Lord Benton!" the queen called when he reached the door.

"Your Majesty?"

"We are thinking a pilgrimage would be of great benefit—a long one, mayhap to the Holy Land. Confine yourself to your chamber. We shall send a priest to you."

He did not answer, and the door closed moments later.

"Lady Laura, I present your betrothed, Baron Soames."

Boots across the floor. The fleur de lis rising to meet her and yet no clearer than before.

"God's arms!" the queen exclaimed as night drew its curtains across day. "We did not mean to frighten her so."

Only because Lothaire saw her sway and did not request permission to leave the queen's side did he reach Laura before she hit the floor. He caught her around the waist, swung her into his arms, turned to the queen.

Eleanor's smile was all satisfaction. "Would she could have seen how you flew to her side." She gestured to the sitting area. "Best she recover here rather than grease squeaky tongues by you carrying her to her chamber."

Discovering Laura was not much heavier than ten years past, wondering if she might be lighter out of her heavily embroidered gown, Lothaire conveyed her to one of the couches.

As he lowered her, her lids fluttered and she met his gaze. "I am going home with you."

Was it a question? Or did she merely acknowledge what she dreaded?

He settled her head on a cushion, slid his arms from beneath her, impulsively hooked a tress off a cheek as smooth as he remembered.

"You are going home with me," he said low. He thought it relief in her eyes, but it was so soon replaced by regret it could have been imagined. Or wished for.

"Why?" she breathed.

He owed her no answer, but he said, "You are my somehow."

She frowned, gave her head a shake as if to clear it. "You think you have won, but I fear not."

"We shall make the best of what we have been dealt," he said gruffly. "You and I."

"Clarice?" she said with such desperation he was ashamed he had not included her.

"And Clarice," he forced the girl's name across his tongue and drew back. "Rest now. We depart on the morrow."

She stared a moment longer, then lowered her lids.

And Lothaire was struck by how little it had taken for his heart to pick up where it left off. But then he remembered he was no longer fewer than a score of years aged. That Laura Middleton had made a cuckold of him.

8

Castle Soaring, England
May, 1163

IT SHOULD NOT have taken three days to reach Castle Soaring.

Laura did not need Lothaire to speak it, and he did not, but she felt his impatience. Unfortunately, not only did Tina sit a saddle poorly, but the maid did so amid numerous packs containing the gowns Laura had taken to court and two more stuffed with the fine material and embellishments gifted the future Lady of Lexeter.

In Lothaire's hearing, Eleanor had ordered a wedding gown be fashioned as befitting the cousin of the Queen of England.

Clearly, Laura's betrothed had been displeased, but he inclined his head, as done often throughout the journey that followed, speaking as few words as possible to his betrothed. And not many more to the knights and squire who had accompanied him to Windsor. But of greater note—and blessing—was he did not present as smug over making good his belief Laura would be his. Because he now regretted his win?

Cease! she told herself as they slowed their mounts before the donjon. *It matters not. It is done.*

Her heart lightened to see she was to be received by Maude's second stepson, Michael D'Arci, and his beautiful wife, Lady Beatrix of the Wulfriths. But when the latter stepped forward and Clarice was not to be found behind the lady's skirts, Laura's heart once more took on weight.

As anxious as she was for Lothaire to meet his future stepdaughter, it boded ill Clarice was not here to greet her mother.

Is it me? Laura wondered. *Or Lothaire?* She had told her daughter the queen was to provide a husband and father, and Clarice had not been pleased. Nor had Laura expected her to be. But she had known it would go worse were no warning given and had hoped during her absence her daughter would settle into the idea of a home of her own where she was not made to feel tolerated as she had been by the Baron of Owen's wife.

Laura moved out of Lady Beatrix's hug, looked to Michael who had stepped forward to welcome Lothaire.

Doubtless, they remembered each other from the one time they met during the first betrothal. After she had flung herself into Michael's arms, Lothaire had corrected her for being too familiar with Maude's stepson. But he had not been harsh, for she had earlier assured him her enthusiasm was that of a sister for a brother.

Blessedly, the missive Laura had inked at Windsor and sent ahead to Soaring had prepared Michael to receive the man who believed himself betrayed. She had also closed the missive with the words—*Lord Soames does not know.* Thus, Michael was assured their secret was safe and prepared for Lothaire's bitterness over the belief Laura had cuckolded him.

"It has been a long time," Lady Beatrix's husband said, his tone telling it could have been much longer.

Laura tensed. Though she appreciated Michael cared enough to worry over the queen's choice of a husband, she did not wish Lothaire offended.

"Not as long as it feels," he gave back.

"Over ten years," Laura forced herself to enter the conversation. "Imagine how blessed we shall be if we look back on this day ten years hence and think it a short time."

Their eyes swept to her, and she pushed a smile onto her lips and wished she could show teeth to make it more believable. "As 'tis past the nooning hour, Lord D'Arci, I pray you will grant us a night's lodging."

"Unnecessary," Lothaire said. "There is an inn four leagues distant."

"Husband?" Lady Beatrix said sharply.

Michael's smile was all for his wife. "We insist you spend the night, Lord Soames, not only for the sake of your travel-weary betrothed but her daughter. Though we received word of your arrival, we could not know which day you would appear. Thus, Clarice's evening was promised to our children, and we would not disappoint them or her."

Laura frowned, looked to Beatrix.

"She is much the little m-mother." The lady brightened her smile as if unconcerned over the bump in her speech. "It has been good for her."

Remembering how angry Clarice had been when told her mother was bound for court, Laura thanked the Lord her daughter had not been miserable all these weeks. "Lord Soames," she said, "pray, let us accept the hospitality of the D'Arcis."

After a long moment, he inclined his head. And she loved him a little more.

"Where is Clarice?" she asked Beatrix.

"Methinks she watches us." The lady put her head slightly back to indicate either an upper floor or the donjon's roof.

The roof, Laura guessed. Since Maude's death, the girl often sought the solitude of that great height. Indeed, it was upon the donjon's roof at Owen the incident had occurred which forced Laura to awaken.

"May I go to her, Lady Beatrix?"

"Of course. She will be glad to receive you."

Laura started up the steps, remembered Tina, and turned to ask Michael to aid the woman in dismounting. But Lothaire was alongside the maid, arms raised.

Wishing he could love her even a little bit, she ascended the steps.

Six years past, here is where I opened my eyes just enough to think it possible to awaken, she thought as she moved through the hall toward the stairs. *Here is where I revealed Lady Beatrix was not alone in her suffering. Here is where Michael learned how much he wronged the lady with whom he was falling in love.*

If not for Clarice and that Laura loved Michael and Beatrix well, she might have resided here rather than seek a husband. And likely would have remained half asleep the rest of her life.

She found Clarice sitting in the embrasure of a battlement that overlooked the inner bailey.

When the girl heard footsteps, she dropped her feet to the ground. "You are returned."

Despite the cool reception, Laura did not slow her step. "Forgive me for being gone so long," she said and wrapped her arms around her little girl and hugged her so near she sensed it was discomfort rather than distaste that made Clarice protest.

"Mother!" She strained backward, stilled when she saw Laura's tears. "What is wrong? Do you not like the husband the queen chose?"

It was not Lothaire she was thinking of. It was that one whose face returned to her time and again whether awake or at sleep. The one *she* would have chosen for a husband. Thinking to save herself from pain and her daughter from the knowledge Lothaire could not wait to rid himself of another man's child, Clarice would have been exposed to the perverse Lord Benton. Rather than secure a good future for the girl, Laura might have caused her to suffer a life worse than her mother's.

"I saw him, though I could see little of his face," her daughter said, eyes moistening. "He is larger than Lord D'Arci. Is he a bad man?"

"Nay!" Laura dropped to her knees, gently gripped Clarice's arms. "Baron Soames is a good man. He may not be of the affectionate sort, but he will protect you. His home will be our home. Our very own. You want that, do you not?"

The girl drew her lower lip between her teeth. "I wish us to live here with Lady Beatrix and Lord D'Arci."

Laura momentarily closed her eyes. "I am to wed within a month, and where I go you go. You are my daughter."

Clarice's lower jaw jutted. "You say that because Lady Maude is gone, and now you must be a mother to me."

Laura started to deny it, but it was the truth. Had Maude not died, she would not be awake. "I am sorry, Clarice. I know often I have been absent from your life, but I am present now and shall remain so."

"How?" She pulled free. "You are to be a wife."

Laura stood. "That does not mean I cannot be a mother."

"What if I need you when he needs you?"

Laura did not know how to answer the question that revealed vulnerability often hidden behind the impression Clarice was older than her nine years. Or perhaps she did know. Lothaire had said he would be gone often. "Baron Soames is much occupied with the administration of his lands. We shall have plenty of time together."

The girl thought on it, said, "Will he like me?"

Laura breathed down tears. "You will need time to become acquainted, but once you do, how could he not?"

Her evasive answer did not escape Clarice, who narrowed her eyes. "Does he like you?"

"He wishes to wed me." More evasion.

Now her lids became slits. "Because the queen told him he should?"

Laura almost wished her daughter were still very little. Such questions she would not ask. She would be unconcerned about what Lothaire thought of her or her mother, confident he had no choice but to like them. "'Tis true the queen wished us to wed, but Lord Soames is quite agreeable."

"What am I to call him?"

It felt as if someone pushed a needle into Laura's heart. "Methinks *Lord Soames* is best."

"Aye, for now. But when you are wed?"

Laura knew what she sought. Though Clarice had ceased asking for a father two years past, and Laura had prayed the man she wed would become that to her, it could never be. But Laura had no cause to mourn lost opportunity. Just as Lothaire could not be a father to Clarice, none of the other suitors would have been. Where her daughter was concerned, Lothaire was safe.

"What am I to call him when he is your husband?" Clarice repeated with annoyance.

"Once we are settled in our new home, we shall discuss that with Lord Soames."

Color shot into Clarice's her cheeks. "He would rather you did not have a child."

Another needle to the heart, this one going all the way through. "I vow he will come to care much for you," she spoke what was only a dream. But the truth boded ill for Clarice's first meeting with Lothaire which could forever mire their relationship.

Clarice looked as if she might fall into argument as she did often since her grandmother's passing, but she seamed her mouth.

Lady Beatrix, Laura thought. Not only had she exerted a good motherly influence these weeks, but the lady must have prepared Clarice for Laura's return and the man who would accompany her.

"I should meet him now?" she asked.

"If you wish. Or later, ere supper."

"We leave on the morrow?"

"We do."

"Then let us be done with it now." Clarice led the way across the roof, down the stairs, and into the hall.

Lothaire was seated before the hearth opposite Michael, Lady Beatrix standing alongside her husband. He leaned back in the chair, a tankard in hand, legs thrust out before him, one ankle atop the other. It surprised that he looked at leisure—as if he were amongst friends. Ironically, he could be had what happened ten years past not. Michael's half brother had been her childhood friend, but ever she had adored Maude's second stepson, and he had been fond of her.

Was this Lothaire's way of showing indifference to his hosts? Worse, Laura's daughter? It must be, and it nearly made her snatch Clarice back up the stairs. However, the moment Lothaire caught sight of what softly slippered feet did not sooner reveal, he drew his legs in, set the tankard aside, and stood.

Laura released her breath. Were he willing to make an effort to hide what he felt about the greatest evidence of his cuckoldry, there was hope Clarice would not know how little she was wanted.

Drawing alongside her daughter who had preceded her off the stairs, Laura sought Lothaire's regard. But his was upon Clarice, and so intently she wondered what he searched for. The one who had fathered her? Her disposition that he had said was all that mattered for how it affected his household? Or did he steel himself for the introduction to one it could not be easy to look upon?

Laura understood that last. After Clarice's birth, she had averted her gaze and held her arms close lest someone try to place the infant in them. If not for Maude's persistence that had been moved to anger, Laura might not have looked upon her child, might not have held her.

It had been difficult, and how she had cried those first times and been repulsed by the babe at her breast, but that had passed. And her heart had opened to Clarice and seen her daughter. Mostly. Clarice did not have her mother's eyes. Unfortunately, though Laura loved the girl, it had been easier to allow Maude to love her better.

As Lothaire stared, he silently rebuked himself for being so quick to gain his feet. He was as saddle weary as he was determined none would see what went behind his face these past days as he drew nearer life with the woman he had believed lost to him.

The moment he had seen the dark-haired girl trailed by her mother, he had reacted as he should rather than as he wished. Here was the one who had lain beneath Laura's hand that day at the pond—the reason for their broken betrothal. But though he had expected to be repulsed, he saw only a girl years from a woman, an innocent tainted by her mother's sin. And as she neared, he saw in the eyes fixed to his that she but tried to appear bold. Vulnerability and uncertainty dwelt there.

"Lord Soames, this is my daughter, Clarice." Laura halted a reach away. "Clarice, my betrothed, Lord Soames."

Lothaire inclined his head. "Clarice."

The girl curtsied. "Lord Soames."

He glanced at Laura and wished away the pleading in her eyes— wished he had not spoken words that made her believe he would behave poorly toward her child. "I am pleased to meet you, Clarice. On the morrow we shall journey to the barony of Lexeter, my—" He smiled tautly. "*Your* home. I hope you will be comfortable at High Castle."

"Are there—?" She closed her mouth.

"What?"

She shrugged. "Other children?"

"I have none of my own." He looked to Laura. "Yet."

His betrothed's eyes lowered, but not before he glimpsed what seemed fear. And wished that away as well. Though she was no longer pure, their marriage would be consummated and he would know her often enough to gain an heir. Mayhap several, though he had said he required only one. But she need not fear him in bed any more than outside it. A child was what he wanted, not revenge.

"However," he continued, "there are servants' children with whom you may play."

"Babies?"

"A few."

"I will have brothers and sisters?"

Feeling Michael D'Arci's gaze, he said, "God willing, those as well."

Clarice took a small step forward. "Mother says I am to call you Lord Soames for now. What am I to call you when she is your wife?"

Lothaire's chest tightened. In looks she resembled her mother, but more so in her forthright manner that Laura had revealed of herself that day they had first walked—then run—to the pond.

He raised his eyebrows. "What would you like to call me?"

"I have long wanted a father. If you are good to me and my mother, that I would call you." She raised her eyebrows. "If you agree."

"I will be good to your mother and you." That was answer enough. He looked to D'Arci and his wife. "If my chamber is ready, I shall refresh myself ere supper."

Lady Beatrix smiled. "If 'tis not, soon it shall be. Come. And you, Lady Laura. Our children shall sleep in the solar this eve so Clarice and you may have their chamber to yourselves."

Laura murmured her thanks and followed the lady, and Lothaire stepped past Clarice who seemed of a mind to remain belowstairs. That made him wonder. Though mother and daughter had been reunited whilst he waited in the hall, they could not have had more than a quarter hour together. Should not the girl wish to stay near Laura after so long a parting?

He could not accurately gauge mother-daughter relations by comparing them to the disagreeable Lady Raisa and his sister, but there seemed something missing between Clarice and her mother.

Shortly, Laura closed the door of the chamber alongside the solar, and Lady Beatrix led him to a room at the far end of the corridor.

"'Tis ready." She motioned him inside.

He stepped over the threshold and started to close the door. "I thank you, my lady."

"Lord Soames?"

He stilled. "Lady Beatrix?"

"I fear I t-trespass," she stuttered as if nervous, "I pray you will forgive me, but my husband and I are fond of Lady Laura and her daughter—so much that were the lady not fearful of being a burden and determined to provide Clarice a home of her own, we would have them remain with us."

Then Laura had not needed to seek a husband she did not want. Because she truly did not wish to burden D'Arci and his wife? Or did she weary of no position of her own, she who was to have been a baron's wife?

"Thus," Lady Beatrix continued, "we would be assured they are happy with you."

He was not going to like this. "Speak, Lady Beatrix. If I can, I will put your mind at ease. If I cannot, you will have to accept I have good cause."

She looked dismayed, then annoyed. "I know once you were betrothed to Lady Laura, and I know you broke the betrothal when——"

"I did not break it."

She blinked.

"Though I would have had Lady Maude not done so."

Her nose wrinkled, reminding him of a rabbit, albeit a beautiful one. "And yet now you shall wed a woman you believe cuckolded you."

Bitter laughter broke from him. "Believe? Are you so slow of mind you forget I just met her daughter?"

Her eyes flew wide, replacing the image of the rabbit with that of a hawk who made prey of that other lovely creature.

"I am but slow of tongue, Lord Soames. *You* are the one slow of mind." She drew a deep breath. "But I make allowances for your ignorance. At least, I hope that is all it is. If 'tis cruelty..." Now she flashed a smile that brought to mind a wolf. "I give warning. Not only does Lady Laura have a friend in my lord husband, but one amongst the Wulfriths."

He should not be surprised. "Abel Wulfrith is your brother?"

"A most beloved brother."

Lothaire nodded. "I met him last year upon the barony of Wiltford the day Sir Durand and Lady Beata wed." Following annulment of Lothaire's marriage to that lady, which could have ended in spilled blood had he not overtaken the men sent by his mother to murder the newly-wed couple, he did not say.

Lady Beatrix appeared taken aback. "Well, assuredly you know our family's reputation, even if you have had no occasion to engage my brother at swords."

"I *have* had occasion. Several. He offered to hone my sword skill at Wulfen, and I accepted. Had the queen not summoned me to court and offered a great incentive to wed Lady Laura, I would be training with Sir Abel now."

She blinked. "Regardless, as I shall count it an offense should you ill treat Lady Laura and her daughter, so shall my husband and brothers."

What offended Lothaire were threats and others' sins cast upon him. He was not Lord Thierry, Lord Gadot, nor Lord Benton. But as anger rose, it occurred to him had Eleanor not pried back the masks worn by the other suitors, he would want such defenders for Laura. And this lady could not know he was not of the same ilk.

"Forgive me, Lady Beatrix. I would not argue with you. And certainly I do not want you to think so ill of me to believe the threat of harm to my person is all that holds me from injuring Lady Laura and her daughter. Our circumstances are difficult, but I am no monster. I am a man wronged, the life promised me stolen and replaced with one that shall ever remind me of how much I lost. I accept my marriage will not be happy, but I am determined neither will it be miserable for either of us. Or Clarice."

She raised her eyebrows. "I am sorry you do not believe in God."

He stood straighter. "I believe in God."

"Do you? Then why is it impossible for your marriage to be happy?"

He blew out a breath. "As told, I do not wish to argue."

"Then listen. Though Lady Laura should have defended herself long ere—" She closed up so suddenly, he took a step forward.

"Of what do you speak, Lady Beatrix?"

She shook her head. "Anger too much loosens my tongue."

"How has Lady Laura not defended herself? And how can you think it possible to do so when—" Now he closed up. It was no secret Lady Maude's ward was seduced by a visiting knight, though it surely would have been had Laura's body not betrayed her as she had betrayed Lothaire. But that he would not speak of. Suffice that he knew he should have listened to his mother's warnings against Delilahs and Jezebels. Suffice he knew he was responsible in part for Laura's sin. Had he not succumbed to temptation, giving them both a taste of kisses and caresses, she might not have fallen prey to desire and given her virtue to a man who left her with living proof of her shame.

Lady Beatrix sighed. "Only one more thing shall I say, Lord Soames, then I will leave you to your rest. Do you gain Lady Laura's trust—give her cause to love you again—I believe God will bless your marriage far beyond the ability to tolerate each other."

He needed to gain Laura's trust? *He* needed to give her reason to love him? "You have said it, Lady Beatrix." He gripped the door's edge. "I shall see you at supper."

She inclined her head and turned so swiftly her fat braid whipped against the door jamb.

The morn could not come soon enough.

9

"I THANK YOU," she said so softly he barely caught the words.

Lothaire looked at where Laura sat beside him at table. "For?"

She touched the tip of her tongue to her upper lip as if to moisten it, but seeing it drew his regard, seamed her mouth.

"For what am I owed gratitude?" he asked again with an edge that had little to do with her delay in answering.

"I know you do not like my daughter, but you hid it well. The appearance of discomfort is far preferable to loathing."

Did she truly believe he disliked a child who had done him no ill? Was that how he presented—as the monster Lady Beatrix also feared?

He angled toward her, creating a wall between them and Michael D'Arci on his other side. "You wrong me again, Laura." He caught the widening of her eyes as her familiar name came off his lips. "I do not loathe...Clarice," he said, though the girl's name was not easily spoken. "I know she is not to blame for the sins of her parents, that she is merely proof of it."

Sparks. Not sparkles.

"It is discomfort with which I am afflicted," he continued, "and considering what I once felt for you that I thought you felt for me, methinks I can be forgiven."

She looked away, reached to her spoon.

Impulse made him catch her hand, the sense of being watched by her daughter who sat at the children's table below the dais made him cradle it. As he stared at her curled fingers, he remembered when she was near on fifteen and he had done the same. As then, he slid a thumb beneath her fingers, eased them open, lowered his head, and pressed his lips to her palm.

He heard her breath catch, and as he drew back, he marveled that her hand appeared smaller ten years later. But it was no error in memory. She was a bit taller and fuller of breasts and hips, but he was the one who had added to his height those first few years following her betrayal. More, his body had broadened to accommodate muscles required of a man of the sword.

He had not thought Laura fragile before, and she would not break as easily as the petite Lady Beatrix, but it would not be difficult to snap her in two.

"Lothaire?"

He opened eyes he had not meant to close, lifted his chin he had not meant to lower, found her gaze near his.

A slight smile touched her mouth, and he wondered if she put it there for Clarice. But then she whispered, "Judge me as you will, but do not think those same memories do not haunt me."

Unsettled at being read, he nearly spoke words that would cause the blossoming of her hand in his to close up tight as a bud beyond hope of opening. But he did not challenge her, nor say it was a pity she had made ghosts of those memories.

"How am I your *somehow?*" she spoke more softly.

He had hoped she would not remember him naming her that following her collapse in the queen's apartment, but it did not matter, especially as it had naught to do with the heart. Indeed, it was all business. "I vowed *somehow* I would save Lexeter," he said all that needed to be told. Then for Clarice, Michael D'Arci, and Lady Beatrix, he retrieved Laura's spoon and set its slim handle across the palm to which the Samson and Ahab in him longed to put his mouth again.

"I am pleased you are eating better," he said, and noting her lips had lost their curve, picked up his own spoon.

"Lord Soames," Michael D'Arci said. "I understand your lands are mostly given to the commerce of wool. My liege, Baron Lavonne, wishes to expand his grazing lands. Have you advice I may pass to him?"

To further remind Lothaire he was no longer a young man made foolish by love, the Lord of Castle Soaring could not have chosen a better topic—sheep, the restoration of Lexeter more possible with the concessions gained from his acceptance that Laura was his *somehow*.

Only that, he told himself. And wished he believed it.

On nights like this, when the air was still and sweet and lowered voices the only evidence she was not alone in the world, she liked to walk the inner bailey. Sometimes the outer.

At Soaring, she ventured to the latter and spent a quarter hour inside the dovecote listening to the gentle birds in their nest-holes, those awakened by her entrance cooing and shushing as if to settle their young ones back to sleep.

Face tipped up, Laura peered at the circular walls lined all around with roosts. And remembered again Lothaire's breath and lips upon her palm. She had nearly leaned in to offer her mouth, as once she had done. Would he have hungrily kissed her as once he had done?

"Lothaire," she spoke his name, and doves to the left and right responded with a whisper of wings.

She slid down the wall onto her knees, clasped her hands before her, and prayed for what only the Lord could grant. "For Clarice's sake above all, Lothaire's next, mine last, help me find the right moment and words to fix what I did not mean to break. Show me your arms are not so full you cannot hold all of us."

Another quarter hour she sought the Lord's arms and would have continued seeking had she not heard a familiar voice ask after her.

She pushed upright and opened the door as Michael D'Arci reached for it.

Concern on his torch-lit brow, he searched her up and down. "My lady wife thinks you gone too long. She sent me to see you returned to the donjon."

During Lothaire and Michael's hour-long discussion of Lexeter's wool operation, Laura and Lady Beatrix had spoken of small things while Clarice occupied the D'Arci children and, later, carried them abovestairs to bed.

After Lothaire excused himself to find his own rest, Laura had told Soaring's lady she wished a walk before withdrawing to her chamber. Lady Beatrix had offered to join her, but Laura had declined. Doubtless, the lady eschewed her own bed to ensure her guest returned safely.

"She is kind to worry over me." Laura stepped from the dovecote and closed the door.

"She is my prize in heaven come to Earth," Michael said, a smile in his voice.

Inwardly sighing over the love shared by him and his wife, she hesitated when he offered his arm. Then assuring herself she would not feel the stomach-churning discomfort experienced with her three rejected suitors each time she forced herself to accept their touch or extend hers, she laid her hand on his forearm and walked beside him.

Neither spoke until they passed beneath the raised portcullis into the inner bailey and the donjon was before them.

"Why have you not told him?" Michael asked.

She faltered, and he turned to face her. "You revealed the truth of Clarice to the queen. Why not Lord Soames?"

She dropped her hand from him and averted her gaze.

A finger beneath her chin returned her eyes to his. "Do you fear him, Laura?"

His question reminded her of the talk they had before she went to court. She had told him what she had witnessed between Clarice and the son of his older brother, Joseph, which awakened her to the necessity of removing her daughter from Owen. When she apologized for overreacting lest Michael believe that of her, he became angry, though not with her, and said the gift of fear was given by the Lord and one should open it as soon as it appeared. And how she wished she had when it was given her the day she descended to the cellar where Simon cornered her.

"Do you fear Soames, Laura?"

She shook her head. "Not that he will do me physical harm, but I do fear for my heart."

"You love him still."

"Aye, and the mere thought I may never again have any part of his heart hurts mine."

"Then why not reveal to him that revealed to the queen?"

"I needed Eleanor. Though certain she would not give aid to a harlot, I hoped she would help a wronged woman with whom she shares blood."

"I believe you must tell him, Laura. Though he is bitter, methinks I like him better than the first time we met. And were he without honor, I do not believe anything would persuade Abel Wulfrith to instruct him in arms."

Laura had wondered how far his conversation with Lothaire had strayed from talk of sheep. "He received training at Wulfen?"

"Indeed. A rarity for one who has earned his spurs, but it speaks well of him that a Wulfrith, especially Abel, expended so much effort reserved for boys and young men. And well that your betrothed is not so prideful he refused the opportunity to better his skill at arms. Doubtless, he has suffered humiliation to be a grown man training amongst squires."

It did speak well of Lothaire, but not so well she was ready to reveal the true circumstances of Clarice's conception, especially the part she had played—that which might not condemn her in Michael's eyes but would likely condemn her in Lothaire's.

Laura gathered breath. "I have prayed over revealing to him what happened at Owen, but ever I come back to the lack of proof and that for ten years I offered none. Now to tell the tale of a man who cannot defend himself for how long he has been in the grave? Most convenient, my betrothed will say."

"You but kept your word to my stepmother, which you should not have given."

"I could not injure her more than already she was by the truth of her son. She was ever kind to me, like the mother I did not have. When my father disavowed me and would not provide funds for me to enter a convent and hide my shame, she remained steadfast. And what of you? Have you not suffered knowing the truth?"

"Not as much as I would now suffer were it never told. Do not forget that Simon's depravity nearly lost me the woman I love."

He spoke true, but still he had been deeply pained to learn his beloved brother had become a stranger—the same as Simon had become to Laura during his knighthood training.

"I would not wish my brother's sin cast wide like seed upon fertile soil," he said, "but if any ought to be told, it is the man from whom my brother stole what was most precious."

"I agree, but I do not know Lothaire will believe me, and if ever he should, certainly not now. Mayhap once I have proven a good and faithful wife."

"Laura, though I could not clearly see Baron Soames kiss your hand, methinks that is a man who still loves even if he does not know it or wish it. He may not believe you now, but I think it the place to start, and ere you wed. If he requires proof, I will stand witness, as will my lady wife."

She drew a shuddering breath. "I know not when, but I shall tell him."

He squeezed her shoulder. It was so reminiscent of when her world had been bright and he was the big brother denied her when she was sent to live distant from those of her blood, that Laura lurched forward and put her arms around his neck and pressed her face to his shoulder.

He went very still, and she knew she questioned the appropriateness of her embrace, but he set a hand between her shoulder blades and patted her back.

She did not mean to cry, but she could feel the rise of that emotion that made being awake so difficult. As if sensing it, he said with teasing, "You should know my sweet wife has threatened Lord Soames with bodily harm if he causes Clarice or you unhappiness."

She lifted her head, blinked away tears. "Lady Beatrix said she would hurt him?"

"Aye." He chuckled. "Though forsooth, I would be her instrument of revenge. And her brothers."

Her laughter was weak, but it was sincere, and it calmed the emotions seeking to tip her into misery.

"You are a good man, Michael D'Arci. I am glad you have been blessed to be so loved."

"I pray the same for you."

Her smile wavered, but she took his arm again and, with a lighter step, crossed the bailey.

Beware the Delilah, my son. Beware the Jezebel.

Lothaire loathed finding his mother here with him—not to offer comfort but force him to see what he did not wish to see. And regret what he ached to regret.

He stared down upon the man and woman until their ascent of the steps delivered them to the donjon's door. Then the cool night air he had sought feeling chill, he stepped back from the window he had unshuttered minutes before Laura and Michael D'Arci crossed from the outer bailey into the inner—her hand on his arm.

He had struggled for a reasonable explanation for the two walking alone in the dark. And likely would have failed to find one even had D'Arci not stepped in front of her, even had she not gone into his arms.

What little doubt might have lingered was swept away by the memory of a younger Laura running to greet Lady Maude's second stepson with enthusiasm that seemed to surpass that shown Lothaire upon his arrival. Later, when he told her such behavior was not befitting a lady, she had once more assured him Michael D'Arci was as a brother. For love of her, Lothaire had accepted her word.

Fool! Was the man Clarice's father? Certes, it was a *visiting knight* who got Laura with child. Were D'Arci the one, more sense it made that Lady Maude had not merely been kind in allowing her scandalous ward to remain in her household. And her stepson was a better fit than her own son whom Lothaire had briefly considered as the offender. Though Laura had shared fond memories of their childhood, the one time he had met Simon, she had been distant with the disagreeable youth who was not much older than she, yet seemed younger.

Were it a D'Arci who made Lothaire a cuckold, it was surely this one entrusted with Laura's daughter while she was at court, he who had hair as dark as the girl's and eyes as pale.

Restrainedly, Lothaire closed the shutters he longed to slam, then strode to the bed and dropped onto it.

Woe to Lady Beatrix who believed herself happily married—more, for her defense of the woman who had birthed her husband's child.

Woe to Michael D'Arci if ever the Wulfrith brothers learned the truth of him—more, if he thought to cuckold Lothaire a second time.

10

WHAT HAD CHANGED since he had pressed his mouth to her palm, making her dare to hope the Lothaire of their youth was not entirely lost to her and ask how she was his *somehow?* It had hurt when he said she was but a means of saving Lexeter, but the next morn prior to their departure from Soaring, he had seemed more distant. And what had caused him to cool toward Michael though their talk of wool the night before had seemed almost friendly?

Though thrice over the past day and a half of travel Laura had asked Lothaire what troubled him, each time whatever lightness could be found about him darkened and he refused to answer. Thus, she feared the nearer they drew to the home he would share with Clarice and her, the more he regretted remaining a suitor.

Clarice also made the journey uncomfortable, but Lothaire was passably civil when the girl made it impossible for him to pretend she did not exist. In his hearing, she grumbled she would not like Lexeter and wished she could live with Michael D'Arci and his wife.

It was obvious she offended, but with flushed face and set jaw, ever Lothaire turned his attention elsewhere.

Laura entreated her daughter to keep her tongue, but though Clarice grudgingly agreed, that grudging was often her undoing after hours in a shared saddle.

"Look, Mother!" she returned Laura to the present. "Is that our home?"

Startled by what seemed excitement, Laura swept her gaze to the distant fortress. It had to be High Castle. Lothaire had said they would reach it some hours after noon, and it was as her young betrothed had described.

Perched on a hillock that resembled a bow with its string drawn all the way to the ear, narrow towers resembling arrows aimed at the heavens, the castle would appear to sit among clouds on days thick with fog. And to the far left grazed sheep who seemed lesser clouds that had lost their way.

Clarice made a sound of disgust, called, "Lord Soames, is that our home?"

Laura shifted her gaze to where he rode ahead and saw his back stiffen, but he slowed, allowing them to draw alongside.

"That is High Castle. There you will live."

Yet he did not name it their *home,* Laura noted.

"It is pretty," her daughter said, though from her tone it was other things as well, pretty being the highest compliment she would offer.

He glanced at Laura. "Pretty, though mostly at a distance. It is in need of repair."

Clarice sighed. "Lord D'Arci repaired his castle years ago. Why have you not done the same?"

A muscle in his jaw spasmed. "That requires funds that have been lacking."

"Have you them now? I do not like ugly things."

Laura grimaced. As Clarice had been encouraged by Lady Maude, and as evidenced by the girl's clothes and gifts that became more extravagant the older she grew, she had a great taste for beauty.

More color rose in Lothaire's face, and when he spoke there was strain in his voice. "Funds are being raised, but as it will be years ere Lexeter is whole, best you become accustomed to less than pretty." He urged his horse forward, and Laura thought he would have spurred away if not for Tina and all the packs.

High Castle proved more distant than it appeared, taking a quarter hour to reach walls that were, indeed, in need of repair. And that was not all. But though many of the buildings in the outer bailey were in poor condition, there was evidence of restoration, primarily to the stables and smithy.

It seemed a good sign the men on the walls and castle folk greeted their lord's return with enthusiasm, and her foreboding eased when some of the lines in her betrothed's face disappeared and he returned smiles and raised a hand.

Laura did not expect his mother to greet them before the donjon, since her inquiry into Lady Raisa's health had yielded she had never fully recovered from the illness that allowed her son to visit his betrothed at Owen absent her escort. But Laura had thought his sister, whom he had told remained unwed, would be among those gathered before the donjon. She had never met the lady, but there were no noblewomen among the servants.

Lothaire lifted Clarice down, then Laura. "Well come to your new home," he said without hint of welcome and crossed to Tina to aid in her dismount.

Laura raised her gaze up the donjon and glimpsed movement at a window on the uppermost floor. Two figures, one wearing dark green, the other pale blue. Lady Raisa and Lady Sebille?

A hand cupped her elbow, and she peered across her shoulder at Lothaire whose gaze had followed hers. Had he also noted the movement? If so, he said naught, but something told her it was that which returned him to her side.

"Come." He guided her forward. "Meet those who shall serve my wife."

Introductions of Baron Soames's betrothed and her daughter were made quickly, and though the household knights and servants were mostly reserved, none were impolite.

"They are not very friendly," Clarice bemoaned as she ascended the steps alongside her mother.

"They are respectful as is required of them," Lothaire said.

The girl clicked her tongue. "As are Lord D'Arci's retainers, but his are more agreeable."

Feeling Lothaire's tension rise, Laura said, "Clarice, it is not for you to—"

"Nay," Lothaire said as they neared the landing, "she may speak as she finds—providing she does so discreetly."

Laura looked sidelong at him, saw his eyes were upon her daughter on the other side of her.

"They must not only earn your respect, Lady Clarice," he said, "you must earn theirs."

"Why? 'Twas not required upon Owen, nor at Castle Soaring."

As Lothaire said something beneath his breath, Laura rasped, "Clarice!"

Her daughter heaved a sigh, and as the donjon's doors were opened by a pock-marked soldier of middling years, surged forward and entered ahead of the man who lorded these lands.

"'Tis obvious you must better learn a parent's role ere being entrusted with mothering my heir," Lothaire rasped as they entered the hall.

Outwardly, Laura did not stumble. Inwardly, she tripped so hard scathing words nearly flew off her tongue. None need tell her she was deficient in raising her child, least of all this man whose losses did not come near to numbering hers—he who had well enough forgotten her that he wed another.

And lost her, she reminded herself. Breathing deep to slow her heart and cool the heat flaying her cheeks, she wondered what he had felt for his wife, something she had tried not to ponder for years. Had he loved her as once he had loved Laura? More? How had the lady died? In childbirth? If so, perhaps his losses did number hers. Might even exceed them.

"The hall," he said and halted at its center.

Laura lifted her gaze she had fixed to the floor so he would not see the effect of his words and caught her breath. The great room was in better repair than what lay outside its walls. Though it evidenced neglect and age that would require much cleaning, polishing, and repair to set it aright, it was extravagant.

A massive hearth faced with beautifully carved stone discolored by soot stretched half the length of one wall, a half dozen sumptuous tapestries marked by stains and dulled by dust hung ceiling to floor, three alcoves boasted disarrayed benches and small tables, many-branched candlesticks wrought of iron as tall as a man stood crookedly in the hall's four corners, the dais constructed of the same stone as the hearth was stained by cast-off food, and upon it sat a table whose front was curtained with gathered material that sagged—at one of those gaps the shining eyes of what was surely a dog.

A shiver of anticipation went through Laura. The household given to another woman would soon be hers, as ever it should have been. No longer would she merely be led through life. She would lead others, ensuring the donjon was comfortable and hospitable—a credit to her husband and his station. For Clarice she had awakened, and though her daughter's happiness and security was of greatest concern, here was something for her. If never she was loved by her daughter or husband, she would have this.

"You are smiling."

Had been, the corners of her mouth lowering as she swept her regard to the man who would give his household into her keeping. "I thought never to be here."

He raised his eyebrows. "As did I, but what Eleanor wants, Eleanor takes."

The freedom to choose the one who ordered his servants and birthed his heir.

Little chance I will know his love again, she thought. *I shall have to be content with being the one who loves, though not by way of words. Too much I would bleed to speak what may never again pass his lips.*

Unless you tell him, she recalled Michael's encouragement.

I shall, she silently vowed. *Though he may not believe me and think more ill of me, when the time is as right as I can make it, I will reveal what would not have happened had I been less foolish.*

She tried for a smile of apology, but it shook her mouth. "I am sorry you felt you had no choice."

"At least 'tis not without some gain," he said of the tax relief that would allow Lexeter to rise above its financial woes. The queen had explained it to Laura and been pleased her cousin had enough wits to understand how great a boon it was for the man who would not otherwise wed a used woman.

Laura inclined her head. "I would like to be shown to my chamber. My daughter and I are travel worn."

He dropped his hand from her. "As I have matters to attend to, Sir Angus will escort you." He summoned a knight to whom she had been introduced minutes earlier.

He was handsome, perhaps a dozen years older than Lothaire, and the smile he once more bestowed upon her seemed genuine.

After receiving his lord's instructions, the knight said in a voice touched with a Scottish accent, "This way, my lady."

Laura motioned to her daughter and maid, and as they fell in behind, heard Clarice grumble over the state of the hall and knew it a futile hope Lothaire did not hear.

As they climbed the stairs, a man garbed in a long green tunic appeared on the landing above and halted his descent. Broad of shoulders and silver of hair yet stranded with the dark of his youth, he stepped to the side so as not to impede their progress.

"Lady Laura," Sir Angus said when they reached the landing, "this is High Castle's physician, Martin." He nodded at the short man who, despite a deeply-lined face that told he was over three score aged, was yet attractive and straight of back.

Guessing by the color he wore he was one of those who had watched their lord's return from the upper window, Laura said, "I am pleased to meet you, Martin."

"And I you, Lady Laura." It was said with little sincerity. Then his eyes sharpened and brow grew more furrowed. "Surely not Laura *Middleton?*"

Her surname almost spat, evidencing he had served this family many years, she stiffened her spine. "*Lady* Laura Middleton, soon to be *Lady* Laura Soames.*"

His upper lip hitched and nostrils flared, but his reaction to the joining of her name with his lord's seemed a small thing compared to the shock that went through her. It was the first time in a decade she had spoken her name alongside Lothaire's.

"This is Clarice, Lady Laura's daughter," Sir Angus said. Though he likely sought to lessen the tension, it thickened when the physician's gaze landed on the girl, causing Clarice's mouth to tighten.

Fearing whatever words formed behind her lips, Laura said, "And here is my maid, Tina." She nodded at the woman.

As though a servant were beneath him, the physician turned away, though not to descend to the hall that had been his destination. But as he set foot on the stairs that accessed the third floor, Sir Angus caught his arm.

"Baron Soames waits on you." The knight's tone evidenced rebuke. "He would know the state of his mother's health."

A flush crept up the man's neck. "First, I must speak with Lady Raisa."

To inform her of the identity of her son's betrothed, Laura guessed.

"Nay, Martin, first you must wait on the Lord of Lexeter, he who pays your wages."

The man's jaw clenched so hard Laura heard the grind of his teeth, then he pulled free and started down the stairs.

"Mercy," Tina muttered.

"I do not like him," Clarice said, blessedly not loud enough to carry far. "I pray I do not fall ill."

"Worry not," Sir Angus said, "though soured by age and circumstance, Martin is accomplished at healing and knows well his medicinals."

Were he of a mind to minister to one who sought his care, Laura thought.

"Martin has tended my lord's mother for over a score of years," he added.

Of course he had.

Grateful for Sir Angus's intercession, Laura managed a smile. "If you would show us to our chamber, we shall allow you to return to your duties."

He turned and led the way down the corridor.

The lady of the castle was distraught. Lothaire did not need the physician to tell him that, nor give his opinion on his lord's betrothed whom he had encountered abovestairs—doubtless, an unpleasant meeting once the man learned the identity of the woman Sebille and he had looked upon from the upper window.

Of course Martin did not like the cuckolding Laura Middleton, protective as he was of Raisa, but just as Lothaire's mother would not long suffer the barony's new mistress, neither would the physician. When Raisa moved to her dower property, Martin would go with her, meaning another physician must be found—further expense to make the bellies of Lexeter's coffers groan. As for Sebille, unless she could be persuaded to abandon the burden of companion and caregiver to their mother, she would also be leaving.

Breathing deep, Lothaire reminded himself his immediate concern was the audience with his mother, which would be more difficult had Angus not insisted the physician report to his lord. Otherwise, Martin would have informed Raisa of who came to High Castle, and she would be beyond distraught.

As Lothaire believed it better he deliver the tidings, he had sent a missive to Sebille and Angus ahead of his return. After informing them to hold close the knowledge of whom he was to wed, he had directed them to prepare the castle folk to receive their new lady, prepare the second-floor room Laura would occupy until the wedding, and move Lady Raisa to the third floor rear-facing chamber to ensure she was not at a window when he returned from court and—of equal import—put distance between her and the lady she loathed.

"This will end your mother," the physician's hiss returned the Baron of Lexeter to the man's presence.

"Not if I am the one to tell her. I shall make her see the good of it."

"What good?"

Lothaire raised his eyebrows. "You shall remain belowstairs until I send for you."

"But Lady Raisa—"

"Until I send for you, Martin." Lothaire gestured at the chairs before the hearth.

The man's stocky body swelled as if to set upon an enemy, but as ever—excepting when Lothaire was a boy and his offenses earned him a shove, a shake, or a cuff to the ear—Martin acceded with a curt nod.

Lothaire lifted his tankard of bitterly warm ale and drank as he followed the physician's progress to the hearth. When the man dropped so heavily into a chair it screeched backward, Lothaire turned his thoughts to the meeting to be had after he conferred with Sir Angus. But not for the first time these two days, his mind veered off its path and conjured remembrance of the night at Castle Soaring.

He hated that it bothered so much to discover Laura yet felt for another what he had once believed she would only feel for him. Turn his stomach though it did to admit it—even if only to himself—from the moment he had caught her up in his arms in the queen's apartment, to the moment he pressed his lips to her palm and she whispered the same memories haunted her, to the moment ere she went into Michael D'Arci's arms, he had thought they could do better than make the best of their marriage. That they might even reclaim a fraction of the love they had once shared.

"Fool," he muttered and nodded to the servant who approached with a pitcher of ale.

Shortly, Angus reappeared. Out of hearing of the physician, the knight reassured his lord that though Laura's encounter with the man had been tense, naught untoward had happened, then he told that the lady and her daughter were pleased with their accommodations.

Next, Lothaire asked after his mother. As expected, Raisa was fitful over her confinement and Sebille bore the brunt of her anger.

That last was told with resentment, a reminder that once Angus had wished to wed Sebille. When Raisa rejected his offer, Sebille refused to go against her mother's wishes despite Lothaire's consent. It was many years since the knight had ceased his pursuit of Sebille after exhausting his patience on waiting for Lady Raisa's wasting sickness to claim her so her daughter was free to wed. Now, even if the tidings the Baron of Lexeter was to wed his former betrothed put his mother in her grave, it would likely change naught.

The Sebille whom Angus had loved was gone. Though she had once been vibrant and joyful, the loss of their father had caused much of the light to go out of the girl deemed a *miracle* by their parents. One would not know she had once had a lovely lilt to her voice and been quick to smile and laugh. As for her appearance, except on the rare occasion she washed the hair severely braided back off her face, one would not know it was golden-red, and her feminine curves had been lost to an appetite so diminished one sometimes had to look twice to be certain of her presence when she stood in profile. Though thirty and one years aged, it was almost more believable she was Lothaire's mother.

"I am sorry Lady Raisa was difficult," Lothaire said.

Angus arched an eyebrow. "I am not the one to suffer for it."

As ever when his sister rose between them, Lothaire longed to apologize for what Angus and Sebille had lost. But it would only unsettle the knight whose attempts to suppress his anger would turn him silent for days.

Deciding it was time to reveal to his mother who would birth Lexeter's heir, Lothaire thanked Angus and strode to the stairs. He took them two at a time, continued past the first landing, and ascended the second flight.

Sebille stood halfway down the corridor, face gaunt, hands clasped beneath barely existent breasts.

As he neared, he saw the circlet of rough-hewn stones by which she counted her prayers spilled over her fingers to gently sway against the worn blue of her gown. "Forgive me for being so long in returning," he said, halting before her.

Her shrug was so slight it might have been merely an inhalation. "Is Lexeter saved, dear Brother?"

He longed to remind her it did not need saving. However, the new taxes that would pass over his demesne like the spirit of the Lord had passed over the Hebrews who marked their homes with lamb's blood to save their firstborns, could have proven the ruin of Lexeter.

"It is saved."

"By Lady Laura." Sebille glanced at the door behind which their mother awaited him. "Lady Raisa will make misery of you."

"More of you."

Once again, a shrug that might or might not be. "Now you shall have to send her to her dower property."

As the queen required and Lothaire did not regret. "You will not be persuaded to remain at High Castle, Sebille?"

"For what? I must have a purpose, and that I have in serving the Lady of Lexeter who shall soon relinquish that title."

"It does not have to be that way. You are still young—"

"I am not, Lothaire." She unclasped her hands, loosed prayer beads that fell against her skirt and swung from the girdle to which they were attached. "Prepare yourself," she said and led her brother to their mother's chamber and fit the key.

11

Laura surged to sitting, looked to wide-eyed Clarice and Tina, then the ceiling.

"Wh-what was that?" her daughter asked.

Was it Lady Raisa's response to learning her son was to wed the woman who had cuckolded him?

"Mother?" Clarice leaned forward in the chair she had dropped into when Sir Angus admitted them to the chamber.

Laura swung her legs over the mattress and stood. "It sounded like a hawk. Did it not, Tina?" She widened her eyes at the maid, entreating her to agree.

Tina frowned and resumed the transfer of her lady's possessions from the packs to a spacious trunk set between the windows. "Certes, hawks screech like that," she allowed. "Mayhap one entered the donjon through an open window."

"It sounded like a woman's scream," Clarice said.

Laura feigned a shrug. "It was a strenuous journey. Do you not wish to lie down?"

Clarice peered at the ceiling as if awaiting further disruption, then dropped back in the chair. "I am not tired. I prefer to explore my new home."

Laura might have acquiesced as often she had since Maude's passing, but this was High Castle, and until she wed Lothaire, it was not truly their home—indeed, might never be if the one who had screeched found a way around Queen Eleanor.

"You may acquaint yourself with it later," Laura said.

"Why not now? I just sit here with naught to occupy myself."

How had Maude responded to argument? Two answers—the first being firm correction of a young Laura, the second less than firm correction of the stronger-willed Clarice. Though Laura had not dozed so deeply she was unaware Maude often yielded to her beloved granddaughter, ever it had been easier to allow another to rear her child.

Now it is for you to do, she told herself. *You were raised well, presented so fine a young lady the foreboding Raisa Soames approved of you wedding Lexeter's heir.*

"Well?" Clarice tossed her hands wide.

"We shall aid Tina in unpacking and arranging our clothes."

"But 'tis for her to do! I wish to look about the castle."

"Later," Laura said firmly and started toward the maid.

Clarice thrust up out of the chair. "Then I shall rest."

Laura longed to allow her to laze on the bed though she claimed she was not tired—far less conflict than exerting authority to teach her daughter responsibility as Maude had done with Laura when she was younger than Clarice—but she set a hand on her daughter's shoulder.

"What?" The girl's demand caused anger to nip at her mother.

"You shall aid with the clothes, Clarice."

"Ah nay, milady," the maid said with false cheer surely meant to ease the tension. "The task is best left to me."

"You are more fatigued than we are, Tina. Thus, we ought to unpack whilst *you* rest."

"I will not!" Clarice gasped.

Laura kept her chin up. "You will. Now come." She started to draw her daughter toward the packs, but the girl pulled free and moments later tossed open the door and started down the corridor.

Laura hesitated amid Tina's entreaty, "Let the child go," then once more reminding herself she was awake, broke free of all that conspired to drag her in a less uncomfortable direction and ran.

"Clarice!" she called when she saw her daughter stood in the middle of the corridor as if also pulled in two directions.

Clarice resumed her course, but her mother's legs were longer, and Laura did not stomp her way to the landing. As she took hold of the girl's arm, Clarice swung around. "I do not wish to be with you."

"Regardless, you are. As I am your mother, you shall abide by my instruction."

"Instruction? You are not Lady Maude."

"True. I am more to you than that. I am your—"

"You are not! You are a shadow."

Laura nearly choked on her next breath. "A what?"

"A shadow." Defensively, Clarice raised her chin. "'Tis as Lady Maude told."

Hurt flooding Laura, she whispered, "She said this to you?"

Her daughter hesitated as if considering a lie, then scowled. "Nay, ever she defended you. I heard her tell it to the baron."

Her stepson, Michael's older brother.

Laura swallowed. "She spoke true. A shadow I was, but a shadow no longer. Though I cannot replace Lady Maude in your affections, I am trying to be a better mother."

"Then you are failing. Try harder!"

Were she alone, Laura would put her face in her hands to muffle her cry of pain. Instead, she suppressed it. "I know, and I regret it." She released her daughter, touched her cheek. "If you will help me—"

Clarice drew back.

Lowering her hand rather than display how empty it was, Laura said, "I know change is difficult, especially our loss of Maude, but—"

"What of Donnie?"

Her affectionate name for the one who had been her playmate the same as Simon had been Laura's. But Donald, nearly three years older than the cousin he did not know Clarice to be, had left behind the playthings of boys as evidenced by his exploration of the playthings of men—that which dealt the blow that awakened Laura.

Clarice made a sound of disgust. "It was just a kiss, but you had to make more of it, and now I have lost him as well."

"You are nine, Clarice! He is nearly twelve. It was not *just* a kiss." *At the time, perhaps,* Laura silently conceded. It had been the same for her at close to the age Clarice now was, but as the years had born out, it had meant far more to Simon. And had been the beginning of the end of Lothaire and Laura.

The tears brightening Clarice's eyes contrasting with her stubbornly set jaw, she said, "Methinks you are jealous that no one kisses you."

Laura lurched back, but when her daughter spun away, recaptured her arm.

"Release me!" Clarice cried as she was pulled off the landing, then she let her legs go out from under her.

Laura stared at the girl at the end of her hand. So much hurt shone from Clarice, as if the one who had born her intended to beat her into submission the same as Simon—

Laura thrust aside the memory. "Forgive me," she said. "I but wish you to return to our chamber."

Her daughter's nostrils flared. "Let me go, and I will follow."

Laura released her, but once more her daughter made for the stairs.

Laura snatched hold of her and pulled her around. "Pray, Clarice, do not make this more difficult than already it is."

"*You* are the one who makes it difficult. Let me go!"

"Nay." Putting in her eyes what she hoped was steel, Laura lifted her chin.

And could make no sense of the flurry of movement until Lothaire barked, "Enough!"

He stood behind her daughter, gripping the wrist of the hand drawn back to strike the one Clarice defied, and when the girl strained against his hold, he said, "Cease this foolery!"

Clarice drew a breath that added to her height, looked over her shoulder at Lothaire where he must have come off the third floor stairs, then yielded up the extra height on a long exhale.

He released her. "Go to your chamber, Clarice."

"You are not my father!"

"I need no reminder of that, but henceforth you will treat me with the respect due one's sire, for that I shall be when I wed your mother. Now go."

Laura could hardly breathe for the ache of what had happened between Clarice and her, the shame of what Lothaire had witnessed, and the judgment to come.

Clarice brushed past her, moments later slammed the door.

"Have I this to look forward to every day until she is old enough to wed away?" Lothaire demanded.

His eagerness to rid himself of Clarice wounded, but blessedly he spoke low enough to ensure his rebuke did not travel beyond them.

Though Laura longed to defend the behavior he had witnessed, it was a waste. She was at fault for the failed relationship with her daughter, and until she remedied it, Lothaire would have to bear whatever cost was passed to him.

"Yet more I must pay for the queen's tax break?" he scorned.

Now his words cut. "A *sizable* break of which you ought not be dismissive, Lord Soames! After all, its reward for wedding me is your greatest chance of saving Lexeter."

How she missed the young man who had regarded his betrothed with dismay when she behaved as he deemed inappropriate but could be teased into accepting her displays of happiness. How she missed the possibility he was not entirely lost to her when he had kissed her palm at Castle Soaring. Now he regarded her with what seemed disgust. There would be no teasing the man he had become. No way of stopping whatever words of condemnation he loosed upon her.

Actually, there was a way. Though her question was unkind, his answer might better prepare her for the reunion to come. "Was that your mother screeching like a hawk defending its territory?"

Condemnation falling from his eyes, he said, "A blow she has been dealt, but she will recover."

"You will send her from High Castle as Queen Eleanor directed?"

He raised an eyebrow.

"I know how to be hated, Lothaire. My daughter does not. Yet. The longer that is delayed, the better."

His shoulders broadened with breath. "In advance of our arrival, I had Lady Raisa moved to a third floor chamber. As she is unwell, you are unlikely to encounter her providing neither you nor your daughter venture above this floor. Once my mother is hale enough to travel, I will deliver her to her dower property."

That was hardly comforting, for it was nothing definite, increasing the likelihood Clarice would be exposed to the woman. Moved to a threat, albeit a gentle one—for now—Laura said, "I look forward to sending word to my cousin that my daughter and I are comfortably and safely settled upon Lexeter."

His lids narrowed.

She inclined her head. "Until supper, my lord."

He let her go. Thus, it was she who halted her progress. Turning before her chamber, she saw Lothaire stood in profile, a hand to the door beyond which must lay the lord's solar.

"I wish a bath," she said. More than wished. She hungered for warmth and weightlessness.

Lothaire looked over his shoulder. "And you wish me to do what? Collect a basin and towel?"

She frowned. "Such I would not ask of you. I but wish to arrange a *tub* bath."

His eyebrows rose.

Feeling herself shrink, she said, "Is it asking too much?"

"This is not Windsor, Lady Laura, and your host is not the Queen of England. This is Lexeter, and as you must know from the state of the castle, few are the luxuries afforded even its lord since labor is far better spent improving the living conditions for all than heating and lugging water for one."

Mayhap I am as spoiled as Clarice, Laura silently admonished. Ashamed by her request that must have sounded like a demand, she said, "I apologize. I did not mean to be thoughtless." She turned aside.

Once she had closed herself in her chamber, she felt such relief that if not for the sight of Clarice sitting back on her heels alongside Tina, she would have propped herself against the door. Instead, she lowered to her knees on the other side of the maid and, ignoring her daughter's sulking, began making High Castle her home.

A bath was not unreasonable, especially after the long journey. However, the audience with his mother who *had* screeched like a hawk upon learning Laura Middleton had come to take from her the title of Lady of Lexeter, had dragged Lothaire's toes—then heels—to the edge of forbearance.

There had been only one screech, then Raisa went lax and would have crumpled to the floor had he not caught her. As he laid her on the bed, she had gripped the neck of his tunic and demanded he return the *Delilah-Jezebel* and her misbegotten daughter to Eleanor.

It had taken some time to reason her down from hysterics which she often scorned as a weapon wielded by women too weak of mind to control a man any other way. But as Sebille and he knew, her aversion had more to do with such displays being ineffectual with her roving husband.

When Raisa had calmed, she grudgingly conceded King Henry's harlot had given her son no choice. Without the tax break Laura Middleton brought to the marriage, it could prove impossible to hold onto Lexeter. As he did not need his twice betrothed to remind him, it was generous compensation—naught of which to be dismissive.

Nor were the hours that remained of daylight. It was time to resume the labors neglected during his absence.

Garbed in homespun tunic and chausses, to which he had become so accustomed he no longer scratched at his skin, he departed the donjon certain he would not join Laura for supper. If he returned ere the middling of night, it would be early. And likely he would once more depart ere she rose to face the first full day of the thousands she would pass upon Lexeter.

12

"CATCH ME!" LAURA called and peered over her shoulder at Lothaire, certain once his much longer legs overtook her they would kiss. If she unbalanced him as she had on the day past, they would find themselves in the grass again. And when their kiss progressed as far as he permitted, they would entwine their fingers and watch the clouds glide in and out.

But this was only a dream, she realized as she rose up through it. A dream made of remembrance. Unlike the other times it had visited, Lothaire would be with her when she opened her eyes. Or nearly so. Were he outside the donjon, he would not be far—even if he rode out to survey his demesne as he had done on the day past. Therefore, he was no longer entirely out of reach.

And what fool you are to think that, she reminded herself of her purpose upon Lexeter and their confrontation over Clarice. *You are a tax break and a womb for the making of an heir, his—*

What did he call you? His somehow. Merely a somehow.

She lifted her lids, found the ceiling above. Though once she had preferred sleeping on her side, after what had been done to her in the cellar, it made her feel vulnerable to give her back even to the walls. From the moment she closed her eyes upon night to the moment she opened them upon day, she wanted the assurance no one was near enough to catch her from behind.

She shifted her gaze to the right side of the bed. She was alone, Clarice surely having set off to explore the castle as had been denied her on the day past. And Tina? There was no humming or movement about the chamber, meaning the maid had gone for viands to break her lady's fast.

Laura stretched, then wondering how late she had slept, pushed onto her elbows. And could not contain her cry of surprise and dismay at finding she was not alone.

She tried to speak the name of the woman who stood before the door garbed in a beautiful, albeit outdated gown, but her voice failed. And the Lady of Lexeter did not look of a mind to make it easy for them to renew their acquaintance.

Laura sat up, turned the covers back from her modest chemise, and rose from the bed. Clasping her hands at her waist, she said, "I am pleased to see you again, Lady Raisa."

They both knew it a lie, so it was not really that, Laura supposed, but it was proper.

With a rustle of skirts that evidenced the gown was not worn often enough to soften its weave, Lothaire's mother slowly advanced.

Wishing Tina were here, grateful Clarice was not, Laura remained unmoving. When the lady and she stood eye to eye with barely a reach between them, Laura wondered as she had all those years ago how such an aged and dour woman had birthed so attractive a son. The lady's young husband must have been pleasing to the eye. And illness and the addition of these past ten years had been even less kind to his widow.

She startled when Lady Raisa lifted a hand and took hold of her chin, held her breath as sharp eyes scrutinized her.

"I did not think you would be so lovely when you grew into your face and body," Lothaire's mother said. "I should have heeded the Lord when He burdened me with uncertainty, but your father was generous with your dowry—at least until you proved the foulest Daughter of Eve."

Laura took a step back and came up against the bedside table.

The lady lowered her hand but followed. "Alas, you are a necessary evil, as is the one you and your lover spawned who will surely prove as much a Delilah and Jezebel—mayhap more a whore than you."

The hand Clarice had raised against her mother on the day past became Laura's hand. But unlike Clarice's, this one landed its slap and turned the woman's head to the side.

Hardly had Laura time to feel the horror of what she had done before Lady Raisa retaliated with such force it was not believable her thin body possessed half the strength required to overpower one thirty-five years younger. Her hand gripped Laura's face, wrenched it to the side, and when her victim's body followed, slammed her head onto the bedside table.

Pain spearing Laura's skull, she dropped to her knees. Not realizing the lady's hand remained splayed over her face—pressing it to the tabletop—until that one's breath was in her ear, Laura floundered for a response. And half senseless, wondered if the assault was her due. Albeit provoked by what the woman said of Clarice, she had struck first. So was this deserved? And was it only the beginning, as when she had refused Simon?

"My son does not want you, Laura Middleton," Lothaire's mother said. "I do not want you. The people of Lexeter do not want you. Though we shall suffer you and the foul fruit of your fornication as long as we must, I warn you—do you even think to cuckold my son again, the pain you feel this day will be naught compared to what I will do to you." She pinched Laura's earlobe. "As now you know, I am not as frail as I appear. And this wasting sickness…Aye, I am afflicted, but not so much you will soon see me in the ground."

She released Laura and stepped back.

Gripping the edge of the table with one hand, Laura slapped her other hand to the bed and pressed to her feet. With a breath that quaked her body, she turned.

A placid smile showing gray-cast teeth, Lady Raisa said, "Heed me well, and do not forget your great weakness. Well, *great* insomuch as you have a care for your brat." She turned, paused at the door, and touched the mark on her cheek. "I will not tell my son you struck a sickly old woman if you do not tell I have yet enough life in me to defend my person."

Her threat confirmed she had sought to be aggressed upon. And foolish, still impulsive Laura had done her bidding.

Refraining from touching her own cheek that would be more marked than the other woman's, Laura said, "Do not come to my chamber again. More, stay away from my daughter."

The woman raised her eyebrows. "Do you give me no cause to visit you or *trouble* your little girl, you need only tolerate me in passing." She opened the door.

"If not in passing, the next time I shall be prepared," Laura called.

The lady chuckled and closed the door behind her.

All of her trembling, Laura looked to the bed to which she longed to return and hold herself close. But she had been vulnerable enough for one day, and were she not more cautious now she was reacquainted with Lady Raisa, she would leave Clarice open to that woman's threats.

She dropped her chin to her chest. She had been grateful to escape Lord Benton's perverse clutches, but now there was this which could prove as dangerous to her daughter. Perhaps more...

"Father," she whispered, "aid me in keeping Clarice safe—in persuading Lothaire not to delay in sending his mother from High Castle." She lifted her head, probed her aching face, muttered, "Certes, she is well enough to travel."

Determined that if her betrothed would not do as bid, she would send word to Eleanor as she had gently threatened Lothaire, she began preparing for the day.

Blessedly, the mirror on the dressing table revealed her face felt more tender than it appeared. Providing a bruise did not rise, none need know an elderly woman had retaliated for the offense dealt her.

"After the offense dealt my daughter," Laura murmured as she smoothed creamed powder over her flushed, lightly abraded cheek. Still, despite Lady Raisa's cruelty, she felt evil as the woman had named her.

"A necessary evil," she whispered. And nearly cried.

One step. It was all she could manage of the stairs that reached from the second floor to the third.

Lungs aching with each draw of air, joints protesting how tightly she gripped the railing, Raisa let her shoulder fall against the wall and clutched her side. So hot had her blood coursed when she stood before the one unworthy of her son that she had thought it a great lie she was frail and soon to have dirt flung upon her corpse. But it was no lie, all of her day's strength wasted on the Delilah-Jezebel.

"Not wasted," she croaked and released her side to finger the mark on her cheek. The flesh had cooled, likely presenting little evidence of the attack, but it had served its purpose. Despite Lady Laura's own threats, the younger woman was afeared enough she would not soon take a lover. But when Raisa was gone...

Catching the sound of humming on the stairs below, she straightened her spine. Certain the noise belonged to Lady Laura's maid whose earlier descent was marked by tune which assured the reunion with Lady Laura would be uninterrupted, Raisa forced herself to mount the steps. With strength scraped from her depths, she made it out of sight and sank to the floor on the uppermost landing.

She disliked the prospect of being found by Sebille who would guess the Lady of Lexeter possessed a key to her chamber, but unless she recovered sufficiently, there was nothing for it. Of course, Sebille might be persuaded she had forgotten to secure the door, especially if Raisa provided a good distraction.

Chuckling at the realization her inability to reach her chamber could prove of benefit, she gave her cheek a more vicious pinch than that dealt the harlot's ear and improved on the injury by raking her nails down her jaw.

Poor old woman. She did what she must to ensure the future of the Soames family as her husband had not—he whose body had yet to be returned by the family who murdered him, he whom she did not mourn as a loving wife should. Had his treachery not led him to seek out his mistress, during his return to Lexeter he would have had no cause to request a night's lodging upon the barony of Wiltford. He would yet live. If never her unfaithful husband was exhumed and replanted in consecrated ground she would be all the happier.

It was a long quarter hour before the one who had once seemed a miracle nearly stumbled over the old woman.

"What—?" Sebille caught her breath when a bruised and scratched face was raised to her, dropped to her haunches.

"The Delilah," Raisa choked. "I sought reassurance she repented of her sins against your brother, but she is less godly than ten years past." With a shaking hand, she touched her face. "I defended myself as best I could—pushed her away. Certes, she would have done me greater harm had she not stumbled and struck her head on the table." She let slip a smile, knowing to suppress it would cause the disbelief rising on the younger woman's face to blossom, then she gripped Sebille's arm. "The whore will further ruin Lothaire."

Raisa did not believe Sebille had a great care for her as she had when she was a girl—when she had good cause to love the Lady of Lexeter and be loved in return—but Lothaire's sister had been devoted to her brother since she first held Ricard's infant son. Thus, the younger woman who was growing old ahead of her years might finally serve a purpose other than that to which she had rightfully given her life.

Clenching her teeth so hard her bony face that had once been softly rounded looked harsher, Sebille struggled to help Raisa to her feet. "Let us get you to bed, my lady."

It was no easy thing, Raisa so weak she could offer little assistance and Sebille so spare of muscle she was huffing by the time she nearly dropped the older woman onto the mattress.

"We must tell Lothaire what that woman did to you," Sebille said.

"Nay." Raisa groaned back into the pillows. "I wish we could, but Lexeter does need what that harlot brings to the marriage, and I would not give him cause to break the betrothal. We will simply have to be vigilant, protecting him as best we can, eh?"

She was pleased by the emotions struggling across Sebille's face that made the younger woman close a hand over the prayer beads hung from her girdle. And further pleased when Sebille said, "I shall watch the lady closely." She drew the covers up over Raisa's shoulders, glanced at the door. "How did you gain a key to your chamber?"

No feat that. As Lady of Lexeter, she had possessed keys to all doors of import—two sets, the one Lothaire took from her when he determined he could manage the demesne better than she and the set hidden in a dozen pockets sewn into the inner lining of her clothes trunk to allow them to lie flat and keep them from rattling against one another.

"Would that I possessed one," she said and let a smile onto her lips as would be expected. Though this one trembled, it was not entirely for show, so fatigued was she. "When you departed earlier, I noted you did not lock the door."

"But I did!"

"Nay. I heard no turning of the key, and it was unlocked when I tried it."

Sebille studied the older woman's face, slowly nodded.

"Worry not," Raisa said. "I will not tell Lothaire you were remiss lest he no longer entrust you with my care."

Something flashed in and out of Sebille's eyes.

Dismay, Raisa named it and drew an arm from beneath the covers and patted the younger woman's hand. "I vow I will not tell him—and most selfishly, for you know I would have naught to live for were you taken from me, do you not?"

Another nod, then Sebille said, "I will have to be more mindful of securing the door," and hastily added, "to protect you should you be tempted to expose yourself to Lady Laura's venom again."

Venom. Raisa liked the word applied to that woman, Lothaire having accused his mother of the same when he brought to ground men sent to punish Lady Beata whose unconsummated marriage to her son had been annulled by Queen Eleanor. "You are right to do so, but more to keep that whore from my chamber lest she seek to permanently remove me from my son's life."

Sebille stood. "I shall summon the physician."

He who had served the Lady of Lexeter since shortly after her husband's disappearance. The man was her dearest friend, though perhaps because he was her only one. Regardless, none could know it from the formality with which each regarded their relationship.

"What will you tell him when he asks about your face?" Sebille asked.

The truth, of course, Raisa thought but said, "The physician is well aware I am not as steady on my feet as once I was."

"And what if Lothaire should visit this eve?"

"If you cannot discourage him, the dim of my chamber shall suffice. But unless Lady Laura is so fool to tell him of my attempt to defend myself, I do not think he will come this night."

"He might on the morrow."

"Not if the physician advises I am not to be disturbed." Lothaire would welcome the excuse to stay away, she did not say. "Given a day or two, I should be presentable again."

The young woman inclined her head. "Rest well."

"Sebille!" Raisa called her around. "Do not forget to watch her closely."

"I shall."

"And her daughter."

"Her as well."

13

"WHERE IS BARON Soames?"

Sir Angus unclasped his hands from behind his back, came around. "Lady Laura."

"I told you, Mother," Clarice said on a sigh. "I saw him ride out at dawn."

The knight inclined his head. "As your daughter tells." He started to turn back to the squires he had been instructing in hand-to-hand combat.

"But that does not inform me as to where he is," Laura pressed.

"Apologies, my lady, but it is not for my lord to give me an account of his whereabouts. Suffice to say he has begun his day's work and will not return 'til late in the day, mayhap the eve."

Laura looked past the training yard to the drawbridge beyond the raised portcullis. "What keeps him away so long?"

"The work of wool, my lady. The heartbeat of Lexeter."

She knew much of the barony's income was derived from the numerous flocks of sheep she had seen as they traversed the demesne on the day past, and that Lothaire's acquisition of a wife had taken him long from his duties. But the possibility he could be gone the entire day and into night seemed much for one who oversaw the operations, especially since he had returned so late on the day past she had not seen him again. Rather, she had taken her supper alongside the vacant lord's seat. Afterward, she had only the company of her pouting daughter at the hearth, Lady Sebille having yet to appear.

"As Baron Soames has been absent nearly a fortnight," Sir Angus said, "he has much to occupy him."

And much to avoid, Laura silently added. He had told he was often away from the castle, but now he had greater cause.

"Is there something with which I may assist, my lady?"

She shook her head, causing the loose braid Tina had worked from the left of her brow down the right side of her face to brush the concealed bruise.

The maid had been shocked by her lady's face. Though tempted to tell it was the result of a fall, for the sake of Clarice, Laura had revealed the truth. Until Lady Raisa departed High Castle, help would be needed to ensure the girl did not expose herself to Lothaire's mother.

"I thank you, Sir Knight, but I have a missive to write to the queen over which I must consult my betrothed. I suppose it shall have to await his return."

"I will tell him you seek an audience."

She blinked. "You do know where he is."

"Not now, but I know where he shall be near the nooning hour. I am to meet him."

"Then I shall accompany you."

He frowned. "My lady—"

"As will I!" Clarice exclaimed.

Laura started to naysay her, hesitated over the expectation shining from a face downcast since her mother had ended her exploration of the inner bailey.

"I am sorry to discourage such adventurous females," Sir Angus said, "but I must. The work of wool is not for ladies, as I do not doubt your betrothed would agree. I shall convey your message to Baron Soames that he return to the castle as soon as he is able."

So firm was he that she wavered, but her daughter's beseeching hand on her arm—the same that had nearly struck her on the day past—made her stand taller. "I shall convey it myself, Sir Angus, even if amidst the work of wool. What time do you depart?"

"An hour hence, but—"

"You would do me a kindness to ensure my horse is saddled alongside yours. An hour, then," she said and turned away.

She heard a low growl above the squires' grunts, knew it sounded from the knight rather than the enormous, bedraggled dog lazing alongside the training yard's fence, but it was naught compared to Lady Raisa's bite.

Clarice tugged on her mother's arm. "You will allow me to accompany you?"

Laura preferred she remain at the castle, but after this morn's encounter, she was loath for Clarice to be out of her sight for long, even though Tina could be prevailed upon to remain near her.

"Mother?"

"A moment." When they were distant enough from Lothaire's man not to be overheard, Laura halted—and was surprised to find the large dog at her daughter's side. Alarmingly, the girl's hand was on the beast's neck. "Clarice, you do not know that dog—"

"But I do. I played with him in the hall this morn. He is Tomas."

As if aware he was the subject of their conversation, the dog turned his eyes on Laura, considered her with what seemed interest, then yawned, revealing the longest tongue and sharpest teeth she had ever seen.

"He is very big and of many teeth, Clarice."

"Aye, but he is gentle and sweet." The girl did not have to bend far to kiss the dog's head. Returning her gaze to her mother, she said, "So I may accompany Sir Angus and you?"

Hoping the dog was as temperate as he appeared, Laura said, "Aye, but we must change quickly."

Clarice smiled, then frowned. "'Tis an hour ere Sir Angus departs."

"It was. Now it may be less."

The girl's eyes widened. "You think he will leave without us."

"Very possible. Let us disappoint him, hmm?"

The last time her daughter's mouth had bowed so wide was when Lady Maude allowed the girl to journey with her to a nearby abbey to present a new altar cloth to show her appreciation for the prayers offered up for her son, Simon. A month later, the lady passed.

Clarice had loved the adventure, unaware it was as personal a journey for her as it was for her grandmother. Laura had remained behind, no invitation wasted on one who would have rejected it as calmly as possible.

"Sir Angus will not like it," Clarice said with a song in her voice that reminded Laura of when she had been young.

True. The knight would not care to be foiled, nor would Lothaire. But her betrothed was not here to gainsay the one who was done being led where she did not wish to go.

And she was fair certain her cousin, the queen, would approve.

What was Angus thinking to bring her here? And of equal surprise and disturbance was her daughter's accompaniment, to which Lothaire was more opposed considering the girl's attempt to strike her mother. She ought to be confined to her chamber.

He muffled a curse. He may not wish Clarice for a daughter, but if Laura would not control the girl's impulses, he would quickly learn the role of a father. Clarice would not abuse her mother and destroy the order in his household—whatever little he had.

He dropped the hammer, spat out the nails pinched between his lips, and snatched up the tunic tossed aside when labor and the day's heat conspired to make it one with his torso and arms. As he dragged on the garment, he heard the giving of a seam forced over perspiring flesh, and when he yanked it down his hips, felt another yield.

Fool, he berated himself. *She who surprises you is not unfamiliar with a man's bared body.*

That nearly made him wish he had not covered himself, but still there was Clarice who would be old enough to wed away in as few as four years. Surely he had done as a father would the longer to preserve a young lady's innocence...

As the half dozen riders neared, among them three men-at-arms who were to repair the aged fence, Lothaire set his gaze upon Angus who would aid him and the shepherd in separating the lambs from this flock's mothers as should have been done a fortnight past.

The knight awaited the look his lord gave him, with apology shook his head.

What had been so difficult about refusing to allow Laura and her daughter to accompany him? And what was of such import it could not await his return?

Determinedly suppressing the shame of a lord reduced to common labor, Lothaire looked closer upon Laura as she neared.

Like Angus, she awaited his gaze. Unlike the knight, her color was high as if she was exerted by the ride. Did he not know better, he would think her flush a result of embarrassment at glimpsing his bared torso and now his dampened tunic embracing his muscles.

But no maiden was she, he once more reminded himself. And no evidence need be offered beyond the girl perched before her, she who was likely of Michael D'Arci.

Lothaire strode forward, gripped the horse's halter, and squinted up at his betrothed. "You ought not be here, my lady. I cannot think why Sir Angus allowed you to leave the castle."

He heard her swallow, sensed her determination to keep her eyes from moving down him.

"As I needed to speak with you, and Sir Angus could offer little hope of your return ere I seek my bed this eve, I insisted." She glanced at the knight. "Much to his regret, I am sure, I gave him no opportunity to depart without me."

Lothaire breathed deep, momentarily savored the scent of moist earth and the grass sprung from it. "What is so important it could not wait?"

She opened her mouth, closed it, glanced at her daughter. "I would speak in private."

If she did not wish Clarice to be privy to their conversation, why had she brought her? Had the girl made it difficult to refuse? Likely.

Patience, he counseled and shifted his regard to Clarice.

To his surprise, she smiled tentatively. "If you would lift me down, Lord Soames, my mother and you can speak whilst I play with the lambs." She nodded at the flock of one hundred ewes and their babies who were to be babies no longer.

He cleared his throat. "I will lift you down, but you will not approach the lambs."

"Why?" she said with offense.

"Their mothers will butt you ere thanking you for *playing* with their babies. And 'tis no mere nudge, I vow."

She sighed and reached to him.

Lothaire lowered her beside him. "Sir Angus, escort Lady Clarice to look nearer upon the sheep."

The knight dismounted and passed the reins to his lord.

Lothaire swung into the saddle. "See to the fence's repair," he ordered the men-at-arms long accustomed to doing the work of commoners. They had not liked it in the beginning and some had left his service, but the Lord of Lexeter made it worth the sacrifice of dignity. Their reward meant the barony was slower to recover from the abuse of its finances and lack of leadership prior to Ricard Soames's son taking control of it, but more often they vied for the opportunity to engage in the labor.

"Come, Lady Laura," he urged his mount ahead of hers.

They rode to the crest of a gently sloping hill and he turned his horse to observe the shepherd moving amongst the sheep, Sir Angus standing alongside Clarice with a wide enough berth to cause the ewes little discomfort, and the men-at-arms wielding blunt weapons against wood as opposed to keen weapons against flesh.

"You have my attention," he said as Laura drew alongside.

She inclined her head. "You were mending the fence."

That was *not* the matter of import which caused her to ride out to meet him. "I was," he said with defensiveness he regretted almost as much as providing proof of exactly how much he needed to wed her.

"And now your men-at-arms shall do so."

He considered her, thought how becoming her hair looked with its loose braid curtaining one side of her face. "They are well compensated," he begrudged, then inwardly sighed. Best she learn the true state of his demesne now rather than later. "I pay them coin when I am able. When I scrape the bottom of my coffers, they are mostly content with an extra day of rest."

Her lips parted, teeth picked at her lower lip. "I did not realize your circumstances were so dire—your need to wed so great. I hope what I bring to the marriage is enough to set Lexeter aright."

"Certes, 'twill be of benefit. Now I do not mean to be curt, but if I am to join you at table this eve, I must resume my work."

"The work of wool."

"What do you wish to discuss, my lady?"

"As I am sure the queen is eager to learn all progresses as it should, I intend to write her this day. I would have her know the announcement of our marriage has been arranged—"

"It has," he interrupted. "Upon our arrival, I instructed the reading of the banns commence immediately. So it shall this Sunday. If none oppose our marriage, we shall wed in three weeks."

She nodded, causing the shadow of hair draping her face to shift—or some of it. That upon her cheek remained dark.

"Anything else?" he prompted.

"As discussed on the day past, I wish to assure Eleanor your mother will soon be situated on her dower property."

"As told, I will see it done when she is well enough."

"I..."The tip of her tongue touched her lips. "I do not think that will satisfy my cousin."

He frowned. "Nor you, hmm?"

She hesitated as if considering denial, but said, "Nor me."

He shifted in the saddle to look closer upon her. "Lady Laura, I know my mother can be unpleasant…"

More than unpleasant, he silently acceded. But he would not alarm her by revealing the Lady of Lexeter had sent assassins to the woman to whom he was briefly wed. Though Raisa Soames no longer had access to men willing to do her dark bidding, he did not think that would be of much comfort to his betrothed.

Seeing the frown gathering on the half of Laura's brow that was visible, he realized he had not completed his thought. "I agree it is best my mother dwell on her dower property, but as it is nearly a day's journey by cart, I must be certain she can make it without great discomfort."

Laura looked down then up, and in a voice just shy of challenging said, "What makes you think she is not well enough. Surely she is not bedridden?"

"She is, though some days are not as bad as others." Days that had become worse since last year's murder attempt, he silently acknowledged. Days that sometimes made him question the soundness of her mind. "The physician believes she is not likely to see another summer. Thus, she will not be a bother to you."

She turned her face away, drew a strident breath.

He leaned closer. "What is it?"

"Naught," she said sharply. "As told, I would not risk my daughter being exposed to your mother's hatred."

Though he wanted to assure her it was not hatred Raisa felt—only concern for her son—he could not lie. And even if he could, it would be a waste. He was not accomplished enough at falsehood for Laura to believe him.

"You would do better to concern yourself over your daughter's behavior than my mother's."

She snapped her chin around. "I would not!"

He barely heard her protest, his attention once more captured by the immovable shadow on her cheek.

He reached and swept aside the braid covering that side of her face. And was moved by anger when he glimpsed what lay beneath a veil of cream thinned by the brush of her hair. "She struck you hard enough to leave a bruise," he snarled and moved his gaze to the girl in the distance who looked too small to inflict such an injury.

"Nay!" Laura gripped his arm as if for fear he would put heels to his mount. "Clarice did not do this. I fell!"

He looked back at her. "You lie."

She shook her head, providing another eyeful of the bruise. "She did not hit me, Lothaire."

He stared.

"May God bear witness!" It was said with such desperation he believed her even less.

"You and your daughter will return to High Castle. Now."

"Lothaire—"

"Clarice requires discipline, Laura, and though I do not wish to be the one to correct her, I will if you do not."

"I tell you, she did not strike me!"

"Do something about her, Laura, ere she becomes the same as—" He did not finish the thought. Though he wished her to understand the seriousness of the matter, he would not have her suffer further injury.

"You fear she will become like me," she herself dealt the blow. But then she said with such bitterness he tasted it, "I am not sure that is such a bad thing—providing her path to becoming her mother is a firmer path than the one upon which I found myself."

Found. As if she herself were not responsible.

"But a firmer one I intend to make it," she continued, "and for that I sought Queen Eleanor's aid in securing a husband." She heaved a sigh. "Woe to you that you must suffer me, Lothaire. And woe to you if you think to correct my child for something she did not do."

She commanded her horse forward, and he watched her descend the hill and argue her daughter up in front of her. When she turned toward High Castle, he spurred forward.

"See them safely back to the castle," he instructed Angus as he dropped out of the saddle.

The knight's brow was rumpled, but rather than speak his question, he mounted his horse and set off.

And Lothaire threw mind and body into the work of a commoner.

14

THE LADY WAS so thin that even at Laura's slightest she might have appeared heavy alongside Lothaire's sister.

Laura rose from the hearth where she had sat following supper the past two nights. And just as Lothaire and his sister had been absent from the meal last eve, so they had been this eve. Now the latter appeared, and she looked almost starved. Too, though she was only a few years older than her brother, she appeared ten or more.

"You must be Lady Sebille." Laura curtsied as the woman halted before her. "I am——"

"I know who you are." Lady Sebille glanced across her shoulder at the girl who sat at a small table with the young squire persuaded to join her in a game of chess. "And that is your child."

"Aye, Clarice."

"The daughter who should have been my brother's," the lady said low. "Now alas, by default she is his responsibility."

I ought not be surprised I am no better liked by her than I am by her mother, Laura mulled, then said, "Most unfortunate, our sovereign gave us little choice."

The lady stepped past her, lowered into a chair, and motioned to the one from which Laura had risen. "We must needs speak."

When the two faced each other, Lady Sebille leaned forward. "Are you as marked by Lady Raisa's violence against you as she is by yours?"

Laura nearly choked. "She told you?"

"Her rendering, which I know to be pocked with exaggeration—likely even lies."

What had Lady Raisa said? And would she reveal it to Lothaire though she said she would not if Laura did not speak of it?

The lady moved her eyes to the braid that was mostly for Clarice's benefit. "Pray, show me, Lady Laura."

She wanted to refuse, but she confirmed Clarice's back remained turned to her and swept aside the braid.

"The cream lightens the bruise but does little to conceal the swelling," Lady Sebille said.

Laura dropped the braid. "'Tis improved over this morn. Your mother is stronger than she appears."

"She is not, my lady. I nearly had to carry her to her chamber. I am sure she but caught you unawares."

An act, Laura silently countered.

"Though I am quite certain she must have provoked you," the lady added with something just short of apology.

Laura frowned. "What makes you think that?"

"I know her, mayhap better than she knows herself—though that may be as she would have me believe."

Just as she wished her daughter to believe her terribly infirm, Laura thought.

"Regardless, I allow she is difficult, not surprising for one who sees her life as mostly wasted, Lothaire her only worthy contribution. Thus, she is fiercely protective of my brother. As am I." She sat back, fingered a string of dark beads on her girdle, the shine of which indicated they were handled often. "What matters to me is that you succeed where Lothaire's first wife failed."

"I know little about her. How did she fail?"

Lady Sebille raised her chin higher, peered down her nose. "I am not surprised he has not told you, and though 'tis not my place, I will tell it. Lady Edeva failed him the same as you."

Did she mean the woman had cuckolded Lothaire? If so, not the same.

"A terrible blow," the lady continued, "especially since he believes he failed himself."

"How?"

"Whereas Lady Raisa could be blamed for choosing you, it was Lothaire who decided on the lady—he who determined she was suitable and pure. A lie." She sighed. "But she is dead and in the past. So the question remains, Lady Laura. Now you are no longer a fickle, indiscriminate girl, can you make Lothaire a good wife?"

It was impossible not to take offense, but since the sister was more tolerant than her mother, Laura answered as levelly and honestly as she could, "It seems where Lexeter's prosperity is concerned, I am capable of being a good wife, but beyond that, I fear not."

The lady's face pinched, then a smile plucked at the corners of her mouth. "Your fear gives me hope."

"What say you?"

"Does it not mean you would like to be a satisfactory wife beyond what the queen and king promised my brother?"

"I would like that, but he thinks ill of me—does not trust me."

Barely present eyebrows rose. "You betrayed him in the worst way."

"Did I?" Laura said and regretted the impulsive response, an unwanted side effect of her awakening. Were she to keep peace in the home where she was to raise her child, her words would have to tread more carefully.

"Are you saying you did not betray my brother?" Lady Sebille glanced at Clarice, whom she believed evidence of that betrayal.

This time Laura suppressed the impulse to speak what was best left unspoken. Though a part of her she had not realized was so lonely strained toward the possibility of friendship with this lady, she must also subdue that. Perhaps she and Lothaire's sister would eventually enjoy each other's company, but not until Laura secured her place upon Lexeter. And that was not possible until the removal of Lady Raisa.

Hopefully, when Laura sat down to write the missive postponed to provide Lothaire time to avoid the queen's wrath, his mother would be gone.

"You do not answer me, my lady."

Laura recalled the question of her betrayal. "I can but assure you I am not the evil your mother names me. I have made mistakes, but those I shall not repeat."

"I am glad to hear it. If you at least strive to be a good wife, you will have my support. If you do not..." She turned up her hands. "I will protect my brother as best I can."

Another threat, and yet it was not quite that. There was too much pleading for Laura to take great offense. "Noted, my lady. Now I must ask, do you intend to tell your brother I slapped your mother?"

"That is not for me to do, and methinks Lady Raisa will not speak of it if you do not reveal she retaliated."

"I will not, though he is aware I..." Laura's smile felt bitter. "...took a fall that did injury to my face." She stood. "I bid you good eve, Lady Sebille."

The woman also rose, and the prayer beads attached to her girdle fell halfway down her skirt to settle amid the folds. "I am glad we spoke, and I hope to know you better in days to come."

Laura opened her mouth to agree, closed it at the sound of booted feet.

Lothaire emerged from the kitchen corridor alongside Sir Angus. Head tilted toward the slightly shorter man, he chuckled at something the knight said and lifted a hunk of bread over which he paused when his eyes found Laura's.

She noted he appeared fresher than when she had drawn him away from mending fences—and not only his hair that was now tightly bound at his nape. Had he washed his garments in a pond? Also bathed there? Imagining that as she should not, she recalled how once she had wanted to swim and bathe with him out of doors—and had believed they would when they wed. Now it seemed so sinful a thought her face warmed.

"Another missed meal," Lady Sebille said low. "He works too hard. I hope your marriage changes that."

"Once we are wed," Laura said, "his income will increase, providing more leisure time."

"Ah, but will it be soon enough for him to recover his dignity?"

Laura had sensed he had not liked her seeing him reduced to the labor of one born to the land, and yet she had also sensed the responsibility did not ride his back as heavily as those of the privileged class might think—that despite the hard work, he was fairly comfortable beneath its yoke.

"It seems one good thing has come of your presence here," the woman said. "My brother may appear the lowest of villeins, but he washed away most of the day's filth ere returning to the hall."

As verified when Sir Angus and he halted before the ladies.

"Lady Laura." Lothaire dipped his head, and his cool eyes warmed when they moved to the other woman. "Sister."

Lady Sebille nodded. "How fares the demesne?"

"Well, though there is much work to be done. How is Mother?"

Her hesitation made him frown. "A difficult day, but she sleeps it away. On the advice of the physician, she is not to be disturbed."

"I shall visit her on the morrow."

"I would not. The physician has ordered several days of rest to allow her to regain her strength." She looked to the bread he held. "That is your supper?"

"More of a dessert. Sir Angus and I filled our bellies in the kitchen."

She clicked her tongue. "Do you not sit at high table on occasion, Lexeter's people may forget you are their lord."

"I shall make a greater effort on the morrow." He leaned down, touched his lips to her brow. "I am pleased you and my betrothed are becoming acquainted."

"We have something in common."

He raised his eyebrows.

She smiled, and though the expression did not turn her pretty, it lessened her severity. "You."

He looked sidelong at Laura. "I am a topic of conversation?"

"You are," Lady Sebille answered. "A worthy one."

"Now I am curious, Lady Laura," Lothaire murmured.

Blessedly, an outburst saved her from satisfying that curiosity. Not so blessedly, it came from Clarice.

"But the game is not finished, Squire Aland. And I am winning!"

"I am sorry, my lady."The young man pushed upright. "Now my lord is returned, I must resume my duties."

"I will see the game to its end, Lady Clarice," Lothaire called as he closed the distance between them. To his squire, he said, "See the solar is made ready. I shall be up shortly." He dropped into the chair vacated by the young man, and the dog Clarice had befriended rose from alongside her chair and set its chin atop the Baron of Lexeter's forearm.

Lothaire patted the beast, said, "Whose move, my lady?"

Clarice looked like Laura felt—a bird wishing to spread its wings and flee, though in Laura's case she would do so with her fledgling lest the one who told he would correct her daughter made good his threat.

"Your move, Lord Soames," Clarice said cautiously, then less so, "but be vigilant, for I plan to take your queen. And there is little you can do to prevent it."

"Perhaps." He bent his head to study the board.

"I have not seen him play a game in years," Lothaire's sister said, returning Laura's gaze to her.

"As I have not seen you play one, Lady Sebille."This from Sir Angus, causing both women to startle, evidence his silence had rendered him invisible.

Lady Sebille's laughter was false and abrupt. "You know me, Sir Angus, never one for games."

"True. For such you have no time."

"As preferred." She dipped her chin. "Good eve, Sir Knight, Lady Laura." She crossed to her brother, who introduced her to Clarice. Then the lady continued to the stairs the physician ascended ahead of her—he whom Laura had not realized had returned to the hall following his departure at meal's end.

"I should have kept my mouth closed," Sir Angus said and gave Laura a sheepish smile. "I should still, but as you are to be her sister-in-law, there can be no harm in you knowing now what you will otherwise learn in time."

Laura felt pulled between this suddenly sorrowful knight and the chess game, but she held his gaze.

"I was very fond of the lady once. She was fond of me." He sighed. "But not enough. So I did the unforgivable. I loved others—or as near to love as I am capable. And with that, I shall leave you, my lady."

She watched him cross to the sideboard where he poured a tankard of ale.

"Oh!" Clarice exclaimed. "I did not see that."

Laura swung her gaze to the two with the board between them, saw it was Lothaire who removed his opponent's piece. It seemed there *was* much he could do to prevent Clarice from taking his queen.

"The next time you will see it," he said.

Grateful her daughter rarely cried over such losses, Laura returned to the chair to await the game's end when Clarice and she could depart together. Though she had instructed the girl not to venture to the third floor lest she disturb Lothaire's ill mother and Clarice had agreed, as Laura now knew, Lady Raisa did not confine herself to that floor.

It took longer than expected to name the winner of the chess game. And it was not Clarice.

Laura stood, started forward.

"Another game, Lord Soames?" her daughter entreated.

Before Laura could warn against further imposing on him, certain it was rest he required not another game that could last an hour, he looked around and said, "That is for your mother to decide."

She halted, wondered if his words were calculated to give her control over her daughter that he believed—with good cause—she lacked.

How was she to respond as a parent should? Though disinclined to agree, eager as she was to retreat abovestairs, she was moved to consent to please her daughter who asked so simple a thing, especially considering how well Clarice had earlier contained her disappointment over being given little time amongst the sheep. She had protested when Laura ordered her back into the saddle, but that had been the end of it. Or mostly.

"Lady Laura?" Lothaire prompted.

She looked from him to her daughter whose teeth were pressed into her lower lip. If not that Lothaire must long for bed, the answer would be easy since it was early enough Clarice would likely while away an hour ere gaining her own night's rest.

What would Maude—rather, what had Maude done with Laura in such circumstances?

She set her shoulders back. "I am well with it, Clarice, but only if Lord Soames truly does not mind. We must be considerate of one who has labored harder than we and will likely rise early again come the morrow."

Her daughter's lip popped from between her teeth. "We shall make it a quick game, Lord Soames. No more than a thirty count per move, hmm?"

Feeling his gaze, Laura looked to him. Had she failed? Did he think worse of her?

He gave a barely perceptible nod she hoped was of approval and turned back to Clarice. "A quick game, though you will owe me a favor."

"What favor?"

"To be named when I need one. Agreed?"

Her nose twitched, but she said, "Agreed."

As she set about returning captured pieces to the board, Laura moved to regain her seat.

"Lady Laura?"

She looked to Lothaire.

"If you are of a mind to seek your bed, I will escort your daughter to your chamber."

"I shall wait."

This displeased him, as told by his frown, but she was not ready to grant him the role of sire. That would take time and assurance his means of correcting Clarice was acceptable. Now if only she were certain of what *acceptable* was...

Within a quarter hour, Laura was easy enough with the bits of conversation overheard between the two and the occasional laughter and chuckle that she eased into the chair's depths. Shortly, she dropped her head back and watched them through narrowed lids.

And from time to time lowered her lids to rest her eyes.

"So much she likes her sleep, she can be difficult to rouse."

Lothaire shifted his gaze from Laura to her daughter who straightened from her attempt to coax her mother awake. "She likes her sleep?" he said.

"Indeed."

Not the Laura he had known. She had seemed never to rest, during his visits to Owen ever at table ahead of him to break her fast, rarely dozing as he had done when they lay on their backs in the grass, always begging for another half hour—then another—at day's end.

Clarice sighed. "I do not think she has ever risen ahead of me—or Lady Maude who was always saying, *Let her sleep, let her sleep. Her nights are so very long.*"

"Long?"

"Aye, restless. For that I mostly slept in Lady Maude's chamber." Her eyes moistened. "I miss her."

"Then you spent much time with the lady."

"I did, more than with..." She lowered her voice further. "...my mother. Lady Maude loved me very much."

Because the girl was the child of her stepson, Michael D'Arci? He let his mind replay the embrace witnessed at Castle Soaring. But only once. Jealousy's bite was sharp.

"I am sure your mother also loves you deeply."

Clarice shrugged, rubbed the shoulder of the big dog who sidled near. "She says."

He looked back at Laura whose cheek rested on her shoulder, lashes threw shadows toward her nose, lips parted enough to permit a glimpse of pretty teeth he hoped his heir would have. His were not unsightly, but neither were they as straight or bright as hers.

In that moment, he acknowledged how much he had missed her smile these ten years—recalled how often it was followed by beautiful laughter and how that smile had felt against his own. Would he see it again? Or was it lost to him forever?

"Methinks you will have to carry her," Clarice said, making him jerk with surprise—more, the longing to fill his arms with Laura as done too briefly when she collapsed before the queen.

"Certes, you look strong enough, Lord Soames."

More than strong enough. And Laura weighed very little.

"Is it not permissible?" Clarice pressed. "You are to wed. And what fun when she awakens and knows not how she came to be abed."

"I do not believe your mother will think it fun."

"Mayhap, but better than finding herself rumpled in a chair come morn."

The solution was to make a greater effort to awaken her, but he was strangely loath to do so. And he did have the excuse it was her daughter who suggested he carry her.

He considered the girl who had kept him from his bed for not one but two more games, having persuaded him to continue when she saw her mother slept. Despite Clarice's disrespect for Laura, he almost liked her as he had not expected of one whose father had reduced him to a cuckold, and was further inclined to like her when her disappointment at being bested at the first two games proved she handled defeat fairly well. Thus, he had allowed her to win the third game. The years until she wed at fourteen—perhaps fifteen—might not test him as much as feared. Providing Laura did her part in training her up into a lady.

"You will have to defend me if she takes offense," he said.

He saw Laura in her smile. "I will tell her I insisted."

"But I would not do it if you insisted, Clarice. As your mother is not yours to command, neither am I."

She had the grace to look chagrined. "At my request, then."

He slid an arm around her mother's back, one beneath her knees, and lifted her.

Laura did sleep as if she might never awaken, and in that moment he was grateful, for he held her nearer than necessary, gazed less guardedly upon her, knew if she looked as near upon him she would see what he did not wish her to see—that he so vividly remembered what he had felt for her he could almost believe it was not all memory.

"You are glad you shall wed her, are you not?"

Berating himself for thinking it safe to leave his face open, Lothaire shuttered his expression. "Methinks it will be a satisfactory marriage."

Clarice wrinkled her brow and nose, then her face smoothed. "Do you make her fall in love with you as she loved my father, 'twill be better than satisfactory."

Jealousy knelling through him, he said low, "Did your father love her in return?"

"Surely I would not be here if he did not." She leaned forward and continued in a conspiratorial whisper, "For love and loss of him, I have only known her to be sorrowful—a shadow of herself, I heard Lady Maude tell her stepson."

She swung around to lead the way across the hall. Had she not, he might have failed to contain the emotions flaying him as he once more recalled the embrace between Laura and Michael D'Arci. Unobserved, he let jealousy run rampant, then shoved it to his depths, ordered Tomas to remain in the hall, and followed Clarice to the chamber shared with her *shadow* of a mother.

I care not what she felt for her lover, he assured himself as he strode into the room.

I care not that she so soon forgot me, he told himself as Clarice entered the garderobe and closed herself in.

All I require of her is King Henry's tax break and an heir. He lowered her to the mattress. *And fidelity. Above all, fidelity.*

As he slid his arms from beneath her, she narrowly opened her eyes. "Lothaire?"

Though she no longer filled his arms, he did not straighten from where he bent over her. "'Tis I."

She lowered her lids, raised them a bit higher. "Did I do well?"

"Well?"

"In allowing her another game?"

Grudgingly moved by her concern over what he thought of her mothering, he said, "I am hardly acquainted with parenting. Still, it seemed an appropriate response."

She closed her eyes, breathed, "I am awake now."

Hardly, he mused.

"I will make it right, Lothaire."

"It?"

She did not answer, but he was fairly certain she referred to becoming the mother she had not been to Clarice.

He started to straighten, but seeing her braid had fallen back from the bruise she claimed her daughter had not dealt, he drew it over that side of her face. Then he pulled the covers atop her and crossed to the door. As he stepped into the corridor, Clarice exited the garderobe.

"I thank you for the games, Lord Soames," she called low.

He inclined his head. "We will play again."

"What of the favor I owe?"

"I shall think on it. Good eve, Clarice."

15

A FORTNIGHT GONE. A sennight to come. Then she would be Lothaire's wife, would each night fall asleep in his bed, each morn awaken in it. And before the sleeping and after the awakening...

Staring at the gown Tina and she fashioned out of Eleanor's material, Laura's heart sped so fast she nearly pressed a hand to it. For this—fear of intimacy that had once been beautiful expectation, time and again she distracted herself from vows that would grant her husband the right to do with her body as he pleased. Were it the Lothaire of her youth and had she not learned by violent means what it meant to be possessed by a man, all would be different.

Laura replenished her breath, fingered the gown's heavily embroidered bodice. "'Tis beautiful, Tina. You must have arisen ahead of dawn to complete it."

"Aye, with yer daughter."

While on and on Laura slept. But no more. As she was to be the lady of the castle, a position of responsibility that reflected on its lord, no longer could she while away the morn that had made her days easier to face.

"Henceforth, I would have you awaken me at first light, Tina."

There was so much approval in the maid's smile Laura was ashamed she had not asked it sooner. "Even if I must drag ye out by yer heels, milady?"

"Even if."

"I am glad, milady."

Laura inclined her head. "After breaking my fast, I will return and help set the gown's sleeves."

Tina smiled and lowered to the chair drawn before the windows to allow summer's light to guide her needle.

Shortly, Laura stepped off the stairs into the hall she would make great again once she was Lothaire's wife.

When a sweep of the room did not bring her daughter to light, she tensed. As reward for good behavior three days past, she had agreed Clarice could leave their chamber ahead of her mother providing she went directly to the hall for her morning meal. So she had, and here Laura had found her. Might she have yielded to curiosity over Lothaire's absent mother and ventured to the uppermost floor?

She pivoted.

"Lady Laura!"

Peering across her shoulder, she saw it was Lothaire's man who called to her. "Have you seen my daughter, Sir Angus?"

He halted before her. "She is with the baron. He instructed me to tell you he has collected on the favor owed by Lady Clarice."

"Favor?" she said, then remembered her daughter's bargain for another game of chess. That same night, Laura had awakened to find herself abed and Lothaire leaning over her. Not until morn had she been discomfited by the realization he had carried her from the hall—and more by words spoken between them she could not recall but must have been adversarial since he had grown cooler since.

"Your daughter aids my lord in moving the eastern flock to the stream where they will be washed ere shearing," Sir Angus said.

Laura frowned. "What aid can a nine-year-old girl give?"

"No aid." This from Lady Sebille whose appearance made Laura startle and the knight stiffen. "Indeed, she will cause my brother more work." She raised her eyebrows. "But unlike her mother, she expressed an interest in the barony's greatest source of revenue, and since Lexeter is to be her home until she weds, my brother did not discourage her."

Concern for Clarice diluted by shame over her avoidance of Lothaire that closed her mouth against questioning the work that rarely saw him returned ere sunset, Laura said to the one whose presence was almost as rare as her brother's, "I appreciate Baron Soames's consideration and sacrifice, and I agree it is a burden he ought not carry." She looked to the knight. "Once more I require your escort, Sir Angus. I shall collect my daughter."

He inclined his head. "My lord said that if you insisted, I should do as bid."

"I insist."

"As would I if not for tidings from Wiltford," Lothaire's sister said and raised a parchment whose upper edge bore the remnant of a wax seal.

Laura frowned over the name of Wiltford, recalled a remark made by one of Lothaire's men en route to Lexeter—that the journey would be hours shortened were his lord permitted to pass over that barony without Wiltford's lord taking offense. And now that offended baron sent word to a man he distrusted.

Sir Angus thrust a hand toward Lothaire's sister. "My lady," he said with censure as if she overstepped in reading the baron's correspondence.

Lady Sebille slapped the parchment in his palm. "As you are too *scrupulous* to read it ahead of my brother, I shall tell its tidings so you may make all haste to deliver it. Baron Marshal writes that—"

"Worry not," Lothaire's man spoke over her, "I will be of good speed." He slid the missive in a pouch on his belt, looked to Laura. "You will accompany me?"

"She will not." Lady Sebille again. "Lady Laura's place is here, readying the donjon to receive Baron Marshal and his wife whilst I prepare Lady Raisa."

The knight caught his breath. "He is found?"

As Laura bit her tongue to keep from asking who was found, Lady Sebille said in a choked voice, "At last, they return him to us."

Sir Angus reached as if to touch her arm but drew back. He looked to Laura. "As my lord will likely ride to High Castle immediately, yours would be a wasted journey, my lady."

At Laura's hesitation, Lady Sebille said, "Better you direct the servants in making the hall presentable should your betrothed's enemy enter here."

"Baron Marshal is your brother's enemy?" Laura said. "For what? And who does he return to you?"

"My lady," the knight began, "methinks it best—"

"Go, Sir Angus!" Lady Sebille said. "The Baron of Lexeter will not thank you for dawdling."

Nostrils flaring, he turned on his heel. As he strode across the hall, Laura caught sight of the physician whose presence often surprised, and not for the first time she wondered if his stealth was purposeful. Had Lady Raisa tasked him with being her eyes and ears to report on Lothaire's betrothed?

"Lady Laura?"

She returned Lady Sebille to focus. "You will explain about Baron Marshal?"

"'Tis not for me to do."

"Nor was it for you to tell me of your brother's first wife," Laura said. "Just as it is not for me to direct the servants until I am their mistress through marriage to their lord."

Lothaire's sister looked ready to refuse, but her eye was caught by the approaching physician, and she called, "I believe the Lady of Lexeter is in need of her medicinals, Martin," then she motioned Laura to follow. Once ensconced in an alcove distant from the eyes and ears of others, she said, "'Tis a private and cruel matter. You know our father disappeared over twenty years past?"

"I know. Lothaire told he was but six."

"I was nine." The lady drew a shaky breath. "With the passage of time, we came to accept his life was forfeited. Now we know it as fact—that he was slain by the Baron of Wiltford."

Laura gasped. "He who comes to High Castle?"

"Nay, that baron is long dead, his title recently passed to Durand Marshal through marriage to the murderer's cousin, Lady Beata." Lady

Sebille swept up her prayer beads, began to pick her fingers over them. "On the morrow, Baron Marshal and his wife shall return our father's remains so he may be buried in consecrated ground."

"For this they are Lothaire's enemy?"

"That is some of it. The rest, methinks, is that ere my brother tried to return Lexeter to prosperity through marriage to you, he sought to do so by wedding Lady Beata against the queen's—*and* the lady's—wishes. Hence, you who were to be his first wife will not be his second but his third."

Laura was grateful for the shadows upon her face. Not only had she been unaware of Lothaire's second marriage, but his sister made it sound as if he had forced Lady Beata to speak vows. It did not seem possible, and yet...

She recalled her audience with Eleanor who insisted Lothaire remain among Laura's suitors. She had said it would allow him to right another of his wrongs. This the other wrong?

"You are saying Lothaire forced Lady Beata to wed?"

Lady Sebille snorted. "She had incentive enough."

"But—"

"He was angered and had cause to be." She harrumphed. "Of course, since the marriage was quickly annulled so our queen could wed Lady Beata to her favorite, Durand Marshal, 'tis worth mentioning so you understand how uncomfortable the morrow will be. Not only are our father's bones to be returned, but Lothaire will face Lady Beata and her husband. Thus, I would not have shame over the state of the hall make it more difficult for him."

Laura glanced across her shoulder at the room.

"You are thinking 'twas not made ready for you, his betrothed," Lady Sebille submitted.

"I am not."

"I would have you know that as much as possible it was prepared in accordance with my brother's instructions sent ahead of your arrival. Unfortunately, I was occupied with Lady Raisa. Though Sir Angus knows well how to direct men in defense of his lord, he is fairly useless in ordering servants—believes a room is presentable if no bones are visible among the rushes." She raised her eyebrows. "Lady Maude taught you the duties of the lady of a castle?"

Laura hesitated. She had been trained in keeping a household, but little practice had she before her life toppled and none since. Just as Maude had undertaken the task of mothering Clarice, she and her stepson's wife had ensured the donjon was comfortable and the business of feeding the castle folk economical, efficient, and palatable.

Lady Sebille gave a grunt of disapproval when the big dog, Tomas, drew alongside and pushed him away. "Your silence bodes ill, Lady Laura."

"As you must know, I have had little experience, but Lady Maude did instruct me."

"Then see to it." The lady released her prayer beads and stepped from the alcove.

"Lady Sebille!"

The woman turned.

"Will Baron Marshal and his wife require a chamber? If so, I will have to do some shifting to accommodate them."

"Nay, they will not pass the night at High Castle. Our hospitality does not extend that far to the family responsible for the murder of a beloved father."

Laura inclined her head. "I understand." And she did mostly. Though the baron and his wife had not murdered Ricard Soames, their presence would likely pick at the scab of a twenty-year-old wound. Were the Marshals to pass the night here, that scab might be torn off—if not by Lothaire, then his mother who was not as infirm as her daughter believed and could attempt to do worse to those of the barony of Wiltford than what she had done to Laura.

"If possible," Lady Sebille said, "I shall return belowstairs to aid you. Much depends on how the Lady of Lexeter receives the tidings." Her brow furrowed. "Lest she requires calming, I must alert the physician."

He who was no more receptive to Laura and her daughter than when they were first introduced, continuing to exude such disapproval that Laura's prayers for Clarice's continued good health had become lengthier.

Laura watched Lothaire's sister go from sight, then considered enlisting Tina's aid, but the woman's time was better spent on the wedding gown—that which would be removed on the nuptial night that too rapidly approached.

She pulled her thoughts back, looked upon the hall with an eye to setting it aright for Lothaire whom she would not have shamed amid the grieving to come.

"This one we call Grandmother."

Clarice frowned. "Grandmother?"

"She is the matriarch. First we deal with her, then the others follow." Lothaire smiled. "Fortunately, she and I are of an understanding." It was an overstatement, for the old ewe had tried his patience and bruised him many times, but he appreciated the challenge, poor substitute though it was for the heft and swing of a sword.

The girl took a step back that placed her to the left and behind Lothaire. "She glares at me."

"Heed her well, Lady Clarice. Just watch, hmm?"

She snorted. "I have no intention of going nearer. She is so filthy I can smell her stink from this distance."

"Hence, our purpose in moving the sheep here." He jutted his chin at the clear-water stream temporarily dammed to form a pool, this portion chosen for its considerable width and graveled bottom that aided in cleaning the sheep without introducing more dirt stirred by the muck found farther downstream.

"It seems a lot of trouble when you could wash the fleece after 'tis sheared," Clarice observed as did many who did not understand the business of wool.

"It would save some time and effort," Lothaire allowed, "but this way there is less waste—meaning higher yield and greater revenue."

The girl wrinkled her nose. "If I watch, my debt is paid?"

"Watch *and* learn. What we do here keeps food in your belly and shoes on your feet."

"What of gowns?"

He glanced at the one she wore. It was too fine for the work of wool—even if only in the capacity of observation—but when he had suggested she change into something simpler, she told this was her least favorite since she had nearly outgrown it. It was tight and showed more of her ankles than would be permissible were she older. Hence, all the more reason not to waste good coin on expensive fabric for the garments of a rapidly growing child.

"Aye, gowns as well, Lady Clarice, though I warn you the cloth will not be as fine as you are accustomed to."

Her brow lined. "I like pretty things."

As did Lady Raisa whose indulgences following the disappearance of her husband were largely responsible for Lexeter's decline. "I imagine that is a taste acquired from your mother. Her gowns are exceedingly fine."

Clarice shook her head. "She hardly cares, though ever she pretended she was pleased with Lady Maude's gifts so she did not hurt her feelings."

Eager as Lothaire was to lead the workers in cleaning the sheep, his impatience slowed to a crawl. "Your mother does not like her finery?"

"I believe she likes it, but I do not think she would be terribly bothered were she reduced to homespun cloth."

Choosing his words carefully, he said, "I am sorry there is strife between the two of you. I am guessing the loss of Lady Maude has been difficult for both."

She heaved a sigh. "Lady Maude was as a mother to me. Now she is gone, all is changed. I have lost my home and my friend. For it I have gained a mother who tries too hard to replace Lady Maude, and you who

I do not believe is truly pleased to become a father to me." She raised an eyebrow. "Nor to wed my mother."

He ought to like that she was so frank, providing insight into the Laura he no longer knew—had he ever—but it made him feel as much a fraud as she believed her mother to be. "Like many a noble marriage, ours will be of great benefit to our land and people, but that does not mean affection will not grow from our union, nor that I am incapable of caring for another man's child." Those last words he had not carefully chosen, but he contained his dismay—blessedly, for the girl watched him with the eyes of one more mature than her years.

But then she rolled them. "Donnie is right. 'Tis good I am misbegotten so I may choose love over *affection.*"

Lothaire frowned. "Donnie?"

"My friend, the son and heir of Lady Maude's eldest stepson, Joseph D'Arci." She lowered her lashes. "Actually, more than a friend."

Lothaire did not like the conversation's turn. Ignoring the men and women who waited for him to escort Grandmother into the stream, he said, "I am sorry you lost your friend. How old is he?"

"Near on twelve. Though I did not see him often once he was fostered away from Owen for his squire's training, we spent time together when he returned home, and more this last visit ere my mother determined she must seek a husband."

He clenched his teeth to keep from prompting her, remembering how his own mother's prompts had roused suspicion and resentment, causing the youth he had been to close up. And still he closed up when Lady Raisa pressed him.

"Methinks she became jealous, and that is why we had to leave Owen." Clarice's eyes widened. "The argument you happened upon our first day at High Castle was of Donnie."

"For that you raised a hand to your mother?" Even to Lothaire's ears his disapproval was rampant.

She flushed. "I would not have struck her."

"Aye, you would have. I felt the force in your arm, Clarice." Though he longed to ask what had caused her to strike her mother later, he determined not to speak of it lest she believe Laura had revealed the assault.

She groaned. "I know 'twas wrong, but she frustrates me."

"You will have to learn to control your frustration. I will not tolerate disrespect of your mother."

Anger flashed across her face, slid off, and in a defeated tone, she said, "I fear I will not see Donnie again, that he will find other girls to..." She blew breath up her face. "...talk to."

It was more than talk, but Lothaire kept his tongue. And waited.

"So Lord Soames, show me how you persuade Grandmother to bathe."

Was it a kiss the *almost* twelve-year-old Donnie had filched from a nine-year-old girl? For certain, it was not jealousy that caused Laura to seek a husband she did not want for the home required to remove her daughter from a boy moving toward manhood faster than a girl moving toward womanhood.

"My lord?" said the shepherd, an outspoken commoner who did his job too well to begrudge him impatience that oft matched Lothaire's.

"Watch, Lady Clarice," Lothaire said. As he strode down the rise where the old ewe stood upon the bank, he was struck by the feeling it would not be enough for the girl to observe. But perhaps he merely cast her in the mold of a young Laura who had sat still only the one time he was first introduced to her in the company of Lady Maude and Lady Raisa.

To lessen the ewe's alarm, he led it backward, but once its hooves met water it began to struggle. Lothaire pressed onward and, thigh-high in the pool, gently tipped her. As she tried to get her legs beneath her, he pulled her to the center of the dammed stream where she came right side up and floated. Immersed up to his chest, he began loosening the dirt and other foul matter from her fleece. Once she abandoned her efforts to swim back to the bank, the workers led other ewes into the stream.

Out of the corner of his eye, Lothaire watched Clarice draw nearer, sometime later heard her screech when a ewe's thrashing wet the skirt of her gown. But the wetting of her hem was of her own doing.

An hour later, she who liked pretty things was nearly as drenched and fouled by the dirt coming off the matted fleece as the rest of them. Standing in the water, she aided a young woman given charge of year-old lambs who had accumulated enough wool to make the cleaning and shearing worthwhile. And scattered across that bank were dozens of ewes whose much brightened fleece dried in the sun.

As Lothaire pushed a ewe back to the shallows where it dug its hooves into the gravel to heave its water-logged fleece out of the stream, laughter brought his head around.

The voice was more childish than that of the one to whom he had first been betrothed, but it sounded of Laura, just as her daughter's smile summoned remembrance of the young woman he had senselessly loved.

In disposition, Clarice was more like her mother than she could know, she whom he should have fathered.

The pound of hooves and a shout turned Lothaire toward Angus whose appearance portended ill.

Soaked through, Lothaire stepped from the stream, strode between the dozing sheep, and halted atop the rise.

Angus swung out of the saddle and extended a missive. "Word from Wiltford, my lord."

Lothaire stared at what remained of the wax seal—doubtless, broken by Sebille who, more than Lothaire and their mother, ached for the tidings likely inked by Baron Marshal.

He reached but drew back the hand over which dripped water from his tunic's sleeve. "You will have to read it to me."

Minimally proficient in letters, Angus grimaced as he unfurled the parchment. He cleared his throat. "Baron Soames, by this missive know the answer long awaited is given," the knight melded the sounds into words and stiltedly strung them together to form a sentence. "That which your family lost has been found, placed in a casket with due respect and...ceremony, and shall be returned forthwith. As my father-in-law has taken ill, my lady wife shall accompany her lord husband to the barony of Lexeter. I trust you will receive us and our...entourage with good will. This missive travels a day ahead of our nooning arrival at High Castle." The parchment rustled. "Baron Marshal signs his name."

Lothaire stared at the dirt darkening about his feet as water ran from his clothes. Though glad his father could be properly interred, he almost wished the old baron's return further delayed. It would be better for Lexeter to receive its lost lord when the disparity between its prosperity of twenty years past and now was not as great, and this was too near the wedding. Not that his marriage would be a joyous event, but it would be further dampened by the burial to take place only days before. Or perhaps it would not.

Lothaire ground his teeth. Sebille would not like it, nor their mother who would not be averse to her son's marriage being more over-shadowed by mourning. However, this day a grave would be dug in the cemetery of the village of Thistle Cross so Ricard Soames could be laid to rest shortly after Baron Marshal and his wife arrived with an entourage Lothaire did not doubt would be sizable and well armed lest they were not received with good will.

"My lord?"

Lothaire met Angus's gaze. "Ill timing," he said. "Hardly am I returned from court and now this."

The knight peered past him. "I will aid in cleaning the sheep so you may—" He blinked, nearly smiled. "There is a young lady washing the sheep, my lord."

Lothaire looked across his shoulder at Clarice who had an arm hooked around the neck of a lamb the village woman bathed. The girl's face was near the animal's, and she appeared to be chatting with it. Then she laughed and kissed the top of its head.

He fought imaginings of Laura doing the same. And failed. She would have, even at the expense of a gown finer than her daughter's. But no longer. She was too changed, surely by abandonment of the one who had made a child on her. And, dare he hope, regret over her betrayal of the one who had loved her? He had believed that last when he returned to her in the garden at Windsor and found her weeping, but after seeing her with Michael D'Arci and the more he learned of this older Laura from her daughter who believed her sorrow a result of being parted from her lover...

"I am thinking her gown is ruined," Angus said, "but she does not look to mind."

"She is much as her mother was," Lothaire spoke aloud his thoughts and grunted when the knight narrowed his eyes. Not that Angus was unaware of what had gone between his lord and the lady. He had served the Soames family since his squire's fostering at High Castle and been knighted by Ricard only months before his lord's disappearance.

Years later, Angus had trained Lexeter's heir in arms after Raisa refused to allow her son to earn his spurs with a fostering lord. Just as Lothaire had protested her decision, so had this knight who believed the loss of a father made it more imperative Lothaire be fostered—and all the better were he accepted by the Wulfriths. But Raisa had been determined to keep her son under her control, citing he might otherwise be led astray, becoming no better than her faithless husband.

How she missed the power she had once wielded, though it had almost been the ruin of Lexeter. Not that she acknowledged what she had wrought, ever blaming Ricard and now those responsible for her husband's death—even Lothaire whose efforts too slowly revived the barony.

"Your betrothed did ask that I deliver her to you that she might retrieve her daughter," Angus said.

Lothaire frowned. "As instructed, you were to comply."

"I agreed, but your sister insisted the lady take charge of the household to prepare for the Baron of Wiltford's arrival."

Whilst Sebille prepared Raisa to receive her husband's bones, Lothaire knew.

"I shall take your place so you may return to High Castle," Angus said.

Lothaire considered the offer but saw little benefit in returning early. "I am sure Lady Laura has all in hand. Thus, my time is better spent here."

"As you will, my lord. Should I deliver Lady Clarice to her mother?"

"You may ask her, but I believe she will decline."

"Might she have wool in her blood?"

That possibility made Lothaire ache. He would wish it of a child he had fathered, but one whose veins carried the blood of the man who had lain with Laura? He had brought Clarice here to acquaint her with the workings of Lexeter and further assert his authority soon to be granted as her stepfather. It was not his intention to foster an avid interest in wool best passed to his heir. He wished her to respect it and be conversant enough that when she was of an age to acquire a husband, she would draw more suitors willing to overlook her unfortunate birth in exchange for one learned in what was increasingly regarded as England's greatest source of wealth.

"In her blood?" he said. "Methinks she is merely bored and will soon tire of the novelty and bemoan her soiled gown."

Once more Angus cast his regard her way, then strode down the rise. He soon returned. "She prefers to wash sheep."

"To which I myself must return," Lothaire said.

Angus set a hand on his shoulder. "Regardless of the ill timing, I am glad your father shall soon be laid to rest."

Lothaire inclined his head. Then he instructed his man to pause at Thistle Cross to make arrangements with Father Atticus to conduct the funeral mass at High Castle followed by burial in the churchyard, send word across Lexeter that work be suspended in honor of the old baron, and inform his betrothed of the morrow's plans that he himself would reveal to his mother and sister.

16

SHE HAD FEARED she would cry. It proved difficult to direct servants, not only due to lack of experience in prioritizing tasks, but the inability to exude confidence which caused resistance toward one who was not yet Lady of Lexeter.

But then Sir Angus returned with the assurance Clarice was not a burden to his lord and tidings the old baron's burial would take place as soon as he was delivered to Lexeter. From that point onward, the task given her was less daunting owing to the knight's assistance with the servants. Though Lady Sebille had said Sir Angus was inept at household management, under his discreet guidance Laura fared well. A nod from him here, a shake of his head there, and the servants to whom she passed on his urgings began to move faster and with greater purpose.

Cook was another matter. He was not exactly disrespectful and acknowledged that in a sennight it was Laura with whom he would consult over the menu, but he did not temper his frustration that the nooning meal Lady Sebille had approved for the morrow would not be served.

"I am sorry to give so little notice," Laura said and glanced past the middle-aged man whose stained apron so well fit him it emphasized muscles more suited to a soldier than one who wielded blades over meat and vegetables. Sir Angus's shake of the head indicating she should not have apologized, she inwardly groaned. She ought to have been kind but firm in informing the man a meal incapable of being stretched to feed

the Baron of Wiltford's party—should they accept Lexeter's hospitality—must be altered.

Laura cleared her throat. "Most unfortunate, only this day were we
informed of the possibility of guests."

The cook grunted. "I've only enough venison for stew—hardly a
meal fit for noble guests, my lady, but there is naught for it."

Laura inclined her head. "I have faith you will ensure 'tis agreeable."
That was as Lady Maude would have said, gently issuing a challenge for
the man to prove worthy of his station.

He scowled and started toward the kitchen.

"Well executed," Sir Angus said low.

She did not agree, but she had done her best. Smoothing the skirt
of the old, plain gown into which she had changed, she said, "I thank you
for your aid, Sir Knight."

"My pleasure, my lady."

Laura looked around the hall. "I wish there were time to clean the
tapestries. They are much dulled by dust and smoke."

"Surely a good beating will suffice."

She sighed. "And see much of the work in the hall undone—dust
everywhere."

"Not if the tapestries are removed and cleaned outside on the donjon's steps."

Laura looked to him. "You are right."

"Then we shall require ladders."

Two hours later, several tapestries had been beaten fairly clean
and were being returned to their hooks, while another was unrolled
on the steps. As women and men took brooms to it, Laura returned
to the hall and, catching Sir Angus's eye, crossed to his side. "I thank
you. The room is much brightened. I dare hope Baron Soames will be
pleased."

"I am heartened you wish to please him, my lady."

"Of course I do. I..." She set a hand on his arm. "No matter the past,
Sir Angus, I hope in time I will prove a good wife to your lord."

He looked to her hand on him. "I am more inclined to believe you than not, Lady Laura. But you must know my first loyalty shall ever be to my lord."

Too late, his consideration of her hand on his sleeve and now his words alerted her to the inappropriateness of such familiarity—especially in light of what he believed of her.

She lowered her hand and retreated a step. "Baron Soames is blessed to have a friend in you."

His smile was slight. "I do not know I am that to him—he has little use for friends—but I watch more than just his back, my lady. Closely."

"Sir Angus...Lady Laura," Lady Sebille's voice sounded, and they turned to where she advanced on them. "Where is my brother?"

Curtly, the knight dipped his chin. "Baron Soames is confident his betrothed can put the household in order and determined his time is better spent preparing for the shearing."

She halted before him. "He ought to be here."

"I but relay his message, my lady. I am sure he will return as soon as he is able."

She shifted her gaze to Laura. "With so much to be done to receive Baron Marshal, I am all surprise you waste precious time chatting."

The lady's disapproval thick as cold soup, Laura felt as if caught in a compromising position.

"I assure you," Sir Angus said, "'tis not idle talk in which we indulge." He jutted his chin to the tapestry being set on its hooks. "Much the lady has accomplished during your absence. And you? Your mother is apprised of the old baron's return?"

She looked between Laura and him, drew a whistling breath through her nose. "All has been made known to Lady Raisa. As expected, she is distressed."

Laura did not doubt that. No matter how severe the lady, no matter it was twenty years since her husband's disappearance, the return of his remains would be painful—and could prove more so when she and her daughter learned they would be interred without delay.

"Indeed," Lady Sebille said, "methinks it may be some time ere the Lady of Lexeter is able to attend her husband's burial—mayhap a sennight."

The knight caught Laura's eye, raised his eyebrows as if to remind her it was for Lothaire to reveal the burial arrangements, then strode away.

Lady Sebille kept her back to him a long moment, swung around, and watched him cross to the tapestry that had been rehung on the wall. When he aided a shapely young woman in descending the final rungs of a ladder, Lothaire's sister sucked a sharp breath.

Then still she wanted the man she had rejected? Laura wondered. Certes, the disapproval to which she had subjected Laura thickened as if jealousy were stirred into it.

"Careful, Lady Laura," Lady Sebille said so low that had she not named the woman alongside her, it would have seemed she spoke to herself. "Gallant and helpful Sir Angus may be, but he has a great appetite for women."

Laura did not know how to respond, on one side uncertain as to why the lady warned her, on the other side surely expected to have no knowledge that once the knight had been fond of his lord's sister.

"As you—and I assure you, my brother—know well, flirtation can lead to ruination."

Now Laura sucked air. The lady's warning was as it sounded. "I was not flirting with Sir Angus."

Lady Sebille *tsked.* "I am sure that woman would say the same." She nodded at the servant. "But look at her. See what she invites."

"Lady Sebille—"

"Look at her," she repeated, this time with beseeching.

The woman laughed at something Sir Angus said, stepped nearer.

"Women like that turn good men bad." Lothaire's sister met Laura's gaze. "Ricard Soames was a good man and father, but he yielded to temptation, just as Sir Angus does. For it, my sire is but bones. For it, Lexeter was nearly ruined by the excesses of a grieving wife."

More laughter that returned Lady Sebille's regard to the woman who glided a hand down the knight's arm. Then the servant turned and, with a roll of the hips, moved toward the next tapestry to come down.

"I shall have to speak with her," Lady Sebille said. "If she wishes to continue feeding her pack of brothers and sisters, she will have to turn her attentions to those nearer her station." The lady's hand closed around her prayer beads. "And of course, more time at prayer would not go amiss."

So much spoken that told there was far more unspoken. But though curiosity eased Laura's outrage over the lady's belief her exchange with Sir Angus had been flirtation, she knew the answers to her questions would not be given.

Patience, she counseled. *And observation.* Eventually, she would better understand the family amongst whom she was to raise her daughter.

Lady Sebille's elevated brow prompting a response, Laura said, "Even unanswered prayer does not go amiss, I suppose."

That brow lowered and the light clatter of beads over which she worked her fingers went silent. "All prayer is answered, Lady Laura. Just because you do not like the Lord's response does not mean you do not have His ear. He sees and hears and feels all."

Hence, the reason His arms were ever too full? Laura questioned as she struggled to press down further offense at being taken to task by one who may have loved and lost but had not been forced down that path—at least, not by violent, painfully degrading means.

Laura drew a deep breath. "You are right. My apologies. I fear I am embittered by a life turned opposite the direction I wished to travel."

"And who is to blame for that, Lady Laura? Certes, not the Lord."

Laura felt her chest expand, pressed her lips so the air straining her lungs did not escape on words she would regret. She had thought she might come to enjoy the company of Lothaire's sister, but now…

"I pray you will excuse me, Lady Sebille. There is much work to be done."

Hardly had she taken a step than the woman caught her arm. "Forgive me," she said. "I am also embittered by a life gone awry—though mayhap I fool myself in believing it was ever mine to direct. And now with the return of my father…"

Laura appreciated her attempt to rectify her transgression, but she needed to distance herself. "I understand, Lady Sebille, but I must resume my duties if I am to do right by your brother, as I know is of utmost importance to the sister who loves him well."

"Of course." She inclined her head. "And I shall consult with Cook lest the Baron of Wiltford avail himself of our hospitality."

"Forgive me," Laura hastened. "It was probably not my place, but I have discussed a change of menu with him."

Lady Sebille's lashes fluttered. "As it is to be your place, 'tis good you did, especially since he can be disagreeable. Thus, the sooner you have him in hand, the better."

Laura inclined her head. "I hope I shall see you at supper, Lady Sebille."

"Likely, I will be with Lady Raisa. Now since I am not needed, I shall seek the Lord's guidance for the morrow."

Which she could not know would be more difficult yet, but that was for Lothaire to tell.

Laura watched the woman's wraithlike figure cross the hall. Had she not been looking for Lady Sebille's seeking of Lothaire's man, she might not have noticed the slight turn of the woman's head toward where he stabilized the ladder climbed by the servant Lady Sebille believed tempted him. It was an advantageous position, one that would allow him a view up the woman's skirts, but he did not tip his head back.

Laura was not surprised. He might give in to temptation, but he seemed too honorable to leer or make lewd advances. And yet, not so honorable in that he allowed Lady Sebille to witness his temptations. To rouse jealousy? If so, was it an act of reprisal or of purpose—that he yet hoped to gain the lady's hand and thought to move her in that direction?

The latter, Laura decided, then set her mind to assuming the role Lady Raisa would unwillingly relinquish.

Wearied and disheveled, a greater contrast the two could not have presented to the great room into which they stepped.

Lothaire halted so abruptly the girl on his heels bumped into him.

"Forgive me, Lord Soames." She jumped from behind. "I ought not follow so—" Her gasp reflected his own disbelief.

Though Angus had met them in the outer bailey as the horses were given into the care of stable boys and assured his lord Laura had set the hall aright as much as possible, Lothaire had not thought *this* much was possible.

Though the shining extravagance that prevailed following the disappearance of his father was far from restored, the smoke-discolored walls yet in need of paint and most of the fine furnishings sold by Lothaire after he took control of Lexeter, the hall was beyond presentable. And it smelled better than he, which said much since he had made an effort to purge the day's filth.

When the last of the flock was washed and the stream undammed one last time to replace the fouled water with fresh, he and the workers, including Clarice, had submerged their clothed bodies and rubbed themselves as clean as possible. But Lothaire had gone further, applying the washing lye used to remove foulest matter from fleeces.

He had done so in preparation to see his father laid to rest on the morrow, but the moment Laura hastened from the kitchen corridor and her eyes fell upon him, he had to admit he had done it for her as well.

She stilled, mouth convulsed as if to suppress a smile, then she saw her daughter. "What has happened, Clarice?"

"Naught ill," the girl said as her mother rushed forward.

"But your hair and gown—"

"Sheep mother! Only sheep."

Laura halted before them, the stir of fresh rushes underfoot causing the herbs with which they had been scented to spring upon the air.

Hands at her sides closing as if to keep them from pulling the girl to her, she said, "Sheep?" and glanced at Lothaire.

It was the first time he had looked closely on her face in over a sennight, the side braid she had worn to disguise her injury abandoned to reveal clear, unpowdered skin. "Aye, sheep," he said.

"I helped, Mother—with the small ones. 'Tis hard work, and I had to rest often, but Lord Soames says I did well." Clarice looked to him. "Did you not?"

"For it, we are returned to High Castle sooner," he said, then to Laura, "I apologize for not earlier delivering your daughter and to have once again missed supper. As we are behind in shearing, and I shall be much occupied on the morrow, I determined to make good use of the hours remaining of daylight."

Guessing from the flick of her eyes at Clarice she questioned if the girl knew what would so occupy him, he gave a slight nod. He had been brief in the telling since he did not think it necessary for one of Clarice's age to know the circumstances of his father's death, but he had prepared her to conduct herself as befitting a member of the Soames family.

"I understand," Laura said. "When your squire told you had returned, I asked Cook to prepare a platter of viands to be served hearthside since the castle folk have begun bedding down."

"I thank you." Disturbed by how pretty she looked in a plain gown surely chosen for the work overseen this day, he started past her but paused. "I am pleased by what has been accomplished in my absence, Lady Laura. I do not know when last the hall appeared so inviting."

Color pinked her cheeks. "The servants were eager to please their lord, and Sir Angus kindly advised me how to direct them." She looked momentarily down. "I have had little experience with such."

He inclined his head. "He is a good man. Forsooth, my best."

"You are fortunate." Before the smile she gifted him could reach her eyes—were that possible—sounds from the kitchen corridor turned her around. "Here is your meal. Come, you must have quite the appetite."

Lothaire did not, having joined the workers in filling their grumbling bellies with dried meat, biscuits, and ale, but Clarice had to be hungry.

Such an interesting girl she was, happily spending the day in the water doing the work of laborers or resting on the bank alongside a sunning lamb she had helped clean. That was the young Laura in her. But as for the one who required a nudge from Lothaire to swallow her complaints over the food and then mostly picked and sipped at the offerings...

That was of this more proper, reserved Laura, she of gowns so elaborate one could not dispute she was kin to a queen. Which was why what she wore this eve so affected him. Though of good cloth, it was beautifully simple, much the way she had dressed in her youth.

"I am starved!" Clarice exclaimed and ran forward.

That was her mother in her as well. Spontaneous, with only enough disregard of propriety to be charming—at least to one who had given his heart to Laura, fool that he had been.

And will not be again, he reminded himself as he watched daughter overtake mother. More than once this day he had wished it was Laura at the stream with him, she who had loved the water and unashamedly spoken of when they would swim and bathe together.

That was the Laura whose betrayal he might be able to forgive were she to return laughter and joy to his life—above all, be faithful henceforth. But if she yet loved Clarice's father and that man was Michael D'Arci...

Cease torturing yourself, he silently commanded and strode to the hearth.

Cheese, bread, and fruit were arranged on a platter alongside a pitcher of wine. Though Lothaire had believed himself sated, he ate as more of the castle folk gained their pallets and, between bites and long drinks, listened to Clarice regale her mother with tales of washing sheep.

"At first, I was upset at wetting my gown, but as I have nearly outgrown it and the work of many makes work light—as Lady Maude would say, would she not?—I decided to help. And the lambs are so sweet, not at all temperamental like Grandmother."

Laura lowered her goblet. "Grandmother?"

"An older ewe. Lord Soames washed her first—walked her backward into the water so she would not be so frightened, then pulled her to the middle of the pool where she could not touch bottom."

"But surely she went under?"

"Indeed not! Sheep float. Can you believe it? Lord Soames says it is because of air trapped in their fleeces."

A seemingly genuine laugh sounded from Laura. "That I would like to see."

"Then you ought to join us the next time. Should she not, Lord Soames?"

Imagining Laura in the water, gown clinging to her curves, tempting his thoughts to the marriage bed before it was that, he could not think how to respond.

"Lord Soames?" Clarice pressed.

He caught Laura peering at him from beneath her lashes before she swept her gaze to her goblet. And remembered their first meeting when she had done the same, her slippers tight together where they peeped from beneath her skirts. His mother had been impressed with her modesty and silence—as had he until his subsequent unchaperoned visits caused the young woman to cast off that mask to reveal someone he had not expected to like but had come to love.

Clarice made a sound of disgust. "Lord Soames, do you not hear me?"

"Forgive me. I am worn and much in need of rest. If your mother wishes to learn the work of wool, she is welcome to accompany us, but do not press her. She is no longer a girl but a fine lady and—"

"I would like to accompany you," Laura said. "That is, if your offer is genuine and it would not be an imposition."

"The offer is genuine," he said, glimpsing no falsity in her expression, "but it shall require that you awaken as early as your daughter."

"That I shall do henceforth, as befitting the future Lady of Lexeter."

"I am glad." He stood. "Now ere I gain my bed, I must see to my mother. Good eve, Lady Laura…Lady Clarice."

"Good eve!" Clarice called, causing several of those settling into sleep to grumble and grunt.

Lothaire raised a hand and continued to the stairs. When he reached the third floor landing, he paused to steel himself for his audience with Raisa. "Lord, grant me patience," he rasped and firmly tread the floorboards.

His sister occupied a chair pulled close to the candlelit bed. As he strode inside, she stood and nodded at their mother. "She does not sleep, only closed her eyes when she heard your boots upon the corridor."

"A body can fall asleep quickly," Raisa hissed and lifted her lids. "Especially one who shall soon take her place beside the husband finally returned to her as but a box of bones."

Halting alongside Sebille, Lothaire met his mother's gaze. "At last, he shall rest in consecrated ground. That is much for which to be grateful."

"Do I live long enough to see it."

It was the opening he required, though he had not thought it would be granted so quickly. "Therefore, the burial shall take place when he is delivered on the morrow."

"So soon?" Sebille exclaimed.

"Disrespectful!" Raisa gasped.

"I do not believe so," Lothaire said. "For over a year we have known with certainty he is dead and mourned throughout. The sooner he rests in consecrated ground, the sooner we can look to the future as I am certain he would have us do."

"You are certain of naught—concerned only with *your* future," Raisa snapped.

As Sebille felt her way back onto the chair, Lothaire said, "My future and the future of Lexeter—hence, your future and Sebille's—is of great concern. If this land is to recover from the excesses and neglect of the past, the sheep must be sheared and a marriage made without delay."

Raisa thrust to sitting and pointed a bent finger at him. "Ever you seek to blame me for the barony's failings, but 'twas your father—"

"Regardless of who is at fault," Lothaire cut across excuses he had heard time and again, "Lexeter has been slow to recover. Thus, as it is past time we do right for these lands and its people, word has been sent to the lesser castles and villages instructing all work be suspended on the morrow so prayers may be offered up for the old baron and any who wish to attend his burial."

As his mother's jaw worked over words she sought to string together, he saw what appeared to be scratches down one side of her face. As they were mostly faded, he was swept with guilt at not noticing them during a more recent visit.

Before he could ask after them, she fell onto the pillows, turned her back to him, and commenced groaning. "Trollops...whores...harlots... The ruin of your father. He the ruin of us. A good wife and mother I was. None dare dispute that!"

Lothaire could but would not. Before Ricard Soames's disappearance, Raisa had shown little regard for her son, so entranced was she with the miraculous daughter made with the young husband who had wed Raisa for alliance and a generous dowry. Thus, the heir of Lexeter had been made to feel a nuisance by his mother and even, on occasion, his father.

Blessedly, Sebille had doted on her little brother just as their parents doted on her. But all changed with Ricard Soames's disappearance. Embittered by the loss of her husband whose faithlessness placed the burden of Lexeter on her, it seemed Raisa no longer had tolerance or time for love. She had divided herself between administering the barony, grooming its heir, and—of great detriment—extravagance previously denied her.

Lothaire had longed for his mother to return her attention to Sebille, and not only because life was suffocating for one accustomed to running about unfettered. His sister having become so sorrowful it was increasingly difficult to remember how joyous she had been, he had thought she would recover if their mother but showed her half the regard she had ere Ricard's disappearance. But Raisa had seemed content to let her miraculous daughter fade.

"Nay, none dare dispute it," that much aged woman returned him to the present.

Though in the past she had dragged Lothaire so near the edge of her void he had defended himself and the stands he took by speaking against her mothering, with her decline in health he had vowed it was a weapon he would no longer wield. Thus, ofttimes it was necessary to withdraw from her lest he break his word.

"It is too soon to bury Father," Sebille said softly, and Lothaire ached over how fragile she appeared. "But methinks you are right, Lothaire. 'Tis best done now."

Raisa sprang upright, landed fierce eyes on her daughter, and screeched, "Get out!"

Sebille gaped.

"Out, I say!"

Anger bolted through Lothaire, but reason prevailed. Too much his sister suffered Raisa's misery and here was permission to escape it—a gift of solitude she needed more than her brother who had known his father's affection but had either been too young to grasp its depth or not been as loved as Sebille.

"Go," he said. "I will stay with Mother a while."

She hesitated, then stiffly crossed the room and closed the door behind her.

"Neither do you wish to be here," Lady Raisa said. "Why do you not also abandon me?"

He dropped into the chair. "You are my mother, I am your son. Now tell me what comfort I can give a grieving widow so she may attend her husband's burial." They were mostly words, for though he had pressed Durand Marshal to discover the whereabouts of Ricard Soames's remains so the Lady of Lexeter could begin to heal, he was fairly certain her anger was too great for her to grieve her departed husband.

"Even for love of your mother, you will not be moved from tossing your father in the ground come the morrow?"

"It has been arranged and will be done."

"That you may sooner send me from High Castle?"

There was that, too, though it had not been a conscious consideration. He had assured the queen it would be done to ensure the safety of Laura and her daughter, it being but a year since Raisa sent men to murder those soon to return the body of Ricard Soames.

He clasped his hands between his knees, leaned forward. "There is to be a new Lady of Lexeter. For both your sakes, distance must be put between you."

Her jaw shifted. "Sebille *will* go with me."

"This I know."

She curled her fingers over the coverlet, slowly gathered it up her chest. "Then who will watch over you?"

"I am a grown man—"

"And Laura Middleton is now a grown woman—one of great appetites."

He narrowed his lids. "What is it you wish me to beg you to reveal?"

A corner of her mouth lifted. "It may not be as dire as feared—yet—but your sister observed something disturbing."

The muscles of Lothaire's legs twitched with the longing to leave. Chances were Raisa would exaggerate what her daughter had seen, but on the chance she did not, he said, "Tell, Mother."

"Your betrothed is too familiar with Sir Angus. Though she denied it when Sebille confronted her, she worked her flirtations upon him."

Jealousy rose through Lothaire, but he pushed it down. There was naught over which to be concerned. Not only was he confident of the knight's loyalty, but Sebille viewed women who received the most innocent attention from Angus as being flirtatious. However, that of which he could not be confident was Laura. She had betrayed him once—

He sliced the thought in two, consigned one half to darkness.

"Worry not," he said. "I will not be cuckolded again."

"As much as you are absent from High Castle, you cannot keep close watch on her, my son. Did Sebille and I remain—"

"Nay." He sat back and thrust his feet out before him. "We will speak no more of this. Now rest. The morrow will be long."

She continued to grumble and snap. But when she finally quieted, the long day had settled into his bones, and the sleep he feigned became truth.

17

STILL LOTHAIRE WAS with his mother. As in his younger years when he prayed in the chapel ere gaining his night's rest, several times this past fortnight Laura had heard him enter and exit the sanctuary beyond the chamber she shared with Clarice. With all he must face on the morrow, he would surely come again this eve.

Lest she sleep through his prayers, she eschewed the comfort of a bench and leaned against the cool stone wall at the rear of the chapel. Each time her lids lowered and knees softened, the sensation of falling returned her to her senses.

Lothaire entered at what she guessed was middle night—and immediately broke stride, gripped his dagger's hilt, and pivoted toward her with an expression so fierce she could not move. But he could.

"'Tis Laura!" she gasped.

That snapped him to a halt and kept the point of his blade from exiting its sheath.

As he peered into her darkness, the flickering candles on the altar revealed one she hardly recognized. He wore the skin of a warrior never before seen. Though the sight made her tremble, she ached for all she had missed of the man he had become in the years since their parting.

Upper lip lowering over bared teeth, he thrust the dagger back into its scabbard. "What do you here, Laura?"

As she approached, she guessed from the deep wrinkles about his tunic's waist he had sat long with his mother, might even have slept. "I must speak with you."

"About?"

She stepped into his light and stared into a face framed by hair that had mostly come free of the thong at his nape. "About the morrow, this day, and what came before."

His lids narrowed. "Before?"

"I did not know I am to be your third wife."

His lids flickered. "Sebille told you?"

"She did."

"Does it matter?"

She might have taken offense were his words not weighted with more fatigue than derision. "Only so I know what I shall face when I stand before Baron Marshal and the woman who was your wife ere she was his."

The breath Lothaire drew adding to his height, he said, "I do not think this the place to discuss it."

"Would it so offend the Lord?" she said and, at his hesitation, added, "The hall is taken with those at rest. Until we wed, 'twould be unseemly for me to enter your bedchamber."

"And you are no longer unseemly, hmm?"

His sarcasm stilled her, but before she could force a response, he said, "Forgive me. I am raw from the audience with my mother."

She swallowed hard. "May we speak here?"

He looked to the altar, the hair brushing his jaw so tempting her fingers she pressed them into her palms to keep them from betraying her. "We may, but first prayer," he said.

She should have expected that, but she was not prepared to kneel alongside him as she had done upon the barony of Owen. Never had she been as eager to pray as during his visits. Hand in hand, they had traversed the aisle. Reluctantly, they had released each other's fingers. On separate kneelers, they had lingered over their conversations with

God. Silently she had bemoaned that soon they would part and the night between them and the morn would be long.

"First prayer," she acceded and, as she followed him, recalled that ten years past the walk had been filled with lovely imaginings of when she would traverse a chapel beside her new husband and a priest would speak the nuptial mass over them.

To her surprise, one that so pained she thought her heart might bleed, Lothaire caught up her hand when they reached the altar. Broad calloused fingers a breathtaking contrast to her slender soft ones, he handed her onto a kneeler. Then as if as surprised by the gesture as she, he immediately released her.

When he lowered to the other kneeler and bowed his head, Laura raised her palm. It had not forgotten his. And never would it.

Clasping her hands hard, she closed her eyes. Over the next quarter hour, she asked the Lord to be with them this night, on the morrow when Lothaire's departed father returned to his family, and a sennight hence when their lives were joined to secure both Clarice's and Lexeter's future.

Ever Lothaire's prayers had surpassed her own, and that had not changed. Her beseeching done, she sank back on her heels and watched him as she had done the young man. Years ago, he had grinned when, upon opening his eyes, she swept back his hair and slid her fingers over his scalp. His reminder such behavior was not appropriate in the house of the Lord had been more teasing than correction. Were she to give in to that impulse when he finished these prayers, would there be any teasing about him?

Not this Lothaire. But God willing, eventually some lightness might be found between them.

He raised his head and looked sidelong at her. "I thought never again to be at prayer with you."

"I thought the same."

He inclined his head. "It grows late. Let us speak and be done with it."

She was also fatigued, but it hurt he was so eager to be rid of her. She glanced at where he knelt. "Here?"

He stood and raised her to her feet.

They were too near, and though she tried to give volume to her voice, it was breathy. "I thank you."

He released her. She thought they might sit, but he remained unmoving, and she guessed it was because even the benches near the altar were in shadow. Whereas she had most often imagined being intimate with Lothaire in daylight, whether the sun cast halos against a wall or sparkled on water, the dark seemed the preferred medium in which lovers became better known to each other. Did the shadows present too much temptation?

She gripped her hands at her waist. "You told your mother and sister the old baron is to be buried on the morrow?"

"I did. As expected, it was not well received—an offense to my sister, an inconvenience to my mother."

That last surprised only for its honesty. It seemed she was not alone in believing the woman who had slammed the face of her son's betrothed onto the table was too unfeeling to love. Had she always been? And was it possible Lothaire would believe Laura were she to reveal her encounter with Lady Raisa—that her slap had been provoked?

She was tempted to test him, but as naught had transpired between her and the lady since, perhaps it was best consigned to the past. But if Lothaire did not soon remove the woman from High Castle...

"For what else did you seek me here?" he asked.

Trying not to be unnerved by his impatience, she said, "This day your sister accused me of flirting with Sir Angus whilst he aided me in directing the servants."

"I am aware."

Of course he was. Sebille *had* warned she would protect him from further betrayal.

"My mother told me," he said, "not my sister."

She pressed her shoulders back. "Regardless, there is no truth to it."

"I am glad."

Glad, but no acknowledgement of her innocence, nor disbelief over the accusation. Now herself impatient to seek her bed, she said, "Your sister indicated Lexeter's financial difficulties are due to the excesses of a grieving wife."

Something not quite a smile touched his lips. "She would not have you believe I am at fault for our reduced circumstances."

"I did not think you were. After all, our first betrothal was sought for my generous dowry."

He frowned.

"Lady Maude was thorough as my father required. Thus, I was aware the dowry was of greater import than the possibility of mutual happiness. It made me sad until your second visit when we——" She closed her mouth. He did not need to be told what already he knew of their beautiful courtship. Though he believed she had cuckolded him in the end, he could not question how enthralled she had been with the young man who, shed of his mother, had proven they could be wondrously happy.

As if Lothaire was also uncomfortable dabbling in a past that had promised much and delivered naught, he said, "What Sebille believes is mostly true. Months following our father's disappearance, our mother accepted he was dead and began indulging in the things denied her whilst he lived—finery like that gifted his mistresses, elaborate furnishings, choice foodstuffs, the best French wines. When the steward protested the lightening of Lexeter's coffers, she dismissed him, took charge of the finances, and cast coin where she pleased. Had our father's wool business been given the attention it required, the barony could have afforded many of her extravagances, but she had not the mind nor care for such. Shortly after you broke our betrothal, I wrested control of Lexeter from her. But too much damage was done."

His tale made her ache, that last more so. She had known she hurt him deeply the day she turned from the pond to reveal her reason for rejecting him, but to learn of the burden he had carried alongside that pain...

"It was a difficult year," he said, "one in which I was able to keep hold of Lexeter by selling off most of the costly furnishings and some of my mother's fine clothes."

She wished she had been at his side…

"The barony's recovery has been slow, so when the opportunity to sooner set it aright was offered in the form of a wealthy heiress—my first wife, Lady Edeva—I took it." He fell silent, then said, "Now we return to the matter of my second wife, if Lady Beata can be named that."

Guessing the tale was not one quickly told, Laura settled into her feet.

"Come." He drew her to the nearest bench, and keeping a respectable distance between them, lowered beside her. "Lady Beata's father, realizing he was about to lose another infant son to sickness, summoned his daughter from France to take her place as his heir. As this outspoken and rather inappropriate lady was widowed by a man of so great an age she was more a daughter to him, she was called The Vestal Wife. You have heard of her?"

"I have, and that after she lost her husband she was called the Vestal Widow."

He inclined his head. "Lest the king and queen undertake to wed her to a favorite, Lady Beata's father attempted to hide the loss of his infant son until he found a husband of greater benefit to his family than to the royal coffers. The lady's reputation being well known, he had few good prospects. Thus, seeing the potential in Lexeter's wool, he approached me, confident my need for funds would cause me to overlook her faults. It could not have been easy for him since my father was last seen alive upon his family's demesne and my mother had long accused them of being responsible for his disappearance."

"As they were," Laura prompted.

"Aye, though 'twas not known for certain until the lady's father enlisted me to aid in stealing her away from Sir Durand, who was to ensure she did not wed without Queen Eleanor's permission."

"You forced her to marry you."

Lothaire eyed her. "I was getting to that, but my trespass against the lady began further back when I required proof she was, indeed, vestal."

"Proof?"

Despite the dim, she saw a muscle in his jaw convulse. "At my mother's urging, her physician accompanied me to the barony of Wiltford and the lady was persuaded to undergo an examination."

Laura had heard such might be done were it suspected a woman would not come to the marriage bed virtuous, but mere imagining of that humiliation so repulsed, her face surely reflected it.

"It was wrong of me, but"—Lothaire's gaze upon her sharpened—"once, for a time, I had a lady pure of heart, mind, and body. A lady turned only to me."

The young Laura Middleton. Were she not sitting, her knees might fail her. Sinking her hands into her skirt, she said, "Twice cuckolded, you wished your second wife pure as Lady Edeva and I were not."

His brow lowered. "Sebille and you talked much."

"Where her beloved brother is concerned, she believes I am in need of counsel."

His searching gaze disturbed her, but finally he said, "I sought purity, in part to salve a battered pride, but more for the chance of life with one who did not long for another as my father had done, one whose arms only opened to me as mine would to her."

"You are saying your first wife longed for another whilst you were wed?"

His tension leapt—so deeply felt she glanced at her hands to be certain they had not strayed to him.

"Of course you wish to know about that as well," he growled.

"Should I not?"

He set his forearms on his thighs, and gripped his hands between them. "It was I who chose the second woman to whom I was betrothed, and I believed I had chosen better than my mother. Lady Edeva had a good dowry, was fine of face and figure, and presented as proper—until the morn after our nuptial night when I discovered my bride had not been chaste. I arose ere my wife and completed my ablutions. Thinking to awaken her, I returned to the bed. Had I not approached her side, I would not have seen the vial amid the rushes that bore traces of the blood she spilled upon the sheet to conceal I was not her first lover."

Laura did not have to imagine how that betrayal hurt, his ache crossing the space between them.

"I confronted her, but she said the vial was not hers and denied giving herself to another. Though I knew she lied, I resolved to make the best of our marriage. However, she was so unhappy that whenever she wished to visit her family I allowed it. But that last time when I was delayed in returning her to Lexeter..." He shook his head. "I arrived at her family's home two days late and went to the office of the master of horses to arrange our mounts to be readied at dawn for our departure. He was there." Lothaire turned his gaze upon Laura. "As was my wife."

She waited for him to continue. He did not, and it took some moments for her to realize he need not. What he did not speak, his eyes and clenched jaw told. Though she had thought herself prepared for a painful revelation, she startled.

"Aye," he said, "and I beat him as never have I beaten a man. Had I not felt a grip on my fist—surely of the Lord, for there was no other to stop me—I might have killed him."

Laura shivered. "What of your wife?"

"The only hand I laid on her was in separating them. 'Tis true Edeva's cuckoldry was the death of her, but it was not my doing."

"How?"

"The beating of her lover was no quiet affair. Hardly did I have my mantle around her than her father appeared. Before I could get her away, he slew his master of horses. Had I not placed myself between him and his daughter, methinks she would have fallen to the blade. Immediately, we departed for Lexeter, though I might as well have left her behind. Countless hours I spent on my knees trying to forgive her—and perhaps there would have been peace between us had she not blamed me for the death of the man she loved. Edeva's unhappiness became misery, her tolerance contempt. I could not even express concern over her wasting away without leaving myself open to accusations and physical attacks she likely hoped would cause me to end her life more quickly than she was capable of doing herself."

Laura's throat tightened. How she had hurt upon learning Lothaire had wed, having hoped he had not done so sooner because he still felt for her...thinking he did so only because he loved again.

"A fever laid low many at High Castle," he continued, "and my fear Edeva would take ill in her weakened state was realized. Every dawn ere departing the donjon, I opened the door of her chamber and listened for her breathing. Then one morn I heard naught, and when I touched her shoulder, she was cold."

Laura slid a hand over his two. "I am sorry. Upon hearing you had wed, I imagined you were happy. That you loved again."

"I am not the fool I once was—at least, where love is concerned. Certes, a fool I made of myself with my second wife."

Laura had forgotten he had not finished that tale. "What happened with Lady Beata?"

He sat back but did not pull free. "Though obvious she had feelings for Sir Durand, her father stole her away from the king's man. En route to the church where we were to wed, she and her sire exchanged words that made me suspect they hid something. Ere the ceremony I listened in on them and learned that after Lady Beata's cousin killed my father over a woman's favors, her sire aided in hiding his body. When I showed myself and the lady refused to wed me, I reasoned the wealth she brought to our marriage was the least owed my family and threatened to reveal her father's complicity." He drew a deep breath. "No sooner were vows spoken than Sir Durand overtook us. Just as Eleanor arranged the marriage you and I will make, she arranged the annulment of my union with Lady Beata—all the more easily granted when I attested to its lack of consummation."

"You did not oppose the annulment?"

"I did not. As it was out of anger I wronged the lady, I was grateful there was no opportunity of consummation that might once more see me sharing my life with one who loved another."

Laura recalled Eleanor saying Lothaire's marriage to his former betrothed would right another of his wrongs. Doubtless, Lady Beata was the first he had made right.

"I am glad you saw your error, Lothaire, though I am not surprised. You are a good man." Further evidence was what Michael had revealed to her at Castle Soaring. "I understand you received training at Wulfen Castle."

His eyebrows rose. "Lady Beatrix told you." Before she could deny it was she, he said, "Aye, though Abel Wulfrith's offer to better my knightly skills was meant as an insult, I set aside my pride and accepted. As you know, my mother would not permit me to be fostered."

It had been the same for Simon, though finally Lady Maude's stepson had sent his brother away. But it had been too late, proving the ruin of the sweet boy he had been.

"Thus, I received my training in arms here," Lothaire continued. "I do not believe I was deficient ere availing myself of the skills taught me at Wulfen, but I am better able to protect those for whom I am responsible."

Which now included Laura and her daughter. She smiled. "Aye, you are a good man. And worthy."

He stared at her so long the weight between them seemed to lighten, then his eyes moved to her mouth, down her neck, and shifted to her fingers upon his. Freeing a hand, he pinched her sleeve's cuff. "I like this gown better than the others."

His finger against the heel of her palm making her shiver, she had only enough voice to whisper, "'Tis plain."

He inclined his head. "The others try so hard to outshine your beauty they offend, whereas this one…" His gaze returned to hers. "… plays well with memories of the young woman I knew."

She could not think what to say.

He pressed his thumb to her wrist. "Your heart beats fast."

"I feel it." She moistened her lips. "Does yours beat as fast?"

He raised her hand to his chest. "Does it?"

She savored the thud—so strong and rapid that now she was the one remembering. The last time she had felt this was during his departure from Owen shortly before her ruin. He had leaned down from his mount and stroked her cheek in lieu of a kiss that could not be given in Lady Maude's presence. When he called her *Laura love*, she had reached up and placed her hand just there. And been happy knowing how much his heart moved for Laura Middleton, soon to be Laura Soames.

"Does it?" Lothaire's voice was so deep it throbbed through her palm and up her arm.

"'Tis like a hammer on steel," she whispered.

He leaned toward her, not close enough to kiss but near enough that if she met him halfway her lips would be upon his. Was that what he wanted? If so and she breached the space, would he still want it? And what of her? She thought it what she desired—certes, for this her own heart threatened to abandon her chest—but the last time she had been kissed...

The memory flashed through her, and as it moved her toward what had come after, Lothaire pulled her to him.

His face before hers. Only his.

His breath brushing her lips. Only his.

His mouth nearly upon hers. Only his.

"Lothaire?"

Lashes sweeping her eyebrow, nose brushing hers, he lightly touched his lips to hers.

"You are sure?" she breathed.

"I am not," he rasped, but before disappointment could deliver its sting, his mouth was fully on hers.

She thought she would know his kiss, but it was barely familiar. Because it was too long since last she had been thus with him? Or because the kiss was more certain than what she had shared with a younger Lothaire? Perhaps both, but certainly the latter. He had been wed, even if to a woman who loved another, and were he at all like his father, there had been others with whom he was intimate. Whereas she...

Once more battling memories, she slid her arms around his neck, pressed nearer, kissed him back.

He groaned and deepened the kiss.

It was exciting...dizzying...wondrous—until there was no more sweet about it, no more coaxing, and hands were where they ought not be. Not rough like—

She shoved that memory aside. Nay, not rough, but desperate. Too desperate. Not cruel like—

Laura wrenched free and stumbled upright. Though so unbalanced she barely kept her feet beneath her, fear of a man at her back made her swing around.

Lothaire had also risen and was reaching to her.

Only to steady me, she told herself, but she retreated further. Not that he would—

Or would he?

Nay, he did not regard her through the eyes of a predator but with regret. And when she managed to remain upright, the hand he reached to her fell to his side with what seemed relief.

"I know better," he said. "Pray, forgive me." He blew breath up his face, causing the hair falling around his cheeks to shift. "But now you know I am no longer a boy, surely you understand why I hesitated to speak here. No matter your betrayal, I want you in my bed." A bitter laugh. "I thought you wished it as well, but perhaps not. Perhaps as when we were first betrothed, 'tis another you want—the one who fathered Clarice."

Feeling as if punched in the belly, Laura could not find her breath, but when she did, it burst from her on words over which she had no control. "I do not want him! If needs be, in my own blood I shall write it!"

Lothaire searched her eyes, but whatever he found beyond their color, his tightening lips told he did not believe her. "You are saying you want me—*my* kisses and caresses?"

Lest what leapt through her present as revulsion rather than fear, she averted her gaze. "I do not know what I say." She ran her hands down her skirt, tugged it back into place. "All I am sure of is that I am glad 'twas you whom Eleanor called to her side. You who shall take me to wife."

"You tell, and yet you fear me."

He might not see it, but he sensed it.

"As you are no longer a boy, I am no longer a girl." Realizing she continued to pluck at a gown that needed no further straightening, she folded her hands at her waist. "You are wrong if you think these ten years have been easier for the woman I am than the man you are. Different burdens, aye, but burdens nonetheless. Still, I shall strive to be a good wife, in bed and out."

Lothaire watched her in the dim, wished she would speak what she did not so he might understand—even if he did not like it. Or perhaps more in the hope he would so dislike it that it would ease the ache of this body wanting hers.

"For Clarice you sacrifice yourself?" he said with more knowing than bitterness. Her relationship with her daughter might have been built on sand, but he believed her attempt to rebuild it on rock was genuine.

"'Tis true I am prepared to sacrifice myself, but I have hope I do not. Just as I have hope that in wedding me you do not truly sacrifice yourself for Lexeter."

He raised his eyebrows. "Perhaps if we both seek to put the past behind us, we shall."

She inclined her head. "I am very tired as I know you must be."

"So I am," he said and led her to her chamber.

At the door, she looked across her shoulder. "I thank you for your honesty. It better prepares me for the morrow."

Lothaire also wished honesty that he might know how he had lost her to Clarice's father and if she had truly loved the man and still loved him though she vowed she did not want him. But those things—and greater insight into Clarice's Donnie—must save for another day.

"I am glad you shall be at my side upon my father's return," he said. "Good eve, my lady."

18

SOLEMN. AS WAS fitting.

Honorable. As expected.

Mournful. Greater than anticipated.

But more than Baron Marshal's impressive procession numbering two dozen armored and sword-girded men astride fine horses, that last was due to the multitude who journeyed from across Lexeter to pay their respects. The common folk had begun arriving shortly after dawn, but those in the outer bailey were outnumbered by the scores ascending the hill behind the greenery-festooned wagon bearing the casket of Ricard Soames.

The ones now come unto High Castle had been gathered along the route Baron Marshal and his entourage had taken. Surely for this—to allow those on foot to keep pace—the projected midday arrival had come and gone.

Though Lothaire had been frustrated by the two-hour delay, mostly for the added grief given Sebille by their mother, now that he knew the reason, he was grateful for the consideration shown those who wished to mourn their long-lost lord. And that their numbers were so great. He had been aware his father was respected but had not realized how much. Even had he known, he would not have thought so many would spend a day free of work on a man twenty years gone.

"I know him!" Laura gasped.

Lothaire looked to where she stood at his side. "Who?"

"Is that Baron Marshal at the fore?"

"It is, and his lady wife beside him."

"I know him—rather, I am acquainted with him, though not as Durand Marshal."

Lothaire returned his regard to those nearing the drawbridge, considered the one who had wed Lady Beata after him. "By what name do you know him?"

"Sir Piers," she said almost too low to catch over the stir of those gathered in the outer bailey behind. "'Twas the name he gave Lady Maude and me when our carriage was lamed en route to Castle Soaring six years past. For his kindness in aiding us, Lord D'Arci permitted him a night's lodging and..." She trailed off.

As she pondered whatever stole her words, jealousy spurted through Lothaire. He was not surprised there had been other visits to Michael D'Arci's home, but learning this now roused him.

"Ah," she said. "It has been so many years I near forgot."

"What?"

"Later, I learned he was in disguise, having disabled our carriage to gain entry to Castle Soaring so he might do the bidding of his lord, Baron Wulfrith. Michael had imprisoned the man's sister, Lady Beatrix, believing she murdered Si—"

She closed her mouth, and what appeared to be guilt flashed in her eyes before she averted them.

The clop of hooves on the drawbridge that would soon sound with the rumble of wheels sought to drag Lothaire's gaze back to the procession, but he was too near something she clearly did not wish him near. "You say Simon was murdered?"

Laura shook her head. "Though Lady Maude and I journeyed to Castle Soaring so she could face the woman responsible for her son's death, it proved an accident had taken his life." She returned her gaze to Baron Marshal. "I had heard Durand was the real name of Sir Piers but did not consider he and this one were the same."

Now the wagon was on the drawbridge, and Lothaire gave his attention to the bearer of his father's remains.

Shortly, Baron Marshal and the lady who had been Beata Soames for a brief time, reined in before Lothaire and Laura where they stood before the raised portcullis.

"Baron Marshal, Lady Beata," Lothaire said, and wished his voice did not sound so tight. "Though a grim duty brings you to High Castle, you are welcome."

Durand inclined his head, but the outspoken Beata said, "'Tis grim, indeed, but the least owed your family. My father sends his regrets that he cannot be here. Most unfortunate, illness sees him abed many a day."

That might be true, but Lothaire suspected it was more than that. Her father had concealed the murder and location of the remains. Now, just as the man had compelled his daughter to wed the son of a murdered man, he expected her to shoulder this burden.

As when Lothaire had risen above anger and come right of mind, realizing he also wronged the lady, he regretted this fell to her. And yet, from what he knew of Lady Beata, she would have insisted on accompanying the procession even were her father present.

"I shall pray your sire recovers," he said. He did not like the man, but he did not wish him ill.

"I apologize for the delay," Durand Marshal spoke. "Shortly after we crossed into Lexeter, your people began following, and 'tis a long walk."

"I am grateful you slowed to allow them to keep pace," Lothaire said.

The baron inclined his head, looked to Laura. "Last Sunday, I had business upon your sire's demesne and heard the banns read for your marriage."

She stiffened, and Lothaire guessed she had not considered the announcement must not only be made upon Lexeter but her father's lands to ensure any who wished to contest the union had the opportunity to come forward. That Lothaire had arranged as well. Though he had not expected to hear from the one who had disavowed his daughter, might Laura wonder about it? Hurt over her father's silence?

Lothaire set a hand on her shoulder. "I understand you are acquainted with my betrothed."

The baron's mouth curved. "We met many years ago and under false—albeit necessary—pretenses."

Grateful Laura had not left him in the dark, Lothaire said, "You called yourself Sir Piers."

"Aye, the easier to save Lady Beatrix Wulfrith from Michael D'Arci of Castle Soaring. Blessedly, that lady did not need saving. Not only was she in love but loved."

"A story I would like to hear, but it will have to wait. Now my father is returned, he is to be laid to rest this day."

The baron's eyebrows rose. *"This* day?"

"Another few days may seem naught in the more than twenty years since he breathed his last, but it is too many for his family. And as Lexeter's people have gathered to pay their respects, a better day could not be had. Too, should your wife and you wish to attend the burial, 'tis convenient."

"I think it a good thing." This from Lady Beata, followed by a soft, prettily gapped smile that hardly detracted from her loveliness. "As we would not impose upon your grief by passing the night at High Castle, it also benefits us."

Lothaire was relieved it would not be necessary to offer lodgings that would distress Sebille and his mother—best for both his family and the Marshals who would not sleep easy beneath High Castle's roof.

"As my mother is ill," he said, "the casket will be placed in the donjon chapel where she and my sister may attend the service to be held once you are refreshed with food and drink. Then my father will be taken to the village of Thistle Cross and interred in the churchyard with his forebears."

"That is well with us," Baron Marshal said.

Lothaire took Laura's arm, and the villagers gathered in the outer bailey crowded left and right to allow the procession to pass.

As Lothaire led his betrothed forward, the heads of those on the ground bowed, but the same could not be said of the men on the walls.

As instructed, the castle garrison were to save their prayers until Baron Marshal and his warriors departed. Not that Lothaire believed they presented a threat, but danger was most effective when it was not perceived as such. That he had learned long ago, but even better during Abel Wulfrith's instruction at Wulfen Castle that, surprisingly, was not all to do with the swing and thrust of a blade. Much was strategy and tactics discussed at night during patrol of the walls or demonstrated over games of chess.

That last made Lothaire grimace. Never had he spilled as much *blood* upon a checkered board than when it was Abel's brother who sat across from him—Everard who had devoted several afternoons to training Lothaire in a darkened cellar. There he had honed his pupil's senses of hearing, smell, taste, and instinct despite Lothaire's initial objections to what seemed a child's game of *Find Me*. That it certainly was not.

Laura was relieved by her betrothed's hand on her that pushed Simon toward the back of her mind, but she dreaded when her betrothed would ask more about Sir Piers's breach of Castle Soaring's walls. Even had she held close her recognition of Durand Marshal, it would have been of no benefit. Likely, the baron would have revealed their previous acquaintance, and it would have been ill of her not to prepare Lothaire. But what was done was done, and what was yet to be done had its own worries.

The inner bailey was not as populated as the outer, but scores of castle folk were assembled before the steps on either side of Sir Angus and Tina who had been given charge of Clarice.

Laura had discussed the day's import with her daughter, and like Lothaire had not told it was by murder the old baron met his end. Clarice had been inquisitive, but Tina had distracted her with talk of which gown was best suited for so sorrowful an occasion and how she would fashion the girl's hair to make her appear more a young woman than a child.

It had not been mere talk. Even at a distance Clarice presented more as a lady in the making than a girl. Thus, it was unlikely Baron Marshal would recognize her. And neither would Clarice recognize him, having been three years aged when, fastened more often to Lady Maude's side than Laura's, she had accompanied them to Castle Soaring.

Still, it would not be long ere the knight whose marriage had elevated him to a great title guessed the girl's identity. Hopefully, he would be discreet so Laura would not have to evade her daughter's questions.

At the center of the inner bailey, Laura became aware of Lothaire's tightening grip and followed his gaze to the window where she had first glimpsed Sebille when she herself arrived at High Castle. The lady was there again—as were the physician and Lady Raisa.

Laura shuddered, certain the latter's eyes were upon her, then more violently at the realization of how long they may have been upon her daughter.

"Laura?"

She swung her gaze to Lothaire. "Your mother is out of bed."

"So she may watch her husband's return. If she is strong enough, she shall attend the service."

Laura nearly protested, chilling at the thought of standing on one side of him whilst his mother stood on the other. And unless she could summon a viable excuse to keep Clarice away, her daughter would be too near that woman.

"She loathes me," Laura whispered.

"As told, she is not pleased by our marriage, but you need not fear her."

Laura almost laughed.

"She knows how important our union is to Lexeter," he continued, "and understands that if she does not properly conduct herself as my father's widow, she will be removed from the service."

Of little consolation.

"For everyone concerned, I have determined it best I escort her and my sister to the service. Hence, Clarice and you and Baron Marshal and his wife shall enter last and remain at the rear of the chapel."

Of some consolation. Though tempted to look to the window again, Laura kept her eyes upon his. "I agree that is best."

Moments later, Tina stepped back to allow her mistress to take her place alongside Clarice on whose other side stood Sir Angus.

"Oh," her daughter breathed, "I thought Lord Soames fair handsome, but Baron Marshal is more so."

Laura did not like her nine-year-old noting such a thing, but considering Clarice had shared a kiss with Donnie, she ought not be surprised.

"Is that his wife, Mother?"

As the lady reined in, her mount danced its backside around. "Aye, Lady Beata."

"She is pretty, I suppose, but not at all like the ladies woven into tapestries who are as beautiful as their lovers are handsome."

Though the volume of Clarice's voice was discreet enough to escape their guests, Laura said, "Do not speak such."

"'Tis true, but they did not hear me. And look, she is a bit fat."

"Enough!" Lothaire growled, peering past Laura.

"Pardon," Clarice muttered. And once more Laura felt inadequate—and irritated by his interference. But only for a moment. Baron Marshal had dismounted and lifted his wife down. Had Lothaire not silenced Clarice, whatever else gaily skipped across her tongue might have been heard.

As husband and wife approached, Laura's dismay slipped at the sight that caused her daughter to believe the lady carried too much weight. She did, but it was not her own, and it was confined to her waist and hips. Within a two-month, the Marshals would be parents.

Beside Laura, Clarice caught her breath, evidence she also realized Lady Beata was with child.

"You are to be congratulated," Lothaire said when the two halted before him. "By summer's end you shall have a babe in arms."

Lady Beata touched her belly. "If I birth early, which is very possible with twins."

"Twins? How know you?"

Her smile revealed more of the small gap between her front teeth than Laura had earlier glimpsed. "Until a month past, we thought it one large babe, but now the movement is so vigorous I find myself kicked by three and four feet at once. Too, the midwife confirms the beat of two hearts."

"We are pleased for you."

Lady Beata inclined her head. "As we are pleased for your pending nuptials, Baron Soames." She moved her regard to Laura. "We shall pray this time next year you are with child."

The start of Laura's own smile was genuine. Its end was not. She wished to give Lothaire an heir, but the getting of one meant overcoming fear of what she had only ever experienced as violation—remembrance of which had caused her to tear herself out of Lothaire's arms last eve.

For that, she must reveal the truth of Clarice ere their nuptial night. He must understand it was not him she rejected but the violence that made memories spread through her like disease. Surely then he would go more slowly, be more gentle and, perhaps, come to love her again. *If* he believed what she told.

Durand Marshal's wife set a hand on Laura's arm. "I am glad to meet you, my lady."

"As I am to meet you." Laura cleared her throat. "This is my daughter, Clarice."

Lady Beata looked to her. "I thought you must be. You are as lovely as your mother."

Clarice curtsied. "I thank you, my lady."

Lest the girl claim she had her father's eyes as she was wont to do when resemblance to her mother was noted, Laura said, "I am sure you must be fatigued after your long journey, Lady Beata."

"Indeed, we are."

"Baron Marshal," Lothaire returned to the conversation, "my betrothed will ensure your party's comfort whilst my men and I tend to my father."

Laura caught the narrowing of the baron's eyes on the upper window ere he returned his regard to Lothaire. Did he sense danger? Did he fear for his wife whose family was responsible for the loss of the man whose wife and daughter watched?

His hand was not on sword or dagger, but she did not doubt his mind was ready to give the command. He could not be pleased Lady Beata accompanied him, especially in her pregnant state, but for that his escort surely numbered more than it would otherwise—and would not enter the donjon were they asked to disarm. Blessedly, it seemed that would not be required of them.

"Laura?" Lothaire prompted.

Glimpsing the vulnerable youth in his eyes, she smiled reassuringly, said, "I shall see to their comfort," and led the way into the great hall.

19

THE EFFORTS OF the day past were more obvious with the afternoon sun casting itself through the upper windows like a beautiful sacrifice. So, too, were its shortcomings that revealed how tired the room was.

Clarice at her side, Laura started toward the high table. And halted when a hand touched her arm.

"A moment," Lady Beata said. "First let us see the casket pass."

Laura's face warmed. Of course it was inappropriate to seat one's self ahead of the procession. She may not have been the best pupil, but Lady Maude had made certain her ward was versed in proprieties.

Grateful for Lady Beata's encouraging smile, she allowed the woman to hook arms with her and draw her toward Baron Marshal's knights and the castle folk who stood on either side of the path cleared between doors and stairs.

Laura glanced at her daughter who had also corrected her course, then whispered to Lady Beata, "I am not accustomed to acting the lady of the castle. I thank you."

Lightly, the lady bumped Laura's shoulder. "It becomes easier," she said out of the side of her mouth. "Ere long, it will seem almost like breathing."

It was some minutes before Lothaire, Sir Angus, and four other Lexeter knights entered bearing the casket on their shoulders. When her betrothed's eyes flicked to her and mouth tucked up slightly, her ache over his loss increased—as did her gratitude toward Lady Beata.

The procession wended past and up the stairway.

As the sound of their boots faded, Clarice tugged her mother's sleeve. "May I go to the kitchen?"

Laura frowned. "Are you not hungry?"

"I could not help myself. I ate an hour past."

"Then go, but do not get in Cook's way."

Clarice hastened opposite.

Laura looked to Baron Marshal. "Let us see you refreshed."

Once they were seated at the high table, their men at lower tables positioned perpendicular to the dais, the viands kept warmed these two hours were served—and not only to those in the hall but Lexeter's people in the bailey as Laura had directed. Hopefully, Cook would be able to accommodate greater numbers than expected.

There was nothing boisterous about High Castle's guests as was usual with visitors, and it became more solemn when those who had borne the casket abovestairs returned to the hall—all but Lothaire and Sir Angus. Talk was in hushed tones, and Laura was so worried over her betrothed that the few bites she took were mostly tasteless.

"I thank you and Baron Soames for receiving us kindly," Lady Beata said. "There has been so much ill between our families that fear for my safety roused an argument between my husband and me over my accompaniment." She made a face. "Even when he found himself bound and at my mercy aboard ship, I do not think he was as angry."

Laura could not imagine the formidable warrior reduced to helplessness. "Truly, you tied up Baron Marshal?"

"'Twas not I who bound him, but he was under my control—until we found ourselves shipwrecked. Then I was at *his* mercy, and much he showed me. I should have gone down with the ship, but he saved my life."

Laura was captivated, and her interest must have shown, for Lady Beata gave a laugh that likely would not be so restrained were it not for the day's sorrow. "A tale to be shared in full in future, which methinks possible now my family has made amends as best we can."

"I look forward to it. I am especially curious about..." Laura trailed off.

"My marriage to your betrothed?" the lady prompted.

"Aye."

"Know this, my lady, Lothaire Soames gave me reason not to like him, but I mostly understand why he did what he did and am grateful he rectified his trespass without prompting." She glanced at her husband on her other side where he conversed with one of his knights. "Thus, all the sooner I was able to wed the man I love."

Laura's throat tightened. "You are blessed."

The lady's brow puckered. "You do not believe you are?"

Though Laura told herself she had no reason to confide in a stranger, she said, "Once I was, then I lost all and thought myself cursed. Now I would like to believe the Lord is providing another chance at happiness. But even were He, I fear I do not know how to take it."

"With both hands and much gratitude to our Creator, of course," Lady Beata said. "'Tis not easily done, but to be truly blessed, do you not think one must be bold? That such is the part the Lord would have us play in our own lives?"

"But if it did not suffice in the past—"

"Ah, the past," the lady spoke over Laura. "As Everard Wulfrith's wife, Lady Susanna, assured me when I thought all lost, the past is not our future. There are better days ahead. And to that I add, be bold."

"I like you," Laura said, unable to keep the childish declaration from passing her lips.

Lady Beata's eyes brightened. "Much appreciated, for many have not a care for me. As oft told, albeit more to my back than my face, I am unseemly."

"Surely your husband does not think the same?"

She shook her head. "Love tolerates—and forgives—much. Though on occasion I unsettle him, he prefers me less behaved than behaved. And for love and respect of him, I am learning to think my thoughts through to their good and bad end ere speaking them into beliefs and opinions." Her eyes widened. "Most difficult."

Laura understood better than the lady knew. Once she had been too free with her own thoughts. Had Simon not changed all, she might be still. And had she wed Lothaire years ago, she imagined his love would have tolerated and forgiven much.

"I thank you for your encouragement, Lady Beata. It gives me greater hope I shall be blessed by the queen's hand in my marriage just as you were."

"Eleanor." She clicked her tongue. "Ever I shall be grateful to our queen though I would not have believed it a year past when she ordered me to return to her court in France. Now..." She set a hand on her belly. "...from love, babes that I pray you will also have." Of a sudden, her smile fell. "Did Lady Raisa receive you well?"

Laura's own smile dropped. "She did not."

"How did your betrothed respond?"

"I...did not tell him of our encounter." Laura hoped she would not be asked to elaborate.

The lady sighed. "I am not surprised, for the queen told that if I remained wed to Baron Soames his mother would make my life miserable."

Laura nodded. "For that, Eleanor insists my betrothed move her to her dower property."

"Wise. Let us hope 'tis done soon."

"Baron Soames assures me it shall be."

"Hold him to it, Lady Laura. Too much I like you to worry over your happiness."

As Laura looked to the bulge beneath the lady's hand, Baron Marshal's fingers covered his wife's.

"Are they restless?" he said low.

"Not at the moment. Methinks them lulled to sleep by good food and drink."

He smiled, looked past his wife. "You shall wed a sennight hence, Lady Laura?"

Determined to suppress her hurt over the revelation her father was aware she was to wed, Laura moved her thoughts to Tina's assurance the gown would soon be completed. It was beautiful—albeit extravagantly so—the maid having worked its embroidery down the bodice into the waist and skirts.

"Aye, in a sennight."

He nodded. "Your daughter has grown much since last I saw her."

"She was but three when you gave Lady Maude and me aid en route to Castle Soaring. Now she is nine."

"I was sorry to hear of the lady's passing."

"Her loss is much felt, especially by Clarice."

"It was obvious she adored the lady and was adored in return."

He could not know how much, few being aware Maude had been Clarice's grandmother—only Michael, his wife, and now the queen.

Laura nodded and, catching sight of the physician coming off the stairs, motioned him forward.

During his ascent of the dais, she felt tension rise, not only from Lady Beata but her husband, and a glance at the two confirmed it. Before them was the man who had performed Lothaire's examination to prove Lady Beata was untouched.

As though unaware the Marshals did not welcome him, he said, "Lady Laura, Baron Soames wishes me to inform you the service for his father will be conducted an hour hence after the family has privately shown its respects."

Feeling for Lady Beata's discomfort, Laura said, "I thank you, Martin."

He dipped his head, then ignoring her dismissal, set his regard on Lady Beata. "I see the Lord has blessed you with what we must pray is a boy."

Slowly, as if exercising control, Baron Marshal leaned forward. "Must we, Physician?"

Had the man been oblivious to the tension before, he could not be now. But more the fool, he said, "'Twill be a sign your marriage is blessed."

"And if 'tis a girl?" the baron said with great measure.

The physician raised his palms in what seemed a gesture of helplessness. "Displeasure, the birth of another Daughter of Eve being God's attempt to correct a woman's—occasionally a man's—path."

Never had Laura seen a man so fast upon his feet. Ere the physician's mouth was fully agape, the neck of his tunic was in Marshal's fist and his face flecked by the spit of a threat more growl than words. "I have not forgotten, you bag of pus and bones."

"Baron Marshal!" Laura nearly upended her chair as she thrust upright, which was no match for the speed with which the warriors of Soames and Marshal rose to defend their lords.

But though hands gripped hilts, no blades were drawn. It seemed those who might either defend or set upon the physician understood he was unworthy of rending the peace—at the moment.

Amid the silence, Lady Beata touched her husband's sleeve, the fine fabric of which bulged with muscles surely capable of flinging the physician far from the dais. "He is of so little consequence it requires but a slap from a Daughter of Eve to render him speechless, Durand. Pray, release him ere he soils himself and further dishonors his lord's hospitality."

A slow, deep breath further broadened her husband's chest, then his high color began to recede. "You will not speak another word to my wife. Ever. You will not move your gaze within sight of her. Ever. You will not breathe the air she casts off. Ever. Do you understand, *Martin?*"

The physician's throat convulsed, but were he trying to summon words, he failed.

"You may nod or shake your head," the baron said. "Either will suffice, though one will see you all the worse for it."

Hardly had the man bobbed his chin than a voice thundered across the hall, "Release the physician, Baron Marshal!"

Laura snapped her chin around, struggled for words to keep Lothaire's sword from exiting its scabbard.

"A disagreement only," Lady Beata's husband said. "As we have come to terms…" He thrust Martin back, nearly toppling him, then gestured to his men to release their hilts.

"I am glad you appreciate the hospitality shown you, Baron," Lothaire said and gestured to his own men.

As all resumed their seats, Lothaire looked to Laura.

She forced a smile she hoped would assure him he had not made a mistake in admitting the Marshals to his hall.

Next, he looked to the physician. Though the man had descended the dais, he had yet to distance himself from the warrior who could bleed him in the blink of an eye. He was surely dazed, though from the quick rise and fall of his shoulders he was coming back to himself well enough to gather anger to him.

"Martin," Lothaire said, "my mother has returned to her chamber. Pray, attend her."

The man stumbled forward, found his stride. "My lord, Baron Marshal—"

"You came to terms, did you not?"

"As forced upon me, my lord."

"That is well with me. Now, my mother is distraught and in need of her medicinals."

The man muttered something, stepped around his lord, and climbed the stairs.

"Baron Marshal," Lothaire called, "I would speak with you abovestairs."

The man looked to his wife.

"Go," Lady Beata said. "Lady Laura makes for good company."

And additional surety, Laura guessed. Her husband need not worry ill would befall his wife whilst Lothaire's betrothed was as vulnerable to Marshal's men as Lady Beata was to those of the Baron of Lexeter.

Durand Marshal bent and spoke something to his knight, then descended the dais and strode toward Lothaire.

"Fear not," Lady Beata said as the two men mounted the stairs. "Methinks your betrothed is aware of his physician's shortcomings and will not be surprised to learn my husband was provoked."

As Laura hoped he would accept she had been provoked if ever Lady Raisa revealed Laura had slapped her.

"Once that is established," the lady continued, "they can move on to Baron Soames's questions about his father's remains."

Laura picked off a crust of her trencher, crumbled it. "As to where they were found?"

"Aye, that is the place to start."

"Where *were* they found?"

The lady sighed. "Where first we ought to have looked."

One could not be certain they were his father's bones, they were so barren, nor his clothes, they were so deteriorated, but the heavy signet ring wrapped in a piece of embroidered linen and bound with a gold cord was of the house of Soames.

"It was found near his hand," Durand Marshal said where he stood at the foot of the table upon which the casket sat. "Lady Beata restored it."

It was so clean and polished Lothaire could only guess what twenty years in the moist earth would have done to the ring whose revelation had caused his mother more distress than the bones she had been determined to look upon. And Sebille...

Though Raisa had insisted her daughter view the remains, Lothaire's sister had refused and asked Sir Angus to assist her to a bench. They were still there to the left of the altar, and though in shadow, Baron Marshal's Wulfen training was evident the moment he entered the chapel. As when Lothaire had sensed Laura's presence on the night past, even sooner Lady Beata's husband had sensed Sebille's and Angus's though they were more distant.

Lothaire closed his fingers around his father's ring he was not ready to place on his own hand. "I am grateful for your wife's kindness, Baron Marshal."

The man inclined his head. There was an air of expectation about him, but were he waiting for his host to demand he defend his encounter with the physician, he would wait forever. Lothaire required no further explanation beyond that deduced when his mother's collapse brought him belowstairs in search of the physician.

He had tolerated Martin for years. Though the man was as near a confidant as Raisa had, he did not like women. Hence, all the greater Lothaire's offense against Lady Beata by insisting she prove herself chaste. Following the examination, she had slapped the physician, and though he had denied offending her, Lothaire had known better then as he knew better now. When Lady Raisa retired to her dower property, the physician would go with her and another physician would be found for High Castle. One more expense, but worth it.

"Now," Lothaire said, "I would know where Lady Beata's father buried mine all those years ago."

"The answer is unexpected," Baron Marshal said. "He did not bury your sire."

Lothaire glanced into the casket whose contents were so lacking substance it was hard to believe that beneath the material of the fine pall provided by the Marshals was the tall, broad frame that had supported Ricard Soames.

"Who buried him?" he asked.

"His wife, Lady Beata's mother."

She who, witness to her nephew's murder of their guest, had dragged the body to a corner of the garden and dug a grave to hold it until her husband returned from his travels to better conceal the crime.

"You are saying he was never moved from the garden," Lothaire said and heard his sister's sharp breath. "Your wife's father did not bury him distant from the castle as told."

"He did not, and methinks he would have taken the truth to his own grave had I not ordered the garden razed and a new one constructed at the rear of the donjon so my wife might find peace and rest out of doors."

Which was not possible in that place where, as a very young girl, she had witnessed the atrocity.

"So we are here with hope that what was broken can be mended to ensure lasting peace between our families, Baron Soames."

Though it was enough for Lothaire, it would not suffice for Raisa. But of greater import, would it be enough for Sebille?

Lothaire looked around, wished he could see more than her slight figure alongside Angus. Not that he required her consent, but he wished it. When she remained unmoving, he returned his attention to Durand. "The Soames are at peace with you and your wife's family, as begun when I did not oppose annulment of my marriage to Lady Beata."

"We are grateful. I know this cannot be easy."

It was more difficult than anticipated, Lothaire having believed himself too young upon his father's disappearance to grieve deeply. But though he knew his loss was not as deep as Sebille's, from the moment he caught sight of the procession delivering their father home, he had hurt—and more as blurred memories sharpened. His father might not have loved his wife, his marriage one of convenience, but he had adored the daughter made with her, and perhaps even the son.

"Once he is in consecrated ground," he said, "we can better leave the past where it belongs."

"Have you further questions for me, Baron Soames?" Marshal asked.

Feeling the edges of the signet ring, Lothaire said, "I am satisfied as much as I can be. Pray, give your wife my apologies for taking you from her side and assure her there will be as little delay as possible between the chapel mass and the burial so you may sooner begin your journey home."

The baron dipped his head and strode from the chapel.

"Under their noses all these years," Sebille said when the door closed.

Lothaire turned and saw her snatch her arm against her side when Angus tried to assist her to standing, causing the prayer beads she had surely been working her fingers over to clatter as they fell down her skirt.

"So great a risk was it to leave him there," he said, "I never seriously considered it might be our father's resting place."

"Rest," she hissed as she advanced. "For over twenty years he has cried out to bring him home and avenge—"

"Say no more," Lothaire commanded. "'Tis over."

She halted alongside him. "Is it?"

He set a hand on her shoulder. "The man who did this is long dead, and by his own hand, so great was his remorse." As Lothaire learned whilst listening in on Lady Beata and her father, Ralf Rodelle had drowned himself at the age of thirty and one, the same age Ricard Soames had been when he was murdered.

Sebille's face opened as if to spew anger, then crumpled and Lothaire pulled her into his arms and pressed her head to his shoulder.

"Leave us, Angus," he said.

The knight did as bid, and Lothaire held Sebille as she poured out her misery between cries of, "Oh, Papa! Papa!"

When finally she exhausted herself, he offered to escort her to her chamber, but she refused. Unlike their mother who had declared she could bear no more before her collapse alongside the casket, Sebille would not allow her emotions to prevent her from attending the mass.

A half hour later, it began. Rather than Lady Raisa on one side of him, it was Laura, and though it was clear Sebille on his other side did not wish the lady in so esteemed a place, she said naught. And when Lothaire closed his fingers around the soft hand that slipped into his as the priest's words resounded around the chapel, he silently acknowledged how glad he was to have Laura at his side. No matter her betrayal.

20

"THE LORD WILL have to do much work in me if ever I am to forgive them."

Sebille's declaration was not discreet, but neither could it be heard by those departing Thistle Cross to begin their journey home to the barony of Wiltford. Once more Marshal's entourage was accompanied by Lexeter's people for the protection afforded by warriors. Though the demesne was mostly peaceful, brigands were not unheard of, especially during the dark hours.

"I shall pray for you as ever you pray for me, Sebille," Lothaire said and looked from his sister at his side to Laura and her daughter where they crossed to the gray-and-white speckled palfrey they had ridden to the village.

At a light trot, it would take over a half hour to reach High Castle, and though the clouds were not so heavily hung they portended a storm, that scent was on the air. Hopefully, whatever stirred above would pass—or at least hold off until the villagers reached their homes and Baron Marshal and his party arrived at a neighboring castle where they would spend this night en route to Wiltford.

"It is sorrowful your mother could not attend the mass and burial," said Father Atticus who stood on Lothaire's other side.

His regret was sincere, though he knew her attendance would have risked the dignity and solemnity due her husband. She was too bitter and her mind increasingly slippery to present well as the grieving widow. Worse, in the presence of the Marshals and the woman who had cuckolded her son, she might have made a spectacle of all. For that, Lothaire had been relieved his mother would not leave her bed.

"It is sorrowful," he said, "but for the best."

The man nodded, sent his gaze in Laura and Clarice's direction. "You are certain you do not wish to postpone the wedding, my lord?"

"I think you ought to," Sebille said, her voice louder, the despair that had nearly suffocated during their father's burial giving way to offense.

"It is past time we rise above our losses," Lothaire said. "Six days hence, Lexeter shall have a new lady."

Father Atticus cleared his throat. "In the scores of years you shall be wed to the lady, God willing," he said, the last surely added in remembrance of the many last rites given to women who died in childbirth, "there is little difference between a sennight and a fortnight, my lord."

"Wait, Lothaire," Sebille urged. "Only a fortnight."

"It is decided, but I thank you both for your counsel."

"'Tis because of Lady Raisa," his sister said. "You are eager to rid yourself of her."

This was not a conversation he wished to have, especially this day. "You know our mother." He moved his eyes from his sister to the priest. "Though she accepts my marriage to Lady Laura is necessary, the sooner she and my betrothed are no longer in close proximity, the sooner there shall be peace at High Castle."

Sebille made a sound of dissent, and he thought she would argue, but Father Atticus said, "In that you are right, my lord," and inclined his head, causing his gray-streaked cap of dark hair to swing forward and conceal his eyes like blinders on a horse.

Sebille gripped Lothaire's arm. "Mayhap you will be as pleased to see me depart."

He ground his teeth. "You know I will not, that I would have you remain at High Castle, but that is your decision. I only pray you will be without regrets."

She withdrew her hand, and when her wet eyes flicked to Angus, he knew her thoughts were of the man she could have wed and with whom she might now have children.

Lothaire sighed, said to the priest, "I thank you for making right all these years of wrong. At last Ricard Soames is at peace."

Father Atticus inclined his head. "Come see me ere the wedding, hmm?"

"I shall try, but with much shearing to be done, it may not be possible."

"Then I should come to you?" Another sacrifice like that made this day—entering the donjon to perform the funeral mass though he disliked being so near Lexeter's lady.

"I will come to you," Lothaire said. "Until then, Father." He took his sister's arm and guided her to her mount. Once she was astride, he moved toward Laura but corrected his course when he saw she had gained the saddle and settled Clarice in front of her.

Lothaire swung atop his horse, considered the church where Laura and he would wed, next the graveyard to which one more Soames had been added. Then he urged his horse forward into what he hoped was a blessed future for all of Lexeter.

"Your sire's?"

Lothaire raised his gaze to the one he had not expected to return to the hall following a somber supper after which Laura and Clarice had retreated to their chamber. He had not meant to linger belowstairs, and yet here his betrothed found him. In the absence of hearing his tread along the corridor, had she come looking for him?

She halted before him where he leaned against the wall alongside the massive fireplace with Tomas at his feet, looked to what he held between thumb and forefinger. "'Twas your father's? Found with his body?"

"Aye, his signet ring."

"Now yours."

"Replaced long ago—twice, in fact."

"Twice?"

He looked to those who had bedded down for the night and those yet to do so. "You wish to speak, my lady, or do you but pass through on your way to the kitchen?"

She raised her chin. "'Twas for you I returned to the hall."

"For what purpose?"

"I thought if you are not ready to gain your rest you would like company."

He almost smiled. "Are you worried for me, Laura? Do you seek to ease my grieving?"

"I am worried. I know your father has been long gone and you were but six—"

"Methinks it best we continue this elsewhere." He glanced at two knights who did not appear to be listening but whose bodies had a lean that revealed their lord and future lady were of interest.

"Come." He tucked the ring into the purse on his belt, pushed off the wall, and strode to the corridor that led to the kitchen if one traversed its entire length. Halfway down, Lothaire retrieved a torch from a wall sconce, turned onto a short corridor, and opened a door at its end.

"Have a care where you place your feet," he said. "The stairs are steep and in need of repair." He was a step down when he realized she did not follow. He looked around at where she stood unmoving. "Laura?"

"Why the cellar?" she said so low he might not have understood in the absence of context.

"At meal you said you liked the wine. It is our finest, a cask held in reserve until opened this eve in honor of my sire. I thought another pour would be welcome."

At her hesitation, he guessed she feared it would be too much temptation were she to accompany him into the donjon's deepest, darkest place. Considering what had happened between them in the chapel, she had good cause.

"Forgive me," he said, "I am not thinking right. I will fill a flask and bring it to the kitchen."

She nodded and turned away.

Lothaire did not keep her waiting long. Upon entering the kitchen, he found it more brightly lit than usual at this time of night, evidencing Laura had stirred the cooking fires.

He crossed to the shelving where less valuable serving ware was stacked scores high and several deep to accommodate the castle folk at meal. With the exception of the rare occasion High Castle hosted noble guests, as done this day with the Marshals, these plates, bowls, and drinking vessels were used to serve Lothaire and his men. What little gold- and brass-trimmed silver and horn ware had not been sold—consisting of pieces passed down through the generations of the Soames family—was locked away when not in use. Thus, Lothaire retrieved two simple goblets and lowered to the stool across the table from Laura.

Her smile almost shy, he was reminded of their first meeting. But then there had been a sparkle in her eyes he had not yet known was of mischief. In the hour of his family's grieving, now was not the time to wish that sparkle returned. But he did.

He filled the goblets half full, passed one to her, and was jolted by the brush of her fingertips across his just as a rumble sounded through the stone walls. At least the storm's arrival was not heralded by a crack of lightning, he mused.

"Do you think the villagers and Baron Marshal's party are safely inside?" Laura asked.

"Aye, 'tis surely an hour or more since all gained shelter."

She raised her goblet, sipped. "Tell me about the ring, Lothaire."

He removed it from his purse and this time she opened her hand beneath his. Wondering if she had been as disturbed by the touch of their fingers as he, he set the signet ring in her palm.

"Why twice replaced?" she asked as she examined it.

He took a drink of the wine, lowered his goblet. "The first time following my father's disappearance when my mother took control of Lexeter. The second time when I took control and she refused to surrender the ring. She hid it, doubtless with other items that went missing as I settled into my title—valuables whose sale would have eased some of Lexeter's financial problems."

"You think she still has them?"

"I do, though not all."

"How know you?"

"On occasion, she wishes some luxury Lexeter's coffers cannot afford. On other occasions, she wishes certain services, which require payment to those who do her bidding."

"What bidding?"

"Those things she does not wish me to know of."

"Such as?"

That he could not tell, at least not while Raisa resided at High Castle. Much coin his mother had surely paid the men who set upon Durand and Beata on their wedding day. "Activities of which I do not approve," he said.

She searched his face, held out the ring.

He did not open his palm beneath it, once more subjecting his senses to her touch and his imaginings to those fingers moving up his arm, around his neck, and pressing against his scalp to prolong their kiss.

A sennight, he told himself and returned the ring to his purse.

"You will not wear it?" she asked.

"Later." Once Lexeter's fortunes were reversed, he would set aside the cheaply fashioned ring that was all he could afford when he came into his lordship—that which had never adorned his hand for its ability to reveal how far his family had fallen.

"After your mourning is done?" she pressed.

"Perhaps." He took another draught of wine.

"But—"

"Tell me about Donnie."

She caught her breath, and her head jerked so violently she would have slopped wine onto the table had he filled her goblet fuller. It made him regret his change of topic. He wished to know what had happened between the boy and her daughter, but he had not meant to distress her. However, what could have waited a while longer was before them now.

She moistened her lips. "I have not thanked you for being so kind to Clarice."

Did *she* now change the subject, or ease into an answer?

"It has been difficult for her since we lost Lady Maude, and though I try not to fail her, my choices have further tipped her world. Whereas you…" She lowered the goblet, clasped her hands atop the table. "You who have no obligation to do so are setting her world right side up."

"I am to be her stepfather."

"Even so, I did not expect you to become easy with her—certainly not this soon."

Now came a crack of lightning that made her glance at the ceiling.

"I am not easy with her," Lothaire admitted, "but neither am I as uncomfortable as expected. Mayhap because she has much the young Laura about her."

She flushed as if pleased, and in her face he glimpsed that younger woman. Once more feeling his body tug toward hers, he said, "Mayhap we ought to leave the matter of Donnie for another day." He raised his goblet to drain it that he might sooner distance himself from the temptation of her.

But she said, "Another day will not make the telling easier."

"Then tell me."

Laura did not want to, the boy's name on Lothaire's lips having been as near a blow one might deliver without actually slamming knuckles against skin and bone, but he ought to know.

"What did Clarice tell you about Donnie?" she asked.

"He is several years older than she, the heir of Lady Maude's eldest stepson, and the argument I happened upon between the two of you was over him."

She nodded. "Much of it."

"She seems to believe he is the reason you left Owen to seek a husband."

"He was not the only reason. Even before I..." Should she reveal what she had seen? Might it cause Lothaire to treat Clarice differently, especially considering what he believed of her mother?

"I can guess what your daughter meant when she said the boy was more than a friend, Laura," he prompted, "but I prefer not to make assumptions."

As she drew a breath, she caught the sound of rain tapping at shutters that, thrown wide, would offer a view of the garden. "Even before I found a twelve-year-old boy pressing a nine-year-old girl against a wall and kissing her, I knew I had to make a better life for Clarice. Donnie was the slap that brought me fully awake—confirmation I must wed to provide a home away from those who would take advantage of a fatherless girl."

She closed her eyes as she once more recalled the snare into which she, desperate to wed any but Lothaire, had nearly led her daughter. And shuddered.

"Laura?"

She returned Lothaire to focus. "Lord Benton," she gasped. "What if I had...?"

The understanding in his eyes caused tears to flood her own. "Eleanor may be the most manipulative female in the history of womankind, Laura, but never would she have given Clarice and you into the keeping of one such as Benton. She aspired to do what was best for you. And she did."

"Aye, but what of you?"

His jaw shifted, and he said gruffly, "Was the boy forcing Clarice?"

She should be grateful for another change of topic, but he might as well have said that had marriage to another provided the same benefit for Lexeter, he would not have agreed to take her to wife. Though he wanted her in his bed, another would slake his passion as well—nay, better.

"Was he, Laura?"

Though her daughter's willing participation would reflect poorly on Clarice, she could not lie. "He did not force her."

Now Lothaire hesitated, but though she steeled herself for a knowing glint in his eyes, it did not appear. "As I can attest, boys—even girls—are wont to test the breadth of adulthood ere they are prepared for the consequences," he said.

To which she could also attest, and not only from the intimacies shared with him.

"However," he continued, "'tis unlikely Clarice and the boy's explorations would have progressed further."

Laura gasped. "Perhaps not then, but eventually he would have ruined her."

"You do not know that."

"Do I not?" She surged to her feet, and though she told herself to close her mouth, the rest tumbled out. "Know you how his mother defended him when I told her what I stopped? She said of course her son did not respect one whom all knew to be misbegotten, especially since Clarice was willing to follow her mother's example. The lady's only concession was to agree it best her son gain his experience with a girl more easily set out of their household should he get her with child." Realizing she was shaking, she gripped the table's edge. "Concession, not consolation. No assurance that what happened to me…" She scoffed. "I need not tell you of my ruin."

The soft went out of his eyes. "Indeed you need not." It was so quietly said she felt the hurt of all those years past when she had turned from the pond to reveal the reason for their broken betrothal. In that moment, she longed to tell him all as Michael advised ere they wed. And she might have had he not said, "Do you love him still?"

"Him?"

"Your daughter believes if I can make you fall in love with me as you loved her father, our marriage will be a good one."

Another blow. Never had Laura spoken ill of Clarice's sire when she was unable to avoid talk of him, just as never had she spoken well of him. "Sh-she said that?"

"Aye, that for love and loss of her father she has only known you to be sorrowful."

It was so far from the truth it was tragic. Was that how Lady Maude had explained Laura's long sleep to Clarice, or had the girl devised the story to fill what might be becoming a widening hole?

She shook her head. "She knows naught of what she speaks."

"Mayhap, but that does not answer my question."

Of whether she yet loved the man with whom he believed she betrayed him. Before she could determine if now was the time to reveal the circumstances of Clarice's conception, he said, "What is Michael D'Arci to you?"

She stared. And understood. But did he truly suspect Michael of impropriety? "The same as ever he has been—like a brother. Why do you ask?" When he did not answer, she said, "Surely you do not think he and I—"

"I know not what to think, Laura."

He *did* believe it possible, and it was painfully amusing how near the truth he was. His only error was that he had the wrong brother. Doubtless, here was the reason he had turned cooler toward Michael and her the morn of their departure from Castle Soaring.

As the rain fell harder, no longer tapping—now slashing at the shutters—Laura felt every one of this day's hours. Or was it every one of the hours since Simon had stolen her happiness? Those too.

Wondering how they had moved from her attempt to comfort Lothaire over his loss of a sire to the loss of his first betrothed, she released her hold on the table. "All I shall say is that you do Michael D'Arci a grave wrong in thinking such ill of him. And now I am most tired." She skirted the table, crossed the kitchen, and left him alone with his ill-founded suspicions.

21

BLISTERS. A DOZEN or more small, red-ringed bumps.

She had not known of them until she scratched an itch and her fingertips tripped over the swellings. Holding her breath, she turned her hands front to back. Both afflicted, the left more than the right.

"Dear Lord," she whispered.

Tina finished lacing the back of her lady's gown and came around. "Milady?"

Laura retreated a step, held out her hands. "There is something wrong with me."

The maid's eyes widened. "So there is, milady."

Laura's next words were choked. "The pox?"

Tina bit her lip, and when she moved closer to examine the blisters, Laura lurched back and sat down hard in the chair. "Pray, come no nearer."

The maid continued forward. "I will not touch, milady. Now hold out yer hands so I may look close upon them, for I have seen the pox at its worst."

Laura did as told.

Tina leaned this way and that, shook her head. "I am fair certain this be not the pox."

"What then?"

"I cannot say." The maid straightened. "Though ye will not like consulting the physician, methinks ye ought to."

Laura snatched her hands to her waist. "Indeed I do not like it."

"He will know more than I, milady."

The thought of being touched by the man whose examination had humiliated Lady Beata made Laura's stomach roil.

"I should summon him, milady?"

She looked to her hands again, hoped it mere imagining more blisters had arisen. "Aye, but after Clarice and my betrothed have departed."

"What should I tell Lord Soames?"

Laura was to have accompanied him and her daughter to observe the sheep shearing this second day following the burial of Ricard Soames. Doubtless, they awaited her in the hall.

"As I would not have Clarice alarmed nor disrupt the baron's day, tell him I slept poorly and require further rest. When they are gone, send the physician to me."

Tina hastened from the chamber.

Clenching her hands to keep from raking at blisters that had begun to burn, Laura tried to distract herself by deciding what to do with a day whose plans were ruined. If the physician allayed her fears and provided a salve to relieve the discomfort, she would make a menu for next week's meals, then once more apply herself to the wedding gown Tina had completed the morn of the burial.

She looked to where she had draped it over the chair opposite. It was over-embellished, Tina determined to make use of every bauble of the queen's generosity. Even had Lothaire not expressed a preference for Laura's simpler gowns, she would have been uncomfortable in such splendor. Blessedly, Tina had not seemed offended when her lady told the garment was too elaborate and apologized for not paying closer attention beyond its embroidery.

Tina had said she would remove the pearls and silver beads, but Laura had declined and sat up late last eve snipping them away. It was no easy task, the maid's stitches and knots tight to the cloth, but another hour and it would be done—providing Laura's affliction did not prove dire.

Shortly, Tina reported Lothaire and Clarice had departed and the physician would come after he gave Lady Raisa her medicinals.

"Did Baron Soames seem upset?" Laura asked where she sat on her hands to keep from scratching at them.

"Nay, milady."

"Tina?" Laura said firmly.

The maid grimaced. "'Twas merely disappointment he expressed, as did your daughter. Certes, they both wished your accompaniment."

More likely, they believed she lazed abed regardless of the promise made her daughter who had seemed pleased by Laura's interest in Lexeter's wool. When the two returned later this afternoon—or this eve—they would learn of the physician's diagnosis and she would be redeemed.

Though the time it took Martin to tend Lady Raisa felt like half a day, Laura did not believe it exaggeration that one hour passed before the man arrived.

He knocked sharply and entered. Halting at the center of the chamber, he jutted his chin. "Show me, my lady."

He so soon offended Laura nearly had to swallow her tongue to keep anger from it.

Dragging her hands from beneath her, she whimpered when the relief provided by the pressure was repaid with pain all the sharper for its suppression. There were more blisters, now spreading down her wrists. She thrust her hands forward.

Maintaining his distance, Martin considered them.

"Surely you ought to draw nearer for a proper diagnosis," Laura snipped.

He grimaced. "I would, but unlike many, I believe close proximity passes affliction to the innocent."

"But you are a physician—or so you claim to be."

His brow lowered. "I am a man of medicine, but not a fool. My first concern is for Lady Raisa, as it should be and as her son requires.

'Twould be unforgivably negligent did I risk her delicate health by passing your sickness to her."

A grunt drew Laura's regard to the hearth where Tina stood flushed and stiff. She did not like the man any more than her lady liked him.

"I cannot say I think highly of your competence as a physician," Laura bit. "Pray, persuade me otherwise by identifying what this is."

His upper lip curled, but whatever ill he wished to speak, he did not. At last he asked, "Have you been in the garden?"

"On the day past."

"Then possibly foxglove, the plant whose stalks drip bell-shaped flowers." He nodded. "Methinks you touched what you should not."

Laura knew the plant and that even if one did not ingest its poison, brief contact could cause a rash. Hence, Lady Maude had removed foxgloves from her garden when Clarice began to walk.

"I saw none there, Martin."

"Did you pick flowers?"

"Roses only." And she had thorn pricks to prove it, remembrance of which made her skin itch more.

Another nod. "Once Lady Raisa's children were of an age to obey, she planted foxglove between the rosebushes. Though the plants did not take well, from time to time one struggles up through the earth as I have noted whilst gathering herbs. 'Tis rare one blooms, which is surely why you did not recognize it as such."

It made sense, and Laura wished it to since the diagnosis could be worse. "You are certain 'tis not the pox?"

"Not the usual pox, but..."

"But?"

He cleared his throat. "'Tis a delicate matter, and I would not wish to offend my lord's betrothed."

"How might you offend?"

He pursed his lips, swung them side to side. "To be certain, a closer examination is required."

"Then draw nearer."

With obvious reluctance, he closed the distance between them and leaned forward. "I am fair certain 'tis foxglove, my lady."

"Then not the usual nor unusual pox."

"That last cannot be excluded without a thorough examination— one I would require my lord's permission to perform."

"I do not understand."

"As told, my lady, it is a delicate matter."

Laura thrust up out of the chair, causing him to spring back on his short legs. "Speak!"

He looked to Tina as if she might offer aid, but the maid said, "Lest ye forget, Physician, soon ye shall answer to milady the same as ye answer to yer lord."

He tossed up his hands. "If Baron Soames is angered by what I tell, 'tis of your doing, Lady Laura."

Suppressing the longing to scratch at her hands, she said, "I take responsibility."

"Very well. When I name that other pox unusual, I do so in reference to those of the nobility who are far less susceptible than common folk."

Laura ground her teeth at the insult to Tina.

He sighed. "But since you have engaged in behavior displeasing to the Lord, embracing the sins of the flesh and making yourself a Daughter of Eve rather than a sister of Mary, it is quite possible you are afflicted with that best known to those whose profession it is to provide favors of the flesh."

Laura was so shocked she could only stare, then struggle to control the urge to slap him as she had been unable to do with Lady Raisa.

"Ye dare!" Tina recovered before her mistress.

"Your lady insisted!"

The maid gave a cry, hastened forward, and struck his arm. "Out with ye, foul being!" As if a broom to the debris he had become to her lady, she pushed and swept him over the threshold.

But before she could slam the door, he turned. "I shall send salve. Whether your lady's skin is afflicted by foxglove or that other pox, 'twill provide relief and aid with healing."

"Be quick about it!" Tina slammed the door and hastened back. "Put from yer mind what he said, milady, hear?" She reached for Laura's hands, but her lady snatched them away.

"I should have known of which pox he spoke," Laura said. "He tried to warn me—"

"I think it more likely he baited ye, milady." The maid wiped her palms on her skirts as if she were more fouled by touching him than she would be had she caught up Laura's hands.

"As it is likely foxglove, it matters not," Laura said. "And as easy as it would be to wallow in anger toward him, my time is better spent thanking the Lord 'tis but a skin irritation. So that I shall do. I only hope Martin does not tell my betrothed he suspects it could be the *unusual* sort of pox." She raked her teeth over her lower lip, considered her wedding gown. "Four days, then I wed, providing I am sufficiently healed."

"Ye shall be, milady. I will tend yer hands and take good care of ye."

"I thank you." Laura nodded at the gown. "I thought I might spend some of the day removing more pearls and beads, but my hands hurt, and if these blisters weep, the cloth might be ruined."

"Worry not, milady. I shall pluck out the rest."

"Nay, I shall do it. Mayhap in a few days I will be well enough healed."

"As you wish, milady."

Lothaire was a mess, and would be more so if he yielded to the impulse to bloody his knuckles against the man's scowl. "You said that to her?" he barked.

The physician's expression faltered. "I told her I am fair certain the rash is from contact with foxglove, my lord, but she wished assurance it was not the pox. Thus, I informed her it was not the usual sort, but to be certain it is not that which afflicts many a Daughter of Eve, I would need to perform a thorough examination." He held up a hand. "Which I would not do without your consent."

Lothaire breathed deep. "'Tis fortunate in this you know my mind, Martin. But most unfortunate you know not my mind in other things. You ought to thank God you are soon to depart High Castle." Not at all satisfied by the man's wide-flung eyes and sputtering, Lothaire strode from the hall.

When Tina admitted him to the chamber, Laura's gaze awaited his, and what he saw there would have been of great detriment to the physician were the man within reach.

"See, Lord Soames," Clarice called from where she perched on the mattress alongside her mother, "here is the true reason she could not attend the day's shearing." She nodded at the bandaged hands cradled in her own. "She but feared needlessly worrying us. Blessedly, 'tis only a rash."

Lothaire moved his gaze from Laura's hands to the sheet drawn up around her waist to her loosed hair whose waves spilled over the shoulders of her chemise. Here an eyeful of what would await him on their nuptial night.

"So the physician has informed me," he said and looked to the maid. "Would you take the young lady to my solar and aid her in washing away the day's labors?"

He knew Tina's hesitation had merit, but unseemly though it was for him to be alone with Laura in her chamber, he needed to speak with her in private. True, the matter could wait, but he could not knowing she suffered in the time between what was appropriate and what was not.

Ignoring the voice increasingly fond of naming him a fool where she was concerned, he prompted with, "I would not ask it were it not of great import and were I not soon to wed your lady."

The maid looked to where Laura sat propped on pillows. "Milady?"

Laura inclined her head. "Go with Tina, Clarice. Lord Soames and I will not be long."

"I shall tell you of the shearing later," the girl said and followed the maid into the corridor.

When the door closed, Laura said in a strained voice, "What did Martin tell you?"

"What nearly saw *him* in need of a physician's services." He strode to the bed. "I apologize for what he suggested could be the cause of your affliction. Never would such occur to me. Never would I believe it."

The easing of her shoulders evidencing her relief, she said, "I am glad in this you do not assume the worst of me."

"But?"

She shook her head, seamed her lips.

He did not think before acting, and then it seemed too late to correct the impropriety. Having lowered his damply-clothed body to the mattress edge, he said, "You expected me to think the worst?"

"It follows."

The accusation tempted him to defend his right to think it, but he checked the words.

"I thank you for seeing me as I truly am," she whispered.

He looked to her hands. "You are in pain?"

"Less so. The bandages and salve provide relief, but 'tis possible the wedding will have to be postponed." To his annoyance, his body liked that less than his mind which would rather argue that the sooner they wed the sooner Lexeter would benefit from the tax break. And the sooner his mother—and Martin—would depart High Castle.

"It is not unheard of for a lady to wear gloves on such an occasion," he said. "Unless you fall most ill, I see no reason to delay the ceremony."

Her smile was hardly genuine. "Lexeter—of utmost importance and consideration."

He should let her believe that, especially as much of it was true, but he said, "As well you know, I desire you."

She looked down. "You wish me in your bed."

"I do, and more now I see you like this with your hair unbound." Though his reach caused her to press back into the pillows, he hooked a finger around a bronze tress. "Here you sit like a bride awaiting her groom, your chemise the only garment that must needs be removed to reveal all of the woman you have become." He let the tress slide away, moved the backs of his fingers down the neckline of her chemise, watched color rise up her chest. "Four days hence, the wishing will be done, Laura. You will be in our bed and know my desire as I shall know yours."

"Lothaire."

He looked up, but though he hoped what he felt might be found in her eyes, that was not what he saw there. It was wariness—and something else. Regret? Distaste? If so, because he was not whom she wished him to be?

Weary of jealousy, resentment, and anger, he told himself he must get past the past and said low, "What is amiss, Laura?"

"I am not comfortable being..." She swallowed. "...desired."

He drew his fingers back up her chemise's neckline, over her throat, across her jaw. "Then you should not present thus, Laura Middleton."

He said it with teasing that would have made the young Laura laugh and tease in return, but this Laura appeared further distressed. And something about that troubled him deeply, and not only because he feared her aversion was exclusive to him. It was as though...

Before he could follow the thought to its end, she said, "I am as God made me. I vow, had I known you would come to my chamber, you would not have found me in such a state." Her tone was defensive, as if he accused her of seduction. "I would have—"

"I know you did not expect me, Laura. I know this is not an attempt to seduce me. I but speak as I find." He slid his thumb in the dip between chin and lip, causing her to draw a quick breath that lowered her jaw and shifted his touch to her bottom lip. He was surprised by how sensuous it felt though it was not his mouth upon hers—the bow soft, full, and touched by the moisture of her inner lip, then there was the light scrape of her teeth across the pad of his thumb. No matter her bandaged hands, no matter the sight and scent he presented, no matter the impropriety of sitting upon her bed, he wanted to kiss her. Even if that kiss became more. Especially if it became more.

That last admission made him gain his feet and berate himself for feelings surely not unlike those that had caused her to betray him. Of course she was not comfortable being desired. Had she not a misbegotten child to prove the folly of desire outside of marriage?

"Forgive me," he said. "Just as I should not have done ten years past, I should not speak thus nor touch you as the lover I do not yet have the right to be, that which made you—" He shook his head. "If you wish to delay the wedding, we shall. Now I leave you to your rest."

"That which made me what?" she called, halting his progress to the door.

He turned. "I know you are not all to blame for Clarice, that it also falls upon me."

"How?"

"Had I been honorable and responsible as one of greater years ought to be, had I respected you more and not yielded to kisses and caresses, you would not have become impatient to experience what comes after that which ought to be discovered in the marriage bed."

She sank back against the pillows. "You think you made me a whore." She sighed. "Rest easy, Lothaire. You had naught to do with Clarice's conception. Even had we never met, methinks it would have happened."

Because she had felt much for Michael D'Arci long before she was betrothed to Lothaire? He wanted to ask when she first realized she was in love with Lady Maude's stepson, but he said, "We shall never know. Sleep well, my lady."

Laura watched him go, and her heart ached more that only now with the distance between them stretching she should notice the state of his clothes and disarray of barely bound hair. He had probably smelled more musty than Clarice, but that had also escaped her though he had drawn even nearer.

When the door closed, she let the tears fall. Never had she considered he would claim responsibility for their broken betrothal, for it was true he had naught to do with it. Though as children Simon and she had played at husband and wife, once she left the girl behind she had not regarded Lady Maude's son as anything more than a friend and brother and discouraged him accordingly. Even had she been betrothed to one other than Lothaire and not loved her intended, she would have resisted Simon's claim on her. And very likely still he would have done as he had done.

She lifted a hand to wipe at her eyes, paused over the bandages that could grant respite from Lothaire's desire. Only respite. Best to have done with their nuptial night and see what could be made of it.

"Four days," she said. "Even if I must wear gloves."

Lady Laura was miserable, and more so than expected. Unfortunately, this was not her wedding day. That had been the plan before all went askew. But providing she did not suspect the source of her affliction, all would come right. This day's misery could double. Or worse.

Those imaginings might have caused the one who turned them over to smile despite the certainty the Lord saw all that went below—including here in this dark crack of existence—but deeper reflection proved them mere indulgence.

Were the lady's wedding day to be spoiled, another means must be found. But between now and then, evidence of this day's trickery must be swept asunder. No easy feat, but neither a great challenge. Timing was all, and there were yet days in which to see it done.

Lothaire would not like it, but he would not know. Father Atticus would not like it, but neither would he know. The Lord would not like it, but he would forgive. As for this conscience that had no cause to be troubled, it would untrouble itself.

The brazier having lost much of its heat—further evidence of little regard for one who had more in common with Lady Laura's daughter than was known—the one made to feel of no consequence drew the covers over chest, neck, and face. And ere sleep deepened the dark crack, determined how best to be shed of evidence that could demand investigation. Now only one thing was needed—opportunity.

22

Only one day more. And on this, the eve of their wedding, Lothaire made of it the same as he had every day past—riding out early to do the work of wool.

Watching him and a handful of men-at-arms grow distant, Laura did not yield to resentment. Too much she admired the man with whom she would spend the remainder of her life. Though many a nobleman would seek to improve his circumstances by tourneying or selling his sword arm to the highest bidder, she suspected few would debase their nobility by laboring alongside commoners. As seen nearly every eve Lothaire returned to the castle disheveled and damp from his attempt to wash away the filth, and as told by Clarice who had accompanied him several times, he did not merely oversee the work. He cast himself into it.

When the sun made to mount the sky in earnest—gripping its pommel, fitting its stirrup, swinging itself atop the horizon—Lothaire and his men went from sight, the only evidence of the path they had taken the disturbance of the morning mist and slow descent of dust kicked up by hooves.

Lingering atop the gatehouse she had ascended unbeknownst to her betrothed, Laura felt the regard of the garrison and castle folk beginning their day's work in the smithy, stables, and laundry. They were curious, and doubtless more so knowing though she was their lord's first betrothed, only now she was to be his wife. She nearly cringed, certain the reason their betrothal had taken ten years to come to fruition was also known. Not that Lothaire would have revealed it, but others would have since Clarice's birth had not been hidden. And certainly Lady Raisa would not wish it believed her son was at fault.

It would not be easy for Laura to earn the respect of these people, but she would—and in doing so honor her husband.

Breathing the scent and warmth of the new summer day, she looked to her hands. They were not entirely healed, but on the morrow it would not be necessary to don gloves. Only if one looked near upon them would they find proof of the discomfort borne these past days, which would have been less tolerable lacking the physician's salve. At least in that Martin was competent. And Laura was further grateful for his near absence, whether of his own will he avoided her or Lothaire had warned him away.

Regardless, there was much to do in preparation for the morrow's wedding and feast. And Clarice, who had made an effort to hide her disappointment over assisting her mother rather than riding out with Lothaire, would learn more duties of a lady.

Minutes later, Laura thanked the porter by name and stepped into the hall in advance of its emptying with the physician's departure by way of the stairs.

"Come see what we have done, Mother!"

Not empty after all, Laura corrected as she followed her daughter's voice to the left corner opposite the high table where the girl stood with two others around one of four many-branched candlesticks. The smithy had returned them to the hall on the day past, having straightened out their bends and mended their breaks. They were elegant again, and more so fit with tallow candles as tall as Laura's forearm and so white they appeared lit in the absence of flame.

"Lovely," she said when she stood with the others peering upward. "The feast shall be all the more special. I thank you, Clarice and Tina— and you, Sir Angus, not only for arranging the repairs, but your height which I am certain is responsible for seeing the candles properly fit."

He dipped his head. "I am glad to be of service, my lady."

"As am I," a voice called, and they looked around at Sebille who moved toward them from the dais.

Doubtless, she had been breaking her fast at the high table, rendered mostly invisible garbed as she was in a gown of nondescript color and by how quiet and still she could be.

The lady halted before Laura, looked to the knight. "Shall we fit the rest of the candles, Sir Angus?"

His smile was taut. "I thank you, but as you see, Lady Clarice and the superb Tina have all in hand." He nodded at the two who held baskets of candles, winked at the latter.

Even had Laura not seen the hurt flash across the lady's face, she would have felt it. "I could use your help, Lady Sebille," she said. "I must finalize the menu with Cook and would be grateful for your..." She trailed off as Lothaire's sister turned on a toe.

"Is she angry?" Clarice asked when Sebille disappeared up the stairs.

"No more than usual," Angus muttered and grimaced when Laura shot her gaze to his.

"She is not friendly," Clarice said. "Nor the physician. Do you not think it too, Tina?"

"Methinks it best I keep my opinion to meself whilst we set the rest of these candles." The maid bustled toward the candlestick to the right of the high table, and Clarice ran to catch up with her.

"I know," Sir Angus said. "I should not have winked at your maid."

Laura sighed. "I think not."

"Fire!" Sebille's cry spun Laura around and caused Sir Angus to lunge toward the stairs.

"Stay with Tina, Clarice!" Laura called as she followed the knight.

Before she reached the stairs she smelled smoke, halfway up she saw its haze, and upon reaching the landing she glimpsed Sir Angus darting into the chamber Laura shared with Clarice and Tina.

"Out, Sebille!" he shouted.

A moment later, the lady exited with the force of one flung. She slapped hands to the wall opposite the door from which smoke puffed, pushed off, and stumbled down the corridor.

"Do not go in," she rasped and caught hold of Laura's arm.

"Sir Angus——"

"'Tis mostly smoke, Lady Laura. Methinks something was set too near the brazier."

"I have put it out!" the knight called and gave a hacking cough.

Laura ceased resisting Sebille's effort to hold her back, and as she waited for the knight to emerge, wondered what had caught fire. There was a chair near the brazier, but not too near, and Tina swept the rushes well back from the source of heat lest a spark set all afire. So what had fallen victim to coals that had little to recommend them after holding back the night's chill?

Shortly, Sir Angus appeared amid the smoke. "Come away," he said and gripped the women's arms. "I used the basin of water to douse the offender and threw open the shutters, but it will be some time ere the chamber is fit to enter."

"My wedding gown is in there," Laura said as he drew them down the corridor.

"If 'twas the same placed near the brazier, my lady, it is too late." He coughed, cleared his throat. "That is what I doused. I am sorry, but it is ruined."

Laura gasped. How was it the gown fashioned of Eleanor's generosity and Tina's hard work was lost? "'Twas draped over the chair's back," she protested as he assisted them down the stairs up which servants bounded. "How could it catch fire?"

"The chair was toppled, my lady." He paused to instruct the servants in remedying the damage, and when he and the ladies resumed their descent said, "'Tis possible a dog overturned it, mayhap the one with whom your daughter likes to keep company."

Had it been Tomas? He was so large and smelled so foul Laura discouraged Clarice from allowing the animal in their chamber. Had the beast ventured abovestairs in search of the girl? That made little sense as Clarice had been in the hall where Tomas dwelt when he was not out of doors.

"Mayhap it was…" Sebille's suggestion died amidst a cough so terrible the knight halted on the stairs to allow her to bend and clear her lungs.

When she straightened, tears streamed her cheeks.

"What do you think it was, my lady?" Laura asked.

Sebille averted her gaze. "Silly me. I thought it might be the wind come through the windows, but Sir Angus told he opened the shutters to let out the smoke."

Absurd, even had the shutters been wide open on a morn cooled by a breeze of so little force one had to close their eyes to confirm its presence. Nay, Sebille had nearly said something else, perhaps of detriment, though not to herself. To her mother who was not as bedridden as she wished Lothaire to believe and who was opposed to her son wedding a harlot? Had Lady Raisa once more descended to the second floor? Tipped the chair into the brazier? Made ruin of a wedding gown befitting a relation of the queen but not a licentious bride?

Laura was barely aware of stepping into the hall until her daughter and Tina rushed upon her.

"What happened, Mother?"

For the first time since Laura had seen Lothaire away, her gaze fell upon the scraggly Tomas who loped alongside Clarice. Was he only recently returned to the hall? She hoped the accident could be blamed on him, for how else could it be unintentional?

"An accident," she said as Lothaire's knight moved past and summoned more servants. "My gown was too near the brazier in our chamber. It caught fire."

Tina gasped. "How, my lady? The chair was—"

"'Tis most fortunate Lady Sebille went abovestairs when she did," Laura talked over her and received a knowing look from the maid. "And Sir Angus so quickly put it out."

"A fine man he is," Tina said.

Sebille stiffened, snapped, "That is not for a servant to say."

Tina cast her gaze down. "Forgive me, my lady. I forget meself."

"Certes, you do." Lothaire's sister glanced at the knight who had paused in directing the servants in what was required of them to set Laura's chamber aright. "I must ensure the Lady of Lexeter is unaffected," she said and turned back to the stairs.

Laura squeezed Tina's arm. "You did naught wrong. She is simply prickly."

"I like her even less," Clarice declared. "Mayhap not at all."

Laura sighed. "Methinks her life has been difficult."

"Once more you sound like Lady Maude, Mother. Why does a difficult life grant one permission to make the lives of others difficult?"

Laura was first struck by the obvious—that in such a way Lady Maude had likely excused the minimal presence of Clarice's mother by telling her life had been difficult. Next, she was struck by how wise the girl's reasoning.

"You are correct, Clarice. No matter our circumstances, we have no right to wield them as weapons that reduce others to our state of sorrow."

Clarice's brow smoothed, and she shrugged. "What will you wear for your wedding?"

"I have many a gown. I am sure one will suit just as well."

Nay, better, she silently amended. She would have been uncomfortable so splendidly garbed that she looked like royalty. Too, Lothaire preferred her in simpler gowns as she also preferred. And then there were the rest of the pearls and beads she would have had to pick free.

"I had near given up hope of seeing you ere the wedding," the priest said as Lothaire swung out of the saddle.

"I pray you will forgive me for not coming sooner." Lothaire looped the reins over the top rail of the fence enclosing the churchyard.

"Ever the work of wool," Father Atticus said.

"Until Lexeter is restored." Lothaire adjusted his sword belt as he followed the priest toward the church. "I will not enter," he said, knowing the man would insist and, as usual, lose the argument. Though Father Atticus was adamant the Lord was not offended to receive within His house one who evidenced hard, honest labor, Lothaire could not cross the threshold even though he had washed in the stream before leaving the bulk of the day's shearing to the workers.

"Then let us sit on the bench." The priest gestured to the left of the church doors.

"That was easier than usual," Lothaire said.

The man chuckled. "Two boys are on their faces before the altar repenting for stealing every last berry from widow Magda's bushes. I would not have the rascals listen in on us."

Lothaire lowered to the bench beside the priest and could not contain his sigh over how good it felt to be still, something he was usually too fatigued to savor when he dropped into bed.

The all-knowing Atticus left him to it until Lothaire's own impatience made him lift his head. "Let us be done with it, Father."

"So you may sooner work through the remainder of daylight?"

"It shall sound prideful, but I am amongst my best workers."

The gently aging man snorted. "Were you not of the nobility, methinks we would have to pray hard for your soul."

Lothaire glanced down his worn, stained tunic and chausses. "My mother would argue that because I am of the nobility we ought to pray hard for my soul."

"So she would. And be wrong, bless her." He did not like Lady Raisa any more than she liked him, but any word he spoke against her was ever with apology and oft followed by a blessing as if to absolve her of wrongdoing. Setting his forearms on his thighs, he clasped his hands. "Lady Laura Middleton."

Lothaire inclined his head. "Twice my betrothed."

"You must know I am remembering the day you spurred past my church as if the devil had hold of your hair, then reined around so violently you were nearly unseated."

"I do know." In this moment, it seemed almost the day past he had cursed and shouted and cried every league between Owen and Lexeter. Until Laura's betrayal, he had thought it fanciful that the thing beating in his chest could break over love lost, but so much pain had radiated from it that all he could think was he must get to High Castle and give himself into the physician's care. But as he urged his horse past Thistle Cross, he had glimpsed Father Atticus.

"You are no longer that young man, Lothaire, and I am proud of who and what you have become. Sometimes you act out of anger and speak words you ought not, but mostly you recognize your errors soon enough that you hardly need my counsel."

Lothaire raised an eyebrow. "I shall always need your counsel. If you are considering leaving Lexeter, pray think again."

The priest tapped the younger man's knee, jutted his chin toward the churchyard. "I shall be buried there, though not for many years yet, God willing."

"I am glad to hear it. Now forgive me, but the sun does not rise any higher and I—"

"Wool," the man drawled. "Very well, I will get to the bone of the matter. Can you forgive Lady Laura her indiscretion? If not, how can I help you make a better marriage than that of your parents?"

Lothaire linked his hands between his knees. "I want to forgive her, and I think I could, but that requires trust. And I cannot give it as long as the one with whom she betrayed me stands between us."

"You speak of her daughter."

"I do and do not. Though when I look upon Clarice she moves my mind to the man who fathered her, more I see her mother. It makes me want my Laura back, for her to long for me as she did ere she longed for another. And still longs for another."

"Still?"

"She denies it, but..." Lothaire shook his head. "It matters not if I reveal what I saw at Castle Soaring. She had the chance to explain it and did not."

"But it does matter, my son, especially if you are wrong about what you saw, which will only raise the wall higher between you."

Lothaire looked to his hands. Should he demand an explanation of what he had witnessed? "Her lies will only anger me."

"*If* she lies. She cannot defend herself or ask for forgiveness unless you show the sword behind your back."

Lothaire pushed a hand through his hair, loosing a hank from the thong—the same Durand Marshal had shortened a year past whilst proving his superior sword skill. "I know you are right, but regardless of whether she longs for her lover, better I could trust her if she told me of her own will."

"If *she* trusted *you.*"

"I am the betrayed, Father."

"Lothaire, do you recall what I said the day you were so broken you vowed not to love again?"

He did, the priest's understanding and discretion having prevented Lothaire from being overwhelmed by shame for the tears he shed and the cracking of a voice he had thought himself long past. "You said I would find earthly love again if I aspired to love the Lord and His ways first and above all."

"Do you?"

Lothaire drew a deep breath. "I do, then I run afoul as I did with Lady Beata. In that the Lord was not first. He appeared only in the vows we spoke that we should not have."

"You found your way back."

"I should not have had to find my way back."

"You think yourself more godly than me, Lothaire Soames?"

"Of course not!"

Father Atticus chuckled. "Could I wager, I would bet a goodly sum when I was the years you are now that a week did not pass I had not to find my way back to the Lord."

Lothaire did not know the man's age, and he claimed not to know himself, but he would not be surprised if much of the priest's struggle was a result of clashes with Lady Raisa.

"Blessedly, the Lord provides a map." Father Atticus tapped his chest. "But—oh!—the times I have tried to excuse my behavior by making as if I misplaced it. If you use your heart and think, speak, and act first out of love for Him, your marriage may prove one that seems of too short duration. Thus, when one of you loses the other, the pain will be bearable knowing your destination is the same, your own journey but delayed."

Lothaire thought that too much to hope for, but he did not gainsay this man who had filled the hole left by the disappearance of Ricard Soames whilst schooling the boy in his faith—until Lady Raisa and the priest clashed one too many times.

"As ever, I am owing to you, Father. I thank you for your wisdom."

A pat to the hand. "Either give your lady the chance to defend herself or let the past go and accept her as she is and will become. 'Tis the only way to move forward."

Thinking his audience with the priest was at an end, Lothaire started to stand, but Father Atticus said, "You shall see your mother situated upon her dower property?"

"As soon as she is well enough to make the journey."

"Her health continues to deteriorate?"

"Aye. She accepts my marriage is necessary, but I think it has been hard on her heart. Though I keep her isolated from Lady Laura and her daughter, she has rarely arisen from bed since my betrothed's arrival—as you know, not even to attend her husband's service and burial."

"She has not forgiven him."

Lothaire shook his head. "And never will, methinks. But I believe she would have been at the service had she been able to arise."

"Her end may be near, my son. At long last, peace for a hurting and angry soul if she will but seek the Lord. I pray when the time is nigh, she will summon a priest."

"Would you come, Father?"

"If she asked for me." He sighed. "What of your sister? She remains determined to accompany your mother and the physician to the dower property?"

"Aye. Though I shall regret Martin's departure only for the need to buy the services of another physician, Sebille..." Lothaire drew breath. "Even if my mother's days are reaching their close, already my sister has given too much of herself. It may be too late for Sir Angus and her, but I would see her remain at High Castle and be cared for as ever she has cared for our mother."

"I understand your feelings, my lord. 'Tis unfortunate she will not be dissuaded from being at your mother's side when she passes."

"Aye. As ill as Lady Raisa is, she could linger a long while. It might be years ere Sebille returns home, and more damaged she may be."

After a long silence, the priest said, "It may be best she not return to High Castle."

Lothaire sat straighter. "What say you?"

"Methinks Lady Sebille will more likely gain her deserved peace and rest within the walls of a convent, whether you are able to persuade her not to accompany Lady Raisa to her dower property or after your mother passes. Of course, such will cost a goodly sum."

"I would pay it if 'tis what she wishes, but I would not refuse her if she prefers to live at High Castle."

"I am not saying to refuse her, but if she is not amenable to entering a convent, you must be prepared to persuade her it is of greater benefit."

"I do not know it would be. High Castle is her home."

"Aye, and there is the man whose affections she has lost, and there is the woman who has taken her mother's place, and God willing there will be the children you make with Lady Laura, reminding her of those she will never make with one she loves."

There was sense in what he said, but little heart. Lothaire raised a hand. "I will not reject Sebille who has greatly lightened my burden by giving herself to our mother's care."

Father Atticus inclined his head. "At least offer the convent as a sanctuary when the time comes. I know you do not see it now, but the family you make with your wife is of greater import, just as you will profess before God on the morrow."

Lothaire did not like being irritated with the priest, but he was, and it surely showed, for the man said, "I pray you will forgive me for speaking thus, but know I do it out of love for you and your sister and concern for your marriage that has enough to overcome without adding to the strife."

"I thank you for your counsel, Father." Lothaire stood. "Now I must see how many sheep I can shear ere nightfall."

The priest rose with a creak of bones that better revealed his age than his face and body. "Ought I remind you 'tis the eve of your wedding?"

Lothaire smiled. "As you have now done so, I will defend myself by saying my betrothed has enough to do in ordering the household without finding me underfoot. Better I increase Lexeter's revenues."

"She might disagree."

Lothaire started to wave away his concern, hesitated. "I know you exchanged few words with the lady the day of my father's burial, but how did you find her?"

"What I saw and heard I liked—and her daughter. If you allow none to come between you, I think she will make a very good wife."

"That is more in her hands than mine." Lothaire bent and kissed the priest's cheek. "'Til the morrow, Father."

"You are a good son, brother, and lord," Father Atticus called as Lothaire strode opposite. "You will be a good husband and father."

Lothaire freed his horse's reins and swung into the saddle. "That is as I intend." He turned his mount in the direction of the shearing. Since soon there would be fewer excuses to distance himself from Laura, he hoped the priest was right about their marriage. But as for sending Sebille to a convent...

Father Atticus was mistaken.

23

"I KNOW NOT why you concern yourself over my regard for other women."

"You know not?"

The shrill rejoinder stayed Lothaire's hand on the garden gate. Though he had no wish to listen in on Angus and Sebille, his destination the kitchen's rear entrance, he was held there by Father Atticus's belief Lothaire's sister should enter a convent.

"'Tis worry for your soul, Angus!"

Curt laughter. "Methinks it is more that you, who did not want me, would have no other want me."

"I did want you."

"Only enough to play—and continue to play—the jealous girl."

"I am not a girl."

"Then behave a woman. Cease snatching up the jagged ties you yourself severed and wrapping them around the necks of servants upon whom I smile."

"You do more than smile upon them! And now I wonder how long ere you do more than smile upon your lord's betrothed."

Lothaire nearly flung open the gate, but the ensuing silence kept him from revealing his presence.

"Oh, Sebille," Angus said with such sorrow Lothaire felt his ache. "You do ill by me, more by Lady Laura. Even were I not unsparingly loyal to my lord and did I not love him well enough not to desire what belongs to him, the lady would not want me. I have seen how she gazes upon your brother, how she goes so still 'tis as if breath is but an afterthought. Regardless of her mistake, I do not believe she ever stopped loving him."

Lothaire closed his eyes, wished it were so.

And it seemed neither did Sebille believe it. She laughed, said, "She lay down for another, Angus. *That* is not love."

The knight sighed. "Neither is this, Sebille. What was between us is gone, and though I have said it before, I have never been more certain. My only regret over your departure from High Castle is how much more it will make of you a martyr."

More silence, then footsteps across the stone-laid path, the slam of the kitchen door, the groan of the wooden bench that told the knight had dropped onto it.

Lothaire started to turn away, but Angus called, "How much did you hear, my lord?"

The knight's senses were honed, perhaps still better than Lothaire's after Everard Wulfrith's training in a darkened cellar.

He opened the gate and moments later stood before Angus. "More than I ought to have, and I am sorry for it. But I am grateful for the insight." And it was true, not only for an eyeful of his sister that gave credence to Father Atticus's belief the convent could be a better fit, but the possibility some of what Angus believed of Laura's feelings for Lothaire was true.

Are you being a fool again? demanded the dissenter.

"You have heard of the morn's great event?" Angus asked, and Lothaire knew the man did not wish to further discuss Sebille.

"Great event?" He shook his head. "As I wished to return to High Castle ere sunset, I did not bathe away my filth and came by way of the garden to gain heated water from Cook so I might be as presentable as possible ere entering the hall."

"There was a fire, my lord."

Lothaire jerked. "Kitchen fire?"

"Nay."

"Then of what do you speak? Is Lady——?"

"Your lady is well. Her wedding gown is not."

The tale was quickly told, there being little to it, but as for the cause...

There could be much to that, though Lothaire prayed not—hoped the toppled chair was of the dog's doing. Hoped his mother was too infirm to destroy the wedding gown of her unwanted daughter-in-law. Regardless, the possibility Lady Raisa's hand was in this further confirmed Queen Eleanor was right to require her removal from High Castle.

"Laura?"

She sprang off the chair, turned to find Lothaire approaching from the direction of the kitchen. "You are back early."

"It is the eve of our wedding." He halted before her. His face and hands were clean. Or mostly. As usual, stubborn darkness edged his nails. As for his clothes, they were fouled with dirt, what appeared to be oil, and a multitude of white hairs that evidenced shorn sheep.

"You look lovely," he said.

Laura felt a pang of guilt over being far more presentable than the Baron of Lexeter. "I thank you, my lord."

"Sir Angus informed me of what happened this morn. I am sorry for the loss of your gown, and that I shall not see you in finery fit for a queen."

"Ah, but you prefer me in simpler garments."

"I do, but it is a loss, and the queen shall be displeased."

"Were she told of it. I see no reason to inform her."

His smile was slight. "I am grateful. When she receives your missive, she will be ill enough with me over the delay in moving my mother to her dower property."

Once more gripped with fear Lady Raisa was responsible for the fire, Laura said, "I have not yet sent that missive, it being my hope once you and I speak vows you will see her safely removed."

Something like understanding flashed in Lothaire's eyes, and she wondered if it also occurred to him the toppled chair was no accident.

"I assure you, Lady Raisa shall depart High Castle as soon as possible."

"How soon?" she asked with more urgency than intended.

"If the physician feels she is strong enough to make the journey, within a sennight of our wedding."

"And if he deems she is not strong enough?"

She felt his struggle and hated that she sounded as if she had no care for his mother's well-being, but the fear that had subsided these past weeks following the woman's attack had returned. And was more pressing. A bruise was one thing, a potentially fatal fire quite another.

"I will see it done, Laura," he said as if that was assurance enough, then cupped her elbow. "Sir Angus tells the chamber has been thoroughly cleaned. Show me."

Eschewing argument, she allowed him to guide her up the stairs.

"Nay," Lothaire said the moment they stepped into the chamber. "It may be clean, but it yet smells of smoke."

The scent did irritate, making her sniff. "There is more of a breeze than earlier." She nodded at the open windows. "When I seek my bed this eve, the smell should be much resolved."

"Not enough. You, Clarice, and Tina shall sleep in the solar."

She blinked. "What of you?"

"Sir Angus will make room for me in his chamber."

Her heart swelled. "That is thoughtful."

Lips curving wryly, he said, "I can be on occasion."

Laura knew she should not do it, and she could have suppressed the impulse the young Laura would not have, but she stepped in front of him, reached her body up his, and offered her mouth.

Though his pupils spread wide as he considered her lips and his head started to lower, he took a step back.

"Lothaire?"

"If you are truly uncomfortable being desired, my lady, you ought not do that—and certainly not in a chamber defined by the presence of a bed."

She loathed herself for not suppressing the impulse. Now he either believed she had lied or had so little control she was more the harlot than thought. "You are right. It will not happen again."

"But I hope it shall, my lady, when the wedding ring on your hand grants me permission to lie down with you and kiss you on your mouth and neck. And other places."

Even if that was all she wanted from him, that would not be all he did to her, she thought. Lest she begin to tremble, she stepped past and said over her shoulder. "I thank you for the use of the solar."

She could not sleep. Not here. Not in his bed. Not knowing what would happen there on the morrow. She wanted Lothaire's kisses, but what came after...

How was she to bear it? For bear it she must to conceive an heir. And if it pained and repulsed her as much as she feared, how was she to conceal her feelings? She had only the one experience, and it had turned more violent when her response was as far from passion as pain was from enjoyment.

She gripped the windowsill, leaned into the embrasure, dropped her chin. Lothaire would not do that to her, but that did not mean he would not be as offended by her response.

If only she had found the words to prepare him for the woman soon come to him. Now it was too near consummation of their vows to lessen the possibility of making ruin of their nuptial night. She had thought he would ask her to elaborate on Simon's death, and then she would chance revelation, but he seemed to have forgotten it.

Aye, too late now. As told Michael, perhaps once she proved a good wife...

Lifting her face, she wished a cool wind upon it. But unlike the night past, these hours of dark were still and nearly warm, almost suffocating.

Or mayhap it is merely me, she thought and slowly drew a breath so she might feel all of it. Then she turned and peered into the solar's moonlit expanse.

This room that served not only as the lord's chamber but a place to conduct business in private was larger than expected and well furnished, though not excessively. The postered bed where Clarice slept was impressive. The rug upon which Tina's pallet was laid—and from which a soft snore sounded—was in good repair. The large table and matching chairs at which Lothaire might meet other nobles or work his journals were of oak. The chairs before the fireplace were worn but sturdy. Two iron-banded trunks that must contain Lothaire's personal effects were stacked against the wall alongside the garderobe. But best of all—because she loved water and had not expected such at High Castle—was a large tub.

As when first she entered the solar, she was drawn to it, and once more she ran her fingers over its bulbous wooden rim and smooth, dry inner wall that evidenced Lothaire had not made use of it for some time.

She longed for a bath—the wonderful weightlessness and liquid heat, rivulets of perspiration coursing her face, sinking beneath the surface and peering up at the ceiling through water and gently waving hair.

Had she not postponed entering the solar until it was time to sleep, she would have had Tina arrange for water to be heated and carried abovestairs. Perhaps then she would have been able to sleep—or at least rest.

Laura pulled her shawl more closely around her, looked to the mattress she had lain upon until certain her daughter and Tina slept. It was where she ought to be found in the morn, but though exceedingly tired, she would not be able to find her rest there. Best she try the chair whose discomfort would ensure any sleep gained was not so deep she was unable to slip back into bed ere Clarice and Tina awakened.

The chair proving fairly comfortable, Laura's wakefulness was short-lived. Throughout the night, she awoke often, and returned to bed only when darkness receded in advance of the dawn. None would ever know her first full night in Lothaire's bed was yet to come.

24

"Praise the Lord ye finally ceased your haunting and gained some sleep last eve, even be it in a chair."

Laura swept her gaze to the upper portion of the mirror in which Tina's reflection hovered above her own. "Did I much disturb your sleep?"

"Indeed. I kept driftin' off, but for what—an hour? two?—ye stood at the window, wandered the chamber, petted the tub."

Laura sighed. "Forgive me. Had I known, I would have tried the chair sooner."

"I wish ye had, though not for me. For ye." She leaned around, looked close upon her lady's face. "We shall have to pinch yer cheeks to put color in them ere ye meet Lord Soames at the church door, else he might think ye afeared of him."

On this day she was...

"And a bit of powder ought to cover the dark 'neath your eyes."

Tina was right. If one looked beyond beautifully curled and braided hair, they might think Lothaire's bride ill. Laura nodded. "Aye, powder and pinches."

"As for the tub"—the woman jerked her head toward it—"on the morn after yer wedding night we shall put it to good use, even if I must needs lug every blessed pail meself."

Laura turned on the stool and threw her arms around Tina. "How I love thee!"

Surprise stiffened the maid, then she went all soft and tucked her lady nearer. "Oh milady, how I love thee." They held each other until Tina sighed and ended the embrace. "Now then..." She reached for the powder. "...Baron Soames will be wantin' his bride."

An hour later, the garlanded wagon carrying Laura, her daughter, and maid halted before the church at Thistle Cross, outside which were gathered far more of Lexeter's people than expected. It would have been an impressive number were Laura of a mind to be impressed, but she was too anxious and became more so when she saw Lothaire before the steps alongside Father Atticus.

"Mayhap my new father *is* as handsome as Baron Marshal," Clarice whispered. "Does he not look fine, Mother?"

As nearly she had once imagined he would look on their wedding day. The blond of his hair was darker, and though he was only slightly taller, he was considerably more muscular than the young man who had courted her. As for the garments his squire had collected from the solar this morn, they were the fine ones he had worn at court and tall boots once more gripped his calves.

It seemed silly to think him the most handsome of men, but weathered though she knew he was up close, he was that to her. "He looks most fine," she said and, when Sir Angus came alongside the wagon, accepted his offer to lift her down.

While he next assisted Clarice and Tina, Laura smoothed the skirt of her dark red gown and adjusted the gold cape pinned to her shoulders with small brooches. Then Sir Angus took her arm and led her toward the church that was flanked by Lexeter's people.

To her surprise, Sebille was present. To her relief, Lady Raisa and the physician were not.

Laura withheld her gaze from Lothaire until she halted before him. She did not care—not overly much—that his smile was more for the benefit of their audience. It seemed genuine and comforted.

"Your lady," Sir Angus said and removed his hand from Laura and stepped back.

Taking hold of her arm, Lothaire leaned down. "Are you well?"

Wondering if she ought to have allowed Tina to apply another layer of powder, wishing she had not forgotten to pinch her cheeks, Laura whispered, "I am. I but had difficulty finding my rest last eve."

His smile curved a bit more. "This night you shall sleep in my arms."

In the next instant, the troubling of Lothaire's brow evidenced she had gone paler. But he said naught and turned her toward Father Atticus.

The man nodded at the bride and groom, and she glimpsed concern in his eyes before he began to question them in a loud clear voice.

He asked them to confirm they were not too closely related to prevent them from wedding. They said they were not. Did their parents consent to their union? Though Laura could not know and Lothaire certainly did, they said they were unaware of any objection. Had the banns been read the proscribed three Sundays? Well the priest knew it was so, but they confirmed it for all present. Lastly, they were asked if they entered into marriage of their own will. Lothaire said he did, and though he did so without hesitation, he surely felt the queen's breath on his neck. As Laura agreed she freely gave herself, she wished for the joy and anticipation of the nuptial night to come as imagined ten years past.

That done, silence followed where the bride's dowry ought to be cited. Though the people would be curious, they would have to remain so, even if they wrongly concluded Laura brought to the marriage only the promise of an heir. As directed, the king and queen's tax break was to be held close.

Father Atticus looked to Lothaire, inclined his head.

A jangle drawing Laura's regard to that which her groom unfastened from his belt, she extended her left hand. He set the pouch in her palm, the coins of which would be distributed to the poor, the symbolism of which was the new Lady of Lexeter might act on behalf of her husband in matters of finance.

Once Laura fastened it on her girdle, the priest said, "And now to plight your troth."

Lothaire took Laura's right hand and turned to fully face her.

She peeked up at him from beneath her lashes, and receiving a smile, tilted her face up.

"I, Lothaire Soames, Baron of Lexeter," he said loud for all to hear, "take thee, Laura Middleton, to be my wedded wife, to have and to hold from this day forward, for fairer for fouler, for richer for poorer, in sickness and in health, 'til death us depart, if Holy Church will it ordain. And thereto I plight thee my troth." Then in a voice for her alone, he added, "At long last."

Tears disturbing her vision, she realized her hand was trembling when he gently squeezed it.

Her vows were identical to his but for the insertion of one that made all the difference. "...to be meek and obedient in bed and at table," she pushed past her lips, "'til death us depart, if Holy Church it will ordain. And thereto I plight thee my troth." Then for him alone, she also added, "At long last."

Did his eyes brighten, or was it only the sun in them?

Next, Father Atticus blessed the ring and passed it to Lothaire. As the groom briefly slid it on each finger of her left hand ahead of the finger it would adorn to her end days, he said, "In the name of the Father... in the name of the Son...in the name of the Holy Ghost...with this ring I thee wed."

The warmed band settled at the base of her finger, then that portion of the ceremony concluded, Lothaire turned Laura toward those gathered to witness the marriage and she removed the pouch from her girdle.

Those in greatest need came forward—the aged, the orphaned, those afflicted with defects of birth, illness, and injuries—and into each palm she pressed a coin. When the pouch was empty, the church doors were opened and Lothaire led his bride inside.

Side by side they knelt at the altar, and when Sir Angus and Sebille stretched the pall over them, they bent their heads and the longest portion of the ceremony commenced. At the end of the mass, Father Atticus gave the groom the kiss of peace, which Lothaire passed to Laura—a chaste kiss, but the salty taste of him was still on her lips when she sat before him on his destrier and the wedding party started back toward High Castle for the feast.

And the nuptial night Laura was determined Lothaire would not find wanting.

The scent of roses. Far different from that of ale, wine, and the oaken casks in which those drinks were stored in a cellar.

The sight of red, cupped petals. Far different from that of earthen floor, barrels, sacks, and burdened shelves.

The sound of silence. Far different from that of creaking wood steps and scampering rats.

"Far different," Laura said.

"Different, my lady?"

Having forgotten she was not alone, she swung around to face the priest where he stood before the window awaiting Lothaire's arrival, after which he would see the married couple situated beneath the covers and pray the joining proved fertile, evidencing any promiscuity on the bride's part was forgiven.

That last made Laura glad she knew what to expect and it was not exclusive to her. Even had she wed ten years past whilst pure, such a blessing would have been spoken over the couple once they were abed. Still, the priest would have excluded the groom from forgiveness of sexual sin.

She smoothed her white chemise whose bodice was pleated around the neck, forced a smile, and was as surprised by her words as he seemed when she said, "Aye, ten years different."

He considered her long, nodded. "How different, may I ask?"

"From what I expected and wanted. But I would like to believe I am here now because God knows me better than my husband and makes a way for us to mend the past so there are yet blessings to be had from our marriage." She tapped her teeth against her lower lip. "Might I believe that? Or do you think...?"

"Tell me, my child."

"Is it too late?"

"For what?"

Her hands hurt, and when she looked down she saw how tightly she gripped them. "For Lothaire to love me even half as much as once he did?"

"You profess to love him, my lady?"

Though she might regret her honesty, she said, "I did. I do. Never did I cease. But if he cannot love me again, I shall pray my heart releases him as his has released mine."

He crossed to her side. "Nay, my lady, do not pray such. Far better to love without profit than love not and reap bitterness."

She stared.

"Better than any, Lady Raisa and her daughter taught me that." He patted her arm. "Love no matter the hurt, else any chance you have at being loved—regardless how small or seemingly hopeless—will be lost."

"I thank you, Father." She was grateful for his kindness though he could offer no assurance of substance Lothaire might love her again. Thus, she was to love in the absence of love returned on the chance it would encourage her husband to feel something more enduring than desire.

She winced at allowing that last word to enter her thoughts, hoped Lothaire would not speak it this night lest she be overwhelmed by memories of her pleading with Simon. When she had declared she did not love or want him, he had childishly retorted he would not love her. He would simply desire her, thus requiring naught of her but that she lie still. But she had fought him, and he had subdued her with violence whose only benefit was bruises, scratches, and torn garments that allowed Lady Maude to see her son as the miscreant he had become during his knighthood training.

"Where is your groom?" Father Atticus returned her to the present. Hands clasped behind his back, he turned toward the door.

Laura glanced at the bed whose rose petals upon white linen was so lovely it was almost a pity only Tina who had scattered them, the priest, and the newlywed couple would look upon them.

Almost a pity. Such relief Laura had breathed when Lothaire announced his wife and he did not require an escort abovestairs. Much to the disappointment of many a reveler, they were denied the tradition of crowding the chamber with as many as could fit so they might witness the bride and groom being put to bed.

When Laura had looked questioningly at Lothaire, he had murmured, "For Clarice. And you."

Minutes later, the door opened and Lothaire entered. His feet were bare and body covered in a tunic that fell just below his knees to reveal muscular calves, but what made her stare was his dark blond hair around his shoulders. She was accustomed to it slipping free of its thong, but never had she seen it entirely loosed, not even when they were younger. And how it shone, as if his squire had persuaded him to remain seated long enough to comb it through many a time. It made her fingers long to feel it.

She was so captivated she did not realize he might be similarly affected by her appearance until he halted before her and she looked up. And saw there the young man who, done with watching the clouds pass, levered onto an elbow and blotted out the sky as he gazed upon her below him. Then kissed her.

She was certain he wanted to kiss her now. But it would have to wait until the priest withdrew.

"My lady wife," Lothaire said low.

"My lord husband."

Father Atticus cleared his throat. "Methinks it time the bride and groom were abed."

Wondering what she had revealed of herself, not only to Lothaire but this man of God who believed she had betrayed his lord with another man, Laura dropped her chin.

A hand cupped her elbow, but it was not her husband's.

"Come, Daughter." The priest guided her to the side of the bed farthest from the door, the same she had stretched upon last eve until Clarice and Tina slept.

As she lowered to the mattress amid rose petals and settled into the pillows stacked against the headboard, Lothaire did the same on the opposite side.

Father Atticus pulled the top sheet from where it had been folded at the foot of the bed, covering Laura up to her waist, then strode to the other side and covered her husband. "Let us pray."

Laura bowed her head. To her surprise and gratitude, the priest did not ask the Lord to remove from the bride any taint of promiscuity. And much too soon the blessing of the bed was done.

"My lady." Father Atticus dipped his head. "My lord." He turned, extinguished the candles save the two on the bedside tables, and exited.

Alarmed by how dim it was, though not so much she would be unable to see Lothaire clearly once she resolved to look at him, Laura held her gaze to the door. And nearly snatched her hand from beneath her husband's when he covered it.

"Laura?"

It sounded like a question, but surely not, for what had he to ask? In the eyes of God, Church, and all those present for the ceremony, she was his to do with as he pleased. And she was to be meek and obedient.

Only when he gently pried open her fingers did she become aware of having made a fist of them.

"Three weeks," he murmured as he slid his fingers between hers and settled their calloused pads against the heel off her palm. "They passed too slowly. But not for you, hmm?"

She looked sidelong at him, wished what must be done this night did not have to be done, that she could curl against his side and fall asleep with the beat of his heart in her ear.

"This is not as once I imagined," she said. "Not that I expected it to be."

He sighed. "Though it was not to have been this way, there is naught for it but to go forward."

She jerked her chin. "Then let us."

Keeping hold of her hand atop the sheet, he turned onto his side and set his face above hers.

She closed her eyes, but when he did not kiss her, she raised her lids. "What is it, Lothaire?"

"I like looking at you. Ever I have." He leaned closer, and his wine-warmed breath made her shudder, then he brushed his lower lip up hers. "Kiss me, Laura love."

She stopped breathing. Ten years. Ten lonely, aching years since he had called her that. Though it could not mean the same as it had then and never would in so great a measure, it gave hope there would be enough crumbs of love in the years to come that she might gain a piece of the whole.

She leaned up, set her lips on his, and holding tight to his one hand, slid her other hand around his neck.

"Laura," he rasped and pressed his mouth so hungrily to hers that what she had felt when they kissed in the chapel seemed but a shadow of this. Here in their bed, this exciting, dizzying, wondrous kiss was just the beginning. And she would not fear the end of it.

This was Lothaire. Her Lothaire. Forever and ever and—

His hand was sliding up her calf as it raised the hem of her chemise, stroking the back of her knee, splaying her inner thigh.

Too soon! She was not ready for this nor the weight of his chest upon hers. Though not so heavy she could not draw breath, still she could not breathe—would surely suffocate if she did not get him off her.

She pressed back into the pillows, cried, "Pray, cease!"

He stilled. "Laura?"

She opened her eyes, found *his*—not Simon's—face above her. She yet felt the prey, but there was little of the predator about him. Indeed, though his breath was fast and shallow and color high, it was not anger upon his brow. It seemed concern.

If only that were enough, for her to lie back and be the dutiful wife as she had vowed to be and needed to be for Clarice, Lothaire, and Laura Soames.

"I am sorry," she gasped. "'Tis just…"

The concern on his face drifted away, and as he raised himself and removed his hand from her thigh, anger moved in. "Do you think me still the boy who thought himself a man? That I cannot please you as well as your lover—or ought I say lovers?"

The first of his question broke the skin, the second cut to the bone, and the hurt of it found shelter in her own anger. "I have been with one man only, and he did not please me—was not even half the man you were ten years past."

Though Lothaire no longer touched her, he remained above her, supported by hands pressed to the mattress on either side. Thus, by swaying candlelight she saw the effect of her declaration—the easing of his jaw, the gathering of eyebrows that told she had thrown open doors to questions best saved for another time and place, and the narrowing of eyes that searched hers for answers.

Still, she was unprepared when he said, "Who was it?"

Oh tongue, she silently bemoaned, *what have you done?*

"Tell me and let us be done with it, Laura."

She set a hand on his jaw. "I will, but this night of all nights let us not speak of it. I did not mean you to stop. Truly I did not. I but wish you to go slow."

"I would know his name."

"On the morrow I will tell it."

He closed a hand over hers, drew it from his face, and pressed it to the mattress. "I will not make love to my wife whilst there is another man with us."

"There is no one here but us. I see only you."

She heard the grind of his teeth, then he growled, "Tell me."

The return of his anger relighting hers, she said, "Your bride is meek and obedient as called to be. Now do what you must and be done with it."

His face darkened further, then with a sound of disgust, he dropped onto his back.

And there they lay side by side until he said, "If I am so disagreeable you are reviled, you should have refused the queen."

She turned her face to his, saw his forearm was on his brow, eyes on the ceiling. Wishing she had been able to hide her fear, hating she gave him cause to believe he repulsed her, she said, "As told, Lothaire, I am glad it was you the queen chose, not..."

He turned his eyes upon her. "It is no compliment to be favored over a deviant, Laura. Do not try to make it one. All I wish to know is why, feeling toward me as you do, you spoke vows. And do not say you had to make a home for Clarice. You did not."

She sat up. "You know we could not remain at Owen after Donnie—"

"You could have made your home at Castle Soaring where Clarice was content."

Laura stared, understood.

"Aye," he said. "Lady Beatrix told me she and her husband offered their home to you."

She nodded. "They did, but I could not accept."

"Why?"

"I could no longer be a burden to others, and I wanted Clarice to have a home of her own so never would she be owing to any. As a wife, I could earn our place by keeping my husband's household and..."

"Suffering his attentions?"

"Nay!" She reached to him.

"Do not, Laura!"

She snatched her hand back.

"You wish to know what I am inclined to believe?" he said.

She was certain she would not like it, but it was not truly a question he asked.

"I think you could not accept the offer to live at Castle Soaring because, unbeknownst to Lady Beatrix, her husband is Clarice's father.

And if that is not deterrent enough, despite what you would have me believe of the man who made a child on you, perhaps you love him still."

Laura's belly churned so violently she feared she would be sick. She weathered silence beneath his regard, then said, "I do not understand why you think 'twas Michael. And again, I tell you it was not."

He sat up, turned to her. "The night at Castle Soaring, I was at my window when you and he returned from the outer bailey. I saw you go into his arms."

That was easily recalled, but not because of any passion between Michael and her. It had not been appropriate, but she had missed the brother he had been to her and been so grateful for his kindness that she acted on impulse. Here now proof of what had turned Lothaire cooler toward her and made him curt with Michael. She should have guessed they were seen and judgment passed on one believed to be free with her body.

"Certes, you were not averse to his touch as you are to mine," Lothaire pressed.

"I was not because I do not fear his touch."

"As you fear mine."

"Yours is…" She dropped her chin, moved her gaze over the rose petals between them. "You want…"

"I want to make love to my wife, just as he——"

"I tell you he did not! He is not Clarice's father and never has Lady Beatrix had anything to fear from me. Indeed, 'twas she who sent Michael to me that night when she thought me gone too long."

He considered her, said, "You deny you care for him?"

"I do not. I love him as a brother."

Finding hope in the uncertainty in Lothaire's eyes, she drew a calming breath. "I cannot fault you for thinking the worst, for that is my doing." *And Maude's,* she silently added. For love of the lady and gratitude for the home provided the woman's illegitimate grandchild, Laura had not revealed the sin of Clarice's conception was another's—or mostly. As long accepted, she had been a party to it.

She returned Lothaire to focus, glimpsed pain in his eyes. Though this should not be the time or place, she had made it so by not sooner telling him as Michael urged her to do.

"But you are right in believing Lady Beatrix's husband is more than a brother to me. He…" She dropped her chin, and he waited. At last as ready as she could be, she said, "Michael D'Arci is Clarice's uncle. That is why he cares so much. That is why I do not fear his touch."

Her words shot through Lothaire, flinging themselves here and there in search of a fit. When it found one, he rejected it more quickly than he had done years ago. But though he once more sent it on its way, it returned and fit the hole even better alongside the boy's slingshot, whatever had nearly struck Lothaire at the pond, and Laura calling out the name of Michael D'Arci's younger half brother.

Still, he said, "You would have me believe Simon and you…Him?"

"Him," she said softly.

A moment later, he was off the bed, his back to her. Simon did fit, but as if forced into the hole. What was he missing? What would knock off the resistant edges? Unlike with Michael, Laura had shown no affection for Simon.

"Lothaire?"

He swung around and found her standing before him.

"It was Simon," she said.

"You lay with that whelp—gave yourself to him? He of blond hair fathered Clarice, not he of dark hair like your daughter's?"

Her eyes lit with sparks rather than sparkles. "For the last time, I tell you 'twas not Michael."

"So you wish me to believe, and how convenient Simon is dead." Though in that moment he realized he had yet to discover the nature of that death, he thrust the curiosity aside. "He who cannot defend himself can easily bear his brother's sin so Lady Beatrix never learns the truth."

Laura's face went livid, and he steeled himself for her denial, but she brushed past him.

"Where are you going, Laura? It is our wedding night."

She halted, turned. "Then do the deed and make an heir on me that you may sooner seek better company elsewhere, just as your father did."

As he had allowed her to believe of him that day in the garden at Windsor Castle when she asked how many illegitimate children he had and he told he would leave it to her to discover once they wed.

"Do it," she prompted.

He shifted his jaw, but it remained so tight it ached. "Were I one to force my attentions on a woman, I could not. You, my lady wife, know well how to cool a man's ardor. Now be finished with your outrage and come to bed that all believe their lord and lady are pleased with each other."

"You are right. Appearance is everything." But it was not the bed to which she retreated. She dropped into a chair before the hearth.

Moments later, his stunned bride was in his arms. Halfway to the bed, she demanded he set her down and began to struggle.

Lest her protests grow loud enough to be heard beyond the solar, Lothaire bent his head and captured them in his mouth. She stiffened before she began to go soft, but there was no time to discover if she would return his kiss. And no need.

He lifted his head as he lowered her to the mattress. "Fear not, Laura. That was but to silence you for the sake of Clarice whom we would not wish to know the true state of her parents' marriage." He snapped the sheet over her, causing the rose petals to rise and scent the air before resettling on the bed where their marriage would not be consummated.

"I want to hate you," she said, tears in her voice as he snuffed her bedside candle.

He did not answer until the second candle was out and it was he who made the chair his bed. "Certes, that would be easier for us both," he said across the dim. "Mayhap in time."

She cried, so quietly he might not have known it were the bed's frame not in need of tightening, her sobs poured into the pillow causing it to creak. When silence fell, excepting the occasional hiccough that made his chest ache, he vehemently wished he did not feel for her any-thing near what he had felt ten years past. But he loved her still.

He dropped his head back, looked to the formless ceiling, ached that the promise of this day had been severed. Should he have rejected Father Atticus's counsel and not shown the sword behind his back?

Nay, better he know Laura's lies now than later so they might sooner go forward. Now they were told, they could put Michael D'Arci behind them, his name never again spoken. And perhaps eventually Lothaire would not see that man in Clarice.

25

It tempted, but she would deny herself until Lothaire departed the castle as surely he must though it was the day after their wedding.

"Not now," Laura said as Tina combed a snarl out of her lady's hair. "Mayhap an hour hence."

"'Tis done already," the maid said. "The water is set to boiling and we may see the first pails arrive ere I finish fixing your hair atop your head."

"But——"

"I promised a bath, milady, and so ye shall have one." Her hands in Laura's hair stilled, and she turned toward the open window from which no morning-after sheet was hung to prove the bride had come to her groom chaste——an impossibility in light of the girl who leaned in the embrasure taking in all manner of activity, the sounds of which included the clang of steel markedly different from the smithy's forging. Earlier than usual, the garrison practiced at swords.

"Lady Clarice," Tina called, "might ye hasten to the kitchen and ask Cook for rose oil to scent the bath water?"

Clarice, whose disappointment in her mother's failed attempt to appear joyous was obvious, sprang around. "I shall."

"Nay," Laura caused her daughter to falter. "Not roses. 'Tis already much upon the air."

Clarice's drooping smile picked itself up, proof she had thought she would not be permitted to leave. "Then?"

"Mint, if he has enough to spare."

The girl ran forward and kissed her mother's cheek. "I am happy for you. And me. I quite like the father you have given me."

Laura's throat constricted. "That makes me happy."

"And what of Lord…?" Clarice frowned. "May I call him Father now?"

"I believe he would like that." Hopefully it was so.

"And what of Father? He makes you happy too, does he not?"

Blessedly, Laura was prepared for the question. "He does. Queen Eleanor chose wisely."

Clarice gave a little laugh. "I shall thank her one day!"

Once Laura was alone with Tina, the maid said, "What is amiss, milady?"

"Naught."

"That ye would lie to your devoted servant!" Tina tugged at the crossings of the braid she had begun to work. "*Tsk,* milady."

"I am but tired."

"And another lie. Mind ye, were you tired for the right reason I could forgive, but I saw Baron Soames come belowstairs this morn to break his fast in the kitchen rather than abed with his bride." She drew the comb through the ends of the tresses, resumed crossing them. "Milord looked as thunderous as ye look miserable, milady. And of course the rose petals are hardly disturbed though they ought to be bruised amid sheets that know not their up from their down."

Laura needed no mirror to reveal how brightly she flushed over imaginings of what would have had to happen for this conversation not to be had.

"So in my thinking, and it may be wrong since never have I wed, yer nuptial night satisfied neither."

Laura sighed. "We argued."

"Ah, milady." The maid stepped to the side, and when Laura lifted her face said, "'Twill be a memorable night only for how much you do not wish it to be memorable. But..." Her smile was encouraging. "...ye have a great supply of nights with yer husband. Hopefully this eve ye will set all aright."

"Certes, we shall try," Laura said. Lothaire might wait a while on gaining an heir, but only a while. The next time, be it this night or a sennight hence, she would be meek and obedient and very quiet.

Hardly had Tina wound the braid around Laura's hair and secured it than the first pails of water arrived, along with mint delivered by one of the three serving women who passed it to Tina and withdrew with the others to refill their pails.

"'Twould seem Lady Clarice has found a distraction," Tina said as she shook green leaves into the tub. "But at least she saw the mint delivered."

"Do you think she has persuaded Baron Soames to allow her to attend another shearing?"

"Mercy, I pray not. Ye and yer husband may have argued last eve, but if only for the sake of appearance, he ought to stay yer side the day after the wedding. 'Twill earn his bride no good regard if he soon abandons her."

She was right, and for that Laura hoped he remained, though not in her immediate company.

"Now into the tub with ye."

Laura glanced at the door. What if Lothaire returned? The thought of him finding her unclothed—

"Very well," the maid said. "Come see what I found." She moved to the left of the tub the servants had placed before the hearth.

"See what?" Laura said and moments later saw.

Around the chamber walls were arched recesses in which candles were set, but one had an additional function. Tina lifted out the fat candle, tugged a small iron ring, and a small door swung inward.

Laura had heard of such means for a lord to keep watch on what went in his hall during his absence, but she had never seen such.

"Look, milady."

Laura leaned forward. The kitchen corridor was to the left, the hall entry doors straight ahead, the high table to the right. And occupying that great room were a score of knights and men-at-arms breaking their fast, served by a handful of servants performing the duties Laura had given them. Lothaire was nowhere among them, nor Clarice.

Forget appearance sake, Laura's husband and daughter had likely departed the castle to devote the day to the work of wool. But she would not be disappointed. She was to have a bath and could linger as long as she liked. And there came the women lugging more pails.

Laura was up to her hips in mint-scented water when the servants arrived. After Tina ensured the water had cooled sufficiently it would not burn her lady, the pails were emptied at Laura's feet, and the level rose to beneath her breasts whose weight she remained more familiar with than sight.

Two more trips, she guessed, and there would be enough water for her to slip beneath the surface if she wished. She did wish it, though her hair was clean, having been washed in a basin yestermorn ere the wedding, and effort having been expended to secure it atop her head.

She leaned her head back against the tub's rim, became only distantly aware of Tina moving about the solar that was now more the maid's responsibility to keep clean and neat than that of Lothaire's squire. Doubtless, the young man would be pleased to spend more time out of doors.

When the water covered Laura's shoulders, Tina began soaping and scrubbing her lady. As ever, the lingering would commence once the water was clouded and Laura could feel without seeing it caress her skin.

As she bent forward to give the maid her back, she remembered how abrasive the brush had been across skin which, in recent months, had been subjected to no more than a vigorous washcloth. She did not miss the brush that had left her with healing scratches that sometimes itched so much she could not leave a room fast enough to rub her back against a stone wall.

She sighed. "I think I am nearly all the way awake now."

Tina squeezed Laura's shoulder. "I am glad, milady."

It was worrisome she had spoken her thoughts aloud. She must not do so in Lothaire's presence. "As am I," she said.

Another squeeze. "Ye are clean. Now rest."

Laura sank back and closed her eyes. And let her thoughts go to the night past, which she had tried to avoid since departing her troubled dreams.

She feared Lothaire knew she had cried herself to sleep. It had shamed that she could not control her emotions, but she had turned the damp pillow wet as she spilled out her hurt over the exchange with her husband and regret over not following Michael's advice. But she would follow it to its cruel end. Regardless of whether Lothaire believed how Simon made a child on her, he would be told. And then...

He could refuse to believe her and resolve to live his life bound to one he thought a harlot and liar, or he could verify Simon's character with Michael and his wife. She almost preferred the former, so much she hated the thought of Michael's pain over his brother's perversion and Lady Beatrix being made to relive what she had suffered at his hands that had seen her stand trial for his murder.

The door opened.

Startling at the possibility it was Lothaire, she gripped the tub's rim and looked around.

But ere she laid eyes on him, Tina exclaimed, "Milord!" confirming it was the one Laura wanted least to see this morn.

He halted just inside the solar, and his eyes received hers the instant they flew to his. In a voice so tight she hardly recognized it, he said, "What do you?"

She tore her hands from the rim and crossed her arms over her chest though he was too distant to see anything below her shoulders. "I bathe, of course! What do you here?"

He glanced at Tina where she stood alongside the bed with the cradle made of her apron holding rose petals plucked from the sheets, looked back at Laura, spread his arms. "Obviously, I require a change of clothes."

She could see that now the shock of his entrance was past. The perspiration darkening the neck and shoulders of his gray tunic tapered down his chest to his waist, and his chausses were dusty and sliced at his left knee.

He had been practicing at swords, here the reason that sound was heard earlier than usual.

"So you do," she said. "Take them and be gone."

His brow furrowed, and she regretted not saying it better. It sounded more a demand than a request, but she was naked in the presence of a man who had yet to know her. And growing colder by the moment despite water so heated steam puffed above the surface.

He strode toward her.

"I bathe, Lothaire!" she cried and clasped her body closer.

"In *our* bedchamber." He halted alongside the tub, stared into her wide-eyed face.

Laura bore his gaze until it moved down her neck to the soap-clouded water, then she lurched forward and turned her shoulder to him. "Pray, leave!"

Out of the corner of her eye, she saw him lower to his haunches. A moment later, he touched her upper arm. "Lest you forget, I am your husband."

She drew what should have been a calming breath, but it pulled his salty, masculine scent into her, and so disturbed that the water no longer soothed. She snatched her arm away. "Not yet you are. Not truly."

His silence was of such depth she thought she might drown in it, then he put his mouth near her ear, a reminder they were not alone. "Something we must needs remedy. And soon."

"Leave!" she rasped. "I do not want you here!"

He stood. His boots sounded over the floor, the lid of a chest banged against the wall, moments later dropped. Boots again, then the slam of the door.

Sinking back against the tub, Laura covered her face with her hands.

"Oh, milady!" Tina hastened forward. "I knew not if I should stay or go—knew not what to say."

Laura dragged her hands down her face. "I said enough, Tina, and I wish I had not, but I could not think. I just…wanted him gone."

"I must say, he was fair tolerant, milady. I thought he would send me away and the two of ye would have done with it."

"As did I," Laura whispered.

"Ah, look! Now I must pick the petals from the rushes."

What had been strewn across the sheet was strewn across the floor between bed and tub. "Leave them," Laura said. "And me. I wish to be alone."

"Very good, milady. I will be belowstairs. I should return in…half an hour?"

Laura nodded. When the door closed, she unpinned her hair, drew the fat braid over her shoulder, and loosened its weave.

Had not the maid appeared, he would have waited until this eve to confront Laura over her behavior in the presence of Tina who was to know more of the intimate details of the lives of her lady and lord than any other. All day he would have borne the roiling. But the day need not be entirely ruined.

Tina had not seen him where he stood outside Angus's chamber seeking to calm himself ere entering lest it was occupied, the knight also having departed the training field to change his clothes.

When the maid turned opposite and quickly descended the stairs, Lothaire determined he need not avail himself of Angus's chamber. The solar was no longer exclusively his, but as Laura's husband he could enter at will.

When he strode inside, surprise at finding his wife absent made him leave the door wide, then realizing she must be in the garderobe, he seated the door and moved toward the bed where he would shed his garments and don fresh ones regardless of how Laura found him when she reappeared.

He was feet from the bed when the trickle of water returned his regard to the empty tub.

Not empty, he corrected when he deciphered the light reflected across the water that had risen so far above the rim it streamed down the outside. He dropped the clean garments, ran, thrust his arms into the tub, and snatched Laura from its depths. There was no need to attempt to revive her, she was all flailing arms and spluttering as he swung her out over the rim.

When he dragged her against him, she cried out, "Lothaire!" and stared at him out of eyes so wide their upper lids were known only by the wet, spiky lashes nearly touching her eyebrows.

"Why?" he barked.

She ceased struggling, the only movement about her the rapid rise and fall of her chest that wet his tunic, the only sound that of panting against his neck and jaw.

"Why, Laura? Is the prospect of life with me so terrible?"

As though her mouth had gone dry, her tongue clicked when she parted her lips. "Nay, 'tis what I want."

Bitterness spoiled his laughter. "So much that not even wed a full day you seek to end your life more quickly than did my first wife."

Eyes widening further, she shook her head, loosening her soaked hair caught between their chests. "Surely you do not think I meant to drown myself?"

"Of course not," he snarled. "You were but rinsing the soap from your hair and forgot to surface. Or mayhap you were taking a swim?"

"I was enjoying my bath, that is all. My word I give."

"You took water into your lungs, Laura!"

"Because of the surprise of seeing you above me."

He could find no lie about her, but that did not mean there was none. However, there seemed no benefit in pursuing the truth—indeed, it would be of detriment to a body that was becoming too aware of the bared one pressed to his.

"I did not know you would return," she said.

He raised his eyebrows. "Certes, that was your intent, and that is why I am here. I will not have you speak to me—"

"I know, Lothaire. It was ill of me and all the worse in front of Tina. I am sorry. I just felt…"

"What?"

"Vulnerable. Like prey."

So sincere was her admission that something at the edge of his consciousness shifted—not enough to step into the light, but enough to throw a long shadow.

"I know I granted you rights to my body, but…"

"Tell me."

Her gaze wavered. "I am afeared."

He believed her. Though he hated she was frightened of his possession, no greater evidence could she offer than she had. Realizing his anger had yielded to compassion he would not have thought possible when he slammed the door minutes earlier, he said, "No matter the past, I will not hurt you, Laura. I will be gentle. I will go slow. Even if it feels I die. My word I give."

Finally, she asked what she should not, especially at this moment when he could not be gentle, could not go slow, would surely die. "Now, Lothaire?"

"Nay, when I can keep my word and we are certain not to be disturbed. But we could make a good beginning of it."

Relief tangible, she said, "How?"

"I would see you. And you would see me."

Her blush was violent, but she gave a slight nod, granting him permission to see beyond the cleft of her breasts framed by wet tresses.

He released her arms, stepped back, slowly moved his gaze down her flushed body. Upon reaching her feet, he closed his eyes. "Heavens, Laura, you are beautiful." Though he wanted to more slowly raise his gaze up her, he opened his eyes upon hers. Seeing gratitude there, he lifted the towel from a chair and set it around her shoulders.

"Now I shall change my garments," he said as she gripped the towel closed at her throat. "If you wish, you may look upon me as I have looked upon you, though at a distance safer for me."

He strode across the solar, swept up the tunic and chausses abandoned to the petal-strewn rushes, disrobed alongside the bed, and drew on fresh garments without looking at her. It was not necessary, for he felt her gaze. And suffered for it. Only after re-girding his sword and starting for the door did he look to her.

She had not moved, nor tried to cover more of herself though her calves and inner thighs were visible between the towel's edges.

"As I shall be at High Castle all day, my lady, I will see you at dinner and supper—and in between if you wish."

She inclined her head.

He opened the door, paused. "I have no illegitimate children, Laura," he said what should have been told sooner. "Nor shall I. I am not the same as my father."

Something like a sob parted her lips. "Nor am I the same as Lady Edeva. Not in any way. I do wish to be joined with you for more than a day. Far more, Lothaire."

Here further assurance she had not tried to take her life. And because he believed her as he had feared doing, he said, "You are my somehow, Laura, and not only for saving Lexeter."

An uncertain smile lifted her mouth, and he did not worry over the tub of water to which he left her.

26

FOUR DAYS SINCE he had said they must remedy their unconsummated marriage. Four days in which they had not, though each night he lay down beside her and on the night past had turned his hand around hers as if to pull her to him. Though Laura could understand the past three nights since he had resumed the work of wool and each day returned after a dozen hours, neither had he moved to make love to her the first night after their wedding.

For what did he wait? Not that she was ready—indeed, doubted she would be until she chanced the whole truth about Clarice's conception. But he could not know that burden she yet carried, so why did he hold himself from her?

Never had they spoken more at supper nor lingered over conversation afterward. Indeed, these past two nights, following what was becoming regular games of chess with Clarice, they had remained at the hearth longer than they should have considering how little sleep Lothaire had. And it was more his—and her daughter's—doing than hers. Laura had but to question him about Lexeter's wool production and he of few words became one of many, and more so with his stepdaughter's prideful comments that revealed the depth of her interest in what was a strange fit for one who liked pretty things—above all, being one of those pretty things.

On days Clarice did not depart the castle, she clothed and adorned herself as she had upon the barony of Owen, but when Lothaire permitted her to accompany him to the shearings, she resembled a very pretty boy, having acquired chausses from Lothaire's squire to wear beneath gowns no longer of a length suitable for a young lady but whose laces could be loosened to accommodate her growing torso.

It made Laura happy to see her daughter settling in well, and she knew it was mostly because of Lothaire. And had yet another reason to love him.

"May I join you?"

She swept her gaze from Lothaire and Clarice's chess game to Sebille as the lady lowered to the chair on one side of the bench Laura perched on with her back to a warming fire. "Of course, my lady."

An uncomfortable silence fell, more so since the two women had rarely encountered each other since the wedding—and the reason the lady was often absent the hall. According to Lothaire, his sister readied their mother for her move to her dower property three days hence, following the celebratory shearing supper that marked the end of the wool gathering.

"You are well, Lady Sebille?"

"As well as can be."

Laura guessed it would be hard for her to leave behind Sir Angus though there seemed no hope for them.

"And your mother?"

Sebille snorted. "Could she convincingly affect an attack of the heart, she would so she might remain at High Castle. She insists only she can keep her beloved son safe from…"

Laura glanced at Lothaire and Clarice, was glad their discussion of a chess move held their attention. "Safe from me," she said low.

The lady sighed. "Her son is all to her."

"She is blessed to have you."

Sebille leaned forward. "That I would not argue, but she would. Though once she called me her *miracle* and loved me well, now I am her daughter only insofar as the duty owed her."

Miracle? Laura mused, but fearing she would trespass in asking the meaning, let it go. Keeping her own voice low, she said, "Lothaire believes you ought to give her into the care of a servant and remain at High Castle."

The lady's eyebrows rose. "So now my brother confides in you."

"I am his wife."

"And you are keeping him content, are you?"

Laura gasped. Though the lady guessed wrong, it offended.

Sebille flicked a hand. "Forgive me. A more difficult week I have not had."

"I understand." Rather, she tried.

"What of you, Lady Laura? Do you agree I ought to remain here?"

"If 'twould suit you. I know it is too soon for us to be friends, but did we spend more time together, I believe it possible."

The lady lowered her chin. To hide tears? Laura wondered.

"Do you truly think so?" Sebille said softly.

"I do. Will you not consider staying? Your brother is most concerned for your well-being."

She looked up and, eyes moist, said, "This I know, and that he believes once Lady Raisa is removed from High Castle Sir Angus and I might find the happiness denied us when I chose a path opposite his."

"It seems you yet feel for him."

"I wish I did not. However, even could I abandon my duty to Lady Raisa, I fear 'tis too late for Angus and me."

"Perhaps in the matter of children, but—"

"I do not speak of babes, Lady Laura." Her voice rose, causing Lothaire to look around.

His gaze moved between the two women, and Laura wondered if Sebille's smile was as forced as her own. Though certain he had known his wife and sister conversed, had he been unaware of what was spoken between them, he would not likely be henceforth.

And it seemed his sister knew it as well. When Lothaire returned to the game, she stood and leaned down. "Not of babes, Lady Laura. I speak of betrayal so sinful it cannot be undone, and for which there is little hope it will not happen again. Thus, my course is set." She straightened and turned toward the kitchen.

Laura was tempted to follow and tell her she believed Sir Angus was honorable enough to forego further dalliances were Sebille to remain at High Castle and wed him. However, before she could yield to the yearning, the physician exited the kitchen corridor and the two spoke low, then they moved back toward the kitchen and went from sight.

"All is well?" Lothaire asked and she found him nearly upon her, Clarice at his side as well as that beast of a dog, Tomas.

"I wish your sister would remain here with us," she said.

"As do I, but one day she shall return."

Laura knew it was wrong to wish for another's death, and she did not, but for Sebille's sake and Lady Raisa's suffering were it as serious as the physician reported, she hoped *one day* would come ere the passing of too many that could seal Sebille's loss of Sir Angus.

"Mother?" Clarice dropped onto the bench beside her. "I know I was to spend the morrow with you, but might I accompany Father to the shearing of the upper eastern flock?"

There seemed an endless number of flocks, each identified by its location upon Lexeter. And still Laura had not accompanied Lothaire to learn firsthand the work of wool. Could she, she would join her daughter on the morrow, but she was to oversee preparation of the great quantity of food that High Castle's kitchen would supply the shearing supper.

Laura wanted to agree to Clarice's request, but though her duties would be more difficult with her daughter at her side, compelled as she was to explain and supervise the girl's contributions, she shook her head. "Had I not great need of you to ensure the supper adequately reflects the Baron of Lexeter's gratitude for those who have labored hard, I would permit it. Too, methinks you will enjoy the celebration more having finished what you and I began."

Clarice's hopeful smile forsaken, her jaw quivered and eyes moistened. And Laura had to resist the impulse to reverse her decision.

Blessedly, it was easier done when she glanced at Lothaire and saw approval in his eyes.

"But Mother—"

"Your mother has spoken and wisely," Lothaire said. "Now I am sure Tina is eager to see you abed so she may gain her own rest."

Resentment flashing in the girl's eyes, she stood. "Good eve," she said to Laura, then to Lothaire, "Good eve, Lord Soames."

When she was gone, he said, "But minutes earlier she called me *Father.*"

"Do not think ill of her. She is but disappointed."

"I do not think ill of her, Laura. I dislike that she retaliates for my support of you by rejecting me as a parent, but she did better than expected. And it seems you made the right decision."

Neck beginning to ache at looking so far up him, she stood. "Seems?"

"I am less experienced at parenting, but I believe I am accomplished at putting men to work whether to defend Lexeter or work the land, and in such a way most are pleased with the results. I do not believe what is required for raising a child well can be that different, though I am thinking it is more difficult." He smiled wryly. "Regardless of the depth of a parent's feelings, they surely go deeper than that felt for one who is an acquaintance or even a friend."

As Laura took in his words, she was flooded with regret. "I wish..." She closed her mouth.

"What?"

Though she feared she would regret answering, she said, "I wish I had been here to see you grow into the man you have become. When you appeared at court, I thought you the same I had known—only older and angry. You are so much more, and I am ashamed I cannot claim the same."

"I think you are wrong." He lifted her hand, and she thought how small and slender it appeared compared to his. Then she noticed the state of his nails that evidenced the work of the commoner and hurt that it was more often the tools of hard labor with which he occupied himself when it ought to be the weapons of a warrior and the quill of a lord administering his lands.

"What is it?" he asked.

She looked up. "I am thinking how large your hand is compared to mine."

He arched an eyebrow. "Is that all?"

Hating she might have shamed him, she said, "And how well I like the way your fingers fit mine."

She did not think he believed her, but he inclined his head, set her hand on his arm, and led her to the stairs.

Was this the night he would make her his wife in full? she wondered and wished all of Simon was told no matter what Lothaire might think of her—*were* she completely honest.

She did not have to be, she reasoned. After all, Simon and Maude were the only ones who knew the whole truth of what had happened. As both were dead, they could no longer defend the ravisher.

You would hide the lie amidst the truth? her conscience prompted.

Would it really hurt? she considered. No matter what she had done, she had not wanted Simon to possess her.

The opening of the solar door made her startle. She could not remember ascending the stairs nor walking the corridor.

"Laura," Lothaire said where he stood on the threshold. "I am worn through. It will not be this night."

He read her wrong, though not entirely. Still, she was grateful, and more so when she determined that once they were abed she would tell him the rest of Simon so when he claimed his rights over her body he would do so knowing—even if not believing—her tale.

She jerked her chin. "I am weary too."

He drew her inside, closed the door, then crossed to the table to perform his nightly ablutions. Laura performed hers alongside him, but when he took up soap and submerged his hands in the basin of water, she stepped nearer.

Feeling him stiffen, she slid her own hands into the water and took the soap from him.

"What do you, Laura?"

She lifted one of his hands between hers, looked up. "Let me at least do this for you."

"I do not require—"

"Pray, Lothaire, let me."

His nostrils dilated, but he did not wrench free, and she bent her head and began soaping one calloused hand then the other.

He was rigid throughout, and more so when she took up a washcloth to aid in removing the darkness from his fingertips and around his nails. But though she was able to lighten them, she could not remove all evidence of his hard labor.

"I thank you," he said as she dried his hands.

"'Tis my honor." She released him and wiped her own hands on the towel as Lothaire extinguished the candles, leaving only those on the bedside tables lit.

Laura had been bared to him the day of her tub bath and he to her, but they had not repeated that intimacy. Though it was Tina's duty to aid her lady and Lothaire's squire's to assist his lord, neither was called upon, and by unspoken agreement they would not be until the marriage was consummated. Thus, husband and wife kept their backs to each other as they shed the day's garments and donned their night wear.

The silence oppressive for what Laura would tell this night, she asked over her shoulder, "What will busy you after the shearing supper?"

"Much."

"But the shearing is done."

"So you think I shall be at my leisure until next summer," he said with what sounded like teasing.

"Of course not. I know much goes into the administration of lands, but the work of wool is mostly done, is it not? No longer must you rush to break your fast, miss dinner in the hall, and be late for supper."

"For a while longer, I must. When the last of the wool is sacked and bundled, the workers given their portion, and three quarters of Lexeter's share sold and sent overseas, I will have to see to the last quarter."

Hearing him turn back the covers, Laura ceased pretending she worked the hooks of her chemise, turned, and lowered to the bed.

"The last quarter?" she said, snuffing her candle as he snuffed his.

"Though most of those whose income is derived from the production of wool sell it for others to work into cloth, some years ago I decided Lexeter ought to retain a portion and expand its business into the weaving of cloth. That is what shall occupy me next."

She turned her face to his, wished she could see him better by moonlight. "It is profitable?"

"Were it, the queen would have been unable to compel me to wed."

That gave her pause. "Then who would I have married?"

That gave *him* pause. "None of those Eleanor sent from her presence with their tails tucked tight. She would have found a suitable husband for you."

Laura nearly argued, though she would not have thought to whilst at Windsor. No matter how well Lothaire received her tale, she wanted none but him.

"If the weaving of cloth is not profitable, why hold back a quarter of wool that could generate income?"

"Few ventures are soon profitable, but if not this year, I believe the income will come next year when the additional funds resulting from Henry and Eleanor's tax break allow me to expand my operations. Too, it is of benefit to Lexeter's people who earn extra income over the cold months by weaving my wool alongside theirs."

"Fascinating."

"You think so?" he said as if he thought she spoke what he wished to hear.

"It is. I would like to learn more. Mayhap there is something I can do to help."

"Mayhap," he said with finality that indicated he wished to sleep.

He was handing her the opportunity to further delay the telling, and she longed to take it, but she said, "Lothaire, there is something I would have told you had you not thought me a liar when I said it was not Michael who fathered Clarice but…Simon."

Of a sudden, the distance between them felt not a reach but the breadth of the great hall.

"Hear me," she entreated. "Even if you do not believe what I tell, I must—"

"You must not, Laura. I do not want nor need excuses and most certainly have no wish to hear those names pass your lips. I am content with where we are now and where we are going. I am done with the past, and if there is to be hope for us beyond the getting of an heir and a well-ordered household, you will be done with it as well."

It was said with such control, command, and threat she nearly bowed to it. "You have to know, Lothaire."

He surged onto his side and leaned over her. "If you will not quiet for the sake of our marriage, you have but to keep your vow to be meek and obedient. Now speak no more of it."

One last try, she thought. *But one more, and if he will not listen, you can do naught.*

She laid a hand on his jaw, felt it stiffen as the coarse stubble of several days' growth of beard pricked her palm, but before she could speak, he rumbled, "Do not."

She dropped her hand, thought how pathetic it sounded flopping to the mattress between them. "As you say," she whispered, "but if ever you wish—"

"Laura!"

She snapped her teeth, put between them, "If ever you wish to know—even if only to understand me—you have but to ask." She rolled away, and when he returned to his side of the bed realized she had given him her back, which she could not stand to give any man so near her. She started to correct the error but talked herself down. Though she did not want to expose her back to Lothaire, it was not for fear of having too little time and space in which to defend herself. It was because she could not stop loving him and even now, despite her anger, wanted to put her head on his shoulder and curl against him.

Over the next hour, she knew he lay awake the same as she, and when she could pray no more and began to drift into the night, she told herself she was glad he had not let her speak. Had she revealed she had not willingly given herself to Simon, and had he not believed her anymore than that Michael was not Clarice's father, the progress made toward a passably good marriage might have been impeded, might even have ended were he so reviled by what he thought fantastic lies he determined she would but serve as a womb for breeding and a servant for ensuring the functioning of his household.

Aye, for the best.

27

A LAKE—NOT A pond, just as the young Lothaire had assured her during his third visit to Owen when she had asked if there was a pond near
enough High Castle and sufficiently private that when they wed they
could swim and bathe together.

He had said there was no such pond nearby, and when her smile fell
told her there was a lake, and they would, indeed, swim and bathe there.
Just the two of them, mayhap at sunset. Then he had been bolder yet and
said he would kiss her there and afterward they would lie on the shore
and watch the stars come out and count them until there were too many
to number.

God willing, that might yet happen. But first Laura must surrender
the hurt of two nights past. And Lothaire would have to release what he
held close.

As she reined in and waited for her husband's long stride to close
the distance between her and the final shearing for which she had been
told to expect two score workers and three score of their family, she
wondered if when they returned to High Castle following the supper
and they passed the lake half a league distant from the gathering Lothaire
would remember his promise to take her there. She believed he would,
though she did not expect he would say anything. But in time...

He was dirty and spotted with wool, having spent the early part of
the day shearing the last of the flock, but it was obvious he had brushed

himself off as best he could when the wagons bearing Cook's feast and its escort appeared over the rise.

Laura did not mind his disarray, especially when he smiled at her, regardless if it was more for her benefit or those accompanying the wagons—half a dozen servants, as many knights, ten men-at-arms, Sir Angus, and Tina. There were two others as well, both unexpected—Sebille who said she never missed the shearing supper when Laura could not hide her surprise, and the physician who was to have remained with Lady Raisa but been summoned to tend one of the workers who had broken an arm.

When the rider appeared shortly before the departure from High Castle, Sebille had arranged for a woman servant to sit with her mother and a man-at-arms to keep watch outside her door.

"Your patient rests in the shade of the trees, Martin," Lothaire called as the physician aided Sebille in dismounting—Sebille whose gaze was on Sir Angus who had lifted Tina down.

"I am glad you came, my lady," Lothaire said, halting alongside Laura's mount.

"Is not my place at your side on such an occasion?"

"It is." He raised his arms and it felt wonderful to go into them, especially as there had been little physical contact these past days beyond the brushing of arms and hands.

As if he also missed the contact, his hands lingered at her waist when her feet were firm upon the ground. "You are lovely," he said.

She looked down the gown fashioned of rich brown samite that had been far from simple ere she removed its embellishments save the gold braid around neck and hem. "I thank you."

"I wish I could pay the same compliment to Clarice." He slid his hands down Laura's waist and off her hips, and she felt the intention.

Returning her gaze to his, she saw a glimmer in his eyes she had not seen for two days. He truly was pleased by her arrival. "She is a mess?"

"Methinks you will be shocked, and I fear her gown may have seen its last wear—not only fouled but torn."

"Torn?"

"At waist and hem. She was determined to put shears to one of the lambs though I forbade it since she has neither the experience nor strength to control even a smaller animal without aid."

Though Laura tried not to be alarmed, she had to ask, "She is not the one who requires the physician, is she?"

"She is not. Only her pride and gown were harmed when she lost the battle and found herself in a mud puddle. Too, she disagreed with her punishment."

"Which was?"

"Sacking the wool, which she much dislikes. But she once more assists the shearers."

"I am sorry she was difficult."

"I am not. She learned more than she would have had she behaved. Now she knows exactly why she must obey me, though she will surely test me again."

"She admires you," Laura said, "and I cannot thank you enough."

He inclined his head. "She told me she worked well for you on the day past."

"She did, though methinks she did it more for you than me."

"Nay, the sheep. I did not expect it, but I am not so certain the excitement of what is new to her will grow old. It is quite possible my new daughter has wool in her blood."

As would have been more expected had she Soames in her blood, Laura thought. "I am glad she is happy here, especially after——" Laura stopped herself from spilling the name of Castle Soaring for which her daughter had expressed a preference. Even if it had not led to her speaking the name Lothaire did not wish to hear, it would have put the man between them. In the next instant, his smile faltered, and she realized Michael was there regardless.

She looked past him to the simple structure whose roof was long and wide and walls few. On either side were pens, the one on the left holding a dozen unshorn sheep, the one on the right nearly bursting its posts and rails to contain what must number two hundred barely clothed sheep. And all in between was where the shearing was done out of the day's heat, and which appeared even more the birthplace of snow than it had when first she laid eyes on it.

"While the tables are erected and the food set out," she said, "will you show me the work of wool, Husband?"

"Providing you do not mind picking the fluff from your gown and hair," he said.

"I will not, though I may require your aid where I cannot reach."

She had not meant that to be suggestive, but she was glad it sounded that way when his smile recovered. "I shall be happy to help however I can, Wife."

And then they would consummate their marriage? Feeling her face warm, she said, "Show me how the Lord of Lexeter saves his lands."

"With much sweat, lack of sleep, and the aid of a sizable tax break, of course."

As he took her arm and drew her toward the shelter, Laura said, "Now I have seen how hard you labor, methinks you would have saved your lands had you gained naught in wedding me."

He looked sidelong at her. "Had I gained naught, I would not have wed you."

Of course he would not have, just as she had not thought—or wished—to wed him until the queen revealed her reasons for rejecting Laura's other suitors.

"This I know, Lothaire."

"Nor would I have regretted not taking you to wife."

Thinking he must seek to hurt her, she averted her gaze.

"But only because I would not know there was anything to regret," he added. "As now I know."

She swung her gaze back to his.

"Do you think it by God's hand what was undone has been done, Laura?" At her hesitation, he continued, "I think it must be, though surely Eleanor would say it was by her hand. I shall never cease to be surprised by those He enlists to do His good work."

"Nor I. My surprise is that…" Laura blinked amid the wool floating more conspicuously upon the air as they drew near the shelter. "…His arms were not too full to hold me as I feared when I determined to leave Owen and find a father and home for Clarice."

"Then you believe you can be happy here? With me?"

"I can think of no place or man with whom I would be happier," she said and silently added, *But happier I could be did you allow me to tell you all and you believed me.* But that little word—if—could make ill of what was good. Again, she told herself Lothaire was right. *If* was too great a risk.

As she passed the pen that held unshaven sheep, she glanced across her shoulder and saw the spouses and children of the workers assisting High Castle's servants with unloading the wagons. Sir Angus and Tina also helped, as did Sebille who appeared to be directing them all.

"It makes me sad your sister has not a husband and home of her own."

"She could have had both. Had she wed Sir Angus, I would have awarded him the keeping of my mother's dower property, but Sebille chose Lady Raisa."

"She must love her very much."

His brow furrowed. "I think it more she is easily controlled by guilt and obligation, both at which our mother excels at dispensing. Sebille wants to be with Angus, but there is something she wants more."

"Her mother's love."

"She will not speak of it, but I believe so. I was but six when our father disappeared, but I knew she was adored by our parents. Though I felt loved as well, I was certain she was the favored child."

"A daughter," Laura said. Sons, whether of the nobility that they might carry on the family name or the common folk that they might better labor alongside their parents, were more desirable—at least until a man had his male heir and one or two more to spare.

"Aye, a daughter," he spoke louder to be heard above the bleating sheep, talk of workers, and rasp of shears. "I do not think I begrudged her, for I also adored her. She was joyous then and played the little mother well, but all changed when our father departed High Castle to visit his mistress and never returned. Our mother became so bitter over his faithlessness she turned it on Sebille and her attention on Lexeter's heir. Suddenly I was the favored child—and liked it not."

Bits of wool swirling more heavily around them, settling on their clothes and hair, Laura stepped nearer. "That must have been difficult for Sebille to lose the adoration of both parents."

"Certainly, but when she was not occupied with Lady Raisa's demands, still she mothered me."

"And had your love. That must have eased some of her ache."

"I would like to believe so," he said, then swept a hand before him. "Here, the work of wool, this the last asked of the flock for near on a year—that is, where their fleece is concerned. Still there is sustenance and income to be had from their milk and the meat of those too aged to weather another winter."

Laura marveled over the chaos of so many workers putting shears to sheep. Some of the animals, likely the older ones, lay on the earthen floor letting be done to them what must be done, whilst others were not of a mind to submit.

Laura watched as one whose fleece billowed every which way was toppled and turned legs up by a male and female worker.

Immediately, the man dropped to the dirt, put a leg on either side of the animal, and bracing it between his knees, drew it against his chest and settled its head on one shoulder. "Shears!" he commanded, but before the woman could pass them to him, the ewe began thrashing.

The man drew his knees up the animal's sides and squeezed until the ewe's struggles subsided.

"William is big and strong," Lothaire said, "as is the man whose arm the physician tends. The difference is that William has been shearing for over ten years, the other man two."

"'Tis why you would not allow Clarice to attempt such."

"Not even on a slighter animal. Blessedly, most of the flock are easily persuaded to give up their oppressive coats."

"How many—?" Laura clapped a hand over mouth, sneezed.

"It is the wool," Lothaire said. "Methinks there is no other activity at which you will hear so many sneeze."

Laura rubbed her nose with the back of a hand. "How many have you sheared this day?"

"Eleven. I hoped to make an even dozen."

"May I watch?"

He grinned. "You wish to see your lord husband hard at labor?"

"I do."

"Clarice thought you might." He motioned to the man who stood before the gate of the nearly barren pen.

Moments later, a large ewe was led into the shelter.

"Mother!"

Laura turned. Lothaire had not exaggerated. Clarice was so fouled—mud spattered across her skirts and chausses—she looked most unladylike. But she was smiling.

"I know," she read Laura's alarm, "but it could not be helped."

"Could it not?" Lothaire said.

She sighed. "Aye, but I have been punished and am behaving." She patted the ewe as it passed. "That is Grandmother," she said.

Laura raised her eyebrows. "The one you told had first to be washed in the stream?"

"Nay, this is a different Grandmother. Every flock has one. This one is bigger and less friendly. I asked Father not to shear it until you arrived."

"Why?"

"So you may watch, and because he will make quicker work of it than the others. He is very good at shearing."

"Not something with which I ever thought to impress a lady," Lothaire muttered and took charge of the ewe. "Forgive me for baring you, Grandmother. When the shame passes, I vow you will be as grateful as the others to shed this heavy old coat."

Laura did not grasp what it meant to be good at shearing, but as she and her daughter watched Lothaire, she did not doubt there were few who could best him.

The ewe struggled and bleated as it was toppled, tossed its head and flailed its legs as it was trapped between knees and thighs, and when it gave up the fight, Lothaire supported its head and upper back against his shoulder and chest. The shears were passed to him, and he set to relieving the animal of its fleece. He parted the thick coat at the center of the ewe's belly, slid the blades close to the skin, and began cutting and pushing aside the shorn fleece.

The animal resisted again when Lothaire finished its belly and rolled it onto its side. Once more, he clamped it between his knees, and the ewe yielded to the shearing of its neck, shoulders, front legs, and flanks. Once the fleece on the opposite side fell away, the ewe was turned right side up and seemed to sulk as its back and rear legs were bared. Then the considerably smaller, much lightened animal was led to the pen to join those gone before her.

"Not a drop of blood spilled," Lothaire said, brushing at his clothes as he advanced on Laura amid a flurry of wool to which the cooling breeze added. "Impressed, Wife?"

"Indeed." Knowing her own hair would appear as touched by snow as his were it not partially covered by a light veil, she had to fold her hands at her waist to keep from brushing at his hair. "You made it look easy."

"Of course I did. You were watching." He halted before her where she stood alone, Clarice having been collected by the women shearers who were to wash in a nearby stream in advance of the men availing themselves of its cleansing water. "But as my clothes reveal and, alas, my scent, it is good Grandmother is the last I shall shear this season."

He did exude a strong odor, the only light about his perspiration-darkened tunic and chausses the white bits of fleece.

Resisting wrinkling her nose, she said, "The women have gone to wash at the stream."

He inclined his head. "By the time we finish here, they will have returned and the men will then make themselves as presentable as possible."

She pressed her lips inward. "I saw the lake on the ride here. The one you spoke of years ago."

He reached, picked fluff from her veil. "You are thinking better I bathe there?"

"Not this day, but..." She cleared her throat. "I thank you for demonstrating the shearing. Mayhap next year I can participate."

"If you are not with child or have one at your breast," he said, then added. "Much can happen in a year."

Laura was struck by his choice of words. She had said the same to him the day their young selves had walked to the pond and he had chastised her for her behavior. The truth of that had been proven. But this time, if God blessed them, it would be Lothaire's child she birthed, a babe born of wedlock.

"Much can happen," she murmured. "Thank you for the demonstration. Now I must assist with the food." She turned away.

Lothaire watched her lift her skirts free of the dirt and upon her person carry away fluff that had escaped the great sacks whose contents would be woven into cloth she herself might one day wear. Though hardly in need of clothes, if much did happen within a year, her lacings would be unable to accommodate her increasing girth and she would require new gowns ere the birth of their child.

That was his hope, though he wished he had not used her words from ten years past. It had not been intentional, determined as he was to go forward and as encouraged as he was by her mention of the lake he could never pass without recall of what his young bride and he were to have made of it. However, he had glimpsed wariness in her eyes and knew she remembered the same.

"Fool," he muttered and turned back inside the shelter. As the last of the ewes yielded up their coats, he joined the other men in gathering swaths of wool shorn since the departure of the women who had sorted the best from the worst, the former being the back and sides, the latter including the breech. Accordingly, the wool was stuffed in sacks, most of which would bring a good price for the high quality for which Lexeter wool was increasingly known.

There was much work ahead—years of it—but Lexeter was saved.

He searched out Laura. She was at the far table arranging platters of food, and even at a distance he could see the flecks of white covering her. She looked good in virgin wool.

One of the worker's daughters appeared at her side, and the Lady of Lexeter turned at the tug on her skirt, listened to whatever the child said, and handed her something from a platter.

The girl bounced onto her toes, laughed, and ran opposite.

Lothaire smiled. Lexeter was saved, indeed. As was he, though he would have sworn he did not need saving.

28

ALL HAD PLENTY to eat and too much to drink. Now they wanted their lord and lady to join in the dance. Such was not unknown to Lothaire who had years ago given himself to the dizzying, unrestrained whirling of the villagers, partnering with many a maiden to celebrate the last of the shearing, but the movements would surely offend a noblewoman.

"Dance with your lady, milord!" This from the shepherd whose skill at shearing exceeded Lothaire's.

"Dance with her!" Called the buxom wife of a worker from the village of Thistle Cross whose flushed cheeks told she would not care to rise from bed on the morrow. "See, she is willing."

Lothaire followed the jut of her chin to where his wife had stood in the midst of other women who had not participated in the last dance. Now she moved toward him with a hand outstretched—just as he imagined the young Laura would have done.

He straightened so abruptly from the tree against which he leaned that many laughed.

"Your lady is a bold one! Dance with her, milord!"

Wishing the lowering of day were farther along so the lengthening shadows concealed the warmth traveling up his face, Lothaire strode forward to meet Laura halfway.

She slid her hand in his. "Too bold?" she said, smile so teasing he wanted to kiss it open.

As those who had brought their instruments to the celebration began to pluck at and blow upon them, he said, "As long as it is my hand in yours..." He drew her nearer, slid an arm around her waist. "...my arm around you..." She settled hers against his broad back. "...my eyes upon yours...my breath upon you...never too bold."

Sparkles were coming out in her eyes ahead of those of the heavens that would not prick the sky for another hour.

"Are you sure you wish to do this?" he said. "As you have seen, the dances are not only more vigorous but more intimate than those to which you are accustomed."

She tilted her face higher. "As never have we danced, I am accustomed to none. So pray, accustom me to those of your—*our*—people."

"Our people, indeed," he said and began to move her across the trampled grass dance floor.

As their bodies brushed, pressed, and withdrew, he held her gaze, and though other men spun their women past their lord and lady, he was only vaguely aware of them.

When the tempo increased, encouraging partners to widen the distance between themselves, he was glad it had become so crowded that the steps through which he guided Laura provided an excuse to hold her closer and feel curves long denied him. And she surely felt the planes of his body, her pupils dilating, breath quickening though far less effort was required from her since more often she was off her feet than on them as he lifted and turned her.

This eve, I will make love to her, he decided. *I will truly accept her as she is and will become, and together we shall throw the last of the dirt upon the past.*

As the dance neared its end, the tempo increased further. Here was where men with sufficient strength and space gripped their partners beneath the arms, lifted them above their heads, and spun them wide. In this instance, Lothaire had enough room, but no other man was going to look upon Laura's legs.

He lifted her high but planted his feet firm to the ground and tilted his head back to look up at her where she looked down at him with a smile so wide he was certain she would welcome his attentions this night.

As he held her there, the outsides of her thighs pressed against the insides of his arms, she laughed and said, "Should you not be swinging me about?"

"Certainly not." He eased her down his chest, abdomen, and hips. When her feet settled atop his boots, she pressed upward, kissed his cheek, and spoke three words he thought he must have heard wrong amid the joyous shouts of a dance at its end.

"Say it again," he said as a dozen dizzy couples dispersed. "I do not think I heard right."

The curve of her mouth eased, and her eyes flitted down his face.

Had she spoken it? Meant it? Did she now regret it?

Her eyes returned to his, then she leaned in and said in his ear, "Do not let me regret the baring of my heart. There is only one man I have loved. And I love him still."

He closed his eyes, lowered his face to the place between her neck and shoulder, and wished away the world.

But it was going nowhere, as evidenced by a tug on his sleeve. "May I dance with Mother and you?"

As the musicians began to play another tune, Laura slipped off the tops of Lothaire's boots and, in her haste to remedy what nobles would think inappropriate, would have lost her footing had he not kept an arm around her waist.

"May I?" Clarice asked again.

Lothaire considered Laura's daughter—*their* daughter. "If my lady wife is not too breathless."

"Say you are not, Mother."

Laura glanced at him. "Methinks I am no more breathless than my husband."

Glad they were moving forward rather than struggling through the mire of past sins, he took Clarice's hand and instructed her to take her mother's.

Where Lothaire had felt desirous minutes earlier, he felt what seemed happiness as the three danced and Clarice's antics made them laugh.

As ever when he loosed that sound from his deepest place, he drew the regard of others who surely thought him incapable of such. And he saw in Laura's eyes what he had seen years ago when she dragged that laughter up out of him—adoration. How he wished he could be alone with her now. Unless he knew her not at all, she would give herself to him without restraint. And they might even make a child.

Since they were far from alone, he attempted to distract his body by shifting his regard to the other celebrants and caught sight of Sebille standing behind a depleted table, beside her the physician who had joined the celebration after setting the worker's arm. Though they were almost shoulder to shoulder, each time Lothaire looked to them, they were not conversing. And when he followed his sister's gaze, he was not surprised it rested on Angus. Earlier the knight had danced with several young women, but now he stood back from the revelry, head bent toward Tina who animatedly related something.

Was it truly too late for Sebille and Angus? If the knight asked her to dance, would she accept and, on the morrow, remain at High Castle rather than depart with their mother? Unlikely, but he must try.

When the dance ended, he thanked his two ladies, said he needed to speak with Angus, and assured them he would return shortly.

As Laura watched her husband weave among the dancers, she heard again the three words she had dared speak to him, albeit much of her daring was surely aided by one-too-many cups of wine. Though he had not spoken the words back, they had pleased him.

"Has Lord Soames made you love him, Mother?" Clarice asked.

She shot her gaze to her daughter. "What say you?"

"Has he made you love him as you loved my father?"

Not wishing to lie, she said, "I do love my husband, and I am glad to be his wife. And you? You are glad to be his daughter?"

"I like him better every day."

"That makes me happy." Laura kissed Clarice's brow. "This is our home now."

Her daughter drew back. "Do we belong as you wished us to, Mother?"

Nearly so, she thought. "Assuredly, you are of Lexeter, Clarice Soames." Lothaire's surname nearly stuck in her throat for how often she could now speak it—more, her husband's Christian name.

Clarice gasped. "A game of ball!"

"Go," Laura said, but already her daughter was on her way to being gone.

As Laura stepped off the heavily trodden grass, Tina appeared. "My heart smiles to see ye and yer husband dancin' and smiling as if never were an ill word spoken between ye. Methinks this the best day I have spent in yer service."

"'Tis a good day, and I pray for many more, Tina. Now what of you? I have not seen you dance."

A grin spread the woman's lips. "Sir Angus did ask me to join hands with him on the dance floor. Had not your lord husband wished to speak with him, we would be there now. But mayhap afterward."

Laura considered Lothaire whose expression and that of his man seemed too serious for a day like this, especially now the sun was all but sunk, the last of it sweeping golden-orange light up the trees beyond the shearing shelter. As she pondered the black of the night to come, she wondered how the moon and stars would look across the lake's surface.

"Tina?"

"Milady?"

Warming at the thought that would have delighted her younger self, Laura said in a rush, "I wish you to do something for me which will also be of benefit to you should Baron Soames's conversation with Sir Angus not soon end."

"Already it sounds agreeable, milady."

"In a quarter hour, regardless if my husband has yet to yield your dance partner, tell him to meet me at the lake."

The maid frowned. "Surely ye do not mean to venture there alone?"

"It is not far, and I shall reach it well ere night falls. You saw the great willow near the shore?"

"I did, but—"

"Tell my husband he shall find me there."

"I do not like this, milady. Though Lexeter seems peaceful, 'tis a great worry for a woman to go unescorted across the land. And dark soon falls and things happen in the night that do not in the light."

"You concern yourself where you need not," Laura gently chided. "A quarter hour, hmm?"

Tina sighed. "I shall be nibblin' and pickin' at my nails, but aye—a quarter hour and not a second more. *Tsk,* ye and yer love of water!"

"And keep watch over Clarice until my husband and I return."

"I shall, milady, even if I have to share my dance partner with her." Tina wagged a finger. "Ye keep good watch yerself, hmm? Does anything ill happen to ye, the Lord shall have to stand between me and yer husband's wrath."

"Be assured I shall."

A quarter hour, Laura mused as she stole away as inconspicuously as possible lest she catch Lothaire's eye. Time aplenty to reach the lake ahead of her husband, though if he rode rather than traveled on foot he would reach it soon after her.

On foot, she hoped, of a sudden nervous now she had committed to swimming and bathing with Lothaire and whatever came after.

Not as planned.

The one who watched the Lady of Lexeter slip away winced, then grunted over a pricked conscience. Whatever happened to Laura Middleton—now Soames—she had only herself to blame. And all the more so if this foolery of hers proved a tryst. And that might never be known did she find herself in the path of those soon to ride upon Thistle Cross to which the day's wool had been transported for storage. Certes, that was the direction the lady headed.

An instant later, something occurred that should have sooner, making the watcher curse as that one rarely did since the devil liked to slip into one's cracks and pry those thin places wide.

Raisa knew that, had learned it from Ricard.

Sebille knew that, had learned it from Raisa.

Angus knew that, had learned it from Sebille.

Accommodating women knew that, had learned it from Angus.

Father Atticus knew that, had learned it from those repentant women.

Then there was the physician, but from whom had he learned it? A good question deserving more thought.

As for Lady Laura, she also knew of the devil's penchant for cracks, surely having learned it from the man she had allowed to plant a babe in her.

Accursed Queen Eleanor! A pure bride Lothaire deserved, not this one who seemed intent on cuckolding him a second time.

The watcher searched out that lady. Finding her gone and wondering how long gone, a third curse opened another crack as what had belatedly occurred only to drift away now returned.

A sign the mind was slipping? Nay, there was much to occupy it, especially with the pieces of the plan screeching and grinding against one another. They would fit, providing Lady Laura's cuckoldry did not ruin it.

Those hired twice now must not be distracted by a pretty woman crossing their path. Hopefully, the men would take the first road on the far side of the lake though the going was rough compared to that which wound around the side nearest the celebration. Only necessary, of course, if Lady Laura ventured as far as the lake. And she might, but were her husband told she had slipped away—

Too late. If he departed the celebration, he might happen on men he would likely recognize as those who failed to end the lives of Lady Beata and her husband. And if he fell to them, the one who saw coins pressed into their greasy palms would ever ache over his loss. All that was done would be for naught.

"Please Lord," the watcher whispered, as ever seeking His understanding of what had to be done. "Let that faithless woman not cross their path."

29

WHATEVER THE TIDINGS, they were of great import.

Lothaire and Angus strode from the gathering to intercept the rider come over the rise across which the light of waning day shone.

"I come from Shepsdale, my lord!" the man called.

Lothaire tensed, certain the celebration's interruption had all to do with wool, the storehouse on the outskirts of the village of Shepsdale crowded with one quarter of this season's shearing, the remainder divided between High Castle and the villages of Wee Wainscot and Thistle Cross.

The rider reined in and swung out of the saddle.

"Deliver your tidings," Lothaire demanded, and hearing his sister call to him, glanced at where she and the physician hastened forward.

"Two—mayhap three—men broke into the wool stores, my lord. Blessedly, the watch put them to flight ere they could make good on whatever ill they intended." The man replenished his breath. "'Twas in this direction they headed."

Lothaire inclined his head. Were they not prepared to cede their loss and quit the barony of Lexeter by way of its southern border, there were only two places they might go—High Castle, which they would not dare for how impregnable it was outside of siege, or Thistle Cross with its own wool stores to which much had been added this day.

"The wool at Thistle Cross," Sebille gasped. "Dear Lord, not again."

Lothaire looked to where she had drawn alongside. "Not again, Sebille? What say you?"

"I am not certain, but..." She snatched up her prayer beads, began to trip her fingers over them.

"Speak, Sebille!"

"What if Lady Raisa is involved as she was with the attempt on the lives of Lady Beata and Baron Marshal?"

"How can you think that possible?"

She drew a quavering breath. "You cannot tell I told, but this morn she was so angry you are sending her away she said 'tis time to stir up more trouble—that if you are to make her life miserable, the one to whom she has given all ought not be spared, nor your harlot wife."

Lothaire believed Raisa would say that, but it did not seem possible her threat went beyond words.

A movement past Sebille drawing Lothaire's gaze to Tina, who halted and looked expectantly at him as if requesting permission to approach, he held up a hand and returned his regard to his sister. "If Mother is responsible for the attack, tell how she could arrange it."

"We think we have isolated her from those who once did her bidding for a coin or pretty bauble, but I fear not." She looked down. "Your wife never revealed the truth of her bruised face, did she?"

Lothaire's heart pounded harder. Though certain Laura had been struck despite her claim the bruise resulted from a fall, Sebille insinuated he had been correct in believing she was attacked, but not by her daughter.

"What is the truth?" he growled.

"I am sorry I did not tell it, but I believed Lady Raisa satisfied enough that she would not bother Lady Laura again, especially when she took so ill afterward. Too, I thought if she caused no further trouble you might allow her to remain at High Castle and I would not have to leave with her."

That last Lothaire barely heard. "Mother attacked Laura?"

"She is not as feeble as she feigns. But in her defense, your wife slapped her, though..."

"What?"

"In Lady Laura's defense, I am certain she was provoked after Lady Raisa stole into her chamber."

"Mother came belowstairs? How? Even were she well enough to do so, I instructed she be secured in her chamber when there was no one to watch over her."

"I have done as directed, Lothaire, as I did that morn. Yet when I returned abovestairs, she was slumped on the landing, fully dressed, face reddened and scratched by Lady Laura. She told I left her door unlocked, but I did not and her chamber accesses no inner passages. Thus, she must possess keys. I know not where, though I have searched."

He pushed a hand through his hair. "You should have told me. My *wife* should have told me!"

"Doubtless, Lady Laura feared you would be angered she had struck an old woman, and Lady Raisa assured the lady that if she did not speak of it, neither would she."

Would he have been angered? Mayhap in the moment, but he knew his mother and did not doubt she had said something cruel to Laura. Too, what was a slap and scratches compared to a bruise that powder and the cover of hair could not entirely hide?

Lothaire breathed deep. "Regardless of whether she hired men to break into the wool stores and thieve—if that is all they were there to do," he added when struck by the possibility they had meant to burn the stores, "she will depart High Castle first thing on the morrow. My only regret is you—"

"Nay!" Sebille's eyes glistened. "I shall not go with her. I hate she will be without family and may pass alone, but no more will I suffer her intrigues." She drew the back of a hand across her eyes. "If still you would have me remain at High Castle, I shall."

"Of course I would." He glanced at Angus who had spoken no word, wished there was hope in his eyes. Wish not granted, he said, "All will be pleased you are to remain with us."

"You are too kind."

Hearing the catch in Sebille's voice, Lothaire wondered if she had also looked near upon Angus. He turned to his knight. "I would have the celebration continue. Discreetly post men around the perimeter, then gather four knights and instruct them to prepare to ride on Thistle Cross."

"I am one of those knights, am I not?" Angus said with disapproval that told he did not believe it.

"Would that you were, but there is none better to ensure the safety of my wife, daughter, and sister."

"Daughter and sister, aye," the physician reminded his lord of his presence, "but your wife...Alas, nay."

Lothaire looked sharply at him. "Of what do you speak?"

"She is gone. I saw her moving along the tree line. Such a pity she so soon proves she remains a Daughter of Eve."

A single stride carried Lothaire so near the physician the man lurched backward, but Tina's shrill cry kept his white-knuckled fist from breaking a nose—or worse.

"'Tis what I came to tell, Lord Soames!" Of a sudden, the maid was at his side. "A quarter hour milady instructed me to wait, then I was to send ye to her at the lake. By the big weeping tree near the shore is where ye shall find her. Alone. Awaiting her lord husband."

Pain lanced Lothaire's chest. At this moment, he would rather Laura was in the bordering wood with a lover than near the lake. If those who had attacked Shepsdale's wool stores made for Thistle Cross, and had they paused along the way to water and rest their horses or conceal themselves from the man sent to alert the Baron of Lexeter, Laura could be exposed to them.

"Dear Lord," he rasped, then to Angus, "Get those knights astride."

Why, Laura? he inwardly shouted as he ran to his mount. *Why this very eve did you have to grant my wish?*

Veil cast off. Girdle unfastened. Gown removed and skirts spread at the base of the tree whose farthest branches hung over the water. Next slippers and hose. But not chemise.

She believed Lothaire would like finding her waiting for him, but it was too bold to bare herself entirely. And though determined to become accustomed to looking upon her body as she must accustom herself to looking upon his, this was enough. For now.

She pushed off the tree and drew the ties of her chemise through her fingers as she approached the water that tempted her toes to test its warmth, then her feet and ankles. She was up to her calves, the hem of her chemise raised to her knees, when movement on the opposite side of the lake drew her regard.

A doe and fawn. They saw her as well, now so still she would not have noticed them across the dusk had they not thought themselves alone moments earlier.

She stared, not wishing to do anything to cause them to seek cover. It was too many years since she had found herself thus, her exposure to the gentle animals limited to those brought to table in various states of venison.

"Beautiful," she whispered, and as if they heard and feared that on the other side of her voice an arrow strained its bowstring, they bounded away.

As Laura watched the last of their pert tails go from sight, she felt a vibration beneath her feet and heard hooves. She turned to the left where Lothaire would soon appear, then the right where he ought not appear. But the latter was the direction from which the rider—nay, riders—came.

Yanking her chemise higher, she ran to the tree. But too late. The white of her chemise having betrayed her, the three riders veered toward her.

As she slipped around the tree and put her back to it, one of them laughed as if excited by the prospect of a chase, and though Simon had not laughed in the cellar, she knew what it meant and her end would be the same if she did not escape.

"Not again, dear Lord," she whispered. "Not ever again. Pray, send Lothaire."

When the riders halted beyond the tree's skirt, all of her was begging to flee. She wanted to, but reason told it would be futile and so deplete her strength she would have little left to fight. Though that would be futile as well, there was one thing that held her together after Simon—that she had fought him all the way.

Sucking air through a throat threatening to close the space between mouth and lungs, she ventured a look around the tree.

"'Twill have to wait," said one who appeared to be of middling years. "If we are to see the rest of our coin, there is a task that needs doing."

"It will not take long." This from a younger man. "Come out, girl! Ye have but to be nice and we be nice to you. That is how it works, don' it?"

"My husband comes!" she called in a voice that barely carried.

"Did ye hear what she said?" the third man asked.

Another laugh. "Aye, that she is happy to oblige us."

Gripping her chemise closed at the neck, Laura forced more breath down her throat and called, "My husband comes. Leave ere he puts you through."

"If 'tis true," the younger said, "there are three of us to one of him."

"One of us," the dissenter once more spoke. "We got business to tend. Ye want somethin' for free when ye could fill your purse full enough to have a woman every night for a week, stay. We are goin' on."

Listen to him, Laura silently entreated. *Pray, go!*

Another laugh. "When the lass and I be done, I shall catch up with ye."

"Then make haste. We will not wait, and yer share be ours if'n ye are late."

The two turned their mounts and spurred around the side of the lake from which Laura had come.

"Show yourself," the man called above the beat of hooves. "I got no time for games, girl."

Laura slipped out of sight. As she searched the ground for something with which to defend herself, she wished she had snatched up her girdle with its meat dagger.

Below her was a hand-sized stone, to the right a fallen branch as long as her arm and as thick around as her wrist.

She snatched up the latter, and as she pried the stone from the earth, peered around the trunk. And nearly cried out. The sound of his companions' retreat having masked his movements, the man guided his horse beneath the tree's skirt.

"I see ye!" He grinned.

Laura slammed back against the trunk and dropped the branch to scrabble at the stone with both hands. She freed it, snatched up the branch, and careened around the opposite side of the tree.

"Where did ye go, girl?"

She drew a shuddering breath, jumped forward, and spun to face him as he urged his horse around.

His eyes moved from the branch to the stone. "I said I got no time for games, girl. And now I see ye better—that ye are a woman in full—I be less tolerant." He tugged the reins and clumsily dismounted as if much drink coursed his blood.

"I vow my husband comes." She backed away. "Do you touch me, he will kill you."

In a less than straight line, he advanced on her.

"Pray, rejoin your friends and live. You need not die."

"Neither need ye, but I am becomin' annoyed."

She thrust the branch forward. "Go!"

He sprang so suddenly she had no time to swing before he slammed a hand around the branch and wrenched it from her. "Now then, how much harder do ye think 'twill be for me to take the stone?" He tossed the branch aside. "Yer too pretty to mess up, so give over."

Laura raised the stone higher, drew her hand back past her ear to more forcefully strike him if he lunged.

He did. And she brought the stone down on his temple, causing him to yelp and stumble sideways.

Still gripping her weapon, praying his companions did not hear his cry above their pounding hooves, she turned to run. But swung back around to consider her assailant's horse. Were she to leave it to its master, she would soon be overtaken.

God willing, the beast would allow her to mount.

Heavenly Father, she silently beseeched as she lunged past the one who stood wide, head lowered and gripped between his hands, *let not your arms be too full. I cannot hold myself much longer.*

30

Two RIDERS AS the man from Shepsdale told. Not the three thought possible, a sweep of the lake revealing no others.

Lothaire knew they had sighted him and his knights against the falling dark, for as the miscreants rode around the side of the lake that presented the better road to Thistle Cross, they bent low over their horses and shouted between themselves.

They hoped to reach the wood, but they would not gain it ahead of their pursuers. Certain there could not have been adequate time for them to harm Laura who must have hidden, he determined he would himself have the satisfaction of taking the villains to ground.

The mounts of the two men no match for a destrier, Lothaire's prey was soon within reach.

Sword drawn, he swung his horse to the left, urged it to greater speed, and drew alongside the one in the lead. Though the slice of his blade would be satisfying, not only did he want these men alive to spill who had hired them—if any—but were Lady Raisa behind their mischief, their crimes might not warrant death. For a few coins, they but stirred trouble.

Thus, he slammed his sword's pommel into the miscreant's head, causing him to slump and tip out of the saddle. But as Lothaire swerved to avoid trampling his prey, the man's companion ducked the blade of a pursuing knight, swung his sword, and caught Lothaire's man in the upper arm.

"He is mine!" Lothaire shouted and spurred after him.

The man surprised, shifting his sword from the right to the left hand and swinging it hard against Lothaire's blade.

For this, the eldest Wulfrith brother had spent days with the Baron of Lexeter, stressing the life-and-death importance of not only battling in the saddle but doing it as well as when one's own legs were beneath him. His pupil had not yet achieved the skill demanded of him but had learned better how to move, balance, and leverage his body to deliver effective blows and fend off another's blade.

Engaging those skills now, guiding his horse with thighs and calves, Lothaire put his shoulder into his sword arm and forced the man's blade off his. His opponent recovered, and over and again their swords met until the miscreant turned his horse into the wood.

The arrangement of the trees, undergrowth, and ground were too unpredictable for Lothaire to soon regain the man's side, but he must. The deeper they penetrated the wood, the darker the shadows and the more likely his prey would escape.

Lothaire bent low, and finding a sizable gap between trees, made it through and once more drew alongside the miscreant.

Teeth bared, the man met him at blades, and something about his face was familiar. But before Lothaire could place him, his destrier lurched over the rock-strewn ground.

Lothaire's mount recovered just in time for his rider to swing a blade up and keep the other man's from slicing him open. And here was the anger Baron Wulfrith had told Lothaire to make good use of. His retaliatory blow nearly sending the miscreant off the other side of the saddle, the Baron of Lexeter prepared to finish him.

Like the dogs of the shepherd who moved the sheep when they were not of a mind to be moved, Lothaire turned his horse in front of the other's and struck with the pommel again—this time to the nose.

The man howled and lost the saddle. As the riderless horse surged forward, Lothaire reined around and saw his opponent lay on his back, a hand over his face. A moment later, he was scrambling for his sword. And thundering toward the miscreant were two knights who had followed their lord.

Lothaire shouted and held up a hand, signaling them to rein in.

Willing to accommodate the one who thought to shift the fighting from atop a horse to the ground, Lothaire loosed a foot from a stirrup, but before he swung his leg over, he caught a sound that would have gone unheard beneath the pound of hooves.

Laura's scream speared his heart. Still, he forced himself to remain aware of the position of the man who had regained his sword, just as Abel Wulfrith had drilled into him while setting numerous opponents at his pupil.

"Kill him if you must!" Lothaire shouted to his knights and put heels to his horse.

As he emerged from the wood, he saw one of the knights who had fallen back to secure the first unhorsed miscreant had regained his mount and spurred toward the lake where there had been no evidence of anyone a short while ago.

Now a horse could be seen standing beneath the drooping branches of the tree where Lothaire was to have met his wife. Atop it, bent over as if resisting being dragged off, was a figure clothed in white.

He would wager it was Laura, and if not for the pound of hooves and that of his heart, he would surely hear more of her screams. As he rounded the lake and drew near his knight, the rest of her was wrenched from atop the horse.

"Protect her, Almighty," Lothaire rasped. Then so she might know he came for her, he shouted, "Laura!"

Still she had the stone. And her assailant yet suffered the effects of the first blow, as evidenced by how effortlessly her struggle had dropped him onto his back when he pulled her from his horse.

She had followed him down and landed atop and well above his head, her splayed arms preventing her chin from striking the ground.

Pressing on the stone in one hand, her palm of the other, she raised her chest and tried to roll off, but his arm that had hooked her waist slid lower and clamped around the backs of her thighs. He might yet reel from her blow, but in that arm was strength greater than her own. And anger. Simon had also been stronger. And angry.

But young Laura had not been able to bring a weapon to hand, and despite the horror of what Simon had done—his body where it was forbidden to go—then she had not ten years of memories to lend her greater resolve.

She thrust her chest higher, exposing her attacker's face that had been buried against her belly, shifted her weight onto her left arm, and once more brought the stone down on his skull.

As he bellowed and loosened her to wrap his arms around his head, she might have heard her name called, but she could not know for certain above the anger pounding through her and someone nearby chanting, "Not again. Not ever again." And there was no time to search out whoever might have called to her—not if she was to beat the man bloody ere he could do worse to her.

Legs freed, she lurched back, drew her knees up to straddle him, and raised the stone a third time.

With his arms protecting his head, it would have to be his face.

That made her hesitate. And provided him the opportunity to shift from defensive to offensive.

Opportunity only, she silently vowed as one of his arms shot up, fingers wide. Though she evaded his grasp, her blow glanced off his cheek and only made him grunt.

She aimed again. Missed again.

And once more his hand closed around her wrist.

"Not again! Not ever again!" Over and over Laura screamed those words as Lothaire dragged his mount to a halt, flung himself out of the saddle, and sword in hand took two running strides to where his wife sat atop her attacker.

Sweeping his free arm around her waist as he moved the point of his blade to the miscreant's neck, he saw it all—her left hand scratching and slapping at the bloodied face, right hand clenching a stone rendered useless by the hand around her wrist. And as he lifted her up and back, still the man held to her and she continued to chant, though now it was her husband she fought, writhing and reaching behind to do to him what she had done to the one on the ground.

"'Tis Lothaire!" he shouted, and with a flick of his blade sliced her assailant's arm, causing the man to yelp and release his prey-turned-predator.

"Not again! Not ever again!" Laura cried as Lothaire struggled to retain his hold on her whilst setting his sword to the man's chest.

Blessedly, with her back pressed to her husband's chest, her aim was off when she flung her hand over her shoulder and tried to slam the stone into his head.

"'Tis me, Laura—Lothaire!"

Still she seemed not to hear him above the words she spilled.

Then the knight he had overtaken was off his horse, sword trained on the miscreant.

Knowing Laura would soon make good on one of her aims, Lothaire lurched back, released his sword, and captured her forearm. "I am here! You are safe."

She convulsed, stilled, then resumed her struggle. Though she no longer expended breath on words, she panted.

He turned her away from his knight who was dragging her attacker upright. Facing the lake across which moonlight surfaced, he entreated, "Laura love, no one can hurt you now."

She tossed her head back against his shoulder and turned her pale face up to his, but though she ceased struggling when their eyes met, it was like embracing a statue, her every muscle bunched as if awaiting the command to return to battle.

He longed for her to fold into him and wrap her arms around him, but she said, "Release me."

"It is me, Lothaire."

"I cannot bear it. Pray, release me."

Her plea hurt, though when he recalled the frantic words she had spoken he began to understand. And did not wish to.

"I shall let you go." He eased her down his body. "Get your feet beneath you, hmm?"

She jerked her chin, and some of the stiff went out of her when he lowered her.

"There. Can you stand on your own?"

"Release me."

He did, and made ready to catch her should she crumple. But she sprang away and swung around as if she thought herself vulnerable in giving him her back. And she was. Neither did he—or any warrior—care to expose that vulnerability to an enemy. But he certainly was not that to her.

Though it had darkened considerably, he saw her gaze go past him to the one who *had* made himself her enemy.

Not again. Not ever again, she had said whilst sitting astride the man and beating at him.

Lothaire held up his hands. "Truly, you are safe," he said and noted a stain on the front of her chemise. Blood? If so, surely her attacker's. He peered over his shoulder. His knight had bound the man and was putting him over the back of his horse.

"Take him to Thistle Cross and hold him with the others," Lothaire called. "I want them in chains."

"Aye, my lord."

Lothaire looked back at his wife who continued to stare past him. Seeing she quaked, he took a step toward her.

Her eyes shot to his, and she clapped a hand to her chest and retreated again, halting only when her heels touched the water rippling over the shore. A moment later, she drew her hand away and considered her palm. "His blood, not mine," she said. "This time I fought harder."

Better understanding the meaning of her words—*Not again. Not ever again*—beginning to hate himself, Lothaire tried to draw near. But she further distanced herself, the water now covering her feet up to her ankles.

Lothaire settled into his legs, gripped his hands at his sides, and waited for his knight to depart. At last, the man was astride and leading the horse burdened by the man it would not be difficult to put to death.

"Laura."

She moved her gaze to him.

"I am coming to you."

She backed away.

He spread his arms. "I will not touch you unless you wish it. You have my word."

"I know. I just..." She touched her bodice above the stain, plucked at the material as if to pull it off her skin. "I want this gone, but I would be unclothed."

"I shall collect your gown and bring it to you."

"Would you?" She nodded. "Aye, bring it to me."

He strode beneath the tree to where she had spread the garment as if to make a bed for them. But as he swept it up, he heard her gasp and swung around to see the white puddle of her chemise on the shore, and just beyond it her bared back as she waded into the cool night-darkened lake.

"Laura!" He ran, dropped the gown, and plunged into the water.

He was nearly at her side when she slipped beneath the surface, nearly caught hold of her hair whilst it floated atop. But then she was somewhere beneath and beyond him.

He dove under, reached wide, but only laid hands on water. Dark, hungry water.

Surfacing to replenish his breath, he cast his gaze around. No sign of her, but as he started to dive under again, she came up in front of him.

"Laura," he groaned. "What do you?"

She did not resist when he drew her to him. Gripping his tunic, she raised her streaming face to his. "Am I clean, Lothaire?"

Emotion flooding him, he choked, "You have ever been clean. It was not you who betrayed me, was it my brave love?"

Her spiked lashes swept down, then up. "I did not mean to. I was only trying to get away. But I should have known—should have yielded naught."

He did not care what she had yielded. She was not at fault, and it made him sick that her silence and evidence of her pregnancy had caused him to condemn her.

"Laura love, let me take you back to the shore. We shall sit and talk for as long as you wish. And you will tell me only what you are able to."

"You do not want to know. You said—"

"I did, but you need to tell me, and I need to listen. Come back?"

"I am cold."

"I will warm you."

They were so near the shore it was only moments before his sodden boots found purchase. Then he lifted his wife, and she slid a hand around his neck and pressed her bare breasts to his clothed chest as he waded ashore.

He carried her to where he had tossed aside her gown, lowered to sitting, and drew the garment over her. As he waited for her to speak, he held her close and watched the moon's languid movement across the sky and thought it like his mantle of blackest blue except someone was busily poking holes in the one above, but not as if to cause ruination. Rather, to give hope that on the other side of this dark could be found light.

Laura stopped shivering, but it was some minutes before she said, "It happened in the cellar at Owen."

He ought not be surprised, here the reason she would not venture into the one at High Castle.

Lowering his chin to the tip of her nose, feeling her breath on his neck, he closed his eyes and beseeched the Lord's aid in concealing the wrath rising through him which would be entirely impotent against a man long dead.

"But it did not begin there, Lothaire. It began nearly six years before when Si—" She gulped. "When Simon was ten and I was nine, he asked to kiss me and I said he could. I did not like it, and he agreed—said he did not understand why men and women did it. Still, he told we would wed when we were older and said I must promise to be his wife. Though I thought him a friend, it seemed a good thing to spend my life with one I liked, so I promised. Then he went away to begin his knight's training at an age much older than most boys since Lady Maude could not bear to part with him sooner. Two and three times a year he returned home, and each time he was more changed, but not…"

Feeling her draw a shuddering breath, he stroked her wet hair, certain even one word from him would make it harder to tell what Simon had done.

"Not in a good way," she whispered. "He was angry, and where he had liked to talk before, he preferred silence and sometimes stared so long at naught he fell asleep. I tried to pull him out of his dark mood by encouraging him to show me all he was learning, but he told me to leave him be. So I did, and it seemed to please him until…" A low whimper sounded from her. "The day before you met him prior to his return to his fostering lord, he learned you and I were betrothed. I could see he was displeased, but I was not prepared when he caught me alone on the stairs. He said I had promised to wed him, and I told him that was years in the past when we were children."

As she drew another breath, Lothaire gathered her nearer.

"He pushed me against the wall and tried to kiss me, but I ducked under his arm and ran to the hall where I stayed at Lady Maude's side the remainder of the day." She tilted her head back, met his gaze. "I had good reason to suspect it was him at the pond—not a dragonfly—that nearly struck you. Certes, 'twas a stone."

Lothaire nodded.

"I did not see him again during your subsequent visits to Owen, and I believed anger kept him away. But he came again when you were unable to visit because your mother took seriously ill. You remember?"

Hardly forgettable, not only since it was during that time he was cuckolded—when Laura should have been with him, not the one who got her with child—but because by the time he discovered his mother's turn of health was a ploy to keep him from Laura, it was too late to journey to Owen. And Lady Raisa had been pleased, she who had believed him too entranced, she who had attacked Laura in her chamber.

"I remember."

She flinched.

Now the tale was begun, the waiting was harder for his imaginings of what had happened in that cellar, but finally she said, "I would not see you again for five months, and when you saw me…" Her voice caught, and she shivered, though surely not from the breeze sweeping off the lake. "…you saw what Simon did."

"Enough is told, Laura. I need hear no more."

"You do if you wish the truth, all of it though 'tis uglier yet. And I would not have a lie between us."

"A lie?"

"That I am innocent." She gripped his tunic, caught up some of his skin beneath. "Had I not encouraged him, I might have prevented what he did."

Lothaire was not expecting that, and before he could think better, he said, "You encouraged him?"

"With what I thought good reason."

"I do not understand, Laura. What good reason could there be?"

"Hold me closer, and I will tell," she whispered. "And pray I need never tell it again."

31

Barony of Owen, England
Winter, 1152

IT SHOULD BE Lothaire come to Owen, but it was Simon. And Lady
Maude, who had been so happy to see her long-absent son, had cried last
eve when he snapped at her for treating him as if he were still a child.

Her fault, he had said. Had she allowed him to be fostered five years
earlier at an age most noble boys left home to begin training for knighthood, he would not suffer the humiliation of being a young man less
skilled at weaponry than many far younger than he.

Then he had turned on the lady's stepson and said it was his fault as
well, that when the father they shared had passed, Joseph ought to have
known it was too late for his youngest brother to be fostered and seen
him trained at home the same as Laura's betrothed.

Last, he had turned on Laura and demanded to know if her *long-
haired Lothaire* could swing a sword better than he could sling a stone.

She could only stare, and he had muttered that Michael—only
Michael—had a care for him, then run from the hall.

This morn as they broke their fast, he had appeared and apologized
for behavior he excused as being born of frustration with mastering
wrestling at which he often found himself pinned by younger opponents.

Lady Maude had cried again as they embraced, then entreated Joseph to spend the morn on the training field with his brother. With obvious reluctance, the Baron of Owen had agreed.

Now, having missed the nooning meal, Simon entered the kitchen that was vacant except for Laura. Dirty and perspiring, a bruise at his jaw, he halted at the sight of her where she sat on a stool near a cooking fire.

"Laura," he said with some of the smile of the boy he had been. "What do you here?"

She summoned some of the smile of the girl she had been and closed her psalter. "I am early for my lesson."

He put his head to the side, causing damp blond hair to shift across his brow. "What lesson?"

"In the workings of a kitchen." She stood, hooked the psalter on her girdle, and clasped her hands at her waist. "As I shall not be long in wedding"—she watched his eyes for anger distinguishable from the reflection of the cooking fire—"my lessons began in earnest last week. Each day I observe the preparation of a meal in its entirety. This day, 'tis supper in which Cook shall instruct me.

He looked around the room. "It looks to me those preparations are hours away. You must be an eager pupil."

"I am, but 'tis only an hour ere Cook returns. There is much more than you can imagine that goes into feeding so many. When I have my own household, I shall be prepared."

"And make your husband proud."

Again, she watched his eyes, again saw only the flicker of the cooking fire. "I pray so."

He nodded. "My mother has been very good to you."

"Like the mother I have not, and for which I am grateful." She gestured to the table where a dozen cooling loaves sat. "You must be hungry. May I cut you bread and cheese?"

He dipped his head, scratched the back of it. "Actually, what I am is thirsty. As you see, my brother took seriously the task forced upon him."

"Then I shall pour you ale." She started toward the sideboard where a pitcher sat.

"Too warm, but wine straight from the cool cellar..." He sighed. "That would quench."

She hesitated. Though Simon and she had played there whilst children, and in its dark corners witnessed the birth of kittens destined to become rat catchers, she did not like to venture alone into the chill, musty depths. But she supposed she ought to since, on occasion, it would be expected of a lady of the castle.

She indicated the table again. "Sit and rest whilst I fetch cool wine." She retrieved a torch and crossed to the cellar. As she set a hand on the door, a feeling she should not go down into the dark made her look around.

Simon raised his eyebrows. "You are too kind," he said and crossed to the table.

She smiled. "I shall not be long, but do eat something." Carrying the torch before her, she stepped onto the landing and descended the steps.

She had to pass through the room that held the dry stores and traverse a long corridor to reach the place where casks of wine and ale were kept. She fixed the torch in a wall sconce alongside the doorway, retrieved one of several ewers turned upside down on a shelf, and crossed to the nearest wine cask. As she reached to its unsealed lid, a sound turned her head.

Was it the closing of the cellar door? Nay, more likely a cat stalking its next meal. Or the rat trying to avoid becoming that.

Laura pushed at the lid, but it was heavy and she had to set down the ewer to add the strength of her other arm to the effort. The lid yielded, and the torchlight that swept into the opening revealed the cask's contents were nearly down to the dregs. Knowing she must disturb the wine as little as possible when she dipped into it were Simon not to gag on stirred up sludge, she reached to the ewer at her feet.

"You are so pretty, Laura."

She spun around, saw he stood with a forearm braced against the doorframe. "Simon! What do you here? I said I would bring you wine."

He stared.

Something in his eyes causing alarms to sound through her, she forced a smile onto her lips and lightness into her voice. "Mother of Mary, are you really so impatient?"

He straightened. "As told, I am thirsty. Very thirsty."

She snatched up the ewer. "Then go, silly. I shall be close on your heels."

He continued forward, and as she closed her other hand around the ewer's belly and raised it like a shield before her chest, he halted over her.

"Silly." He turned his mouth down. "Once I was, but I am no longer the boy Mother and you think me. I am a man—like your Lothaire Soames." He frowned. "I am right in thinking him a man, am I not?"

All of her jangling, she wished herself on the other side of him and gasped when he brushed his fingers down her cheek and across her lips.

"You like him, hmm?"

She unstuck her tongue. "He is a good man, will make a good husband."

He sighed so heavily his breath moved the hairs on her brow. "You have forgotten something."

"Have I?"

His hands closed over hers on the ewer. "That you belong to me. You promised."

She had to clear her throat to regain her voice. "That was years ago, and we are no longer children. Soon you will be a knight and I shall become the wife of Lothaire Soames."

"Nay, you will be my wife."

"I am betrothed, Simon."

"Easily undone."

"I do not wish it undone. I love Lothaire."

His nostrils flared, face darkened, then he wrenched the ewer from her and closed his hands over her upper arms. "You kiss him, do you not?"

She braved eyes she no longer knew. "You are frightening me. Pray, cease."

"Aye, you do." He slid fingers down her chin, beneath it, pressed them to the tops of her breasts.

"Simon!"

"What else do you with Lothaire Soames?"

She strained backward, came up against the cask. "Let me go!"

"More than kisses, eh?" He gave a short laugh. "Still, methinks not what you shall do with me." He lowered his head.

She snapped her chin aside and his lips fell to her ear, the heat of his breath making her shudder.

"I vow you will like my kisses and touch better, Laura."

She strained to the side, but in some ways he truly was a man, her strength no longer rivaling his.

"Bargain with me," he rasped.

She returned her gaze to his. "What?"

"Let me kiss you, and you kiss me back. If you do not like it, I will let you go and bother you no more. We shall just be...friends."

Not after this, Laura thought. "You would have me betray my betrothed?"

"He need never know, and 'twill hardly matter, for you will like my kiss. 'Tis me you shall wed, Laura Middleton."

Perhaps she could wait him out, but what would he do? Strike her? She felt that violence in his hands. And the scream she held in was so forceful she could hardly breathe past it.

"Agreed?" he said.

It was a mistake, but his grip was so hard there seemed no other means of escape. "You promise you will let me go if I allow you to kiss me?"

"If you kiss me back."

Though her stomach twisted at the thought of his lips where Lothaire's had been, she said, "I agree."

The tension in his face eased, and in his seemingly genuine smile she saw her old friend.

He released one of her arms, drew her to the wall, and settled her back against it. "I love you," he said and tipped up her chin.

With the first touch of his lips, she had to swallow to keep her stomach from emptying itself.

He drew slightly back. "Our agreement is that you return my kiss."

She leaned up, set her mouth on his, and tried to kiss him as she kissed Lothaire. But even with her eyes closed there was no pretending she was not revolted. And no denying it was wrong.

She dropped onto her heels, shook her head, and staring at Simon's throat said, "I am sorry, but I do not feel what you wish me to feel. 'Tis the same as...when I kiss Michael's cheek. Brotherly."

His hands gripped her hard again, and she looked up. "The bargain struck is completed, Simon. I do not love you as I love Lothaire. I do not want you for a husband as I want him."

His eyes moistened, lips trembled, and she thought he would cry, but he shook her, causing the back of her head to strike the wall.

"You are hurting me!"

"If you will not love me, I will not love you," he spat, and once more she saw the boy in him—this time the one who had not liked that she could run faster and swim farther. "Hence, I shall simply desire you."

Desire. Somehow he made the word Lothaire had also spoken sound foul. But Simon's intentions were far different. Lothaire had used it to explain why he suddenly ended a kiss that had progressed to an embrace and tested the boundaries of their garments. Simon used it to tell what was to come. And moments later she found herself on the floor.

"Cease, Simon! You cannot—"

"'Tis my right!" She tried to turn from him, but he thrust her onto her back. "Lie still. That is all I require of you."

She dragged her nails down his cheek, and he slapped her so hard her opposite cheek struck the floor.

"Be still!"

She punched and slapped and writhed, and he cursed and punched and slapped back. And when she lost her breath, his hands were all over her and she heard the tearing of cloth.

Then he howled and collapsed atop her.

Guessing her knee had struck him between the legs, she wriggled out from beneath him, but he kept hold of her—until she bit his hand.

She made it to her knees, sprang upright, stumbled toward the doorway, and stopped when she heard him sob, "Forgive me! I did not mean to do it. You know I did not!"

Leave him to his regret, instinct shrilled, and she meant to run as far as she could get, but her heart that had adored the boy would not allow her to distance herself. Peering over her shoulder, she saw he was on his knees, bowed back convulsing, head hung between his arms.

Thinking it strange only now she felt the true depth of the pain dealt by his blows and how in need of breath she was, she leaned forward and braced her hands on her thighs.

"Why did you do that?" she croaked. "Why, Simon? We grew up together. Were friends. Told our secrets to no others. We—"

"Because you promised," he said, just above and behind her. Then he had her again, this time facedown, the grit of the floor raking at her face, his calloused palm capturing her scream and undeterred by the teeth she sank into it, even when his blood sprang onto her tongue.

As he did what he did to her, beyond struggling that proved as futile as prayer for the Lord to deliver her, she told herself she was asleep—only dreaming a terrible dream from which she would soon awaken.

32

Barony of Lexeter, England
July, 1163

"Forgive me." The moment he said it, he wanted the words back. They were the same with which Simon had fooled Laura when she had but to keep running to save herself. And even were they not the same, they were so inadequate they offended.

"Forgive you?" she whispered in a voice weary from the telling, throughout which she had several times paused to cry quietly. "For what have you to be sorry? You did naught but believe as you were meant to."

The anger tempting him to seek hell over heaven so he might hunt down Simon D'Arci began to shift toward Laura. And he heard it in his voice when he said, "Why did you not tell me the truth? Why did you allow me to believe you cuckolded me?"

She drew back, and even by moonlight he could see how red and swollen her eyes were. "I am sorry you are angry, but there are many reasons it was for the best."

"Or so Lady Maude persuaded you." He grimaced over that woman's name.

"I was not yet ten and six, Lothaire. She knew the world better than I. And she was right."

"How could she be? Ten years, Laura! Ten years I believed you a—"

She pressed fingers to his lips. "But now you know I am not, aye?"

He did not doubt his glower was ugly, but he could not temper it. Drawing his head back and lips off her fingers, he said, "Why do you make that a question? Of course I believe you, as I would have had—"

"I think you might have, but Lady Maude reasoned the truth would not change that I was ruined, and with proof of that ruin growing in my belly, your mother would reject me regardless if my babe was conceived through ravishment or consent."

Seeking to calm himself, he momentarily closed his eyes. "You said *many reasons*. What other reasons bought your silence, allowing me to believe as I did the day you revealed you bore another man's child?"

"Though I did not wish to be with him like that, Lothaire, I am not blameless. I knew I should not go down in the cellar with no others near. I should not have let him kiss me nor returned his kiss. When I escaped and he beseeched my forgiveness, I should have kept running. When I saw he wept, I should not have given him my back. I knew it here and here." She touched her chest and head. "Michael says it is the gift of fear the Lord gives us, one we ought to open as soon as it appears. But I did not even untie the string. The underserving fool I was tossed the gift aside as if I wanted—" She caught her breath. "I vow I did not want what he did. But why did I not run when I could have?"

It was a question to which Lothaire also wanted an answer, and he nearly demanded she look harder to find it, but Father Atticus supplied it. How many times had Lothaire denounced his mother's divisiveness and threatened to send her from High Castle? How many times had he let her stay though her presence disrupted the household and made life more difficult?

The priest had named Lothaire's weakness *guilt and fear*—of hurting his mother's feelings, of being disliked, of Sebille's sacrifice that had ever been greater than his.

Laura's situation was different, but like Lothaire she also sought to salve her guilt and fear. Rather than open the Lord's gift, she had yielded it to one who had proven so untrustworthy he was dangerous.

"What other reasons?" he pressed.

She looked down. "Lady Maude is the one who found me in the cellar, and never did she suggest it was my fault, even when Simon claimed I was willing."

"Of course she did not think it your fault. You were beaten!"

She drew a quaking breath. "I loved her like a mother, and she would have been further hurt were the truth of her son known far and wide. And when she later learned why he was so changed from the boy I grew up alongside and why he did that to me..."

"What did she learn? How did she excuse such depravity?"

Laura drew her lower lip between her teeth. "He was not merely humiliated during training for being older than other squires. Terrible things were done him not unlike what he..."

Lothaire was jolted by the horror of what she could not finish, but it did little to assuage the longing to hunt the knave through hell. "Had I known," he growled, "I would have killed him."

"Maude said you would—yet another reason to hold close the truth. It would have ruined your life more than mine. And here is another reason. It is ill enough to be misbegotten, so the fewer who know how my daughter came to be, the less likely she will learn of it and suffer for it."

Lord, douse this fire, Lothaire silently prayed. "When Simon heard you were with child," he said, "did he offer to wed you?"

"He did, and Lady Maude believed it the best and responsible thing to do. But I could not even bear his voice, so how was I to bear his person? More, his bed? And what kind of father would such a man be?" She shook her head. "Though ever I would be known for a harlot, I refused him."

Imaginings of how much worse her life could have been dampening the fire, Lothaire said, "In that instance, perhaps when it mattered even more with Clarice to consider, you opened the gift of fear."

After a long silence, she said, "I suppose I did, though I must confess I did not yet love her. Indeed, I did not think I could since she was got by violent means. But though I have not been a good and present mother, I did come to love her. And easier it was when Simon died."

Lothaire's mind was turning, and it took the next corner fast. "You told he was not murdered, that his death was an accident whilst in service to his lord, but I never learned how he died."

"Aye," she breathed as if relieved to leave behind talk of Simon and her. "When he earned his spurs, Michael persuaded his lord, Baron Lavonne, to enlist his brother as a household knight. As there was much conflict between the Lavonnes and Wulfriths, King Henry ordered a marriage between the families, and so Baron Lavonne sent men—among them Simon—to collect his bride. The two sisters fled, and though Lady Gaenor escaped, Simon overtook Lady Beatrix and sought to ravish her. They struggled and fell into a ravine, and though the fall killed Simon and Lady Beatrix sustained a head injury, she was accused of murder, and Michael believed her guilty. Wishing to confront her son's murderer, Lady Maude traveled to Castle Soaring where Lady Beatrix was held. I accompanied her, as did Clarice, who was but three. It was then we met Baron Marshal disguised as Sir Piers."

Lothaire nodded for her to continue.

"When Lady Beatrix told her tale, Maude and I knew Simon's death was not murder. I told Lady Beatrix I could not reveal the secret of my own ravishment by speaking in her defense, but assured her I believed her. And Michael, who had fallen in love with the lady, had to accept the little brother he had loved was not the same who died."

"If neither you nor Lady Maude lent your voice to Lady Beatrix's defense, how was she acquitted?"

"I was not there, but Maude said that despite her head injury, she told a convincing tale."

Remembering his audience with Lady Beatrix at Castle Soaring, Lothaire now understood her faltering speech. And knew what she had nearly revealed before closing her mouth—Laura's ravishment.

"Too, she had Michael at her side," Laura continued, "and Maude testified for her. She gave no details but told her son had ravished another."

Lothaire gripped the back of his neck. "I am glad she did right by Lady Beatrix, but she did not do right by you."

"She gave my daughter and me a home and was the best grand-mother—"

"That Clarice never knew," Lothaire inserted.

"It could not be helped."

"Your daughter—*our* daughter—believes you loved her father, that it was the loss of him that made you a shadow." Recalling Clarice had told Lady Maude encouraged the girl to allow her mother to sleep because her nights were long, Lothaire ached more for all Laura had suffered. And now he better understood why she had sacrificed herself to remove her daughter from Owen and the boy she feared would ruin Clarice.

Only when he trusted his voice to carry did he ask, "Will you tell Clarice the truth when she is older?"

"I was certain I would not, that it would disturb her to know the circumstances, and still I do not think I shall, but she is stronger and more determined than me and I fear—"

"Nay, Laura, she is not stronger nor more determined, though we shall aspire to make her so. For now she is a girl, and you...I saw what you did to your attacker. Had I not come—"

"He would have done to me what Simon did."

Lothaire shook his head. "I do not think so." It was something of a lie, but only *something*. He believed she would have prevailed as much as he feared she would not have. But if she thought it possible she herself could have prevented the ravishment, perhaps she would sooner heal from the horror of once more finding herself an object to be desired and taken.

"I thank you," she said softly.

He kissed her forehead. "What do you fear for Clarice?"

"That one day her curiosity may have me so pressed into a corner I shall have to tell her just enough about her father for it not to be a lie. But even that seems too much."

"Perhaps if I am the father she needs, she will not be so curious," Lothaire said. "Regardless, whatever you must tell, you will not tell it alone. We have found each other again, and we will take back every year lost to a secret that should not have been made nor kept." He ground his teeth. "I should have let you tell me sooner."

"I should have tried sooner. Michael believed you ought to be told ere we wed as discussed the night you saw me embrace him. I did wish to tell you, and I meant to, but fear you would not believe me and think worse of me stayed my tongue. When finally I determined to reveal all, you believed Michael had fathered Clarice, and the truth seemed even a lie to me since the only ones who could support my claim were Michael and his wife. And I feared you would think he was merely trying to place the blame on a brother who could not defend himself."

She was probably right. Had he been told at the wrong time, his defenses could have flung terrible words at her. And for so much more he would now require forgiveness.

"Laura," he groaned, "however long it takes to pardon me for the wrong done you, I will wait."

Her breath caught, then she slipped off his lap and rose onto her knees beside him. As she set a hand on either side of his face, the gown draping her shoulders slid down her back, revealing her in moonlight as he could only bear by keeping his eyes firm upon hers.

"If there is anything to forgive, Lothaire, 'tis forgiven. Love is like that."

He would not have thought his chest could tighten further, but his next breath was a struggle against what seemed iron bands.

The moisture in her eyes threatening to overflow, she continued, "Only you have I loved. Though for years I tried to stop, that first day at Windsor I knew I loved you still." Tears slid off her lashes onto her cheeks. "You are as much me as I am—mayhap more." A sob stole the warmth of her breath from his face. "Do you think...Can you love me again?"

He could not give his lungs what they demanded in return for words, could not loosen his jaw to mouth them. And now his muscles quaked as the boy he no longer was sought to make him one again. Her emotions tempting him to tears a man ought not shed no matter that Father Atticus told even the Lord wept, Lothaire lowered his head and found a breath of air between them, but it spent itself on a groan.

Her hands slid from his face and around his neck, and he felt her cheek settle against the side of his head.

"Too soon," she whispered, "but when I have proven a good and faithful wife, there will be love again."

He lifted his head.

Laura moved her hands to his shoulders, leaned in, said against his lips, "Make love to me, even if 'tis not yet truly love."

He jerked back. "Here? Now?"

She blinked, and he saw that though her eyes were moist and bright, tears no longer fell. "Aye, show me desire is a good thing between a man and a woman."

He was ashamed that his body stirred. Though this was to have been the time and place to consummate their marriage, surely not after what had nearly happened here. Not after all she had been made to relive in the telling of what she had too long held close.

"Just as once we imagined," she said and angled her head.

Her sweet kiss further awakened him, but he gripped her arms and eased her back. "Not now, not here, not after what almost—"

"Almost, Lothaire. Being with you will help me forget that and... the other."

Or it could ruin all, he thought. "I want it to be right and good for you, Laura. I want no regrets."

"I am stronger than you think, and all the more for unburdening our present and future by revealing the past. More, for being believed. And redeemed." Her smile was hopeful. "This eve I came here to be your wife. Do not let them take this from us—not ever again."

She did not want Simon or that other miscreant to win this night— to once more steal *what should have been.* Neither did he wish it, and more greatly he wanted her this night knowing what those others sought to do. But if it proved a mistake to make love to her, it might be more difficult for her to recover.

"It has to be right, Laura."

"With you, the man I love, how can it not be?"

"Easily, I fear."

"Then go slowly." She leaned near again. "Go gently."

He wanted to, but he knew his body, and those words—Heaven help him those words!—moved him toward a place he now feared going. More than ever he wanted this woman, but she needed him to prove desire could be a good thing, and that was only possible if he revealed the heart that beat so powerfully it was no longer subordinate to his head. Indeed, one day it might rule his head. If they were to become one this night and were there to be no regrets or memories of how wrong it could be, she had to know what he felt.

"It is not too soon for me to love you again," he said, "and blessedly, not too late."

Her eyes widened.

"You have naught to prove, Laura love. Though I would not have allowed myself to believe it until this night, I do not think I ever stopped loving you. I feel as if I have but opened a door against which I set my back, that ever I had one hand upon it and had only to be welcomed back inside."

Tears again, but these were the stuff of stars, and their trails on her cheeks were like those bright lights that shot across the dark. "Truly?" she whispered. "'Tis love you feel for me?"

"Aye. You are the Laura I have loved and still love, she who wished to swim and bathe with me, she whom many a time I tried not to imagine here believing never would she be. And yet you are."

"Now and forever, Lothaire."

He pulled her to him and slowly…gently kissed her.

Slowly…gently stroked the arms she wound around him.

Slowly…gently slid his palm down the back she arched toward him.

Slowly...gently lowered her to the bank.

Slowly...gently made love to his wife.

"You are more beautiful than I imagined."

"Am I?" Laura murmured where she lay on her side, head pillowed on his shoulder, all of her wonderfully exhausted against the warmth of Lothaire's body and beneath the gown she had pulled over them.

Lothaire chuckled. "Not enough for you?"

"Hmm?" she murmured, sleep's hand heavy upon her shoulder.

"Very well," he said. "I can do better." He rolled toward her.

Of a sudden, she was on her back, the gown fallen to the side, and it was no longer the hand of sleep on her shoulder. It was Lothaire's. And she recalled she had questioned her beauty which had not been an attempt to gain further flattery.

Leaning over her, loosed hair falling between them to shadow his own face, he said, "I shall not speak of your face, for ever I have known it to be beautiful, and your neck as well. But your shoulders...Would that my fingers were not so hardened that I might feel as much as my eyes see in moonlight."

Carefully, as if for fear his rough skin would mar her, he trailed his fingers down her collarbone and into the cleft at the base of her throat. She did not fear his touch—not anymore—but there was something else she needed to tell him before he went further.

"Lothaire," she said as his fingers moved downward, "I hardly know my body."

He stilled.

"Certes, now you know it better than I. After..." She shook her head, and Simon fled. "I could not bear to look upon it, especially as it grew round with child. Even after Clarice was born—when once more it was mine alone—it was hard to gaze upon. Will you be patient with me?"

He splayed his hand above her breasts as if to feel the beat of her heart. "You need not ask that of me, love. As I am most willing and you are most willing, and providing God is as willing, we have so many years ahead of us there is no need to rush anything. You have but to tell me what you want and need and 'tis yours."

He made it sound easy, but it could not be, especially if she wounded his pride.

"Tell me, Laura."

She laid a hand over his above her heart. "I now know desire can be wondrous, that where there is love it is not to be feared, but I am not yet enough at ease to..."

"Feel as much as I felt," he finished, and there was no anger in his voice as of one offended.

She nodded. "I felt things I never knew I might, and I would like to feel them again, but there seems something more, meaning I am not fully awake as thought—and I want to be for you. For us. Do you think I will awaken all the way?"

"Methinks this night you nearly did, so aye. And I will be patient, Laura. I will go slowly and gently until you are fully awake."

"You are not disappointed?"

"In ten years, I have not been happier. So now, if you are comfortable, may I continue to tell you how beautiful you are?"

"You do not think we ought to return to the celebration?"

"All are full of food and drink, song and dance, and the satisfaction of the end of shearing season. I do not believe they will miss us. And certes, one of my knights will inform Sir Angus of the events that transpired here, and he will see Clarice and Sebille safely home."

She trailed a hand up his arm, loved that her fingers could hardly begin to span his muscular shoulder. "Then pray, tell me so I might find the words to tell you how beautiful you are."

He laughed, and she so loved that sound from the deepest of him that she would have happily traded his words for more of that rumble. "Methinks I would rather be told how handsome and virile I am."

"*Beautiful* and virile, Husband. If you wish to be merely handsome you will have to cut your hair."

After a thoughtful moment, he said, "You wish me to?"

She smiled at how accommodating he sounded. "You would do it for me?"

"Only you, Laura love."

She slid her hand up his neck, drew her fingers through his damp hair out to the ends. "But then I could no longer wear your hair," she said.

"Wear my hair?"

She felt her body blush. "Wh-when you are like this with me."

"So I ought not cut it?"

She fixed a thoughtful expression on her face. "Since you are far more Samson whose hair was his strength than King David's usurping son whose hair proved his downfall, methinks it best you not cut it. Certes, I shall not."

He kissed her long, raised his head. *"You* are my strength."

Though she thought he exaggerated, she felt stronger despite being bared and as vulnerable as a woman could be. However, this was her Lothaire—lost to her and now found by the grace of God who had surely made Queen Eleanor His instrument.

"Your strength," she mused. "Not merely your *somehow?*"

"That is important too, but not for how Lexeter is saved. For how I am saved. I love you, Laura. Now allow me to continue so you will know how beautiful you are and wish to see what I see. Then one day I shall wear *your* hair."

33

SHE SLEPT THE sleep of a small child, having barely stirred after he lifted her onto his destrier and she gained his promise they would soon return to the lake.

Now Lothaire stood beside the bed cradling his wife, thanking the Lord she was safe, and praying he would never fail to keep her from harm—that he would prove worthy of this precious gift returned to him.

"My somehow, my strength," he rasped and gently lowered her to the mattress and turned the coverlet over her. Though he longed to curl around her if, in sleep, she trusted him enough to give him her back, he must leave her.

A short while later, Angus and he departed the hall.

"I know what you have to tell must be serious to keep me from my marriage bed," Lothaire prompted when they stood in torchlight alone but for guards patrolling the walls.

"Most serious, my lord. Sir Chastaine, who saw your captives delivered to Thistle Cross, recognized two of the three men. He is certain the older ones are the same hired by your mother to murder Lady Beata and Baron Marshal."

Recalling the flash of recognition in the wood, Lothaire stiffened. Sir Chastaine was correct, meaning Raisa once more worked her ill.

"Then my sister was right." He breathed deep. And knew what must be done. Though his mother was to depart on the morrow, he would give her another day—mayhap two—but not to incriminate herself. He required no further proof. What he needed was to uproot the one who aided her within these walls.

"You are thinking a trap," Angus said, "as am I."

"Aye. Under heavy guard, have the miscreants moved from Thistle Cross to High Castle's outer dungeon. Then once again we shall be arrogantly confident our cells can hold them. When my mother's accomplice tries to free the men, we will have him and ensure Lady Raisa's machinations do not infect her dower property the same as High Castle."

The knight inclined his head. "'Twill be done on the morrow."

"I thank you and..."

"My lord?"

"No one but you and I are to know of the trap."

"Not even your sister?"

Lothaire considered, shook his head. "Not even Sebille."

Awakened with kisses.

Laura lifted her chin to move her husband's lips from the side of her neck to her mouth. But they went only as far as her cheek.

She opened her eyes, and before the dawn-lit room came into focus realized she was on her side, the one kissing her at her back.

Lothaire, she told herself even as she sought to move away. Blessedly, he released her, and she scooted and dropped onto her back. And was grateful for the understanding in his eyes.

"Thus, I held you through the night," he said and levered onto an elbow. "Until this moment, you were content."

"Forgive me. I..."

"I know, Laura love. But see, 'tis our nuptial chamber."

And you, she thought. *Ever you.*

"As methinks it is too soon for you to wear my hair again," he said, "I would but hold you if you would like to linger abed."

She wished it were not too soon but was glad he was content to wait. "You do not need to rise, Husband?"

"The shearing is done. Though there is yet much to occupy me, for many months you will more likely awaken to me than not—so much you may sooner wish for spring and summer."

"Never." She moved onto her side to face him. "Hold me like this— for now."

He drew her nearer, made a pillow of his forearm. "There is something of which I would like to speak that I meant to last eve but could not find the right place to do so," he said.

"Something is amiss?"

"Nay, something is explained that ought to have been sooner, though I understand why you did not—why you felt you needed to lie."

Her heart stuttered. Did he not believe Simon had fathered Clarice after all? He must have felt her fear, for he hastened to explain, "I speak of the bruise on your face. Last eve Sebille revealed it was gained by my mother's attack."

She gasped. "Then you also know I slapped her. I should not have, but—"

"I know she provoked you, Laura, would have known even had my sister not revealed it. Will you tell me how?"

The beat of his heart beneath her fist alerting her she had gathered up a handful of his tunic, she opened her fingers and pressed her palm to his chest. "I know she worries for you, that you are precious to her, but when she said Clarice would become a harlot like her mother...I am sorry I slapped her, but though I know she is old, she is not as infirm as she would have you believe." And for which Laura was endlessly grateful the lady would depart High Castle this day, though she would take Sebille with her.

"That my sister also confirmed," Lothaire said, "but you are not to be sorry. It is I who regret my belief Clarice struck you. I thank the Lord there was time and distance between that belief and when next I was near enough to confront her. Had I accused her..." He sighed. "I like her, and my word I give I will not seek to wed her away until she is of a very good age and herself wishes it."

Laura's eyes teared. "I thank you. I have so much to make up with her methinks I shall need every day you provide."

"Not as many as you think. She cares much for you, oft seeks assurance I take seriously the need to make you fall in love with me so you will be happy again."

"I shall assure her 'tis done."

"As shall I. Now another thing." A muscle in his jaw convulsed. "My mother will not depart High Castle this day."

She startled. "Why?"

"You need not ink your quill, Laura. What the queen ordered and to which I am agreeable, shall soon be done. Do you trust me enough to accept my word for it, or would you have me further explain what I prefer not to at this time?"

She longed for an explanation but said, "Of course I trust you."

He touched his mouth to her brow. "One thing more, then I would savor holding you."

She smiled. "Tell me quick."

"Sebille has decided she will not accompany our mother to her dower property."

Laura blinked. "Then she and Sir Angus...?"

"I think not, but does not the Lord enjoy making belief of our disbelief?"

"I pray He shall so they may find each other again as we have been blessed to do."

Lothaire lowered to the mattress and tucked her head beneath his chin. Holding to the woman with whom he would spend his life, he savored her back to sleep.

"They are silent to a man, my lord, the same ere their first escape."

Lothaire sighed. "Either they have not the proper inducement or they are confident of their escape."

Angus shrugged. "The jailer broke the younger one's nose ere I could stop him, but it only served to close their mouths tighter."

That angered Lothaire on two opposing fronts. He had told Nigel there was to be no violence, and if all went to plan there should be no need. But had there been, it was the husband of the lady nearly ravished who ought to have the satisfaction of driving a fist into the miscreant's face. However, certain it would not end there, Lothaire stayed away. And perhaps Nigel should have as well. A great grudge he bore his prisoners, having been knocked unconscious by whoever had freed the assassins last year.

"How did they react when told it is the queen's cousin who was attacked?" Lothaire asked.

"I could see the prospect of being transported to the king's prison alarmed, but they refused to name who hired them and reveal the extent of the damage they were to inflict."

It hardly mattered, Lothaire supposed, having known the best chance of learning who meant to aid Raisa again was to lull the offender into believing it possible to free his accomplices in the same manner as before.

Lothaire had been tempted to confide the plan to Nigel, but the man was not known for discretion, especially when he had a tankard of ale too many.

Lothaire looked around the outer bailey, did not see who should not be seen—four of his most trusted men paired off to ensure they remained worthy of his trust. Of the plan, they knew only they were to keep watch on the dungeon's entrance, and if they could not identify who entered, must learn who exited by whatever means necessary without revealing their hiding places.

"Methinks we shall have our answers," Lothaire said. "Hopefully, this eve."

"I will keep watch as well, my lord."

Lothaire started toward the inner drawbridge, came back around. "I must ask something, but ere I do, I would have you know naught is required that you do not wish."

Wariness flickered in Angus's eyes, but rather than give his consent to proceed he said, "I am sorry, my lord, especially for your sister, but though I have a care for the memory of her, my feelings are not what they were, and I do not believe there enough rain and sunshine to revive them. If you can accept that, and can she should she need to, I shall remain in your service. Otherwise, I must seek to serve another lord."

Lothaire longed to argue he had believed the same—or worse—of his relationship with Laura, that the Lord had provided the warming sunshine and gentle rain to revive it. But he would simply have to pray Sebille and Angus found their way back to each other. "You cannot tell me not to have hope, Angus, but I accept your decision."

The knight inclined his head.

Heart heavy, Lothaire strode toward the donjon where his beloved awaited him.

This sense. This feeling it best to wait. Or perhaps do naught and let be what was to be. But there was danger in that as well, and there seemed not enough trippings of the fingers to begin to rouse the Lord's sympathy.

At this moment no longer the watcher, far more the worrier, the one who needed to make a decision tucked into the chair, drove elbows into sides, and bent forward on a groan so pitiful it sounded like a hurting dog.

What to do? Stay the course or change course? Though this one was long tried and true, something told it had become littered with obstacles.

Pressing deeper into the chair. Driving elbows harder into sides. Bending farther forward. So slight a groan it was as if the dog had died. Then slamming back, splaying arms, and sighing as reason prevailed. As this was the culmination of all, thus of greatest import, this feeling was worry only.

Stay the course, run faster now the end was near, and win the prize for which all had been done.

It could not be too late to be happy. Could it?

34

Lothaire would not have guessed who sought to once more render the jailer unconscious, but there could be no doubt who did Lady Raisa's bidding.

The man was seen entering the dungeon an hour ahead of the prisoners' escape. Not that there was anything unusual about that since he and Nigel sometimes visited each other during the daylight hours and often met at night at a tavern in Thistle Cross where they tipped tankards of ale and patted and pinched serving girls.

Unfortunately for Nigel, his drinking companion was not above endangering the jailer's position. A half hour after he received this man bearing gifts, the perpetrator departed the dungeon. Shortly thereafter, amid the dusk of approaching night, the three prisoners stealthily exited. And Lothaire's men were rewarded for their vigilance.

The prisoners were returned to their cells, and all attempts to rouse the jailer were for naught, his head on the table alongside a decimated platter of viands and an overturned cup.

"The last time you were such a good friend to Nigel," Lothaire said, "it was by the same means, hmm?"

Having not moved from the chickens spitted over a cooking fire since his lord entered the kitchen and ordered the other servants to leave, Cook stared out of twitching eyes.

Advancing on him, Lothaire said, "I am guessing the first time Nigel himself dealt the blows to hide the fact he imbibed too much and slept through the escape."

The tip of the poker with which the man had been shifting the logs rose.

"But he did not sleep through the escape, did he? Something in his food or drink rendered him as unconscious then as he is now. This time is different only in that the prisoners were recaptured."

The poker rose higher, and Angus and the other men at their lord's back drew nearer.

Cook was no easy prey. He was of middling years and nearly as tall and muscular as his lord. Still, Lothaire did not doubt he could better the man who likely had little if any training at arms. As for his brawling over women that sometimes broke bones as easily as chairs and tables, Lothaire believed himself superior as well, though lacking Wulfen training that might have been questionable.

The cook shifted his regard from Lothaire to his warriors, then lowered the poker's tip. "I but followed my lady's orders."

Lothaire halted before him. Though his eyes were fastened on the other man's, he remained aware of the poker's position. "You speak of Lady Raisa."

"Aye, your lady mother. As ever, I do her bidding, whether it is a special food she requires or…other things."

"As ever?"

"Since you took Lexeter from her when I was but a kitchen servant."

"You were paid well, hmm?"

"Well enough."

Confirmation it was more than loyalty that bound him to Raisa. "Always you receive your orders directly from her?" Lothaire tensed as he waited on the answer that would confirm Sebille and Laura's belief his mother was not as infirm as she appeared.

"Aye, until…" The man shrugged. "It has been over a year since Lady Sebille began delivering your mother's private messages."

"My sister?" Lothaire could not contain his disbelief.

"Aye, the same as she did entreating me to once more engage the men sent to avenge the dishonor dealt you by Lady Beata and Baron Marshal. And again this day to aid in their escape."

"Your sister could not have known the contents of the missives, my lord," Angus said. "She must have thought—"

"You are right," Cook said. "I am sure Lady Sebille believed she but delivered a request for special food or drink."

"Show me my mother's messages."

"I would, but ever I am to burn them after reading. And so I have."

Inwardly cursing that he could not verify Raisa's handwriting, Lothaire said, "This is serious what you have done. Your position is lost, mayhap your life."

"I am but a messenger doing the bidding of my lord's mother. Where is the death sentence in that, my lord?"

There was threat in his words. Were he to receive punishment for his role in attempting to harm Lady Beata and Baron Marshal, Raisa's involvement would be exposed. Though she was too old and seemingly infirm to suffer severe punishment, shame would fall upon the family.

Moving slowly as if very aware of the sword Lothaire could easily bring to hand, Cook reached the poker to the side and set it in its stand. "Too, no great ill was ever intended, my lord. Just as those men were but to appear assassins, they had but to appear to threaten the fleece stores."

"What say you?"

"Your mother likes to cause trouble, my lord. I do not ask why. I but take her coin and make the arrangements."

Did he speak true? Or was he thinking fast in hopes of lessening his punishment?

Likely the former, Lothaire thought, remembering Sebille had said their mother muttered it was time to stir up more trouble.

The man grunted. "And when there are complications as twice there have been with your prisoners, I rectify the situation ere any can be made to talk."

"This time you failed."

"This time was one time too many, just as feared. But coin is a great tempter."

Lothaire motioned his men forward. "I am sure we shall speak more on this. Until then, you shall become acquainted with the inside of a cell."

Cook tensed as if to resist.

"Do not," Lothaire said. "If what you tell is true, the loss of your position should suffice and you will be freed."

Resentment flashed in the man's eyes, but his shoulders eased on an exhalation of acceptance. "'Tis true, my lord. Do not forget me in that cell."

As the men took hold of the cook, Lothaire instructed them to remove him by way of the garden. He did not wish to alarm those in the hall settling in for supper, especially Laura. Though she was not as fragile as she ought to be considering her past had nearly repeated itself last eve, he would not have her worry over what was set in motion. When it ground to a halt would be soon enough for her to learn of the breadth of plotting he would never have thought to find himself in the middle of.

"Angus," he called as his man followed the others.

"My lord?"

"Ensure Cook's cell is within speaking distance of the others and discreetly set yourself near to listen. Providing they are not overly cautious, the truth may be known all the sooner."

"Aye, my lord."

"It could prove a long night."

"Whatever is required," the knight said.

After summoning the kitchen servants from the corridor and informing them urgent business had taken Cook from High Castle, Lothaire set the most experienced over the others and returned to his wife at the high table.

"Something is wrong?" she asked.

Angus had been heedful in requesting his lord accompany him to the kitchen, but the event was too unusual to escape notice, especially since the knight had not returned to the hall. Also absent from the table was Sebille, though that was not unusual. Likely, she was with their mother and would yet be there when Lothaire ascended to the third floor. Hopefully, she had not revealed the plot against the stores of fleece nor her suspicion Raisa had arranged it. Lothaire had told her to hold it close so he could himself gauge their mother's reaction that would be more difficult to mask the longer she was denied word of what she wrought.

"What was wrong is being made right," he said and caught up his wife's hand and kissed her knuckles. "Naught to worry over."

Her smile was uncertain.

"Later I will tell you," he said and was relieved when Clarice drew her mother's attention.

It could not be too soon for the servants to deliver the viands and the meal to be done. There were questions without answers and answers without questions. This eve, the unknown and known would meet and this foul business concluded so never again would his family suffer for it. And he and the woman he loved would make good on all the years lost to them.

"You have decided to allow me to spend my final days in my home, have you?"

They were the first words his mother spoke when Lothaire closed the door.

He glanced from Sebille perched on a chair beside the bed, fingers moving over her prayer beads, to Martin who stood on the opposite side, medicinal bag open and vials sitting atop the coverlet.

"Mother," he said.

At his approach, Sebille stood and offered him the chair.

He declined and halted alongside the bed.

Lady Raisa, whose head was so far sunk in the pillow it appeared she had lost the rest of her hair, frowned. "That is as you have decided, is it not, Lothaire?"

She looked worse than he had seen her, and he had to remind himself of what she had done. "Nay, Mother. It is but another delay in moving you to your dower property."

Her lids narrowed. "You do not love me, do you?"

He did not want to yield to her the questions needing answers, but to this he would respond. "I love you, Mother, though you make it difficult." He had not thought he could be angrier with her than when she hired assassins Cook would have him believe were not truly that, but he was. For attacking Laura in her chamber...for hiring men to *stir up trouble* that had nearly seen his wife ravished a second time...

But he could not loose cruel words on her as he might have done had he come to her last eve or this morn.

Lady Raisa sighed, and in a voice softened by weariness, said, "Of what would you accuse me now?"

Lothaire looked to Sebille who gave a slight shake of her head to indicate she had remained silent on the matter. "During the shearing supper last eve, the men hired to work ill on the stores at Shepsdale were thwarted and instead turned their attention to the fleeces at Thistle Cross. That attempt was also foiled but not before one of the men sought to ravish my wife."

Raisa's eyes widened, his sister gasped.

"They failed and are now in High Castle's dungeon. A short while ago, Cook was imprisoned as well for hiring them to do your bidding and attempting to release them as he did when two of these same men were sent to murder Lady Beata and Baron Marshal."

His mother blinked. "So once again I am blamed."

He stepped nearer the bed. "Cook tells it was under your orders he made the arrangements both times."

"He lies. Just as I did not hire assassins to kill Lady Beata and Baron Marshal, I did not—"

"Now you would deny it, though you did not a year past?"

She came up off the pillow but immediately fell back. "How could I? I had to protect—" Her lids fluttered.

Of course he was expected to pry out of her what she would not speak. "Tell me, Mother."

She drew a breath that seemed laborious, and Lothaire could not ignore the need to aid her. He lowered to the mattress, slid an arm around her, and raised her. As he dragged pillows behind her, he felt her hand flatten against his chest as if she searched for the beat of his heart.

Wishing she were worthy of affection, he eased her back against the pillows.

He was about to repeat his question when she said, "I would not tell it if not that my days are few and it hurts knowing when you put me in the ground you will not be sorry because of how evil you think me to be. Aye, I was angered by the annulment of your marriage to Lady Beata—of the funds lost that could have returned High Castle to prosperity—so I cried out, *Will no one avenge this offense for me?*" She looked past him. "You remember, Sebille?"

The prayer beads ceased clicking. "You were very angry, but your words I do not recall."

Lady Raisa scowled, returned her attention to Lothaire. "The day you revealed the assassination attempt and without proof of my involvement accused me of hiring those men, I was hurt."

What Sebille had overheard had been proof aplenty, but then as now he would not reveal his sister had alerted him, giving him time to overtake the assassins.

Lady Raisa looked to the physician. "I guessed it was you who answered my call for aid, that you hired the men."

The physician straightened abruptly.

Lothaire's mother looked back at her son. "As I could not bear to lose the only friend I have, I determined it better you thought it me. And 'tis not as if I did not approve."

"I did not hire those men!" Martin voiced the outrage reddening his face. "You must believe me, my lady...my lord. Much I dislike that Daughter of Eve, but I would not seek her death. I am a healer, not a killer!"

Lothaire did not know whom to believe, but he found himself leaning toward the physician. Certainly he was greatly offensive, but he did not seem one to seek another's death.

"I vow I did not do it, Lothaire," his mother said. "And how could it be me? I can barely move from this bed."

It would have been better had she not resorted to that argument, then Lothaire might not have walked through the door she flung wide. "A year past you could, Mother. Indeed, months past you did. It is only since my wife's arrival that saw you moved to the third floor you have not ventured belowstairs—at least not to the hall." He leaned nearer. "Pray, do not further your lies by denying you went to Lady Laura's chamber and did injury to her."

"She slapped me!"

"After you insulted her daughter and her. I do not condone her retaliation, but she is sorry for it, and methinks it the response you sought."

In her eyes he could see she wished to argue, but she did not.

"Regardless," he said, "Cook has revealed it was by way of Sebille he received your instructions."

"Me?" His sister jumped to her feet. "I am not a party to her..." She snapped her teeth, glared at their mother.

Lothaire set a hand on her arm. "The messages she had you deliver Cook were not always food requests."

Finding her voice, Lady Raisa said, "Though that man was useful in making arrangements after you snatched Lexeter from me, 'tis more than a year since I enlisted his aid. As you put a watch on me, and I cannot trust Sebille not to run to you with my private messages, the only ones I send now are meal requests."

"That is not what Cook tells."

"He lies!"

"He said the message Sebille delivered several days past instructed him to once more hire the men who were to kill Lady Beata and her husband so they might work ill on the fleece. And this day he received another message to aid in their escape."

"Lies! Tell him, Sebille. Tell him I have sent no messages for over a sennight, not even for food."

A sob escaped Lothaire's sister, and she dropped her prayer beads and pressed a quaking hand over her mouth.

"I know you are distressed," Lothaire said. "I am sorry for it, but if you can verify what Mother tells, else deny it, all the sooner we shall be done with this."

She lowered her hand to her side, and her tongue clicked as if her mouth was dry, then she said, "It pains me, but what Cook tells is true."

Raisa made a choking sound.

"Three—or was it four days past?—I delivered what I believed was a meal request, and again this day." She looked to her mother. "How could you use me like that? To do evil?"

Raisa's eyes were all on Sebille. Nostrils flaring, upper lip curling, she cried, "I thought you but disliked me, but 'tis worse. You loathe me."

"I do not, but I cannot lie for you. And I am done being a party to your hatred."

Raisa struggled onto her elbows. "I know you, Sebille."

"Mother!" Lothaire urged her to lie back.

She shoved his hand off and pointed at her daughter. "This is all you, you foul useless thing."

"Cease!" Lothaire erupted.

"You are the one who paid men to murder Baron Marshal and his wife—the one who sent them to work ill on the fleece."

Face crumpling further, shoulders bowing, Sebille caught up her prayer beads. "Of course you would see me bear your sins as I have long borne your care—because I speak in truth, because I will not allow you to lay further waste to my life by accompanying you to your dower property."

Face flushed, brow beaded with perspiration, Raisa said, "You are not my daughter. You know that, aye?"

Sebille burst into tears.

Lothaire was tempted to curse the old woman, but she looked so ill he resisted. "Martin, settle my mother as best you can," he ordered the physician who had nearly made himself one with the opposite wall, then put an arm around his sister. "Come away, Sebille."

"Pretender!" Raisa screeched as brother and sister crossed to the door. "Not my daughter. Never my daughter!"

Hardly did they make it into the corridor than Sebille collapsed. Lothaire swung her into his arms and was jolted by how light was this sister who had carried more weight as a young woman despite the demands their mother placed on her. In the years since she had refused Angus, she had nearly gone to bone.

"Do not listen to her," he said as she buried her face in his tunic.

Though he knew she had slept in the small chamber across from his mother's since Raisa was moved to the third floor, he carried her down to the second floor.

It proved ill timing, Laura exiting her daughter's room as Lothaire strode the corridor.

His wife's gasp drew Clarice to the threshold before Laura could close the door. "Clarice, go back inside," she entreated. "I—"

"What is wrong with Lady Sebille?" The girl started forward, but Laura pulled her back.

"Naught to worry over," Lothaire said. "She but feels unwell." He shouldered open the door of his sister's chamber, entered, and pushed it closed.

"I am sorry," Sebille cried as he lowered her to the bed. "'Tis just I am so weary." She patted a hand across her waist, found the prayer beads, began tripping her fingers over them.

"I shall see you restored, Sebille." Lothaire swept tear-dampened hair off her cheek. "The decision is made. Even do you think to change your mind and accompany Mother to her dower property—"

The door opened and Laura stepped inside.

He returned his gaze to Sebille. "I will not allow it. This is your home."

"I wish to remain, but..."

"It is done, Sebille. Here you shall stay and grow strong again." True, Father Atticus had suggested it would be best for her to enter a convent, but if ever Lothaire could have seen that, he could not now.

He looked to Laura where she came alongside. "My sister has given enough of herself to our mother's care, do you not agree?"

"Of course." The smile Laura gave Sebille was genuine. "I am glad you shall remain with us, Lady Sebille. I shall appreciate your companionship."

A sob escaping Sebille, she turned onto her side and pressed her face into the pillow.

Lothaire drew the covers over her and laid a hand on her head. "Sleep, Sister. All will be better come morn."

She nodded, and he drew Laura into the corridor. Neither spoke until he closed the solar's door.

"What has happened, Lothaire?"

To save her from worrying over his mother's presence, he would not have chosen to tell all that transpired this day. But since she had been exposed to Sebille's misery, it would be cruel to make her wait on an answer.

He took her hands and drew her close. "You are not to worry. On the morrow, my mother departs, aye?"

"Tell me."

"Lady Raisa's lies are unraveling, and she looks for someone to blame."

"Sebille."

"Aye, my sister whom I will have suffer no further abuse."

"What has Lady Raisa done? Did she strike Sebille?"

"Nay, though I believe she would have given the opportunity."

"Then what?"

"Most recently, she hired men to attack the wool stores, the same you encountered at the lake."

Laura startled.

"Aye, though it is certain what nearly befell you was not by her orders. You were simply in the wrong place."

"Dear Lord, why would she do that? The wool is all to Lexeter—to you."

"No longer all to me, but it means much to the barony and people of Lexeter. Who can know the workings of a mind that is not right, but she has ever been vengeful and all the more for being forced out of High Castle."

Laura considered this, said, "That is what she has done most recently. What did she before?"

He sighed. "You want all of it, hmm?"

"Surely the Lady of Lexeter ought not be ignorant."

"Then I shall tell you that which Baron Marshal and his wife know not, how my mother sought vengeance against them for the annulment of my marriage." He drew her to the hearth. "Sit with me."

Was that the mark seen on her mother's face that she had tried to conceal? The mark Clarice had accepted as the result of a fall?

So it seemed. And the witch had done it to her.

Clarice removed her sore, creased ear from the door's seam and looked to the ceiling as she tried to draw breath to her churning depths.

Lady Raisa was up there, likely greatly displeased with her failed attempts to kill Lady Beata and her husband, attack the wool stores, and harm Clarice's mother. What might she do between now and her departure on the morrow?

Clarice shivered. Hating herself for the fear urging her to bolt herself in her chamber until the night passed, she told herself to be brave and go up there and warn the witch that if ever she even looked at her mother she would find her eyes clawed out.

Told herself once...twice...a third time, then absolving herself of weakness with the reminder she was not even ten, hastened to her chamber. And barely suppressed a cry of alarm when Tina, who had taken ill this morn with a cough and running nose, groaned and turned on her pallet.

As Clarice remained unmoving, waiting for the maid to go back down into sleep, she promised herself that if that hag was still at High Castle on the morrow, she would confront her then. In daylight it would not matter so much that her years numbered less than ten. No one was going to hurt or take from her the mother she had only just found and meant to keep.

35

THE PHYSICIAN WOULD be in his bed now, as were all those within the donjon excepting the few warriors who kept watch over the hall. It was dark. And safe.

Grateful for the slight weight that hardly disturbed aged floorboards, the one who had been waiting a long time for this moment stepped onto the dimly-lit landing to the soft click of that which hung from a girdle.

A guard was posted outside Lady Raisa's chamber—to be expected, though it had not been.

I truly am as weary as I would have Lothaire believe, Sebille excused the slip of her mind as she advanced on the man who straightened from the wall.

She halted before him. "All is quiet?"

"Too quiet, my lady. No snoring, meaning she is likely unable to sleep."

She patted his arm. "Gain your rest. I shall sit with her."

"The remainder of the night?"

"Aye, her last night here."

He inclined his head and stepped past.

Sebille gathered strength to speak words long unspoken, then stepped inside and closed the door.

"You," Lady Raisa croaked where she sat propped on pillows, the light of candles on a bedside table revealing how pale she was.

It made Sebille's heart hurt as she did not wish it to. Not for this woman. Such hurt ought to be all for Angus.

"Aye, 'tis Sebille," she said as she walked forward. "Not your daughter. Never your daughter. This I know."

"How?"

Sebille settled on the bed beside Raisa, and as the older woman sank further into the pillows, covered an aged hand with her own.

The old woman snatched it away, said again, "How?"

You will not cry, Sebille told herself. *Words. That is what you came to give, not tears one such as she does not deserve.*

She angled her body nearer and, fighting the longing to take up her prayer beads, gripped her hands in her lap. "I do not truly hate you. What I hate is what you did to me—the childhood you stole." She closed her eyes. "Oh, my beautiful childhood." She returned her gaze to the one staring at her. "My youth. The husband and children I ought to have. Your love—"

"Tell me how," Raisa barked.

"More than anything, I hate that you stole my father." Sebille frowned. "I confess I did hate you until we learned it was Lady Beata's cousin who murdered him. Until then, I thought it very possible you killed him."

Raisa was quaking, color seeping into her skin. "How?"

"How, indeed." Sebille sighed. "The night he left never to return, I heard the two of you arguing."

Raisa gasped, wheezed as if she had taken spit into her lungs.

"That is how I know who I am, who I was to father, who I am not to you, and who you are not to me. I know it hurt when you learned the truth, but I was innocent and undeserving of vengeance. All you had to do was love me as you had before—even half as much would have been enough."

"You who did foul deeds in my name are the daughter of a whore!"

"Only by birth. Until you found that missive, I was the daughter of your heart. Your miracle."

"Miracle! You are deception. Disease. You are—" A gust of air exited her mouth, and the hands she refused Sebille began to clutch at her head.

Her antics nearly made Sebille retch. "Pray, cease. I know what you do—what *ever* you do to gain pity and prolong your stay at High Castle."

Raisa moaned. Familiar as well. But then her eyes began to jerk, and it looked as if one side of her face slid down.

Sebille sprang off the bed. "Is this real, Mother?" she surprised herself by how thoughtlessly she claimed kinship with the woman. "Is it?"

"You!" Raisa said with a slur and pointed at Sebille. "You!" Then the arm with which she pointed dropped. Hand hooked, she gripped the fallen arm and jerkily rubbed it elbow to shoulder.

Was this truly her end? Sebille wondered as she stared at the one she did not have in common with her beloved brother.

Leave her to it, urged the anger sown deep. *Why make hell wait when it can have her now?*

"Is this real?" Sebille asked again, and receiving no response beyond the sound of suffering, reminded herself it mattered not if this was a ploy to deliver Lothaire to his mother's side. Regardless what Raisa told of her meeting with Sebille, he would think it born of further spite— would never believe his sister had composed messages in his mother's name in the hope they would reflect ill on Raisa.

The older woman made a sound even more terrible, one never before heard.

"I shall summon the physician," Sebille cried and ran.

Guilt. Such an appetite it had.

Lothaire had been certain Sebille was duped again, that her own guilt which had returned her abovestairs near the middling of night made her believe the unbelievable. But the physician's confirmation Raisa Soames had suffered a stroke was not needed. One had but to look upon her to know she was truly near the end of her life. And no matter how hard she tried to form words with a terribly misshapen mouth, only her eyes were speaking—with desperation and pleading. When she slept finally, Lothaire loosed the hand he had held for hours and followed Martin into the corridor.

"It has been a long night, my lord. You ought to sleep while you can. I believe 'twill be a longer day."

"You do not think she will survive it?"

"Unlikely."

Lothaire nodded. "You will send for me if she turns for the worse?"

"Of course, my lord."

Lothaire traversed the corridor, descended the stairs, and after checking on his sister who slept in the middle of her bed with knees clasped to her chest, entered the solar whose shutters were open to let in dawn's light.

Laura hastened to his side. "Is your mother as ill as Sebille feared?"

"Aye, she will not make it to her dower property. The remainder of her life shall be spent here."

She cupped his face. "As it should be."

He nodded. "I am tired. Will you let me fall asleep holding you?"

"You need not ask." She drew him to the bed and aided in shedding his garments. When she removed her own, he was pleased, not so they might be intimate again, simply that he could be that much closer to her.

A quarter hour later, she slept where he held her against his chest, and he knew she had lain awake since Sebille threw open the door and told Lady Raisa was dying. Laura had offered to accompany him, but he had declined lest he further expose her to his mother's venom. Though that was no longer possible by way of word, Lady Raisa's eyes remained expressive.

Had he wronged his mother as those eyes told? Though all evidence said otherwise, that not only had she endangered the lives of Lady Beata and her husband, but worse, Laura's, the Lord would not allow him to abandon her in her time of greatest need.

True, there is not much about her to like, he imagined Father Atticus saying, *but she is your mother and shall remain so even in death.*

Lothaire closed his eyes and remembered a younger Raisa— before his father's disappearance. He had been only six, and yet he had known she was not happy, just as he had known his father had greater affection for a pretty serving girl than his wife who could never be called pretty. Still, sometimes his mother had smiled and laughed, and just as Lothaire had felt loved by his parents, there was no doubt Sebille felt it more.

Then Ricard Soames did not come home, and of a sudden Raisa had only enough time and regard for her son—naught for her daughter whom she no longer named a *miracle*.

Why? Lothaire wondered as he had ceased to wonder years ago. What had caused his sister to be reduced to little more than a servant— and on the night past denied entirely?

He sighed and, accepting he would never know, slept.

Finally, the physician departed.

Though the opportunity to confront the witch now lay before Clarice, she hesitated where she stood at the door inside the small chamber into which she had slipped an hour past.

Go, she told herself. *Now ere he returns with whatever concoction he thinks will save a life not in need of saving.*

But her feet remained fixed to the floor as she peered through the crack at the door behind which lay the woman who feigned sickness so she might remain at High Castle and further threaten the Baron of Lexeter's new wife.

You are weak, Clarice, she silently scorned. *It is daylight. Go!*

A sound of distress slipping from her, she opened the door, crossed the corridor, and entered the witch's lair.

As seen when the physician exited, the chamber was barely lit and turned dimmer when Clarice started to close herself in. Fear urging her to leave the door open a hand's width, the more easily for her scream to be heard were she roused to one, she clung to the shadow in which she stood. Heart racing, she swallowed so loudly she was certain the still figure at the center of the bed would open her eyes. Did she sleep? Or merely lie in wait, ready to spring upon her prey?

"Be brave," Clarice whispered and winced at how stiff her legs were as she advanced. Upon reaching the center of the room, she heard a soft moan and halted.

Lady Raisa's eyes remained closed, but now Clarice could see there was something wrong with her face. Was this what was called a stroke? Regardless, she looked near death. And it made her sad as she ought not be for one like this.

"I care not!" she rasped, and the woman lifted her lids. Clarice wanted to flee, and could have in the time it took those frantically flitting eyes to land on her, but once again she could not move.

The eyes of her mother's tormentor widened, bent lips parted, and now her moan had volume. But no words.

Clarice resumed her advance. Reaching the bed, she closed her trembling hands into fists. "I am Clarice, the daughter of Lady Laura Soames and now your son. I..." She searched for moisture in her mouth. "I know you hurt my mother—and I wish you to be aware that if ever you even look at her again, I shall..."

She blinked, wished she could say what she meant to say, but the woman was so pitiful it was not believable she could hurt anyone. It had to be true death came for her. "You will not look at her again, will you?" she said softly. "You will not rise again from this bed."

Another moan, this one very long.

Clarice did not understand why her chest hurt and eyes stung, and it angered her. "You are not a good person, but I am sorry you are hurting."

The old woman gasped, mouth worked.

"And I am sorry for your son and daughter."

The woman grunted and one side of her mouth rose in what seemed a sneer.

"I know not how, but surely they care for you."

A sibilant hiss spilled the lady's foul breath across the air. Was she trying to speak?

Though Clarice longed to flee, she leaned forward, though not so near the woman could reach her were she capable of doing so. "I do not understand, Lady Raisa."

Another hiss, then a moan as she sank more deeply into the pillows as if her battle were lost.

Clarice gave her time to recover, and in the silence heard a familiar click from beyond the chamber.

Lady Raisa made a choking sound and lids that had begun to lower flew wide. Her frantic gaze struck Clarice's, but the bit of speech she pushed past her lips was not needed. "Se…Se…"

Of course it was that lady who came, as told by the sound of her prayer beads. What was not known was whether it was the old woman who whimpered or herself. Regardless, Clarice must not be found here. Lady Sebille, who did not seem to like her, would name it trespass.

Hoping Lady Raisa would not be able to express herself any better with her daughter to reveal who hid inside, Clarice sprang across the room and crouched behind a chair steeped in shadow.

Lady Sebille entered, closed the door, and crossed to the bed.

Peering out from behind the chair where she knelt, Clarice saw fairly well the face of the woman who was now her aunt. The only color about it was splotches that evidenced she had been weeping.

With what seemed sorrow, Lady Sebille said, "How was I to know this time it was real?" Her eyebrows rose, fell. "Not that it would make much difference had I sooner summoned the physician and Lothaire."

As if Lady Raisa had been holding her breath, she expelled it on a groan at whose end Clarice thought she tried to speak her son's name.

Lady Sebille lowered to the mattress. "Aye, Lothaire. He sat so long with you I fell asleep waiting for him to leave."

"Lo," the old woman said.

"Aye, whom we both love—rather, I do. Methinks 'tis more pride and possessiveness you feel for him than anything of the heart. *That* you wasted on me, did you not—ere you hated me?"

As Clarice pondered that last, Lady Sebille reached to her mother and swept back wisps of hair that did naught to soften the lined, age-spotted brow.

The younger woman nodded. "Since now you can keep a secret even better than Father Atticus, I would have you be my confessor. What think you?"

Slowly, Clarice sat back on her heels to better observe the women. Though Lady Raisa's face was very crooked, there seemed interest in her widening eyes and the arch of an eyebrow.

"I thought you would like that." The younger woman lifted a lax hand between hers. "You know 'twas me, so that is already told, and you know much of it was vengeance. But ere you leave us, I would assure you the greater part of it was done out of a sister's concern for her brother, even though we are siblings by only half. I had to save Lothaire from you who should have been gone from High Castle years ago." She shook her head. "You nearly ruined him. Had your convenient illness not kept him from going to Lady Laura ere the weather turned foul, all these years she would have been wed to him."

Clarice caught her breath, blessedly not so loudly she disturbed Lady Sebille. However, if the woman followed her mother's gaze that shot to the girl's hiding place, her presence might be discovered as easily.

"Would she have proven more faithful than Lady Edeva?" Lady Sebille shrugged. "That cannot be known, but the burden she brought with her as Lothaire's third wife is of your doing."

Of what did she speak? Clarice wondered. Had her mother had the opportunity to wed the Baron of Lexeter sooner than she had done? If so, why had she not? And what burden was brought to her marriage?

The lady sighed. "Long I have known where you keep your keys and, more importantly, the household items you hid from Lothaire when he took control of Lexeter. Quite the trove that could have been sold with what you could not hide and which would have eased the financial difficulties caused by your extravagance."

Lady Raisa mumbled something, shook her head.

"Oh, it is true," her daughter said. "You know it, as do all. So when you are gone, I will conveniently discover that secret compartment in the solar from which many a time I have taken an item to pay for necessary things like…"

Though more and more Clarice grasped what was said, this she did not understand.

"I hesitate to be specific," Lady Sebille said, "but you are my confessor, and if the Lord cannot put a seal on your lips, the stroke shall." She caught up her prayer beads. "From out of your trove I paid the assassins to set upon Lady Beata and Baron Marshal."

Clarice pressed a hand over her mouth to keep from crying out.

"But ere you rejoice in believing I am as foul as you, those men but played a part. Never were they to commit murder, only to make Lothaire believe that was what you sent them to do. And 'twas I who alerted him to your plans." She held up a hand as if to prevent her mother from interrupting. "Of course I know they were not your plans, but I was certain you would approve had you thought to do more than snap and snarl and demand Queen Eleanor honor the marriage made between Lothaire and Lady Beata. And I alerted my brother again the day of the shearing supper when two of those same men were to make it appear the fleece stores were under attack."

Clarice's head lightened as all she was privy to whirled through her head. And though she felt guilty for eavesdropping on her parents on the night past, she was glad she had. Otherwise, her shock could have revealed she once more listened in on what was to have been a private conversation.

"Thus, Lothaire was going to send you away at long last, and though I do not trust Lady Laura to be a good and dutiful wife, far more difficult that would be with you here. So you had to go. But I never…" She drew a shuddering breath. "I did not mean you to go like this."

"Lo," Lady Raisa said again, then more forcefully, "Lo!"

Lady Sebille clapped her hands over her face, and with her prayer beads pouring between her fingers, began to weep. Moments later, a choking sound came from Lady Raisa as if she wept as well.

Clarice crossed her arm over her chest, caught up handfuls of her bodice, and squeezed. In that moment, she wanted what she would have declared she did not—to remain a girl, womanhood so distant she need not give it more than a passing thought. She did not like the world she had forced her way into. It was too complicated, despairing, and dark.

Far more than a young man's kisses, she wanted to play with the lambs no matter how muddy they made her. More, she wanted arms around her and kisses atop her head, to be enveloped in her mother's freshly bathed scent rather than the smell of a boy laboring to become a man.

It was almost enough to make her scramble from her hiding place and run. She was fairly certain of success since surprise ought to see her away from the chamber before Lady Sebille could make it off the bed, but two things held her there—fear of the lady whose depth of deception was frightening, and the horror and shame Lady Sebille would feel knowing she had done far more than bare herself to her mother.

Be still, Clarice told herself. *When she departs, then you can, the silent Lady Raisa the only witness to your duplicity.*

Lady Sebille did not cry long, and when she dried her eyes on her skirt, her mother returned to silence excepting the occasional hiccough.

"Worry not for Lothaire," Lady Sebille said and touched her lips to her mother's brow. "I shall keep watch over him, and if his lady wife fails him again, I will make her life so miserable she will wither away the same as Lady Edeva."

The threat against her mother made outrage suffuse Clarice's being. It was not the old woman who should be warned Lady Laura's daughter would claw out her eyes, it was Lady Sebille.

"And if that misbegotten girl proves no different from her mother," Lady Sebille continued, "I shall find a way to remove her from High Castle. We would not want her to corrupt my brother's legitimate children."

"Witch!" Clarice did not know how she made it to her feet before Lady Sebille's gaze flew across the space between them.

The woman snapped back so hard she nearly tumbled off the bed, but then she was also on her feet and, belatedly, Clarice lunged toward the door.

"Sly, deceitful child," Lady Sebille screeched and wrenched the girl back. "Filthy, misbegotten—"

"Nay!" Lady Raisa protested. "Nay, Se!"

Lady Sebille flung the girl onto the bed, causing her to fall facedown across the old woman's bony legs. Clarice rolled to her back, brought her arms up in front of her chest and face.

But Lady Sebille stood unmoving alongside the bed. "You have ruined all," she snarled.

"*You* ruined all," Clarice retorted.

The lady jabbed a finger at the old woman. "Because she ruined all—my father, me, nearly my brother. It began with her, she who is incapable of feeling deep enough to hold onto love when what was thought a miracle is but a mistake, even when that mistake still loves her."

"I know not what you speak of!"

The lady turned away, came swiftly back around as Clarice started to rise. "Do not move! I must think." She nodded. "I can fix this. I just have to think." She slapped a palm against her forehead. "Think, Sebille!"

"I want to go." Clarice scooted to the edge of the bed, but before she could drop her feet to the floor, a hand thrust her onto her back.

"I said do not move!"

Clarice had no intention of obeying, but as she pushed onto her elbows, the lady gripped the hilt of a meat dagger on her girdle opposite her prayer beads.

Clarice stilled, glanced at Lady Raisa.

Though the old woman's face appeared further misshapen, there seemed sorrow in her eyes.

"I cannot think!" Lady Sebille shrilled.

Clarice's own thoughts were so murky with fear that the only thing she could think to save herself was a childish act that had oft brought Lady Maude and her mother running. Unfortunately, it would be effective only were someone near.

It was mid-morn, and Clarice had left her mother in the hall and ventured to the third floor as she had promised she would not. Too distant, especially had the Lady of Lexeter gone to the kitchen to oversee the nooning meal. As for Clarice's new father, did he yet sleep, he might hear. Or a chambermaid. Or the physician returning to administer medicinals.

Clarice returned her focus to Lady Sebille who picked over her prayer beads with one hand while the hand that had touched the meat dagger scratched at her brow. Next Clarice looked to the old woman.

Lady Raisa's eyes were closed, but tears pooled in their corners as her chest slowly rose and fell.

Clarice wanted to assure the woman that her son would come. Instead, she swung her legs up and to the side, rolled, and as she dropped her feet on the opposite side of the bed, screamed—high pitched piercing wails that made Lady Sebille fling herself around the bed.

Three. That was all she had time for, then the lady's hand was over her mouth and the force of her body drove Clarice back into the bedside table, toppling two candles and leaving only one to light the chamber. But it was enough for her to see the fury in the face over hers. And fear the meat dagger that would soon be at her throat.

36

It sounded like the screech of a mouse, but it was much more. Laura did not know how she knew—whether the sudden heaviness of her heart was responsible or an angel whispered in her ear, but she knew. And she knew who.

"Clarice!" She turned from the corridor to which she had ascended, yanked up her skirts, and took the next flight of stairs two at a time. Reaching the landing, she stumbled and went down on a knee, landing so hard her teeth snapped and she tasted the blood of a bitten tongue. She lunged back to her feet, and though there were no other sounds to guide her, she knew where to find her daughter.

Wishing she had thought to call to Lothaire who, were he not deeply asleep, would have been fast on her heels, she beseeched, "Lord, please!" and flung open the first door on the corridor. The chamber was empty, as was the second. But not the third. That one's door banged so hard against the wall it rebounded and nearly struck her in the face as she charged inside.

She did not understand what she was seeing, only that it was frightening. Though the shadows were thick to the right of the bed upon which lay Lothaire's mother, Laura saw it was Clarice there and Sebille at her back, the forearm the latter pressed to the girl's throat holding her captive, the hand over the girl's mouth silencing further screams.

"Come no nearer!" Lothaire's sister cried. "I do not wish to hurt her."

Reaching the foot of the bed, Laura halted and met Clarice's wide-eyed gaze. "I am here," she said, then looked to the woman over her daughter's shoulder. "Of course you do not wish to hurt her." She splayed her hands. "This makes no sense, though I am sure you can explain, but for now all I ask is that you release my daughter."

Laura heard Sebille swallow. "I shall. I just need to think. To fix this."

"We will." Laura took a step forward. "Let Clarice come to me, and we will sit and mend whatever is broken."

"Everything is broken. Because of her." She jerked her chin at her mother.

"She is leaving, Sebille. And you are staying. With us."

Lothaire's sister closed her eyes, and Laura returned her gaze to her daughter's. Aching over the fear there, she hoped Clarice was somewhat reassured by her mother's presence.

"I can stay at High Castle only if I make this right," Sebille said. "And I cannot think how to do it."

Laura advanced another step.

"Stop!" Sebille dragged Clarice closer.

"She is only nine, Sebille," Laura beseeched. "She is a child, and you are frightening her as I know you do not mean to."

"I was only nine, and so much more I bore!"

Laura's mind scrambled to understand, but all she knew was nine was the age at which the woman lost her father. "Pray, Lady Sebille, release my daughter."

"She listened in on Lady Raisa and me, heard things she ought not."

"For which she is very sorry. If you will allow her to speak, she will apologize and we can make this right."

Sebille shook her head, and Laura saw the fingers of the arm against Clarice's neck begin to move as they often did over her prayer beads. She glanced at where they hung from the woman's girdle.

"I know you are faithful with your prayers," Laura said. "Were you to give yourself to them now, you would find comfort enough to do as I ask—nay, beg."

Sebille's fingers stilled. "She will scream again. And I vow I did naught to make her do so."

"I know, Sebille, just as I know she will not scream if you let her come to me."

"I-I will have naught to hold to."

Was that the answer? Laura wondered, then nodded at the chair to the right of the two. "You will have me. I will sit there, you will loose Clarice, and I shall stay as long as you wish. My word I give."

Sebille frowned, slowly nodded. "Sit."

Laura gave her daughter an encouraging smile and crossed to the chair. Though she longed to perch on its edge, she sat back. And prayed Clarice would soon be freed.

Sebille walked the girl to the chair. "Do not scream," she said and removed her hand from the girl's mouth and set it on Laura's shoulder. "You are certain we can fix this, Lady Laura?"

Laura looked up. "I am."

The lady's arm moved from Clarice's neck to her waist and fell away.

And Lady Raisa loosed what sounded like a breath of relief.

But the girl did not run. "Mother?"

Knowing the fear in Clarice's voice was now more for one other than herself, Laura said, "All will be well. Leave us." *And bring Lothaire,* she dared not say, nor needed to, certain Clarice would go directly to him.

"Truly, I should leave you?"

Cautiously, Laura reached up, laid a hand atop Sebille's, and felt the woman stiffen. "My sister-in-law and I shall talk a while. I will see you soon."

"But she has a meat dagger."

"As do I." Laura glanced at her waist. "But since we are not at meal, they are not needed, are they?"

Still the girl did not move.

"Go, Clarice," Laura said as evenly as she could.

"I will not hurt her," Sebille said. "Do as your mother says."

Clarice gave a gasp. "I love you, Mother."

Tears sprang to Laura's eyes. "As I love you, Daughter."

The girl stepped away, but when she reached the door, Sebille called, "Summon my brother."

That jolted Laura. And comforted. Surely it meant the lady intended her no harm—that Laura would not have to defend herself in a manner similar to that with which she had thwarted the one who had failed to ravish her.

"As he and his mother are not likely to meet again in heaven," Sebille continued, "he must needs speak his farewell now."

Clarice opened the door.

"And tell my brother to send for Father Atticus," Sebille added. "Lady Raisa and I are in need of ministering."

Clarice met her mother's gaze, and it made Laura ache that she might fear it was the last time they looked upon each other. Then she was gone, leaving the door open.

"It must be told," Sebille said and loosed Laura's shoulder and moved around to stand in front of her. "He has to know that for as cruel as his mother is, she is not as sinful as believed."

His mother, not *our* mother, Laura mused.

"I will not have him think he had anything to do with her passing. 'Tis my burden."

Laura inclined her head. "Of course."

"Tell me and her"—Sebille jerked her head toward Lothaire's mother—"what you feel for my brother."

This was something Laura did understand. "I love him. Ever I shall. My only wish is that he would have known it ten years longer."

Sebille searched her face, and Laura knew she looked for a lie that would not be found. Then something of a smile lifting her lips, the lady said, "You hear that, Lady Raisa? She tells your son has what you and I have not. If she speaks true, I am happy for him. But you are not, are you?"

Laura looked to the old woman. Though her face was lax, her eyes were bright, and she moaned as if in response.

Of a sudden, Sebille was upon her sister-in-law, knees to the floor, chest on Laura's thighs, head tucked against her abdomen, hands on the chair's seat, one gripping her prayer beads.

"Make him forgive me," she cried. "Do I lose his love, I shall die."

Laura stared at the woman, and only when she glimpsed her own hands out to the sides, fingers splayed as if to fend off an attack, did she know where they belonged.

"Sebille," she said and placed one hand on the lady's back, the other on her head, then folded forward and embraced her. "Once given, methinks one cannot lose Lothaire's love. Though he may be greatly angered and hurt, he does not toss it out. He buries it deep, but he knows exactly where to find it."

"Promise me," the lady sobbed.

That was not for Laura to do, but it was what this broken woman needed. "I promise you."

Thankfully, Lothaire was clothed when his daughter threw open the door, and that was only due to Angus rousing his lord to inform him that what he had overheard between Cook and the three other prisoners corroborated the tale told.

Holding up a hand to silence the knight, Lothaire looked to the girl and found her nearly upon him. "Clarice! 'Tis inappropriate—" In the next instant, he strode forward and took hold of her arms. "What is it?" he demanded as she fell against him. "Your mother?"

She lifted her wide-eyed face. "Lady Sebille will not allow Mother... would not allow me..." She tapped her throat with a shaking hand. "I feared she meant to hurt me, and now she has my mother."

It made no sense, but there was only one thing he needed to know in that moment. "Where is your mother?"

Clarice looked to the ceiling. "Lady Raisa's chamber. Your sister says you must come and tell your mother goodbye. And s-summon Father Atticus." A sob burst from her. "I know I should not have gone in. I promised."

"Remain here." Lothaire released her, and as he started for the door gestured for Angus to follow.

"It was her, Father," Clarice called. "Lady Sebille hired those men, not your mother."

He was certain she misunderstood, but when he entered the chamber with his knight on his heels, the sight was so unexpected he knew he was the one who did not understand.

A glance at his mother confirming she was alert, her eyes wide with distress, he halted mid-stride when his wife raised a staying hand where she sat in a chair, a sobbing Sebille draped over her lap.

Patience, he told himself as Angus halted alongside. *All is well. Likely Mother said something cruel.*

"My lady"—Laura spoke near Sebille's ear—"your brother is come. And Sir Angus with him."

Sebille reared back onto her heels and looked across her shoulder. "Nay!" she cried, then snapped her chin around and sank into her shoulders. "Do not look at me, Angus. Pray, leave!"

He started forward. "What is this, Sebille?"

Lothaire caught his arm. "Let us honor her request. Go to Father Atticus and tell him he is needed."

Lothaire knew his man wanted to argue, that though he had said it was too late for Sebille and him, he still cared enough to wish to comfort her, but Angus grudgingly acceded.

"He is gone, Sebille," Lothaire said when the door closed. "Now tell me what has happened."

Leaning into the hand Laura returned to the side of her head, she said, "Sit with your mother. Hold her hand, for I cannot."

He looked questioningly at Laura, but she said naught, and he supposed it was best since it was obvious Sebille was in a fragile state.

When Lothaire lowered to the mattress beside his mother, he saw it was where he ought to be. There was little light in her eyes, and her skin was so white he wondered if she bled out onto the mattress, and then there was that soft rattling from her chest.

He took her cold, curled hands in his and kissed her cheek. "I am sorry, Mother."

She gave a slight jerk of her head as if to refuse his apology.

"And I am sorry you were denied the happiness I lost and have found again. But it will surely be all the sweeter for you in heaven. For that I am grateful."

He thought she tried to squeeze his hand, and out of one side of her mouth she said, "My...bo."

"Aye, your boy." He looked to his sister whose head remained lowered. "And your girl. We are both of us here."

"Se..."

"I will bring Sebille to you."

She whimpered and her head ticked side to side. "No Seb."

"She does not want me, Lothaire," his sister said. "I do not belong."

He frowned, and when she gave him her red, moist gaze, he said, "Of course you belong. You are her—"

"I am not."

He sighed. "Just because she—"

"She spoke in truth. Though once I was hers and loved for the miracle I am not, never have I been her daughter in blood. That which flows through me is only half of what flows through you."

More senselessness, but now was not the time to demand an explanation. His mother's rattling was louder.

He set a hand on Lady Raisa's forehead. "Be at peace, Mother."

"Pe...Seb..."

"You want Sebille?"

"Nay. You..." She gave a weak cough. "Fo...give...huh."

— 354 —

"Forgive her?" That could not be what she meant, but it was the only sense he could make of her words, and when she jerked her chin as if to confirm it, he said, "Sebille?"

She eased a hand from his, and its fingers slowly crawled up her chest to her collarbone. "I...made...huh."

"Aye." This from Sebille. "You made me into this. But I allowed it."

"Fo...give...huh."

"Of course, Mother."

"An...me."

He touched his lips to her brow. "All is forgiven. Now rest. Father Atticus will be here soon." Hardly were the words spoken than one last rattle left her and all that was yet hard in Raisa Soames went soft.

He drew her hand from her chest, settled it atop the one on her abdomen, and looked around. "She is gone from us, Sebille."

His sister sighed long and set her cheek on Laura's knees.

He would have liked to allow her to remain thus, but there was a frightened girl who needed to know her mother was safe.

He rose from the bed, kissed the top of his wife's head, then gently lifted his sister.

She did not sleep, as evidenced by eyes so tightly closed it was as if she feared she would be made to explain what she herself did not understand.

"Clarice?" Laura said low as she pushed up out of the chair.

"In the solar. As soon as I have settled my sister, I will join you."

She walked ahead of him and down the stairs, paused before the solar door to touch his arm as he carried Sebille past. As she closed the door of their chamber, he heard Clarice's cry of relief and knew the girl was in her mother's arms.

37

SEBILLE DID NOT keep them guessing long.

Between the meals of dinner and supper, she sent word by way of Father Atticus that she wished to speak with her brother and his wife.

Accompanied by the priest, she came to the solar with the rest of a tale she knew had too many holes to be believable. Thus, she would fill those which Lady Laura and her daughter had surely been unable to do in relating what was revealed to them, knowing even then it might be inconceivable. Perhaps that was because the tale was heartbreaking... hopeless...cruel. But it would soon be done and no further chapter or word added once she departed High Castle.

Lothaire placed a chair in front of the one into which Father Atticus had handed her, glanced at the priest who went to stand behind his sister, then his wife who had taken the chair alongside Sebille.

Praying Lothaire and Lady Laura would be as understanding and forgiving as Father Atticus who had received her confession of all she had done in Lady Raisa's name, Sebille curled fingers around her prayer beads.

When her brother lowered to the chair and caught up her hand, she nearly fell to weeping again for fear he might soon toss it aside.

Not Lothaire, she told herself. *Not he who loves me nearly as well as I love him.*

"I am here." He smiled. *"We* are here. Speak when you are ready—or not at all if you are not."

She glanced over her shoulder at the priest who responded by settling a hand on her shoulder.

"For years Father Atticus has kept the secret a nine-year-old girl entrusted to him after returning to High Castle from which she thought herself banished," she began.

As expected, Lothaire's face mapped confusion. He had been too young to comprehend a connection between his missing father and his sister's absence—perhaps did not even remember she had been gone a fortnight.

"Do you recall how much once I was loved and favored for being a miracle, Lothaire?"

"You were our parents' joy, far more than this boy who did not behave as he should have."

She had to smile, for that was the boy she had adored, perhaps as much as she had been adored by Ricard and Raisa Soames. "What you do not know was that our father's feelings for me had naught to do with a miracle. As he knew well and his wife would not for years, there was naught miraculous about me. And when I was nine, his secret that would become mine was discovered. Now I shall tell it to you."

"Ricard of my heart, my soul, and my ache, it is done," Sebille's mother heralded, turning the heads of those in the hall to where she stepped off the stairs. Continuing forward, she looked up from the parchment she carried, but not at her husband who had paused in breaking his fast—at Sebille, who had been slicing an apple to share with her little brother.

Never had the Lady of Lexeter looked at her daughter that way, the same as she regarded the dog who had messed in front of her a week past and for it received a kick to its soft place.

"Mother?" Sebille spoke into a silence that felt as if all held their breath.

Lady Raisa's upper lip curled, and the knife Sebille held slipped and sliced the tip of a finger with which she gripped the apple. But she was so shaken she felt only a sting and the warmth of blood running down the other fingers.

Returning her regard to the parchment, her mother continued, "The child is born."

Ricard Soames thrust upright, causing his chair to screech backward and nearly upend. "Clear the hall! Now!"

As knights, men-at-arms, and servants abandoned their places at table and around the great room, Lady Raisa halted before the dais. "But such enlightening reading I have happened upon, Husband. Surely all ought to know the Lord is not as merciful as we were made to believe." Once more her gaze fell on Sebille who, along with her brother, could only stare.

Of a sudden, their father was behind them, snatching his children off the bench and, with one beneath each arm, descending the dais.

"Aye," Sebille's mother called, "see our *miracle* safely away lest the deceived harm her. Quite wise, Ricard."

Harm? Sebille wondered, heart beating so hard she whimpered as her father's long strides carried Lothaire and her across the hall. *Who is the deceived? Why would he wish me harm? And what has so angered Mother she looks at me like that?*

Her father lowered her and his son to their feet. "Sebille, take Lothaire—"

"Our daughter is beautiful," his wife said. "Her hair golden red."

Thinking whatever had turned her mother's mood dark was past, Sebille touched her golden-red braid falling over her shoulder, then peered around her father. But it seemed those words were not directed at Sebille. They were read like those others.

"And just as it is the same as her mother's," Lady Raisa read on, "so is her pretty round face."

"Close your beak!" Ricard Soames thundered, causing sister and brother to startle and their mother to laugh. But that which sounded from Lady Raisa was not joyous. It was as cruel as the kick to the dog, making Sebille pull Lothaire against her side. Though her bloodied finger stained his tunic, it was where he needed to be. No tears fell or cries parted his lips, but he was so tense she knew his emotions were trying to get out.

Sebille's father bent near. "My dear girl, take your brother abovestairs and see him into bed, then you as well."

Though it was morn, she did not ask after so peculiar a command. "What is wrong with Mother?" she whispered as her own emotions caused her father's handsome face to appear distorted.

"Worry not, Sebille. I will fix this. I promise." He turned them toward the stairs. "Make haste."

It was strange, but Sebille was almost afraid to leave him alone with his wife. Perhaps because she sensed fear about her tall, handsome father who was never fearful. However, his gentle push made her take her brother's hand and lead him up the stairs.

As they neared the landing, she heard her mother scream something—a word that sounded foul though it was not one Sebille knew.

Then her father bellowed, "Give it to me, Raisa!"

More laughter, though in the midst of that was what sounded like a sob. "Too late!" the Lady of Lexeter cried. "I know its every word. I know what you did."

"Sebille?" Lothaire said, and she realized they had halted on the landing, and she was ashamed she was not protecting him as entrusted to her.

"Worry not," she said, "Father will fix it. He promised." As she urged him forward, a thought struck and she glanced at the solar's door. It was a bad thought, and her father would be disappointed if he caught her, but it might be the only way to learn why her mother had looked at her as if...

As if she hates me, she thought and drew Lothaire into his chamber. "Quick to bed, and I shall be quick to mine."

Her brother looked around, and amid the worry on his face was confusion. She no longer aided with clothing and unclothing him—at six he was far from a baby—but on the increasingly rare occasion she escorted him to his chamber, she often lingered to read or sing to him or simply talk.

"We must do as father bid," she said and stepped into the corridor, closed his door, and did not do as told. She entered her parents' solar and crossed to the wall recess with its little peek door hidden behind a fat candle.

She removed the candle and carefully opened the door. It was silent in the hall below, her mother unmoving on the dais behind the high table, her father on the opposite side. It appeared as if the two were engaged in a game of chase and had paused to catch their breath.

Still her mother held the parchment. A moment later, she raised it triumphantly.

"Raisa!" Ricard Soames barked.

"I have not finished reading it to you, my lord husband." She set it low before her eyes to keep him in sight.

"Curse you!" he spat.

"Cursed I am, Ricard. Now where were we? Ah!" She cleared her throat. "She was born at the convent of Bairnwood Abbey on the third day of May." Raisa looked up. "Remarkable, is it not? The same year and month I birthed *our* daughter, though this whore's child arrived three weeks earlier."

Ricard Soames lowered his head, gripped the back of his neck, his figure so defeated and diminished Sebille pressed a hand to her mouth lest she call out to him.

Raisa continued reading. "I have left her there to be raised by the good sisters and am now returned home with none but my mother aware of the true reason for my absence these three months. In a fortnight I shall wed my betrothed and, henceforth, be faithful. I did love you, Ricard, and I believe you loved me, but we were never possible."

That line sank into Sebille, and she disliked herself for how slow of wit she was, only then realizing the one who wrote to her father was a mistress. That he had one was not surprising since his wife sometimes railed against his infidelities. What surprised was that he had made a child who, it seemed, was nearly Sebille's age and had golden-red hair the same as the daughter of the lord and lady of Lexeter.

As Sebille's mind fumbled over the curiosity that she and her father's illegitimate daughter had hair the same unusual color, she fingered her chain girdle and winced over the sliced tip of her finger and the slick left upon the links.

"I shall think of you as little as I am able that you may sooner fade from memory," Lady Raisa continued to taunt her husband with another woman's words. "Oh, Ricard, the whore was so very brave."

Sebille saw her father raise his head, but he did not move. "Do not stop now, Raisa. Be done with it."

She shrugged. "She wished you a good, long life with your wife," she said, then gasped. "That would be me, at that time wed to you for…near on nine months, I believe."

"The babe was conceived weeks ere you and I wed, and I was faithful to you thereafter."

She snorted. "For a time."

"Two years!"

"Why, that is something of which to be proud. Two years, and now we have been husband and wife for ten. And how many mistresses have you had these eight years?"

Her father's shoulders broadened with breath, then he thrust a hand across the table. "You have entertained your sorry self, now give it to me."

Taking a step back, she pressed the parchment to her chest. "So you may destroy it as you should have done years past?" She made a sound of disgust. "Fool. A bit of flame and never would I have known you exchanged that whore's daughter for ours."

Sebille was glad her hand was over her mouth to capture her cry. Her mind had been moving in this direction but refused to arrive. As she began to shake, she prayed this was only a terrible dream, that her mother was her mother in truth.

"Dear Ricard, until your dying day you shall regret not allowing me to go to the grave all the more certain of heaven believing God healed our babe—made a miracle of her."

"It seemed the thing to do," he said with pleading Sebille had never heard from him. The hand gripping her mouth so hard it might bruise, she began to rock her body.

"How could it be the thing to do?" Lady Raisa said so calmly it was more frightening.

"I did it for you—"

"Me?"

"The girl child you birthed was deformed, Raisa—a hole in her lip nearly up to her nose. Do you not recall how you screamed when you saw her? You demanded she be taken from your sight, and when the midwife told the babe could not suckle and was not likely to survive beyond two days, do you not recall what you said? I do—*If God will not work a miracle, put the babe out.* And I said unlike many a man who would set their deformed child out in the night to feed the beasts of the dark, I could not. With your face turned from our babe, you said, *Then pray for a miracle so the child's suffering will not be long.* And that is what I did."

Raisa thrust a hand across the table, shook the parchment. "Nay, whilst I recovered from a birthing that nearly killed me and the shock over what came from my body, you exchanged our daughter for your wrong-born child and came home from that convent spilling lies of the days you spent on your face praying for our child's healing. Ah, the miracle the Lord worked, rewarding his faithful servant for a belief so holy that flesh was perfectly healed! How you must have laughed at how eagerly I accepted our hideous-turned-beautiful daughter that I did not question why she was so much larger, narrow face round, hair where there had been none of a color neither of us possess."

"I did not laugh, Raisa. I made something good out of bad, and you were happy as never have I seen you."

"Because I thought her special—touched by God, not the devil—"

"Enough!"

It was the same Sebille was screaming inside, but no matter that she told herself to retreat to her chamber, she had to know all.

"Nay, not enough," said the woman who was not truly her mother, whose adoration had turned to loathing. "You fooled me into raising your mistress's child." She slapped the parchment to her chest. "From my own breasts I fed her. No wet nurse for her—not for our miracle of a daughter."

Her husband stepped nearer the table. "I know this is a blow, and I am sorry to have hurt you, but Sebille is a good daughter, and she loves you as you love her. That need not change."

"Of course it must change. I cannot love her now. Will not! It makes me sick to think of all I wasted on her that should have been Lothaire's. Instead, I loved her better, just as you have, though for you it is because she is of your mistress." Raisa thrust the parchment forward. "Lady Honore!"

He did not respond, and she said, "I know only one of that name, she of the family Nevarre. She who is wed to Baron Graville."

Again, he did not respond.

"He will be distressed to read this, especially were he made to believe his wife came to him untouched."

Sebille's father moved so quickly she did not see what he did until he swung away and bounded off the dais.

"Give it to me!" Raisa cried as he strode to the hearth with the parchment in hand.

His wife ran around the table and across the hall, but all evidence of the truth of Sebille was upon the flames and beginning to blacken when Lady Raisa reached to retrieve it. Empty-handed, she jumped back and turned to her husband.

"Still I will tell him and ruin Lady Honore's life as she has ruined mine!"

Sebille's father grabbed her and shook her. "You will not. You will keep that sharp beak of yours closed. You will accept the blessing of a beautiful, healthy, loving daughter and—"

His wife whipped her head down, and a moment later Ricard Soames thrust her away and gripped his arm.

Crying softly into her hand, tears running over it, Sebille guessed her mother—nay, not her mother!—had bitten her father.

"I will not!" Lady Raisa cried. "She is as dead to me as…" She took a step toward her husband. "Our cursed child is dead, is she not?"

Sebille's father's chest was heaving, face florid, eyes like flames.

"Tell me!"

Was he purposely refusing to answer, or did he not trust himself to speak?

"I would know, Ricard!"

"Why? So you may reject her again? Have her set out in the wood to suffer teeth and claw?"

"Does our daughter live?"

A smile turned his mouth. "She does, is this moment abovestairs in her bed."

Lady Raisa screamed, her rage and frustration paining Sebille's ears, though it seemed not to move her father. When she quieted, bending forward as if to recover her breath, her husband leaned near. Only by holding her own breath was Sebille able to hear what he spoke.

"I did not set out the babe whose face was as desolate as your heart. I held her close as I rode night into day, and when I reached the abbey I gave her into the care of the good sisters. Gently, quietly, in the arms of the old abbess, Sebille whom you could not bear to look upon died the following morn. And I returned to you with the miraculously beautiful Sebille who sooner healed you and loves you as never have you been loved. And never again will you be loved if you do not set your mind to forgetting what was written on that parchment."

Forget, Sebille silently entreated. *Pray, Mother, forget and I shall ever love you—ever make you proud, ever be your beautiful Sebille.*

Lady Raisa remained bent over, each minute that passed giving Sebille more hope her angry, hurt heart would heal as she remembered all the embraces, kisses, smiles, and words of love spoken between them.

Finally, the Lady of Lexeter straightened, and Sebille could see the shine on her face that evidenced she had been crying.

All will be well, Sebille assured herself and slowly lowered her hand from her mouth and clasped it with the other over her heart.

"I cannot forget," Lady Raisa said. "Every time I look at her I shall see the woman who lay with my husband, and you who made a fool of me. And one day..." She shrugged. "You will not always be here to protect her, Ricard."

"Raisa!" His shout covered his daughter's pained gasp before she could get a hand over her mouth.

The Lady of Lexeter laughed again, and her husband shoved past and strode toward the stairs.

Guessing the solar his destination, Sebille pulled back, but not before her father's chin came up and she saw the determination on his face turn to alarm. Had he seen her in the opening? Or merely noted the little door was ajar?

She longed to run to her chamber but hesitated over whether to close the little door and return the candle to its place. If he had seen her, it would be of no benefit. If he had not and were it left open, he—or Lady Raisa—would know they had been observed.

Sebille closed the peek door, set the candle in the recess, and ran across the solar. She made it halfway down the corridor before her father's boots on the landing announced she was seen.

She whimpered, turned.

"Ah, Sebille," he said as he closed the distance between them. Then she was in his arms, her face pressed to his shoulder. "Why did you do it?"

"Sh-she looked at me as if..." A sob escaped. "...she hated me. And she does." Then came wracking sobs she did not realize resounded around her own chamber until her father lowered her to her bed.

"Cry into the pillow," he said softly and turned her face into it. "We do not wish to disturb your brother."

Pressing her mouth into the sack of feathers, she looked up.

"I must gather your things, Sebille. I am taking you from here."

She wanted to ask where they would go, but all her breath was spent on sobs.

When finally she went silent, head aching too much to cry further, her father enfolded her in a blanket and carried her out into a day that seemed like night with her head covered. Then she was atop his horse and cradled against his chest as they rode into the night.

Bairnwood Abbey, where her real mother had birthed her in secret nine years past.

She did not need to be told that was where she awakened. Even had she not heard the bells calling the sisters to prayer she would have known. Where else would her father have brought her? Where else would she be safe from Raisa Soames?

"Drink," he said.

She looked into the cup he had handed her after propping her on pillows.

"Warm honey milk. Your favorite, Seb."

She sipped, wished she could feel its warmth and taste its sweetness. But at least it wet her mouth.

He did not speak again until the cup was drained, then he set it on the stool alongside the narrow bed and scooted his chair nearer. "Did you hear it all, beloved?"

She jerked her chin.

"I did love your mother—your real one. But she was to wed another as was I. Our families needed alliances. And so we sinned."

As still he sinned, Sebille thought and, despite Lady Raisa's hatred of her, felt that pain of betrayal as ever she had since first becoming aware of her sire's infidelities.

"Unless your mother…" He momentarily closed his eyes. "Unless Lady Raisa reconciles her mind and heart to the truth—and she may the longer she is parted from you—you shall remain at Bairnwood Abbey, and I will visit as often as I can. When you are a woman, I shall see you properly wed as befitting the legitimate daughter of a noble, which none can dispute now the parchment is destroyed."

"I am frightened, Father."

He took her hands in his. "Providing you never reveal the truth—what you saw and heard in the hall—you need not be frightened. Here you will be safe and well cared for."

"I am frightened," she repeated.

His smile was sorrowful. "Then I shall sit with you until you sleep again."

She gasped. "And then?"

"I shall leave."

"Why?"

"To alert your real mother that our beautiful secret has been discovered so she may be prepared should I fail in keeping Lady Raisa from revealing your existence to her husband. Then I must return to High Castle—to our people and your brother who shall need me more now his beloved sister is gone."

"Lothaire," she whispered. "I shall miss him nearly as much as you."

"When 'tis safe, you will see him again." He kissed her cheek, eased her down the lumpy mattress, and drew the blanket up to her chin. "Now sleep."

She did not, knowing once she drifted away he would be gone and she might not see him for weeks…mayhap months. But he stayed as promised and, hours later, without realizing she had closed her eyes, sleep stole her father from her. Forever.

38

LOTHAIRE'S HEAD WAS in his hands, though it was his chest he ought to be gripping for how many wounds it had sustained throughout his sister's tale of a day so long gone he could hardly recall it. But then, there had been little cause for it to burn itself into the memory of a six-year-old.

He opened his eyes, stared at Laura's hand on his knee, then set a hand over hers.

"Forever," Sebille repeated.

He looked from her to the man over her shoulder. "All this you knew, Father Atticus?"

"Upon your sister's return to High Castle, she needed someone to confide in and chose a man of God who could keep her secret whilst praying for and counseling her. However, only this day have I learned those things she did in hopes of permanently removing your mother from High Castle. Though I do not condone them, I understand her desperation. And now I can tell you it was not only Lady Raisa's disapproval of how near you drew to me that led to my departure from High Castle. Though your mother was unaware Sebille and I knew the circumstances of her birth, oft I corrected her behavior toward her daughter until…" His eyes moistened. "…she cursed me, near shouted down the chapel, and pushed me so hard against the altar I fell."

Lothaire felt Laura jerk. Certain she recalled his mother's attack on her, he squeezed her hand.

"Still, I would have stayed at High Castle had Lady Raisa not demanded I leave," the priest continued. "So I might remain near should Sebille and you need me, I went only as far as Thistle Cross. Blessedly, Sir Angus and others of your father's knights were discreet in arranging for me to meet with Sebille from time to time—and you as your relationship with your mother grew strained."

Lothaire remembered. The priest had listened, advised, and prayed for him. And the wary boy he had become following his father's disappearance had known not to reveal those meetings to his mother.

"I did what I could," Father Atticus said. "As I do what I can now."

There was no question he cared for the siblings, just as there was no doubt the years of Lady Raisa's vengeance had damaged Sebille. For that, the priest worried over the family Lothaire now had with Laura and to which they would add. For that, he believed Sebille ought to enter a convent.

"Do you remember when I left High Castle, Lothaire?" his sister asked.

"Aye, I missed you, felt your absence and Father's all the more for how difficult Mother became. She was angry and often at tears, and never had she spent so much time with me as she did whilst you were gone. It seemed I could go nowhere without her following and assuring me of her love for me and mine for her. Though I did not wish to be carried, oft she fixed me on her hip as if I were a babe."

Sebille's tear-swollen face convulsed.

"I was pleased to discover I could sooner climb down from her did I ask when Father and you would return. Then, finally, you came home." That was something he remembered clearly—barreling into his sister and hearing the click of prayer beads that would sound from her person thereafter. "It seemed like months you were gone."

"'Twas a fortnight. For as much as I cried, it felt months to me as well. When Lady Raisa arrived at the convent and said Father had decided I should not give my life in service to the Lord and had sent her to collect me, I tried to hide how frightened I was since I had vowed not to reveal I knew the truth of my birth. Though in the presence of the abbess she behaved as if pleased by our reunion, her eyes were cold. Still, I thought if I tried very hard I could make her love me again. Not until our return to High Castle did she reveal Father had never come home and said his disappearance was a result of fornication—that he had been with a mistress and the Lord punished him for sinning against his wife."

Sebille pulled a hand down her face. "She watched me closely, as if I might reveal my knowledge he had gone to the woman who birthed me. I said he would surely return soon, and she revealed he had passed a night at the castle of Lady Beata's family and not been seen since. She was certain ill had befallen him there." She sighed. "So it did, though until a year past when we learned of his murder, ever I suspected her hand in his disappearance. I wronged her."

Not as much as Raisa had wronged Sebille, Lothaire reflected. "She neglected you, reducing you to little more than a servant."

His sister peered down her body that had been pleasingly plump as a girl and prettily curvaceous as she grew into gowns never again as fine as those worn whilst Raisa believed her a miracle. She had been lovely, but following her refusal to wed Angus she had become gaunt, face and figure trading softly rounded edges for sharp ones that made her appear sunken, golden-red hair dark and lax from too little grooming.

"And she lied," she said low. "As did he about the night he exchanged his dead daughter for me."

"What lie did Father tell, Sebille?"

"He..." Her eyes widened, and she gave a quick shake of her head. "Not Father—Mother. She lied."

Hardly convincing, but Lothaire could see it was useless to press her. More, perhaps, it was too painful for her.

"But still I had you," she said in a rush.

"Better, Sebille, you could have had Angus."

She raised and dropped a shoulder. "Lady Raisa said he would be as faithless to me as my father was to her."

"Tell me you did not believe her."

"For how much he likes women, I thought it possible. And lo, has he not time and again betrayed me?"

Determined not to argue that since the knight and she had not exchanged vows it was not she whom Angus betrayed, Lothaire allowed, "He does like women, though that was never as apparent than when you refused his offer of marriage."

She considered this. "Regardless, that is not why I would not wed him. Would you know the reason?"

"You said Mother required too much attention for you to be a good wife."

"Aye, but more true was she would have made Angus and me miserable had we taken her to live with us at her dower property that you meant to give into his keeping. No marriage would that have been. True, you said she could remain at High Castle and you would hire a companion, but no life would that have been for you. Without me here to mop up her bitterness, I feared you would sink in it. And she would ruin you as she nearly ruined all of Lexeter."

He retrieved her hand, squeezed it. "For love of me you refused Angus."

"Love of you."

"And thereafter, you ceased trying to regain Mother's affection."

"Finally, I accepted it was futile, and I was so angered by the years wasted on trying to love her back to me that I embraced her vengeance, mostly by way of little things that frustrated her. It was not to have lasted long, the physician having said her years were few. But they were not, Lothaire. I felt every one of them, though with each that passed I assured myself I was that much nearer a life with Angus." She swallowed. "I know 'tis wrong, but I longed for her sickness to be as serious as she made it appear, for it to free the living of her. But only now that I have lost my youth and Angus no longer wants me are we freed."

Lothaire wished he could assure her his knight would yet have her, but it could easily prove a lie. "Sebille, you know it was not only Lady Raisa's illnesses that time and again turned me from sending her away."

"It was concern for me—that you did not wish me to follow her—but I also know how great your sense of responsibility and faithfulness. Had she not family at her side, soon you would have brought her home, else taken the burden of her upon yourself, visiting often though you were needed at High Castle. Therefore, I committed to serving as a barrier between her and you here, and still I would be that if not for Lady Beata."

He frowned. "Lady Beata?"

"Surely you remember how your mother railed over your refusal to contest the annulment?"

"I do."

"It made me realize she was nowhere near the end of her miserable life. And when you said you must find a wife else the queen would force one on you, I knew that marriage would be as doomed as your first with Lady Edeva. It was no longer enough for me to serve as a barrier. I knew I must leave High Castle with Lady Raisa."

Momentarily, she closed her eyes. "When she cursed Lady Beata in front of Martin and me and bemoaned no one would rid her of the foul woman, I conceived the idea of assassins to which I would alert you so you could prevent the attack. Though the men hired to play the part were not to have been captured, it unfolded beautifully, convincing you of your mother's duplicity. Thus, you were determined to send her away though I would accompany her. But she foiled me. Was it truly a stroke as Martin told? I but know it looked very different from what finally took her life. By the time she deigned to regain her strength, her offense and endangerment of Lexeter had faded sufficiently that once again you allowed her to remain. And my plans..."

"More plans, Sebille?"

"I would not have harmed her, but I believed her removal from High Castle would speed her passing." She dropped her prayer beads, touched her fingers to her lips. "It sounds evil, and ever I pray for forgiveness, but I knew life would be better without one who made me want to sleep away every minute of every day."

Lothaire turned her hand up and slid his fingers between hers. "Dear Sebille, I am sorry."

She drew a shuddering breath. "If only Father had not exchanged his deformed daughter for me. If only Lady Raisa had not brought me out of the convent. A better, more useful life I would have led serving the Lord."

That he could not dispute. "The men sent to attack the fleece stores were also pretense to move me to banish our—*my*—mother?" He hated having to correct himself, but it was surely best he cease associating Sebille with her tormentor.

"Aye, first Shepsdale, and when the hue and cry was raised, on to Thistle Cross. I thought the attempts to attack the wool, met with revelation of the assault on Lady Laura in her chamber would prove so dire you would accept your mother must be moved to her dower property. Indeed, I was so certain that I agreed to remain at High Castle. Though I knew it might be too late for Angus and me, I believed I would find happiness enough just being your sister and..." She glanced at Laura. "I thought if I became your friend, I could turn you back to Lothaire should you think to stray again."

Though Laura had good reason to be offended, she leaned near and said, "Good, godly counsel I would welcome, my lady—to be reminded of how much I love your brother and he loves me—but I assure you never shall I want any other than Lothaire. As never have I wanted any other."

Confusion grooved Sebille's brow. "But the flesh is weak, Lady Laura. Is not your daughter testament to that?"

Laura's hesitation made Lothaire tense, but she said, "I am ten years older, ten years wiser. I love and am loved, for which I thank the Lord and shall ever seek His guidance to ensure my vows remain as true as the day I spoke them."

Sebille looked to Lothaire. "Already it is a good marriage?"

"It is beyond blessed."

Her eyes brimmed. "Then more I am glad your mother shall no longer dwell at High Castle, though I vow I did not mean her to depart as she did."

"This I know."

She looked over her shoulder at the priest who inclined his head, then angled toward Laura. "There is something else of which I must be unburdened."

"Aye, my lady?"

"I hated you for cuckolding my brother and hurting him so, but I mostly ceased years ago, thinking it emotion better spent on Lady Raisa than one he would not see again. Then it was you he brought home and the anger returned. And yet, I could not make it stick to you. It kept sliding off. Though you had the daughter to prove how ill you had treated my brother, the more I observed you, the more I found myself well disposed and thought you might make Lothaire happy if you would but remain faithful. But when I saw you with Angus—flirting with him…" At Laura's gasp, she held up a hand. "I accept 'twas not your intention, but at the time I felt betrayed. And I wanted to punish you for fooling me."

"Punish me?"

"Your wedding gown. It was not the dog. Nor was it Lady Raisa as I hoped you would suspect were you unconvinced Tomas was the ruin of it."

"You burned it?" Lothaire said sharply.

Her eyes swept to him. "I had no choice."

He breathed deep, managed one word. "Why?"

"When it was so perfectly stitched and embellished it was certain not to be worn until the wedding day, I rubbed foxglove over the bodice's lining." She returned her gaze to Laura. "I wished you to be terribly uncomfortable on the day you wed, not only as retribution for cuckolding my brother but that it serve as a reminder of the vows you spoke when next you thought to betray him. But in undoing the pearls and beads, you touched that tainted fabric ere you should have."

Laura studied her hands. Though they no longer evidenced affliction, she surely recalled the pain and likely wondered how much worse it would have felt upon her chest and abdomen. "The physician believed it was in the garden I came into contact with foxglove."

Sebille's shoulders sank further. "I am ashamed to say it, but I was pleased by what I wrought, that it was no mere itch or discomfort you suffered. And further pleased knowing the shame the physician would impart, since he oft diagnoses rashes as sexual disease ungodly women inflict upon men. But when I realized the gown would be suspect were you further afflicted, I knew I must burn it and find another means of ruining your wedding night."

Lothaire ground his teeth.

His wife drew a deep breath. "I do not understand how you could have set the fire, Lady Sebille. Shortly after I entered the hall, you came from the high table."

Lothaire's sister nodded. "From your window, I watched for your return to the donjon. When you appeared in the bailey, I tipped the chair, draped the gown over the brazier, and slipped belowstairs. You were so occupied you did not see me. Thus, I made it appear I approached from the dais. So you would think that mangy dog responsible—or Lady Raisa—I soon withdrew abovestairs to raise the alarm ere the fire got out of control."

Laura nodded slowly. "You say you meant to find another means of ruining my wedding night."

"I did, but unbeknownst to Sir Angus, he persuaded me to leave you be. The day ere your wedding, I accused him of pursuing you."

In the garden, Lothaire realized, recalling the conversation to which he had been privy.

"He claimed never would he betray my brother, but were he so foul to do so, you would not want him—that one had only to see how you gazed upon him to know 'tis with love. Though I feared he was as fooled as I thought myself, for Lothaire's sake I longed for him to be right. But at the shearing supper..."

"What of it, Sebille?" Lothaire asked.

"I saw her slip away, and thinking she went to a lover, determined she had only herself to blame did she encounter the men sent to threaten the stores at Thistle Cross." She turned back to Laura. "When I learned 'twas Lothaire you were to meet, I thought I would die. Sir Angus was proven right, my plans exposed you to danger, and more, my brother might soon find himself in the path of those men." She shook her head. "I am sorry, as I am for frightening your daughter. I like her for how fond she is of my brother and how hard she tries to please him. Indeed, she reminds me of my younger self."

This Lothaire remembered—how hard Sebille the girl had tried to please the woman who no longer believed her worthy of worship.

"We have much in common—born outside of marriage, longing for a father, seeking a mother's love. I was nine when I lost all. She is nine when what is lost might yet be found." She bit her lip. "I did not mean her harm, but when she screamed I was confused and needed time to determine how to mend what was broken. I so ached to keep hold of my brother's affection as 'tis all the love I have. Do I still, Lothaire?"

"Ever you shall, Sebille. Naught can change that."

She gave a little sob, drew his hand to her mouth, and kissed his knuckles.

Lothaire pulled her to him and wrapped his arms around her. "How I wish you had told me this years ago. Did you think I would no longer care for you?"

She gulped. "I knew only that I was dirty, as Lady Raisa made me feel from the moment she rejected the daughter she had loved."

He tipped up her face, and just as he had assured Laura at the lake, said, "You were never dirty. You were wronged. Now tell me what I can do to help you."

She glanced over her shoulder. "Father Atticus and I believe I would be content at the convent of Bairnwood Abbey. He tells the abbess who administered that place when our father left me there yet lives. She was very kind." She lifted her prayer beads. "These were hers, but too long for a girl, so she cut the necklace and gave me half."

He forced a smile. "That was kind of her. But are you certain you wish to leave your home?"

"Dear Lothaire, this has not been my home since Father took me away. Thus, I would return to where I was born and should have remained. All I ask is that you visit, and when I am better, bring your wife and children."

"Of course," he said, unashamed by how choked he sounded. "You shall be missed."

She eased out of his hold. "I would leave on the morrow."

"So soon?"

"I am glad it seems that to you, but 'tis a long time coming for me, and I prefer not to be here when Lady Raisa is put in the ground along-side our father. Though I shall pray my heart softens enough that one day I forgive her, I am not able to now. And 'tis hard to bear even the thought of her being nearer our father than I am."

"As you will."

She drew a sharp breath. "I have something that should ease your financial difficulties, allowing you to spend more time with your family."

He raised an eyebrow.

"The coins and valuables Lady Raisa hid when you took control of the barony—that which she used to purchase what Lexeter's cof-fers could no longer supply—and from which I took to work ill in her name."

Minutes later, the removal of the sill of a candle recess to the right of the one which held the peek door revealed the stash. The space was nearly as wide as Lothaire's forearm was long and twice as deep. Inside were two pouches of coins, a box of jewelry that included the replace-ment signet ring his mother had refused to yield, all manner of silver ser-vice, a small tapestry woven through with gold thread, a finely wrought misericorde, and a dozen leather-bound books. Some of these had been in the family for generations, but most were purchased by Lady Raisa following her husband's disappearance.

Lothaire felt a lightening about his heart. Those items acquired following the death of Ricard Soames would be sold to provide Sebille a place in the Church. Whatever remained would be used to advance the barony's production of wool cloth.

It seemed, at long last, the worst that had befallen Lexeter might come right. Certes, the worst that had befallen its lord was over, nearly enough to make him feel barely a score of years as when he had first been in love. But not the same love as this love. He looked to his wife, his beloved, his future.

This love was abiding.

"Do you think she truly wishes to leave High Castle?"

Lothaire had begun to believe Laura slept, so relaxed was she. Pulling back, he peered into her face lit by moonlight. "I do. There is naught here for her but ill memories made more painful alongside the beautiful ones of when she was a miracle."

"You are wrong. Her brother is here."

"As promised, I shall visit her often." He stroked his wife's cheek. "Though much of what she did was for love of me, you do not seem angry with her for endangering Clarice and you."

"Knowing her tale, 'tis hard to be angry, but I do think it best she depart High Castle, not only to find peace and prayer amongst the sisters, but because her need for healing seems so great 'tis worrisome what she might do in its absence. I believe she means well, but her mind may not be right. I am sorry if that offends."

"It does not. I also hope for her healing and happiness, and it seems Bairnwood Abbey is the best place for that."

After some minutes, Laura said, "What do you think she meant when she said your father lied about the night he exchanged his dead daughter for her?"

He had also tripped over that but tucked it away. "The first thing that occurs seems unlikely. And yet I think it possible the girl child my mother birthed did not die—at least, not when our father told. If the lie was about the first Sebille's death, I question how the sister I have loved learned of it. Would our father have told a nine-year-old so recently traumatized by the truth about her parentage?" He shook his head. "Hence, if she learned of it, it would be from someone during the fortnight she was at the abbey or... This seems less believable, but perhaps she met her half sister."

"It does sound fantastic," Laura said, "and yet plausible. If you are correct, do you think Sebille is drawn to Bairnwood by her half sister? That the girl—woman—may yet reside there?"

"Mayhap. If so, I hope that a good thing. I do not know the abbess will discuss anything with me we do not already know, but she must be made aware of what my sister endured these years so she is prepared for how damaged Sebille is."

Laura caught his hand up, kissed it. "I love you."

"I love you, Laura."

She slid a finger across the base of each of his fingers. "A ring that ought to be upon your hand is missing."

"When Lexeter is whole—"

"It is whole, Lothaire. What else is required but you, me, Clarice, and your people?"

"'Tis not prosperous—"

"Prosperous enough." She rolled away, opened a small box on the bedside table. When she returned to him, he did not resist when she once more captured his hand. "May I?" She touched the cool band to the tip of his finger.

"You are certain I am worthy?"

"You have ever been worthy," she said and slid the ring on his finger, worked it over his knuckle, and settled it at the base.

Lothaire laughed low and eased her onto her back. "This worthy lord is thinking he would like to make love to his wife. May I?"

"Here? Now?" she said, just as he had done at the lake when she was the one seeking intimacy.

"Here, now, my lady. Providing you are awake enough."

"Wonderfully awake," she said and drew his head down to hers.

Epilogue

Wulfen Castle, England
Fall, 1164

Thomas Becket, Archbishop of Canterbury, had fallen far in King Henry's estimation.

Lothaire Soames, Baron of Lexeter, had risen high in Abel Wulfrith's estimation. Even if the trainer of England's fiercest knights would not admit it, approval glinted in his eyes.

"Methinks I liked you best when you were predictable, Soames," the warrior said and strode with a slight hitch to where his sword had skittered across the training field. He retrieved it, slid it beneath his belt, and turned. "A pity, for you are easy to dislike. Now it may better serve me to seek friendly terms."

"A pity, indeed." Lothaire returned his own sword to his hip. "Far more than fear of yielding up blood, your dislike inspired me to improve my skill. But if we are reduced to friendly terms…" He shrugged. "…I suppose I can find enemies elsewhere."

"Always. Never forget it." The Lord of Wulfen Castle halted before him, and something of a smile moved his mouth. "Providing you show no mercy as you showed me none this day, I think it very likely you shall vanquish any threat to your person—more importantly, your family, people, and lands."

Unlike the past three days when Abel Wulfrith had incited his pupil to anger by naming him a coward, Lothaire had done as commanded—this time giving no quarter when the opportunity presented to take advantage of injuries the warrior had sustained years ago which seemed to have little effect on his ability to defend himself.

Blessedly, Lothaire now knew how to engage all his senses such that he was almost unerringly able to anticipate his opponents' moves and vulnerabilities. Thus, he had struck, and as Abel Wulfrith's sword flew, set the point of his own to the man's neck.

"Then I am Wulfen worthy?" Lothaire said, only to wish he had not fallen into banter with this man who would scorn him, ever holding out of reach the award of a Wulfrith dagger. Grinding his teeth the better to control what might come off his tongue, he waited to be denounced.

That something of a smile eased, strangely contrasting with eyes that continued to shine with what Lothaire had been certain was approval. Mayhap it was mockery.

"Wulfen worthy," Abel Wulfrith said. "That you are, Baron Soames."

The air turned so thick it was hard to breath. No mockery, and the man had titled him. It was disconcerting how much it made Lothaire feel like a boy receiving praise from one he revered.

Then Abel Wulfrith clapped him on the shoulder. "Have I shocked you, Baron?"

The air thinned, and Lothaire said, "You have. You do me great honor."

"And you make much of it—as you should." Abel Wulfrith strode past. "Come!"

Thoughts flying ahead to Laura with whom he would soon be reunited after nearly a month of training more intense than any before, Lothaire followed. Moments later, he passed from the training yard in which he had proven himself into the one in which his old adversaries, Durand Marshal and Elias de Morville, were hard at quarterstaffs.

Legs braced apart, arms crossed over his chest, Abel Wulfrith watched his friends who had arrived at Wulfen Castle last eve. Time and again, the men shifted from offensive to defensive amid lengthening shadows that marked the setting of the sun.

Just when it seemed neither would best the other, the Lord of Wulfen said, "One more thing to prove yourself worthy, Soames. Tell me who shall win this contest."

Lothaire nearly laughed, but it was no joke. Abel saw what his pupil did not. And now again Lothaire must prove he possessed that which was among a warrior's greatest weapons—observation.

"You do not see it?" Abel pressed.

He did not, and he hated he might shame himself. True, he was greatly distanced compared to when he was the one engaged in combat, but that was the point—know thy opponent even whilst he is not yet that.

"Keep watching, Soames. Watch as if you were Baron Marshal, then as if Sir Elias. It is there."

So it was, Lothaire observed moments later. "Baron Marshal shall prevail."

"Why?"

"They are well matched, but Sir Elias's swings and thrusts are not as smooth nor as timely, though not for lack of skill, methinks. It is as if..."

Abel looked sidelong at him. "As if?"

"He is distracted. If Baron Marshal is as bereft of mercy as is required of him, he will soon land the deciding blow."

And so it came to pass. Still, Lothaire suspected the victor had shown the defeated mercy. It would have required little effort to drop Elias de Morville to his knees, but the baron was content with knocking aside the opposition's quarterstaff and thrusting his own against the man's chest.

"Well met, Durand!" Abel called. "As for you, Elias, we shall have to get a good quantity of drink in you to learn what so distracts."

Sweating profusely, tunics and chausses darkened with the foul moisture also dampening their hair and beading their faces, the men advanced on Lothaire and their friend.

"You read me near as well as your brother, Everard," Elias said, halting before Abel. "But drink is not required to loosen my tongue." His gaze shifted to Lothaire, and he considered him some moments. "What distracts is the reason I asked Durand to accompany me to Wulfen."

"Ah, I thought something afoot. But if it can wait a while longer, first I would have the two of you bear witness to the award of a Wulfrith dagger." He nodded at Lothaire.

"It can wait," Elias said.

"You agree to bear witness?"

"I would be honored." This from Durand, and without hesitation.

"Elias?" Abel prompted.

The knight inclined his head. "I trust your judgment."

"As well you should." Abel swung away, said over his shoulder, "Once we are shed of this filth and stink, we shall meet in the solar."

An hour later, all four men were as groomed and well-clothed as Sir Rowan who also bore witness. Then the priest prayed over the Wulfen-worthy knight, beseeching the Lord to ever hold Lothaire accountable for all he had gained at Wulfen—that it never be questioned he was worthy of his faith, country, people, and family. Then the Wulfrith dagger was fastened on Lothaire's belt.

As they ate their supper in the solar whilst the young men who had yet to earn a Wulfrith dagger filled their bellies in the hall, Lothaire was awarded something else…something more valuable than the jeweled weapon…something he had not known he coveted, especially now he had Laura.

Friendship. Not in the truest, deepest sense, he suspected—especially where Elias was concerned—but it seemed a good beginning.

Eyes so dark they might haunt did they not sparkle like stars on a moonless night…

"Lothaire!"

He had known Laura was aware of his approach, though not because she had set High Castle knights on the road to ensure their lord passed by the lake. Because knowing she was here—that much nearer to being in his arms—he had pushed his destrier harder and its thunder had surely been heard ere he saw she stood near the shore with her back to him.

Not until his breath moved her hair had she turned and thrown her arms around him.

"You, Wife, are eager to welcome your husband home," he said and was certain the sparkles in her eyes were reflected in his own.

"It has been a month, Husband!"

He touched his brow to hers. "Much too long. But as I know what years feel like in the absence of you, I dare not complain."

She rose to her toes. "You are right. But still 'tis too long to wait on your kiss." She angled her head and opened her mouth upon his.

He gathered her closer, and feeling like a man nearing starvation, kissed her back.

They could have gone much further than kisses and hands desperate to reacquaint themselves with every curve and hollow despite the heat of the sun reminding it was daylight, but one particular curve made Lothaire draw back.

He looked down, back up.

Laura's thoroughly kissed mouth parted with a smile. "I am showing. And this morn methinks I felt our wee one move."

There was not much to her belly, but as she was barely halfway through her pregnancy, little was expected. But in the months to come...

"Do you know if it is a boy or a girl?"

She grinned. "Too soon to tell—if ever one can. Though the midwife is certain she will know by the lay of the babe when I am further along, methinks we shall have to wait until our child is in our arms."

Imagining that day, Lothaire's eyes burned, and he did not mind that his wife saw he was moved. Indeed, he would have her know. Though a warrior ought to hold close his vulnerabilities, not where his wife was concerned.

"Make love to me?" she said.

He blinked. "Here? Now?"

"Once we have washed away the dust and scent of your ride." She touched the purse on her girdle. "I brought soap."

He laughed, and as the joy trailed off, she said, "Laugh again, Lothaire."

He hiked an eyebrow. "I must needs have something over which to laugh."

She smiled. "We had quite a disturbance a week past."

"Oh?"

"You know Clarice loves her lambs."

"'Tis the wool in her blood."

"True, but in this instance, it was the wool in her *bed."* She nodded. "Poor Tina went to rouse Clarice and found the chamber a mess, the rushes sparse. When she drew back the covers, our daughter was curled around the lamb you entrusted to her."

The one whose mother had rejected it, and whose care was to have been provided in the stables. He gave Laura the laughter she wished, then scooped her up and carried her to the water's edge.

They were not long in divesting their garments, pausing only long enough for Laura to exclaim over the Wulfrith dagger and proclaim Abel Wulfrith had been derelict in not sooner seeing her husband fit with one. Then they stepped into the lake and lingered in water that was too cool—though only for a short time.

Later, as Lothaire cradled his fully awakened wife, she said, "I like the new physician. When he is not attending the complaints of the castle folk, he is all about the demesne caring for the villagers."

"I am glad he is worth the coin paid him."

"Ever so."

"And Cook?" he asked since the one he had chosen to replace Raisa's man had proven incapable of that responsibility. Thus, Laura had herself named a new cook.

"She is wonderful, Lothaire. And not overly reliant on expensive spices to render her dishes appealing.

"I am glad," he said, and as he began to drift, reflected on the three prisoners he had not released with the cook. The two older ones had served six months of hard labor upon Lexeter in order to gain their freedom. The younger one was sent to the queen to dispense justice for the assault upon Eleanor's kin. Lothaire did not know what form that had taken, but the queen had written that justice was served and never again would the man harm a woman.

"I received a missive from your sister," Laura said.

"Sebille?" he murmured.

She turned to face him. "Aye, she who is now a bride and professes to be more loved than ever she thought possible."

Pulling himself up out of sleep, he opened his eyes and saw sparkles. "I must visit her soon."

"Did you not stop en route to Wulfen Castle?"

"Aye, a fortnight ere she was to speak her vows. But this next visit will be less personal. I have a favor to do Baron Marshal's friend, Sir Elias de Morville."

"At Bairnwood Abbey?"

That place which had well enough healed his sister that she now wore a nun's habit. "Strangely enough, aye."

When he did not elaborate, she said, "'Tis not for my ears?"

"Though I am to be discreet, I see no reason I cannot share what I know. But later, hmm? Now I just wish to hold you." He tucked her nearer, and she fit so perfectly he praised the Lord so much could, indeed, happen in a year.

Laura captured his hand and drew it over her hip onto the bulge of their child. "I thank you, Husband."

"For?"

"A life blessed with far more laughter than tears."

He nuzzled her neck. "'Tis a beautiful day to be in love. A beautiful life."

THE RAVELING

Age Of Faith: Book Eight

From USA Today Best-seller, Tamara Leigh, the eighth book in the AGE OF FAITH series—featuring Sir Elias de Morville of *THE LONGING* and *THE VEXING*. Releasing Spring/Summer 2018

1

Forkney, England
Fall, 1164

HE HAD LOST a son he had not known he had—providing the child was
his. After all, there was a reason he had not married the mother. More, a
reason she had not wished to wed him. And it appeared that reason had
not changed.

"Dead," she repeated, then lowered her voice. "'Twas the devil took
him."

Elias had reached for his purse to put coins in her palm, money he
prayed would not be spent on drink, but he stilled over those last words
sent past teeth no longer pretty.

He considered her thin, pale face lit by a torch outside the alehouse
from which she had stumbled minutes earlier, drew a deep breath. "The
devil, you say?"

Fear leapt from her jittering eyes.

"Why the devil, Lettice?"

She moistened colorless lips, glanced around as if to ensure no others listened. "Marked by evil, he was. I had no choice. Ye must know I
did not."

One question answered only to breed more. "How marked, and for
what had you no choice?"

She opened her mouth, left it ajar as if reconsidering. Then she raised trembling fingers to the corner of an eye and swept them down her cheek to her jaw. "All red and purple was he, as if kissed by...ye know. *Him.*"

Elias dug his short nails into calloused palms. A mark of birth, possessed by many—though rarely so large or visible—did not a devil's child make. But as ever, superstition ran rampant.

"That would alarm, indeed," he said with control lest he frighten her away. "What did you do?"

"I couldna keep him, Elias." She shuddered. "Though lovely one side of him, that other side...that mark..."

Lord, he prayed, *no matter were it my son or another's, let her not have set the babe out in the wood. Let her not be so cruel.*

"What would have been said of me?" she bemoaned.

Would it have been much worse than what was said of her when she took coin for the use of her body? he wondered with resentment he should no longer feel for a woman he had ceased loving years ago—or mostly.

He unclenched his jaw. "How did the babe die?"

Lettice flinched, drew a shoulder up to her ear. "I did not wish to know. It...was taken care of."

It.

Pain. Anger. Disgust. All set their brand upon Elias. It seemed naught remained of the woman he had loved. In looks, speech, spirit, and heart, she was unrecognizable. And just as he had been unable to save her then, he could not save her now. Worse, he could not save the babe who might have been his.

Though he longed to walk away, remembrance of what he had once felt for this woman bade him open his purse. "Promise me," he said as her gaze shot to the leather pouch, "you will take what I give to better your circumstances, not—"

"How much?" she gasped.

He hesitated, then cinched the strings, and as she whimpered like a child shown a sweet and denied it, removed the purse from his belt.

"Much," he said. "If you spend wisely, 'twill last through this season into the next."

He reached it to her, and she snatched it to her chest, pivoted, and ran.

He was tempted to follow, but for what? Just as her life was hers to live, the coin was hers to spend.

"Lord," he groaned, "let it not become a stone upon which to stumble. Let it bless her."

Once darkness stole her from sight, he lowered his head and felt the sting of tears of which he would not be ashamed even had the one who knighted him told he ought to be. But Sir Everard Wulfrith of that family known England to France as the mightiest trainers of knights said only those unworthy of defending king and country were bereft of tears for the hurts and sorrows of their fellow man.

"Lettice," he breathed.

"Milord?"

He jerked, cursed himself. Tears were naught to be ashamed of, but succumbing to them in this place at this time of night—leaving himself open to thievery and gutting—was far from worthy. And now the one who had stolen upon him knew better than to quietly approach a warrior.

Back against the alehouse's wall, a Wulfrith dagger at his throat, the man who had gone as still as the dead gaped at the man above him.

Elias assessed him. He was attractive and fairly well groomed, near his own age, shorter by a hand, more bone than muscle, and of the common class as evidenced by a tunic fashioned of homespun cloth—albeit of good quality and showing little wear.

"What do you want?" Elias growled.

"But to earn a few coins." The man splayed his arms and opened his fingers to show empty hands. "No harm intended, milord. None done."

Elias thrust his face near. He smelled drink, though not of the sour sort. "I have given the last of my coin."

A loud clearing of the throat. "Surely a lord so fine as you can get more."

He could. His squire awaited him at the inn which lay opposite the direction Lettice had fled, in Francis's possession several purses fatter than the one with which Elias had parted. "Why would I wish to do that?"

"The harlot's babe. I can tell more about him than she."

What else was there to know? Elias wondered, then asked it.

The man moistened his lips. "There is much to be told that none but straight-fingered Arblette can reveal, milord."

Straight-fingered, Elias silently scorned. Could a self-proclaimed honest man truly be that?

"Buy me a tankard of ale, milord?"

Elias considered the face below his, released the man. "One, and if you think to play me for a fool, I shall spill every drop from your belly."

"How know you of the babe? And what?"

Straight-fingered Arblette raised one of those fingers, and Elias thought it ironic there was a bend to it, then the man looked to the pretty girl who approached the table chosen for its relative privacy in the back corner of the inn Elias had insisted on over the stinking, dilapidated alehouse.

"There ye be!" She set down two of four tankards—so hard ale slopped and dripped between the planks onto Elias's boots. "I be back for me coin."

As she turned toward a table occupied by a half dozen men, several of whom were overly interested in Elias and his companion, Arblette slapped her rear.

She gasped, teasingly protested, "Naughty!" and swayed away.

Lifting his tankard, Arblette returned his regard to Elias. "Not as naughty as she wishes me to be." His grin would have been all teeth were he not missing several. "But I aim to marry better, so unless she defies her brute of a father, she must needs be content with pats and pinches."

Then given the chance, he would ruin the lass without ruffling his conscience. Disliking him more, Elias searched out the owner of the inn in which he and his squire had taken a room for the night. The man was of good size top to bottom, his fat bettered by a greater amount of muscle which bunched as he stared at the one who was too familiar with his daughter.

Arblette was not the only patron to trespass, a recipient of ale at the nearby table hooking an arm around the young woman's waist as she set a tankard before him.

Again she protested, though without teasing, then swatted free. And yet it was at Arblette her father continued to stare.

"You have your ale," Elias said. "Now tell how you know of Lettice's babe."

He took a long draught, belched. "I know 'cause my grandsire disposed of that devil-licked thing."

Though rarely moved to violence outside of defending himself and others, Elias curled his fingers into a fist atop the table. "Disposed?"

"Ah, now!" Arblette splayed a hand as if to ward off an attack. "Not that way, milord, though 'twas as my grandsire was paid to do."

Then the child was not dead? Or had he been snuffed out in a supposedly more humane manner than exposure to the elements and beasts of the wood?

"What way?"

"The way of a good Christian." The man took another drink, winked. "Albeit one in need of funds."

As Elias further tensed in preparation to lunge across the table, the serving girl reappeared. "Give over, milord."

He drew breath between his teeth, opened the purse his squire had delivered him upon his return to the inn, and dropped a coin in her palm that more than covered the ale. "Go."

She gave a squeak of delight and trotted away.

"That there coin buys me three more fills!" Arblette called.

She laughed and flicked a hand as if to rid herself of a fly.

He sighed, lost his smile. "Tell milord, how much would you pay for a look inside my head?"

Elias shifted his cramped jaw, dug two more coins from his purse, and pushed them across the table.

Arblette grunted. "Since it seems we are talkin' about yer son, surely more is warranted."

Elias raised his eyebrows. *"If* what you know proves useful."

The man blew breath up his face, causing his straight black hair to fly upward and settle aslant on his brow. "Certes, you are good for it?"

"As told, *if* what you tell bears fruit."

Arblette leaned across the table, rasped, "Seven, mayhap eight years gone, the mother of your harlot—er, Lettice," he corrected as Elias's face warmed, "sent for my grandsire. 'Twas to him all around these parts turned when they could not stomach ridding themselves of undesirables."

Senses warning he and the other man had become of greater interest, Elias glanced around. Though the voices of those unconcerned with what transpired at this table ensured privacy, he lowered his own voice. "Undesirables?"

"Unwanted babes, whether of the lesser sex when 'tis a son a man needs, sickly, deformed, misbegotten, or devil-marked like your boy."

"Continue."

"My grandsire was paid for the disposal of Lettice's newborn son." Hastily, he added, "Though as told, not the usual form of disposal."

"What form?"

"Whilst setting out a babe some years before, my grandsire was approached by one who offered to pay him for all those destined to breathe their last in the wood." He raised a hand to keep Elias from speaking. "He agreed, as ever it was with heavy heart he did what needed doing and he was certain whatever their fate it was better than death by abandonment. A decent man he was. Now what she does with the babes…"

A woman then, but for what purpose did she buy *undesirables?*

"I pray…" Arblette's voice caught, and he gripped his hands atop the table as if to address heaven here and now. "I pray the Lord forgives my grandsire and me for whatever parts we played in that woman's ungodly schemes."

The chill seeping into Elias became ice. He was not superstitious—
rather, not foolishly so—but he knew there was evil in the world eager
to manifest itself through weak men and women, whether they acted on
behalf of the devil or in their own interest.

Arblette looked up from his white-knuckled hands. "Though in the
beginning my grandsire thought her intentions good, that she provided
for the babes as best she could, he began to suspect she was sent by the
devil to claim his brood and those undesirables whose only sin was of
being born of poverty and shame."

He believed she gave the babes to the devil? How? Surely not
through sacrifice.

Now it was Elias who addressed heaven. *Lord,* he silently prayed, *not
that.* Heart pounding, he said, "What roused his suspicion?"

"Ever she denied him her name. Ever she kept her face hidden. Ever
she appeared within hours of him marking the tree beneath which he was
to leave the babe."

"How was the tree marked?"

"As instructed, a rope tied around its trunk."

Elias jutted his chin. "What else?"

"Were she not walking hand in hand with the devil, she would have
to dwell near to daily pass that portion of the wood to see if the rope
was present, and only once a month at most—more usual every other
month—was the tree marked. And yet ever she appeared when summoned, and for all the babes given into her care over the years, there is
no evidence of her or them in these parts."

"You are saying no others have seen her?"

"Only my grandsire and I."

Elias narrowed his eyes. "Once he suspected her intentions, why did
he continue selling her babes?"

Arblette raised his palms in a gesture of apology. "Not being of a
superstitious bent, I dissuaded him from such thinking. And when I began
to believe as he did, I reminded myself—and him—the undesirables

were destined for unconsecrated ground. Thus, already their souls were lost." Moisture gathered in his eyes. "It was selfish, but her coin put more food in our bellies, clothed us better, and made the lean winters more bearable."

Elias wondered how much he spoke in truth and how much was false. And hoped the latter was heavily weighted, that this was but an act to gain more coin. Not only did the life of the boy who might be his son depend on it, but the lives of other innocents.

"I would speak with your grandsire."

Arblette blinked. "Did I not say?"

"What?"

"A slow sickness laid him abed two years past, and last year I put him in the ground, God have mercy on his soul." He touched a hand to his heart. "Hence, the business is mine."

"You call it a *business?*" Elias struggled to contain anger so sharp he hardly knew himself—he who preferred to laugh, tease, riddle, and arrange words pleasing to heart and soul.

Arblette grunted. "What else to call it, milord? A business it was, and a fair good one with coins from the wretched mothers one side and more coins from the unseen woman on the other side."

"Was," Elias snapped up the word. "'Tis no longer your business?"

Arblette winced. "Still I perform a much-needed service, but no longer do I take coin from the one who paid me better than the mothers."

"Why? Have you now proof of those babes' fate? Not mere suspicion?"

Arblette rubbed his temple as if pained. "The last time I delivered a babe to..." He trailed off. "Well, let us call her what she is—a witch. The last time I prayed for the Lord's protection and followed her, and what I saw..."

"What?"

"I did not stay for it all. I could not, it grieved and frightened me so. But 'twas a most unholy ritual. She danced around a fire in the wood, chanted, and held the babe aloft as if in offering. I vowed then to never again summon her no matter how great my need for coin. And I have not these three months, though my purse can hardly be felt upon my belt."

Elias continued to watch him closely for evidence he lied, well aware one of his own shortcomings was gullibility resulting from the need to believe the best of others, even when they were at their worst. It was the poet in him...the teller of tales...the composer of songs. But as for the actor, that side was of little use in determining if this man he hardly knew wore a face not his own.

"You think all the babes dead?" he asked.

"I do not. Though 'tis likely a great many have been consigned to the dirt, methinks some rove amongst us in search of good Christians to enlist in service to the devil."

Vile superstition, but therein the possibility the babe, who would now be a boy, lived. A boy surely in need of a father.

Arblette leaned farther across the table. "Then there is the rumor of recent." He moistened his lips. "Most unusual twins were born in our village a year past. Joined they were—here." He tapped his chest. "Though sickly, I gave them into the care of the witch thinking they would be comforted as life left them. However, not long ago I heard talk such babes are being exploited by a troop of performers who charge to look upon the spectacle, and for it have been ordered by King Henry himself to leave England."

"You believe the woman sold the babes?" Elias said through met teeth.

Arblette sighed. "I know not what to believe, but it makes one question if the babe I gave—"

"*Sold!*"

The man lowered his chin, nodded. "And now I wonder if 'tis a business for her as well and what other babes suffer that fate. If your son..." He fell silent, providing too much time in which to imagine Lettice's babe exploited for his marked face.

Elias wished the man would look up so his emotions might be better read, but Arblette was slow to raise his chin, and when he did he immediately went behind his tankard and drained its contents.

"I must needs know more about the woman," Elias said.

Arblette lowered his vessel, tapped the table. "As told, my business is not as lucrative as once it was."

Holding back a curse, Elias removed two more coins and pushed them to the man who swept them into his palm.

"I know not her face."

"As already told."

"I know not her name."

Elias glowered.

"I know not whence she hails."

"But you know how to summon her to *dispose* of babes," Elias growled.

"True, but do you recall, I vowed to never again do so no matter how much she offers."

"*She* offers. What of my coin?"

Arblette raised his eyebrows, motioned to the serving girl. "All this talk makes me dry."

Grudgingly, Elias waited as the knave's vessel was refilled. This time Arblette pinched the girl, eliciting a squeal, and once more Elias commanded her to leave.

Seemingly unconcerned by the anger leveled at him by the inn's owner, Arblette said, "What do you propose, milord?"

Elias set before him a purse of a size similar to the one given Lettice, this one holding a quarter of his remaining coin. "Half now, half when you deliver the woman to me."

Arblette stared at the offering. "May I?"

Elias loosened the strings and spread the leather just enough to reveal the contents against a silken red lining.

Arblette whistled low.

"Agreed?" Elias said.

"I can but summon the witch under pretense I have another babe to dispose of." He raised his eyebrows. "'Tis for you to capture her ere she disappears in a sudden fog—which she does sometimes. I would not have the wrath of one such as that fall on me, especially as I am no mighty warrior as your blade tells you to be."

The Wulfrith dagger, prominent on his hip, not only as a matter of pride but to warn any who thought to set upon its bearer.

"When I have her in hand," Elias said, "you shall gain the second half of your coin—though no clearer a conscience unless you continue to delude yourself in believing the Lord approves of leaving his most lovely creation in the wood to die."

"Most lovely…" Arblette snorted. "Ye may say that of babes merely unwanted for poverty's sake, the lack of food taking them a bit later than were they left to the wood, but you cannot say that of those sinful creatures born out of wedlock and abominations come forth with misshapen heads and bodies and marked faces." He nodded. "I do the Lord a service."

Who crawls beneath my skin? Elias wondered. Not even when foul trickery caused him to yield Lady Beata Fauvel—now Marshal—to an unwanted marriage had he so longed to harm another. Prayer was what he needed. And assurance the boy he may have fathered was not in need of rescue.

He cinched the purse, shoved it nearer the man. "Summon her."

2

Six months. They felt like years.

Honore of no surname lowered her forehead to the floor. Gripping her beads, she prayed, "Almighty, You are all. You see all, hear all, feel all." She drew a shaky breath. "You can do all. I beseech Thee, wherever Hart is, turn his feet back to us. Deliver him to these walls unharmed and smiling his sweetly lop-sided smile. Bring him home."

To give the Lord time to consider her request in the hope he might finally act on it, she waited several minutes before setting before Him others in need of grace and healing.

When the bells called the sisters to prayer an hour later, she pressed upright. Soon the chapel would fill with holy women, one of whom Honore was not and would never be. She had work of a different sort—and of equal import, she believed.

She stepped out the side door and paused to allow the sun's heat burning away the clouds to warm places grown cold whilst she prostrated herself before the altar. It felt wonderful, tempting her to delay her duties, but she had been gone too long and Lady Wilma was generous enough with her time.

Honore bounded down the steps and headed around the rear of the chapel so she might sooner reach the dormitory. And halted a step short of colliding with a squat nun.

"Forgive my recklessness, Sister Sarah." She bobbed her head deferentially. "I am late to——"

The nun raised a staying hand, and when Honore seamed her mouth, tapped her own lips.

"Dear me!" Belatedly realizing she had spoken louder than usual as she was in the habit of compensating for a muffled voice, Honore drew up the cloth draping her shoulders which respect for the Lord—and the abbess's assurance He thought her beautiful—bade her lower before addressing Him.

"I was at prayer," she said as she arranged the covering over her head. "In my haste to relieve Lady Wilma, I neglected to set myself aright." She drew the trailing end across her lower face and fastened it on the opposite side. "I thank you, Sister."

It was not cruelty that caused the nun to remind the younger woman of what was best kept concealed. It was kindness, Sister Sarah well-versed in the superstitions of many within Bairnwood Abbey, be they nuns, lay sisters, servants, or residents—especially those of the nobility who resided here because of advanced age, a babe whose birth must be concealed, or to escape an unwanted marriage.

"How fares your good work?" the nun asked.

"Well." It was true, though it felt otherwise these six months.

Sister Sarah inclined her head. "I pray thee a good day, Honore." She stepped around the younger woman and continued to the chapel.

Resuming her course to the dormitory, Honore muttered, "You must cease this grieving. It does him no good. It does you none. Hart is gone. Pray for him and leave him to God. The Lord can protect him far better than you."

Easy to say. Hard to do. The loss of the boy hurt deeply, and worry over him nibbled at her every edge. If she did not gain control of her emotions, soon she would be eaten all the way through.

Honore jumped out of the path of a cluster of nuns also destined for the chapel. As they passed, she landed beneath the regard of a middle-aged woman bringing up the rear, she who was not yet garbed as a bride of Christ. But soon, it was told, the novice's family having supplied the funds necessary to make an esteemed place for her at Bairnwood.

Honore held the woman's keen gaze, refusing to be cowed by one who was her equal—or nearly so. Had Honore wished to become a nun, for a dozen years now she would have worn a habit. Instead, she had been granted her request to use the funds paid for her keeping in a way surely as pleasing to the Lord.

As the novice neared, the woman moved her eyes to the swath of material covering the bottom half of Honore's face, then lowered her gaze further.

Honore reached up and closed a hand around the short string of prayer beads she usually kept beneath her gown's bodice. As noted months past, it was similar to the ones hung from the girdle of the novice who was now past her.

Honore slipped the beads beneath the neck of her gown and continued to the farthest dormitory which housed the abbey's female lay servants.

As soon as she entered the building whose northern end had been converted from a dozen individual cells to one great room a decade past, Lady Wilma moved toward her. "Settle yourselves, children," she called over her shoulder, "else there shall be no honey milk with your dinner."

As moans, groans, and mutterings answered her, Honore noted the woman's anxious eyes. "What is amiss?"

Lady Wilma halted before her. "The raggedly lad was here."

Honore drew a sharp breath between her teeth. She had hoped she would not see him again, that the abbey's plans to render the boy's master useless would be completed ere she was called upon to once more leave the safety of these walls.

"He said his master bids you meet him two hours ere matins," Lady Wilma continued.

Midnight, then—a perilous hour, especially if the dense fog that had arisen these past nights returned.

"He told you are to bring twice the amount of coin."

"Twice?" Honore exclaimed.

"For two, he said."

"Twins?" she asked, thoughts flying to two such babes born in the village of Forkney a year past—rather, the rumor of them.

"I asked the same. The boy said he did not know."

"Is he still here?"

"Nay, I fed him a good meal and sent him away with a coin."

How many times had Honore offered the lad a home here? As many times as he had declined. And now he was too old to be granted sanctuary inside these walls.

She bit her lower lip. She did not want to go to the wood, especially after what had happened the last time, but she had no choice.

Lady Wilma touched her shoulder. "Methinks you ought to take big Jeannette with you."

She wished she could. But she dared not.

Honore was no slight thing, but increasingly she felt dainty alongside the young woman who accompanied her. Lady Wilma had argued it was time to give Jeannette more knowledge of the world beyond the abbey so she was better informed in deciding her future. Still, Honore had resisted—until the lady suggested Jeannette clothe herself as a man and remain visibly distant during the exchange. The young woman's accompaniment would make it appear Honore had a protector whilst ensuring Jeannette had space in which to flee if necessary.

Now beneath a three-quarter moon and amidst fog so thick they could hardly see their feet, Honore looked sidelong at her charge and felt a flush of pride for all she had become. When she could not have been more than one, she was set out in the wood, either due to illegitimacy, poverty, a drifting eye that frightened the superstitious, or perhaps all.

No longer the babe in fouled swaddling clothes whom Honore had hastened to Bairnwood fourteen years past, she stood over a half foot taller than her savior's five and a half feet, was as broad-shouldered as

many a man, had a figure surprisingly feminine for one of such propor-
tion, and possessed a fairly pretty face made all the prettier when she
smiled. Not that she smiled often, of such a serious nature was she.

Of further surprise to those who judged her by appearance was
her intellect. Her size, wandering eye, and tongue of few words lulled
many into believing her simple-minded. She was not. And Abbess
Abigail knew it, encouraging Jeannette's studies beyond writing and
reading to include numbers and Latin. The abbess did not say it, but
she implied a way could be found for the young woman to become a
bride of Christ.

As the two negotiated the wood, Honore once more wondered if
Jeannette would wish to take holy vows were one of common birth given
that rare opportunity.

She hoped not and immediately repented for being selfish and
silently explained to the Lord that her work with foundlings would be
much furthered were Jeannette to fully come alongside her.

Honore had help from a few lay servants and several kind-hearted
convent residents—Lady Wilma for one—but more could be done.
And once alterations to the abbey's outer wall were completed, as they
should have been weeks past, more would need to be done. But that was
not to ponder at the middling of night in a dark wood and soon to be in
close proximity with Finwyn.

Though Honore assured herself the exchange would be over soon,
she shuddered.

"Are you afeared, Mine Honore?"

Mine Honore, as Jeannette had called her since first she could speak.
It was the same as the others coming up after the young woman called
the one whose unseemly birth denied her the title of *lady.* But far Honore
preferred it over the loftiest title. Ever it reminded her she belonged to
someone—many someones.

"A little frightened," she admitted. "The one I meet, hopefully for
the last time, is not to be underestimated. Thus, do not forget you are to
remain distant enough he will not know you for a woman."

Jeannette's white teeth flashed in the dim. "I could become accustomed to such garments." She plucked at tunic and chausses borrowed from a male servant who dwelt outside the abbey. "I feel all held together."

"Are they truly so comfortable?"

"Ever so. I have naught flapping about my legs and feet, naught to hinder my stride."

A very long stride, though Jeannette patiently kept pace with Honore's shorter reach.

"Do not tell Abbess Abigail," Honore said. "She will think it unnatural you are clothed as a man."

"And sinful?" the girl said warily.

Were Honore not so tense, she would laugh. "An abbot might name it sinful, but not our abbess, especially considering your mission."

"Mission," Jeannette repeated. "I like that."

As expected, Honore mused and wondered as sometimes she did why the Lord had not made Jeannette a Jean. Not that she wished it. Had her first foundling been a boy, he would no longer dwell at Bairnwood. As required, males left the community of women upon attainment of their tenth year. Blessedly, thus far all had been placed in good homes well before that age.

Fewer females were as fortunate, but as yet there was no great need. As long as Bairnwood—and Honore—could support their numbers, they were welcome to remain. However, that would not always be so, and all the sooner those numbers would become unsupportable once the man who summoned Honore became dispensable. She would have to work harder—a daunting prospect, but it was not as if she had anything else to live for or fill her heart so full.

Returning to the present, Honore instructed Jeannette that if she must converse henceforth, she ought to whisper.

The two crossed a stream, keeping their shoes and hems dry by traversing the immense rotten tree that had toppled from one bank to the other long before Honore took her first forbidden walk outside the abbey and found Jeannette. It had been two years before she dared approach the one she had seen set out the little one, but her task had become easier thereafter—until the old man took ill and his grandson determined to make more profitable what he called a *business*.

However, though Finwyn required greater compensation than had his grandsire, Honore had not been summoned as often since the old man's passing. Until recently, she had thought it was because the grandson was not as trusted to discreetly dispose of unwanted babes, but that rumor about twins born to a newly widowed villager a year past made her think it could be something else. Were it—

"Mine Honore?" Jeannette forgot to whisper.

"Quiet now," Honore rasped. "We are nearly there."

They continued to traverse the wood until the ground rose before them, then Honore veered to the right. "Remain here. Once I am over the top, follow and place yourself between those trees so the moon is full at your back." She pointed to the top of the rise where two ancient oaks stood like royals before their lessers. "You have only to stand there," she repeated what had been told ere they departed the abbey, then tapped the tapered stick tucked beneath Jeannette's belt. "Hold this to the side, its point down as if 'tis a sword."

"I will look a fierce warrior," the young woman whispered.

And all the more threatening amid moonlit fog, Honore imagined and hoped it would prevent Finwyn from trespassing as he had done the last time when he wrenched the covering from her face.

"No more is required of you," Honore said. "Now I would have your word that if anything goes afoul, you will run straight to the abbey."

"Already I gave my word, Mine Honore."

"I would hear it again."

The young woman sighed. "If all goes afoul, I shall return to the abbey as quickly as my legs can carry me. My word I give."

Honore leaned up and kissed Jeannette's cheek. "God willing, this night we shall each have a babe to sing to sleep." She stepped back and lowered her chin. "Almighty," she prayed, "bless us this eve as we seek to do Your good work. Amen."

"Amen," Jeannette said.

After ensuring the cloth covering the lower half of her face was secure, Honore lifted her skirts and ascended the rise. Upon reaching the crest, she set her shoulders back and increased her stride.

There was no disguising herself as being other than a woman, but she refused to appear meek. If Finwyn drew too near again, she would do more than slap him. She touched the stick beneath her belt that was half as long but twice as thick as Jeannette's. In addition to coin, the knave would depart the wood with lumps and bruises. Or so she told herself, Finwyn being the first and last person she had ever struck.

I shall do so again if I must—and harder, she assured herself and set her eyes on the distant tree, a portion of whose aboveground roots served as a cradle. As the fog creeped thicker there, she would have to draw near to confirm the exchange was possible. On occasion it was not, the cradle empty due to the babe's death.

"Lord, let the wee ones be hale," she whispered and sent her gaze around the wood in search of movement whilst straining to catch the sound of fitful babes. Were they in the cradle, Finwyn would be watching.

She glanced over her shoulder and saw Jeannette had placed herself as directed. The young woman did look to be a fierce warrior—the moon's glow at her back outlining her hulking figure and what appeared to be a drawn sword. She would not go unnoticed, and Finwyn would know exactly why Honore had not come alone. Hopefully, once more he would honor their agreement and collect his coin following her departure.

When Honore was near enough to see the humped roots near the tree's base, she silently thanked the Lord. Amid the fog, two bundles lay side by side. Blessedly, neither babe was fitful, for she hated that they might be frantic and frightened.

Though careful to pick her way amongst the roots that extended a dozen feet from the tree, twice she nearly twisted an ankle, causing the coins to clatter.

When she stood before the bundles, she raised her pouch to show the one watching that she paid the price required to save two innocents, then set it in a patch of moss. God willing, it was the last payment she would make.

As she straightened, she noticed a rope tied around the tree's trunk. Did Finwyn seek to tell her something? Might this be a threat? She considered it a moment longer, then brushed aside the curiosity with the assurance it was not fashioned into a noose. And nearly laughed at allowing her mind to wander in that direction. She did not like the man, but he gave her no cause to fear for her life.

She positioned the sling she wore over her short cloak so it draped one shoulder and rested on the opposite hip, then reached for the first bundle.

"There is naught there for you, woman."

She stilled. Someone showed himself, and it was not Finwyn. Counseling calm though her heart thought itself a drum, Honore slowly turned.

3

SWEEPING HER GAZE over the wood, Honore saw Jeannette's dark figure on the hill, moonlight appearing to radiate from her, then the one whose shadow glided across the fog, swept up over her skirts and bodice, and covered her face.

Though less than twenty feet distant, the only sense she could make of the large figure backed by moonlight the same as Jeannette's and the ring of chain mail, was that here was a warrior.

Fifteen feet.

Grateful his shadow masked the fear in her eyes nearly as well as the cloth hid her trembling mouth, she pulled the stick from beneath her belt.

Ten feet.

She thrust her weapon forward. "Come no nearer!"

Though she doubted he felt threatened, he halted. Even without the sword and dagger hung from his waist, he could make a quick end of her. And all the more easily were he not alone.

Honore shifted her gaze past his shoulder, saw Jeannette had yet to run as instructed. But then, nothing ill had happened. At least, not that the young woman could know with certainty.

Wishing she had better prepared her for what constituted *afoul,* Honore said, "What is it you want?"

When the warrior finally answered, he punctuated each word as if it did not need any other to be understood. "I want my son."

Honore nearly looked behind at the babes, but she dared not move her gaze from this man. Too, she would wager the quiet bundles were only lures—a trap set by Finwyn. Doubtless, he had learned of the abbey's plan and thought to gain every last coin possible ere being rendered obsolete.

What she did not understand was this warrior. Surely he was not meant to kill her. Unless...

Might this be Finwyn's attempt to preserve his business? If so, it would be for naught. Abbess Abigail would see the plan through to its good end. However, Honore's death would serve another purpose were Finwyn even less worthy of his grandsire's name than already believed—revenge. And yet in light of this warrior's words, that made little sense.

"I know naught of your son, Sir Knight," she afforded him a title he might not be owed since he could be but a mercenary of the lower ranks. "I fear Finwyn has misled you for his own profit."

"Finwyn?"

"Finwyn Arblette."

"Ah. Certes, I do not like the man, but thus far all has come to pass as told."

"All?"

"Are you not here to buy unwanted babes?"

She could not see his eyes move to the pouch she had deposited, but she sensed it there. Wishing Jeannette would run, she said, "I am here for an exchange—the coin Finwyn requires for the children whose parents wish to dispose of them."

"How kind of you." His sarcasm was not subtle. "Tell me, how do *you* dispose of them."

Though she longed to rail against the insinuation she was of ill intent, she said as calmly as she could, "I assure you, not as Finwyn would have you believe."

"Then you will have no difficulty delivering my son to me."

That all depended on the boy's identity. "It is possible. Tell me how he became lost to a warrior when those for whom I give coin are of the common class."

For some reason, his hesitation lessened her fear. She had no experience with men of the sword, but they had a reputation for being forceful, brutally decisive, and short on shame. And in this man's silence she sensed none of those things. She felt emotion, sorrow, regret.

"Only in recent days was I made aware of his existence," he said. "I am not certain he is mine, but if he is..."

"Then like many a man, you made a promise to a maiden to persuade her to lie with you and the next morn left her with child. I suppose I am to think it honorable you now wish to take responsibility. Or is it something else? Mayhap you seek to harm the boy to ensure your sin remains hidden?"

"I wish to retrieve my son. *If* he is, indeed, mine."

"How think you to prove that? You believe he will have your eyes? Your nose? Not that it is impossible, but it may be too soon to tell. Nay, Sir Knight, methinks it best for all you tell yourself you tried and pay a priest to put finish to your troubled conscience." She raised her chin. "Now step aside so I may sooner be shed of this farce and gain what sleep remains to me."

He tilted his head, and she felt the intense gaze of one seeking to see beyond her eyes. No chance of that, cloaked as she was in his shadow.

But then he moved to the side, and moonlight poured over her, making her startle.

She did not know how it was possible to move so sure of foot amongst the fog-ladened roots, but of a sudden he was before her, his shadow once more covering her as he grasped her forearm and rendered the stick impotent—had it ever been of benefit against such a man.

Fearing for Jeannette, Honore strained to the side and saw the young woman ran forward as if to give aid with a sword that would soon prove another stick.

"Run, Jean!" Honore cried, surprised by the clarity that caused her to speak the male form of the young woman's name. Then she saw a figure emerge from behind a tree to the right. Sword drawn, the man lunged toward Jeannette.

"Run!" Honore screamed.

Blessedly, the young woman swerved and reached her legs opposite.

"I thought he was here to protect you," the warrior said as he looked across his shoulder. "Not what he appears to be, hmm?"

Honore did not struggle against his hold. It would only drain her of strength better saved should an opportunity for escape present. "You have me," she panted. "Pray, let him go."

He did not respond, and a moment later his companion disappeared over the rise.

"Jean is but a boy," she protested. "He cannot defend himself—"

"*That* was no boy."

Then he guessed her protector was a woman? More likely, he thought Jeannette the man she was made to appear. "Regardless, Jean is no warrior."

He shrugged. "Providing he does not seek to harm my squire, he is in no danger. Francis will bring him back, and whatever you will not tell, I will learn from your man."

She swallowed loudly. "You wish to know of your son."

He inclined his head, then turned her with him into moonlight.

To her surprise, he was almost boyishly handsome, the wavy hair brushing his shoulders framing a face fit with dark eyebrows, long-lashed eyes, a well-shaped nose, and a mouth whose compression could not hide how full-lipped it was. Doubtless, his years fell somewhat short of her thirty and two.

"You are young," he said, and she caught her breath at the realization he studied her as intently. Though she spent no time in front of a mirror, on occasion she caught her reflection in water or on the silver platter with which Abbess Abigail and she were served light fare when they met to discuss the foundlings. She did appear younger than her years and might even be lovely—providing one viewed only what was visible above her covering. Thus, she was grateful this man made no attempt to divest her of the material slung across her lower face.

"Not the crone I expected," he murmured, and she was struck by the resonance of a voice deprived of accusation. Though deep, it was almost gentle and held a note of wonder, causing heat to sweep up her chest, neck, and face.

Honore did not understand her reaction—and did not wish to, it being uncomfortably foreign, though it had not always been. In her younger years she had felt something akin to this in the presence of a handsome young monk who accompanied his bishop to Bairnwood to meet with the abbess once and twice a year. Time and again she had repented for imagining how it would feel to stand near him, clasp his hand, tuck her head beneath his chin, feel his arms around her. She had even wondered at his mouth upon hers. And ever that imagining returned her to reality—her reality. Such could never be.

The warrior before her raised his eyebrows.

Realizing she stared, she recalled the words he had spoken and said, "Nor are you the miscreant I expected, though I suppose you will do as well as Finwyn."

His lids narrowed, though not so much she could not see where his eyes moved when they left hers. Her masked lower face roused his curiosity, the weather too temperate to warrant the warmth the material provided in addition to its true purpose.

But he stayed his hand, and when he spoke again, once more accusation sounded from him. "Where is my son?"

Were the boy amongst those Finwyn and his grandsire had sold to her, there were three places he could be, one readily accessible, one barely accessible, and one impossibly accessible—the abbey, the home of adoptive parents, and the grave. She prayed it was not the latter, though perhaps it was for the best if this man meant the boy ill.

Honore raised her chin. "Regardless of what Finwyn told—"

"He tells you are a witch."

A chill rushed into her, slammed against her spine with such force it should have doubled her over. His words surprised though they ought not. And frightened as they certainly ought. It was not mere cruelty to be named one who consorted with the devil. It was deadly.

She moistened her lips. "You think me a witch?"

"I do not believe you possess ungodly powers, but that has little bearing on whether *you* believe yourself so equipped and commit foul deeds in the hope of strengthening those powers."

"You do me ill to suggest such a thing!"

"Then for what do you buy unwanted babes?"

"To save them. Their parents hire Finwyn—as they did his grandsire before him—to set them out in the wood. For a dozen years I have paid to deliver those innocents from cruel deaths."

"You are saying *you,* who look to be fortunate to clothe and feed yourself, have a brood of children?"

Honore resisted the temptation to peer down her figure. Though simply dressed as befitting her station, her gown and cloak were in good repair. But she supposed one who could afford to leave pouches of coin for abandoned babes ought to possess the resources of a noble. And she did—or *had,* there being little remaining of the wealth that had accompanied her to the abbey thirty and two years past.

"Oft appearances are deceiving," she said, "especially when the one in possession of a good fortune pleases the Lord by spending it to do His good work rather than indulge her vanity."

"Twelve years," he said as if she had not spoken. "How many babes is that?"

She glanced at the motionless bundles. "Were this not trickery, those two would have grown the number to sixty and six, including the few I was able to save ere striking a bargain with Finwyn's grandsire."

He snorted. "Unbeknownst to those of the village of Forkney, you reside nearby with that many children?"

"I do not."

Before she could explain, he demanded, "Then where are they? Where can I find my son?"

He would not like this, but there was only the truth. "As some are sickly and tragically ill-formed when I receive them, many have passed." Ignoring his harshly drawn breath, she pressed onward, "Of the thirty-seven who survived infancy, either they have been placed in good homes or yet reside with me."

"Where?"

She hesitated lest she endanger those of Bairnwood, but as he was one warrior and the abbey's walls were high and secure, there seemed little risk in telling all—and perhaps it would prove Finwyn was the one who should not be trusted. "I am of Bairnwood Abbey."

His eyebrows scissored. "A nun?"

"Nay, a lay servant who answers to the Lord and her abbess."

More hesitation. "Your name?"

"Honore."

"Only Honore?"

She inclined her head. "Of no surname."

He moved so swiftly she barely glimpsed the movement, giving her no time to tighten her grip on the stick. But after he tossed it aside, he released her.

Honore stepped back and her calf struck a humped root. The distance between the warrior and her was slight, but she felt safer. Determined to gain more ground with him since her escape was not yet assured, she said, "Now I would know your name."

"Sir Elias de Morville come from France to learn the fate of the boy born to Lettice of Forkney. You know her?"

Denial sprang to Honore's lips, but something made her hesitate. She knew the name, but did she know it beyond that of the elderly lady who had arrived at Bairnwood ten years past intent on spending the remainder of her life in the peaceful confines of the convent?

"Do you?" the knight pressed.

"I do not. The agreement is the parents remain unknown to me, not only to ensure their privacy but the protection of the one who breaks with them to give their babes into my care. Too, Bairnwood is fairly isolated, and I leave its walls only when summoned."

Not true, she reminded herself of those first years she had ventured farther on her own, but before she could correct the lie, he said, "Summoned?"

She blinked. "Of course. How else would I know when a babe is to be abandoned? You think I haunt the wood nightly?" She frowned. "Is that what Finwyn told to convince you I am a witch?"

"The rope tied around the tree," the knight said. "He told that alerts you to leave coin for a babe."

More and more Honore disliked—and feared—what unfolded. "He lied."

"If 'tis not the rope that summons you, what?"

"Who," she corrected. "Finwyn sends a boy to the abbey, and that night I bring coin and pray 'tis not too late for the babe given unto me to thrive."

"Was it too late for my son?"

"As told, I know not whence the babes come. But if you tell me how old he would be, mayhap I can reveal his fate."

"He would be seven and some."

She startled, for some reason expecting the one he sought was much younger. Were he seven, that would be the year she paid Finwyn's grandsire for three male infants spaced several months apart. And among them was one she could not account for with any certainty.

"What else can you tell me about him?" she asked and heard desperation in her voice. Hoping his delayed response was not born of suspicion, she held her breath.

"On the day past, I spoke to Lettice who revealed the babe is dead. She said he was left to the wood because of a stain upon his face she believed was a mark of the devil."

Honore was grateful she was somewhat prepared for his answer. Had she not been, she might not have locked her softening knees and remained upright.

"After her departure," the knight continued, "Finwyn Arblette appeared. Having overheard our conversation, he told his grandsire did not leave Lettice's babe in the wood but sold him to you."

Hence, the ruse. Doubtless, Finwyn had been paid to deliver the one who had last seen the babe alive. Mere coincidence he overheard this knight and Lettice? Or did he yet earn coin as his grandsire rued years ago—selling the intimate favors of women? Might this Lettice be one of those whose sin he promoted?

"Have you this boy?" the knight pressed. "Does he yet live?"

Silently, she bemoaned he spoke of her beloved Hart. Why not the boy adopted by a childless husband and wife in the village of Dunwidden? Or even the babe laid in consecrated ground after a six-month battle to survive?

"You are too silent," the knight said. "Why?"

She considered telling him his son was the one who had passed, but she could not lie. She unstuck her tongue from her palate. "I know the one you seek."

"Where is he?"

Glad she was not short, wishing she were taller, she said, "Regrettably, he ran away six months past."

A shifting of chain mail, then his hand was on her left arm, moonlight revealing anger about his eyes and mouth. "I am to believe you?"

"'Tis true." As she tried to free her arm, she caught a flash of red on his hip and identified it as a jeweled dagger a moment before he dragged her close.

"Why would he run away? Did you mistreat him?"

"Of course not! I am fond of him."

"Fond, and yet he did not want to be with you."

It was wrong, but Honore wished she had lied. She drew a deep breath. "He did not like his discipline for inappropriate behavior.

We argued, and the following morn he could not be found inside the abbey—nor outside it, the abbess having sent men in search of him."

"Methinks you lie. Did you sell him?"

"Sell?" she exclaimed.

"Sacrifice him?"

"Neither! Never would I harm my charges. 'Tis the Lord in heaven I worship, not the evil one."

He fell silent, and when he spoke again, there was no mistaking the threat in his voice. "You have three options. Give me my son—"

"I do not have him."

"Take me to the one to whom you sold him."

"I did not sell him."

"Or deny me altogether, and I will hand you up to be tried for a witch."

Fear and outrage were terrible playmates, Honore acknowledged as the two careened toward each other. A moment later they collided, flooding all reason and leaving her with naught but the need to survive.

She thrust her free hand between them, closed it around his dagger's hilt, and dragged the blade up out of its scabbard. She had no experience with weapons, and it seemed almost a miracle he wrenched backward. Otherwise, she might have opened his throat.

An instant later, he captured her dagger-wielding wrist, and she had only a moment to note the anger sharpening his face and a whistling across the wood before he fell upon her.

"Almighty!" he erupted as he carried her down toward roots that might snap a back or neck if one landed wrong. If not that he released her, she would have borne the brunt of the fall, but she had just enough time to twist to the side and thrust her arms before her to break her fall.

Blessedly, her hands landed on moss-covered ground, but her hip was not as fortunate. With a loud crack, it struck a root, but though it hurt, she was surprised the pain was not ten-fold greater considering how loud the sound of bone on wood. It might even be broken.

Was this shock? If so, De Morville would have no difficulty subduing her, especially as she was no longer in possession of his dagger. Where had it flown?

She thrust onto her side, and as she searched for silver amid the fogged roots was further astonished the movement did not more greatly pain her. And before her was the reason, though it took a moment to understand.

The knight lay face down on roots that formed the near rim of the cradle which held the bundles that had presented as babes. The crack had not been her hip but his head striking a root. But what sense to be made of the shaft protruding from his upper back? How had that come to be? And was he dead?

Dear Lord, she silently despaired, *what evil is afoot?*

The rustle and squelch of fallen leaves on moist earth brought her chin up, and she followed the sound to a figure who approached from far to the left of where De Morville's squire had earlier concealed himself.

He carried a bow, and as he advanced, hooked it over his head and an arm and let it fall across his torso like the sling Honore had brought to carry the foundlings to the abbey.

Recalling the whistle heard before the knight fell upon her, this she also understood. De Morville had not attacked her. The force of Finwyn's arrow burying itself in the knight had driven him against her. And in saving herself, he was the one victimized by the roots—were he not already dead by way of the arrow.

About The Author

TAMARA LEIGH HOLDS a Master's Degree in Speech and Language Pathology. In 1993, she signed a 4-book contract with Bantam Books. Her first medieval romance, Warrior Bride, was released in 1994 and nominated for a RITA award. Continuing to write for the general market, she was published with HarperCollins and Dorchester and earned awards and spots on national bestseller lists.

In 2006, Tamara's first inspirational contemporary romance, Stealing Adda, was released. In 2008, Perfecting Kate was optioned for a movie and Splitting Harriet won an ACFW Book of the Year award. The following year, Faking Grace was nominated for a RITA award. In 2011, Tamara wrapped up her Southern Discomfort series with the release of Restless in Carolina.

When not in the middle of being a wife and mother, Tamara dips her writer's pen in ink and nose in a good book. In 2012, she returned to the historical romance genre with Dreamspell: A Medieval Time Travel Romance, followed by the Age of Faith series, which now includes the seventh book, The Awakening. Tamara's #1 Bestsellers—Lady at Arms, Lady Of Eve, Lady Of Conquest, and Lady Betrayed—are among her general market romances to be rewritten as clean reads. Baron Of Blackwood, the third book in the #1 bestselling series, The Feud, is now available.

Tamara lives near Nashville with her husband, a German Shepherd who has never met a squeaky toy she can't destroy, and a feisty Morkie who keeps her company during long writing stints. And then there's Boog, her grandpuppy...

Connect with Tamara at her website www.tamaraleigh.com, her email tamaraleightenn@gmail.com, Facebook, Twitter, and Instagram.

For new releases and special promotions, subscribe to Tamara Leigh's mailing list: www.tamaraleigh.com

CPSIA information can be obtained
at www.ICGtesting.com
Printed in the USA
LVHW031056241118
598135LV00002B/775